THE ROOM OPPOSITE

And Other Tales of Mystery and Imagination

THE ROOM OPPOSITE

And Other Tales of Mystery and Imagination

F. M. MAYOR

Edited and with an introduction by

Gina R. Collia

Published by Ṇezu Press
Queensgate House,
48 Queen Street,
Exeter, Devon,
EX4 3SR,
United Kingdom.

This edition published 2023

The Room Opposite: And Other Tales of Mystery and Imagination first published by Longmans, Green and Co. Ltd., 1935.
Life in a Touring Company first published in *The Queen, The Lady's Newspaper*, 8 April 1905

ISBN-13: 978-1-7393921-0-9

Due to the historical nature of the text, some language used within this collection of short stories has the potential to cause offence to the modern reader. However, in the interest of preserving the original text, it has not been altered. For the same reason, the punctuation and spelling of the original text has been maintained, and the original formatting has been used wherever possible. Only minor publisher errors in the original text have been corrected.

CONTENTS

F. M. Mayor: Author, Actress & Champion of the Superfluous Woman

by Gina R. Collia

Flora Macdonald Mayor was born in Twickenham on 20 October 1872, and, according to her father, both she and her identical twin sister, Alice, to whom she remained devoted throughout her life, were 'very small and weakly' at birth.[1] Flora's father, Reverend Joseph Bickersteth Mayor (1828-1916), was forty-six years old and the Chair of Classics at King's College, University of London, at the time of his daughters' birth; later, he became the Chair of Moral Philosophy. Flora's mother, Jessie Mayor (née Alexandrina Jessie Grote, 1831-1927), was forty-two years old when her daughters were born. She was a talented musician and linguist; she spoke Italian, German, Spanish, Portuguese, Danish, Dutch and Gealic, and she translated some of the Icelandic Sagas into English.[2] Flora and Alice were the Mayors' only daughters and the youngest of four children; there were two older brothers: Robert (referred to as Robin, 1869-1947) and Henry (1870-1948).

The Mayor family lived at Queensgate House, 30 Queens Road, Kingston Hill, in Kingston-Upon-Thames, in a large house overlooking Richmond Park, along with a staff of servants, including a cook, maids, a nanny and a gardener. The four Mayor children were all bookish and spent their time reading, making up stories, putting on amateur theatricals, debating and writing for the family newspaper, the *Queensgate Chronicle*. And when they were not amusing themselves at home, taking lessons or attending church and Sunday School (which they were required to do regularly as part of a clerical household), they spent time at the Hampstead home of their seven unmarried paternal aunts—Anna, Lizzie, Charlotte, Kate, Emily, Georgie and Fanny—all of whom were well-read and cultivated.

Flora and Alice were initially schooled by their mother, with whom they were never close, but they later became some of the first pupils to attend Surbiton High School, which was founded by the Church of England in 1884 with the aim of providing a 'superior education for girls in accordance with the principles of the Church of England'.[3] It was at Surbiton, at the age of fourteen, that Flora discovered her love of acting, when she took part in the school production of Molière's *L'Avare*. Two years later, she starred in the school's production of *Little Lord Fauntleroy* and was a great success, receiving some of the admiration and applause she longed for. In 1888, when they were almost sixteen years old, Flora and Alice were both awarded Third Class Honours in the Oxford University Local Examinations,[4] and in 1890 they were sent off to perfect their French at the Moravian School of Montmirail in Switzerland. But Flora and her sister found they were not suited to their strict Protestant finishing school, where they were constantly in trouble, and they left just after the New Year of 1891.

The twins had always been inseparable, but they were parted for the first time in October 1892 when, now twenty years old, Alice chose to remain at home when Flora went off to study history at Newnham College, Cambridge. They wrote to each other every day, and Flora imparted every detail of her goings on at Newnham, of her accomplishments there (social rather than academic), and of the compliments she received, including those about her acting. Flora took the title role of Nan in John Baldwin Buckstone's *Good for Nothing* and was a great success, and she played Mrs Malaprop in Richard Brinsley Sheridan's play *The Rivals*. She thoroughly enjoyed her adventures at Newnham, but as her time there came to an end her family got into financial difficulty, and each of the Mayor children was informed that they'd need to do their bit to help. Her father hoped that she would secure her future by getting a First or a good Second and taking up a post at the college, but Flora got a Third and, though by that time she already had aspirations of becoming a writer, decided to follow her passion and go on the professional stage under the name of Mary Strafford.

Much to her disappointment, Flora found, as she scoured the theatrical papers for acting jobs, that there were very few to be had, and for those that did exist there was an awful lot of competition. She had great difficult getting anything other than walking-on parts, some of which she paid for. In addition to this, she faced opposition to her career choice from her family, on moral and religious grounds, and her health was deteriorating; she was beginning to experience serious Asthma attacks. In February 1897, Flora seized the opportunity to join a small theatre company as it went on its Hastings run; the dressing rooms, she wrote to Alice, were horrid, the conversation was dull, and the play was 'rather immoral in places'.[5] But she was not put off the stage; despite repeat rejections, and her failing health, she continued doggedly to haunt the agents' and managers' offices in pursuit of her dream.

In December 1900, just prior to Christmas, Flora received news that she was to have a part as a 'lady walker-on' with F. R. Benson's theatrical company at the Lyric; it was while working with Benson's company that she met Arthur Machen, whom she liked very much.[6] Her first appearance was in *The Taming of the Shrew*; she had to 'crouch and pray and cover my eyes'.[7] In *The Merchant of Venice*, she was required to throw flowers. Unfortunately, during the latter she repeatedly missed her exit and was dropped when the company went on to do a season at Stratford in the spring of 1901. Before going off to Stratford, Benson told Flora that she lacked spontaneity and was too literary to act. He asked if she had any ambition aside from being on the stage, and she told him she wanted to be a writer; his suggestion was that 'it would be better to stick to that',[8] advice that she subsequently ignored.

While attempting to establish herself as an actress, Flora had continued to pursue her hopes of becoming a writer. Her first book, *Mrs. Hammond's Children*, a collection of short stories intended for adult readers about the relationships between children, was published under her stage pseudonym, Mary Strafford. After being rejected by several publishers, it was finally taken on by a small firm called R. Brimley Johnson in September 1901. A second printing was put out the following year, but the book received very little attention, aside from a few lines in *The Gentlewoma*n,[9] and was soon forgotten.

Around the time her first book came out, Flora was given a walking-on part with Mrs. Bandermann-Palmer's company in Henry James Byron's three-act play *Our Boys.* But during the months that followed she found herself back to being without work. She continued badgering agents and answering advertisements in the theatre papers, but she suffered rejection after rejection. In the spring of 1902, feeling frustrated and desperate, she paid to join the acting classes of Ben Greet. Greet, who used to choose members for his touring company from those who took his classes, promised Flora a part in *Sherlock Holmes*, but when she turned up to rehearsals the following day she was told that there had been a mix up; there was no part for her after all. She wrote in her Stage Journal that the disappointment was so great she was reduced to tears, but still she persevered. In the autumn of 1902, she managed to secure a walking-on part in Laurence Housman's *Bethlehem: A Nativity Play*, produced by Gordon Craig. And finally, in January 1903, after claiming she could play the organ in order to get the job—she'd taken a handful of lessons at finishing school—she joined Herbert Beerbohm Tree's production of Hall Caine's *The Eternal City* and went on her first and only provincial tour. She played several parts, including that of Nattalina,[10] the maid of Donna Roma Valonna, and critics made positive noises about her performance.[11] Flora was not impressed with the play itself—'I never saw anything so despicably dull'[12]—but it received glowing reviews in the newspapers and was very popular with audiences; theatres were repeatedly reported as being packed.

Touring with a theatre company, Flora discovered with dismay, was an uncomfortable business. She was shocked by the often squalid conditions that the company was expected to work in at the theatres themselves, exhausted by the constant travelling from one venue to another loaded down with heavy suitcases, and continually frustrated by the effort required simply to find lodgings to stay in at each location. Worst of all, she missed Alice and home; she missed being around people she cared for and who cared about her. She was at a decidedly low ebb when, on 24 March 1903, during the Macclesfield leg of the tour, she received and accepted a marriage proposal.

Ernest Shepherd was Henry Mayor's best friend when they were at Clifton College together as boys, and the Shepherds and Mayors had remained close. Ernest had been in love with Flora for years, but as a young architect without prospects he'd not been in a position to marry. Things changed when, at the beginning of March 1903, he was offered a post on the Architectural Survey of India and was finally able to propose. Of course, Flora had to give up the stage. On the subject of leaving the theatre, she wrote to Alice, 'it is curious how uninteresting it seems now… and the privations seem much more disagreeable'; Providence, she wrote, had arranged things in 'such a delightful way'.[13] Ernest sailed for India a few weeks later, while Flora, who wanted to spend time with Alice before moving overseas, remained in England, and the couple wrote to each other regularly for the following few months. They were in the process of planning their wedding, their honeymoon, and discussing the prospect of Alice living with them in India, when disaster struck. Ernest fell ill with Malaria and, on 22 October, died in a hospital Simla.[14]

Flora's chronic bronchial asthma and the shock of losing Ernest combined to bring about an almost complete mental and physical breakdown, so Alice took her sister to Bordighera in Liguria, Italy, to recuperate for the first quarter of 1904. Then, in April, Flora's brother Henry, who was by then classics master at Clifton College, asked her to set up house with him, so she moved from Queensgate House to 43 Canynge Square and threw herself into making their house a home. But she found the daily domestic routine at Clifton boring and, so sorely affected by the loss of Ernest and the life they should have shared together, needed something more to occupy her time and mind. Her health failing and often confined to a sickbed, she returned to writing. She began her *Reminiscences* of childhood,[15] and in the spring of 1905 she contributed a long article to *The Queen* entitled 'Life in a Touring Company, by One Who Has Tried It', based on her own experiences of the hardships of off-stage life during a theatrical tour.[16]

In December 1905, during one of their regular Sunday meetings at Frascati's restaurant on Oxford Street, the Dramatic

Debaters, a club of around one hundred members, announced their first competition for playwrights.[17] Members of the D. D.s, as they were called, were invited to submit one-act plays to be put on the following year, the goal being the promotion of unknown talent: the advancement of the 'Great Unacted'. Sixty entries were received, and the judges, Jacob Thomas 'Jack' Grein (the club's founder) and Henry Hamilton Fyfe (the author and journalist), chose four winners, three of which were subsequently performed at the New Royalty Theatre on 25 February 1906. One of the winning entries was *Miss Vere D'Arsay* by F. M. Mayor. The play, about 'a horrid, vulgar, unsuccessful actress',[18] received mixed reviews. Whilst the critic writing for *The Stage* was kind enough to comment that all three plays 'showed a certain amount of promise',[19] others were less than complimentary. According to *The Era*, Flora's play was 'badly constructed and badly written'; the critic went on to say, rather brutally considering the fact that the writers and actors were all amateurs, that if the other entries 'were worse than *Miss Vere D'Arsay* and *The Death of a Soul*—two of the chosen pieces upon which it is impossible to bestow praise—then we sympathise with Mr. H. Hamilton Fyfe, upon whose shoulders fell the onus of selection, in having to wade through what must have been a shoal of "Shockers." '[20] Flora wrote two other one-act plays around this time, both about the off-stage life of an actress, *Behind the Scenes* and *Going Downhill*; the former was performed at Caxton Hall in December 1906 and February 1907 and received brief but kind reviews.[21]

In 1910, Flora moved to West London and set up home with her brother Robin at 11 Campden Hill Square;[22] Alice took over her place in Clifton with Henry. It was while living there that she wrote her short novel *The Third Miss Symons*, which was published, with an introduction by the future Poet Laureate John Masefield, by Sidgwick and Jackson in March 1913. It is the story of Henrietta Symons, an unmarried, unloved woman who longs to love and to be loved but, due to failings in her own character, hasn't the talent for it. It is the chronicle of a futile life; Henrietta, like so many spinsters of her time—like so many superfluous women—'has the fate to be born in a land where myriads of women of her station go passively like poultry along all the tramways of their parishes'.[23] The novel was widely acclaimed, and it was shortlisted for the Edmond de Polignac Prize.[24] *The Daily Telegraph* wrote that Flora's study of a spinster's life 'is brilliantly clever, actual and sincere… Without the slightest attempt to play upon the feelings, it reaches to the very heart of things, and leaves the reader with an aching sense of the intolerable waste of human nature'.[25] The *Free Church Suffrage Times* wrote, 'The story is set down with great beauty, truth and skill… it is partly to give illumination in such lives that our woman's cause exists.'[26]

On 14 December 1912, a few months before the publication of *The Third Miss Symons*, Flora's brother Robin, who was forty-three years old at the time, married Beatrice Meinertzhagen, who was only twenty-seven.[27] When Beatrice moved to Campden Hill Square to begin married life with Robin, Flora moved back to the family home at Kingston Hill and lost what little freedom she had acquired while living with her brother in London. She persevered with her writing, and on 1 June 1914 the first instalment of her novella 'Miss Browne's Friend: A Story of Two Women' appeared in the *Free Church Suffrage Times*; the fourth and final instalment was delayed by the war until 1 March 1915. Then, in January 1916, Flora's brother Henry was appointed Housemaster of Watson's House, Clifton College, and, as he was unmarried, she and Alice were forced to take it in turns standing in as Housemaster's wife, dividing their time between Clifton and Kingston Hill. Unfortunately, neither sister was ideally suited to their new role. Alan Napier, best remembered for portraying Bruce Wayne's butler in the 1960s Batman series, was a student at the school from 1916 to 1921, and he wrote in his autobiography that Henry Mayor, though a splendid classical scholar, was 'so incompetent a hotel-keeper' that he had to call in his two spinster sisters 'Flora and Alice… Of course we called them Flora and Fauna'; they were 'dear, wonderful women—but totally incompetent housekeepers.'[28]

There were entertainments at Watson's every Saturday evening, and sometimes Alice sang Scottish folk songs; for some of the boys, her singing was 'excruciating'.[29] At the end of one term, it was suggested that the boys should celebrate with a theatrical performance; Flora directed the play and cast Napier, who was a tall, thin sixteen-year-old at the time, as a lovesick housemaid; she recognised Napier's potential, coached him and gave him the encouragement he needed, and he stole the show.[30]

It was during Flora's years at Clifton College that she began writing ghost stories, sometimes reading them to the boys.[31] But while at the school, with her time taken up working hard for her brother, in what must have been a rowdy and distracting environment, she found it difficult to write; she wrote to Alice, 'it's most disintegrating intellectually… I should have no powers of concentration left if I led this life for long.'[32] Additionally, when Flora and Alice were apart—when Flora was in Clifton, Alice was at the family home, and vice versa—both found the separation very difficult. In 1919, Henry suffered a nervous breakdown and had to take several months off work, and Flora and Alice left Clifton for good and returned to Queensgate House. Alice took care of their elderly mother, by then a widow, their father having died in 1916, and Flora began work on what was to become her masterpiece: the novel she entitled *Dedmayne*.

Flora's sister-in-law, Beatrice Mayor (herself a playwright and poet), was linked to the Bloomsbury Group, and it was by her introduction that Leonard Woolf came to read *Dedmayne* at the beginning of 1924. On 14 January 1924, Flora wrote to Woolf asking for his opinion of the novel and explaining that it had just been returned to her by Chatto & Windus, who 'while speaking favourably of it, do not think it could be successful commercially'.[33] In the correspondence that followed, it was decided that *The Rector's Daughter* should replace *Dedmayne* as the title; *Dedmayne*, Woolf explained, was hard to remember and described nothing.[34] It was agreed that the book would be published by Virginia and Leonard Woolf's Hogarth Press, on a commission basis and at the author's expense; the funding actually came from Flora's family.[35] Much to the Woolfs' surprise, the book was an instant success; Leonard Woolf wrote on 12 June to say that, of the five hundred copies of the novel already bound up, more than two hundred had already sold, so he'd ordered another two hundred copies in anticipation of 'quite a rush of orders'.[36] One month later, the number had risen to around four hundred and forty copies,[37] and by the beginning of September over nine hundred copies had sold, a second impression had been produced, and the book had been sent to Macmillan and Knopf for possible publication in America.[38] The book was so popular that Boots' lending libraries were forced to restrict borrowing access.[39] The following year, the novel was shortlisted for the Femina Vie Heureuse Prize.[40]

The Rector's Daughter is the story of an unconsummated love affair between Mary Jocelyn, a dowdy, bespectacled spinster and owner of 'uninteresting hair', and Robert Herbert, the sensitive and scholarly curate of a neighbouring parish, who marries the young, beautiful Kathy Hollings. When it was published, the reviews were overwhelmingly positive. *The Westminster Gazette* thought Flora's writing reminiscent of Trollope, *The Gentlewoman* considered it 'a novel of unusual power, brilliancy and depth' and 'not to be missed'.[41] Sylvia Lynd wrote, 'it is like a bitter Cranford. Mrs [sic] Mayor explores depth of feeling that Mrs Gaskell's generation perhaps did not know and certainly did not admit to knowing.'[42] In a letter to Flora, Virginia Woolf wrote of the number of people who had spoken of their admiration for the book, including the critic and biographer Lytton Strachey, the artist and designer Duncan Grant, and the critic Raymond Mortimer.[43] E. M. Forster wrote that the book had interested and moved him very much,[44] and John Masefield wrote, 'It is a remarkable book and confirms you in your remarkable rank.'[45]

On 9 January 1927, Flora's mother died at the age of ninety-eight. It was the end of an era; the family home at Kingston Hill was sold, and Flora and Alice moved to 7 East Heath Road, Hampstead.[46] Shortly after the move, Flora underwent a serious operation, after which she suffered a bout of pneumonia and was admitted to Braintree Cottage Hospital; she was pleased to be the occupant of her own room, commenting in a letter to Alice that she was certain 'all patients in wards are treated like children'.[47] A chronic asthmatic and sufferer of recurrent bouts of bronchitis, every illness left her severely weakened, and she became increasingly frail.

Flora's last novel, *The Squire's Daughter*, was published by Constable in February 1929. It is the story of an old English county family in decline in changing economic circumstances. The novel wasn't as well received as *The Rector's Daughter*, but one critic wrote, 'the real charm of the book lies in the picture it gives of the life of the old-fashioned English countryside and the unavoidable sadness of its passing. The author is writing of what she knows and loves, and her characters are real people whom one may meet any day in rural England.'[48] Another wrote that the novel 'is full of unobtrusive excellence and a patient sincerity which stands Miss Mayor in good stead.'[49] And Sylvia Lynd was a firm supporter of the novel when it was shortlisted for the Femina Vie Heureuse Prize.[50]

In January 1932, both Flora and Alice caught the 'flu. Alice recovered. Flora developed pneumonia, and she died on 28 January 1932; she was only fifty-nine years old. She was buried on 1 February 1932 in Hampstead Cemetery,[51] alongside her seven paternal aunts; on her gravestone were inscribed her favourite words from Bach's Mass in B Minor: *Exspecto Resurrectionem* ('I look forward to the resurrection'). John Masefield wrote her obituary for *The Times*, but, as Flora's work was already largely forgotten, the newspaper refused to print it. The only printed obituary notice appeared in the *Newnham College Roll Letter*, written by her friend Melian Stawell in 1932.

At her death, Flora left the sum of £12328 1s. 10d. and a selection of short stories for which she had never managed to secure a publisher.[52] Some of the unpublished stories had a supernatural theme; she believed, or at the very least wanted to believe, in the immortality of the human soul, and several of her ghostly tales focus on the possibility of communication between the living and the dead. Flora herself thought her ghost stories to be some of the best work she had produced, but they were rejected by publishers time and again.[53]

In September 1933, Robin Mayor attempted to rekindle interest in his sister's work and suggested to the Hogarth Press the possibility of publishing cheap editions of her novels, but by then there was little interest in her writing.[54] Flora Mayor had been all but forgotten by the time that, in March 1935, Longmans, Green and Co. Ltd. published *The Room Opposite: And Other Tales of Mystery and Imagination*, a collection of sixteen of the tales that had been left unpublished at her death. It was issued with a recommendation from no less eminent a critic of ghost stories than M. R. James, who wrote: 'The stories in this volume which introduce the supernatural commend themselves to me very strongly.' Though, one reviewer wrote, 'Approval by such an authority must carry a certain weight, but no such commendation is required, for the stories can stand on their own merits.'[55] On the whole, the collection was well received; one reviewer wrote, 'Here is a collection of tales of mystery and imagination which, without setting out to arouse the mind of the reader to a pitch of horror and hair-raising thrill, yet succeeds in doing so.'[56] Another praised the stories for being "written with a quiet forcefulness which conveys to the full a sense of horror in perfectly natural surroundings.'[57]

Six of the stories contain no hint of the supernatural or uncanny; the misery or fear that their protagonists suffer is brought about by purely human action or inaction. The fate of Mrs. Gwynne in 'Christmas Night at Almira', for example, reminds us that the horrific can be found in mundane human existence, that dread and anxiety can thrive in loneliness, and the simple absence of care and kindness can leave us feeling hopelessly isolated and fearful without the involvement of any supernatural agent. Mrs. Gwynne's torment comes from having outlived her own usefulness;

she is the superfluous woman: ignored, unloved and unnecessary. 'Innocents' Day' and 'Mother and Daughter', as with 'Christmas Night at Almira', concern the loneliness associated with having reached that 'last, most cheerless stage in the journey of life'.[58]

The spinster takes centre stage in two other tales: 'Letters from Manningfield' and 'Tales of Widow Weeks'. Both centre upon the everyday goings on of Miss Corbett, unmarried daughter of the Vicar of Manningfield, who finds 'just living all day with old people is a drain on one's vitality', but these tales also involve some fantastic element: fairies in the former, an epistolary tale, and witchcraft in the latter. And in another of the strange tales, 'There Shall Be Light at Thy Death', James Clarkson, a gambler who needs money in a hurry in order to replace the large amount he has stolen from his employer, finds that doing away with an elderly spinster can have unwelcome consequences.

Another type of superfluous woman - the unmourned wife - is the subject of 'The Dead Lady', in which Lady Wild, who dies believing 'True love dost last for ever', discovers that her husband, Sir Harry, has replaced her less than a day after her death. And in 'Miss de Mannering of Asham', the focus of the haunting, sad tale is the abandoned woman, unloved and unprotected by her father and ill-used by a Wickham-like rake who wouldn't have been out of place in an Austen novel.

But some of the best tales of the collection involve no women at all, or at the most the merest whiff of one. The title story is set mainly in an old English inn and is a tale of robbery and murder with a hint of the supernatural. William Stanley is on his way to Cambridge when he is caught in a snow-storm, loses his way, and finds himself at the One Tree Inn in the ugly village of Swinford. The room opposite his is occupied by a man who, according to his two doctors, is not long for this world, and throughout the night Stanley is disturbed by terrible cries from the sickroom. The story is told in such a matter-of-fact manner that the crimes described within it are rendered all the more brutal and horrific.

In 'The Kind Action of Mr. Robinson', young Charles Marsden is in debt to a money-lender and in urgent need of funds. It is a winter afternoon, and he is waiting at a coaching inn when Mr Robinson—'a tall man in black clothes, with somewhat the appearance of a clergyman'—appears out of the darkness and offers him a packet of cash; 'You need not trouble yourself with an I.O.U.,' says Robinson, 'for I myself will remind you from time to time'. And that he does, every ten years, on the night before the anniversary of their first meeting, until the much-dreaded repayment falls due.

In 'Fifteen Charlotte Street', James Dence has travelled to London to look for work. He is lost when Mr Morell offers assistance and, as it is late in the day and pouring with rain, Dence accepts the offer of a room for the night at 15 Charlotte Street. Once at that address, Morell informs his guest that he is a doctor, that he is concerned for Dence's health, and he proceeds to examine the young man before whispering, 'You are now coming upstairs with me. What happens there is a secret, which no one must ever know.' *The Aberdeen Press and Journal* considered this tale to be 'outstanding among other creepy tales',[59] and quite rightly too.

One reviewer felt that the supernatural stories were as effective, 'as anything I've seen for some while'.[60] Another wrote, 'the author of The Third Miss Symons has, in "The Room Opposite", given an intensely interesting and original performance.'[61] But by the time that *The Room Opposite* was published, its author was so little remembered for her previous successes that some reviewers mistook her for a man. And, as her great masterpiece *The Rector's*

Daughter sold only a couple of hundred copies between 1933 and 1941, it appears that the publication of *The Room Opposite* in 1935 did little to increase awareness of, or interest in, Flora's other work.

On 28 February 1941, *John O'London's Weekly* published a tribute by Rosamond Lehmann entitled 'These Novels Should Live', in which she described *The Rector's Daughter* as timeless and 'a piece of history'. As a result, the final ninety-four copies of *The Rector's Daughter* were sold, and the title went out of print at the publisher; this, compared to the solitary two copies that had sold in the preceding twelve months and the fact that the title had been on the list for pulping.[62] But the surge in interest was short-lived, and there was no further mention of Flora Mayor's work until, in 1967, Leonard Woolf published volume IV of his autobiography, *Downhill All the Way*, in which he referred to *The Rector's Daughter*, by then completely forgotten, as 'remarkable'.

Leonard Woolf's comments inspired Flora's nephew, Andreas Mayor, to approach Penguin about the republication of *The Rector's Daughter*, and it was issued as a Penguin Modern Classic in 1973, after being out of print with the original publisher for thirty-two years. *The Third Miss Symons* remained out of print until it was issued as a Virago Modern Classic in 1979. *The Squire's Daughter* remained unavailable until it was republished as a Virago Modern Classic in 1987. *Mrs. Hammond's Children*, following its second printing in 1902, has never been reissued. And, until now, *The Room Opposite* remained out of print and almost impossible to find as a secondhand book. It is my fervent hope that, with the republication of this collection of short stories, Flora Mayor will receive a large portion of the admiration and applause she so desired, and so richly deserved.

Notes

1 Excerpt from Joseph Mayor's Commonplace-Book. Quoted in Sybil Oldfield, *Spinsters of This Parish* (London: Virago Press, 1984), p. 10.

2 Oldfield, op. cit., p. 15.

3 Surbiton High School, *The Jubilee book of the Surbiton High School, 1884-1934* (London: Favil Press, 1934).

4 Reported in the *Surrey Comet*, 8 September 1888, 'Oxford University Local Examinations', junior candidates list, p. 3.

5 Letter from Flora to Alice, 1897, quoted in Oldfield, op. cit., p. 60.

6 Machen was a happy member of the company from 1901 to 1909.

7 Flora's Stage Journal, quoted in Oldfield, op. cit., p. 78.

8 Flora's Stage Journal, quoted in Oldfield, op. cit., p. 82.

9 28 December 1901, p. 40.

10 *The Era*, 14 February 1903, p. 9

11 For example: *The Era*, 14 February 1903, p. 9, 'Miss Mary Strafford and Miss Daisy Markham successfully sustained the characters of Francesca and Nattalina respectively'; and the *Dover Express*, 17 April 1903, p. 7, 'Miss Mary Strafford, Miss Daisy Markham, and Miss Frances Bainsford all treat their parts excellently'.

12 Flora's Stage Journal, quoted in Oldfield, op. cit., p. 87.

13 Oldfield, op. cit., p. 101.

14 *England & Wales, National Probate Calendar (Index of Wills and Administrations), 1858-1995*, 1904, Sabatier to Tzitzika, p. 74.

15 The manuscript has not survived.

16 *The Queen, The Lady's Newspaper*, 8 April 1905, p. 32.

17 *The Referee*, 17 December 1905, p. 3.

18 *The Stage*, 1 March 1906, p. 19.

19 Ibid.

20 *The Era*, 3 March 1906, p. 15.

21 Oldfield, op. cit., p. 303.

22 *London, England, City Directories, 1736-1943*, Kensington, Notting Hill, Brompton, Knightsbridge, 1910, p. 392.

23 John Masefield's introduction.

24 Victoria Gray, preface to *The Rector's Daughter* (Bath: Persephone Books, 2021), p. xvii.

25 11 April 1913, p. 4.

26 1 June 1913, p. 8.

27 *London, England, Church of England Marriages and Banns, 1754-1938*, Parish of St. Luke, Chelsea.

28 Alan Napier and James Bigwood, *Not Just Batman's Butler: The Autobiography of Alan Napier* (Jefferson: McFarland & Co., 2016) p. 57.

29 Ibid., p. 59.

30 Ibid., p. 60

31 Gray, op. cit. p. xvii.

32 Oldfield, op. cit., p. 204.

33 Penguin Random House UK Archive and Library owner of the Hogarth Press archive collection, held by the University of Reading Special Collections. Document MS 2750/277/1.

34 Ibid., Document MS 2750/277/2. March 1924. Flora explains that *The Rector's Daughter* was actually the original title and that it had been changed to *Dedmayne*.

35 Ibid., MS 2750/277/13 (27 June 1924).

36 Ibid., MS 2750/277/11.

37 Ibid., MS 2750/277/15 (13th July 1924).

38 Ibid., MS 2750/277/19 (6 August 1924). Both Macmillan and Knopf refused the novel. Arrangements were finally made for Coward McCann to publish in the States in February 1930.

39 Gray, op. cit., p. xix.

40 1925, E. M. Forster's *A Passage to India* won. Originally established as an annual prize for a French novel, from 1919 the Femina Vie

Heureuse Prize was also awarded to English works 'calculated to reveal to French readers the true spirit and character of England'.

41 *Westminster Gazette*, 17 July 1924, p. 6. *The Gentlewoman*, 13 September 1924, p. 330

42 *Time and Tide*, 18 July 1924, quoted in Oldfield, op. cit., p. 241.

43 29 May 1924, quoted in Oldfield, op. cit., p. 239.

44 Letter to Flora, 16 June 1924, quoted in Oldfield, op. cit., p. 239.

45 Letter to Flora, quoted in Oldfield, op. cit., p. 24

46 *London, England, Electoral Registers, 1832-1965*, Hammersmith and Fulham, 1930, p. 19

47 Quoted in Oldfield, op. cit., p. 277.

48 *Yorkshire Post and Leeds Intelligencer*, 6 March 1929, p. 6. This was later used in Constable's advertising.

49 *Montrose Review*, 1 March 1929, p. 7.

50 N. Wilson, ' 'So now tell me what *you* think!': Sylvia Lynd's collaborative reading and reviewing - the collaborative work of an interwar middlewoman'. in *Literature & History*, 28 (1), 2019, p. 58.

51 *UK, Burial and Cremation Index, 1576-2014*, 1932, Hampstead, p. 3205.

52 *England & Wales, National Probate Calendar (Index of Wills and Administrations), 1858-1995*, 1932, Labram to Pywell, p. 282.

53 Oldfield, op. cit., p.275.

54 Penguin, op. cit., document MS 2750/277/34 (27 September 1933).

55 *Montrose Review*, 19 April 1935, p. 7.

56 *Montrose Standard*, 15 March 1935, p. 6.

57 *Hampshire Telegraph*, 22 March 1935, p. 21.

58 'Christmas Night at Almira'.

59 21 March 1935, p. 2.

60 *Birmingham Daily Gazette*, 10 April 1935, p. 8.

61 *Kington Times*, 13 July 1935, p. 3.

62 Penguin, op. cit., document MS 2750/277/42, internal memo at Hogarth Press, March 1941.

THE ROOM OPPOSITE

IN the flattest part of Cambridgeshire there lies the ugly village of Swinford. Owing to its paper mills the old thatched cottages have been shouldered out of existence by white houses with slate roofs and a line of red tiles along the top. The bicycles and motors tear by, and take no notice of anything, but the carrier's roan horse is wiser, and sometimes at dusk he shies at the One Tree Hotel, and will not go on. He seems to know that a hundred and fifty years ago events happened on that spot which made Swinford notorious in all the country round.

The following is a record of the events.

In the autumn of 17—, three friends sat together at supper; James Monkhouse and Robert Wenlock, men of thirty, and William Stanley, a youth of twenty-two. Monkhouse and Stanley divided their time between London and their estates in the country; Wenlock was a barrister. They were now in Stanley's rooms in Fitzroy Square.

"When shall we three meet again?" said Wenlock.

"Not till the last fox in Leicestershire has been hunted for the season," said Monkhouse, "and then I shall creep back to your beloved London as sadly as a schoolboy after the holidays. I mean this time to escape my aunts', Lady Maria and Mrs. Cumberland's, kind hospitality, and make a little voyage of discovery. Some people discover the Tartars; I am going to discover our rural inns, not the magnificent inns on the London Road, but the rude inns of the hamlets, and I dare say the inhabitants will be quite as barbarous as the Tartars."

"If you like villainous roads," said Wenlock, "and still more villainous beds, and wine and spirits most villainous of all, you will be very happy in your rural inns, but London is good enough for me."

"I leave you to the joys of intellectual companionship, Wen, and Stanley to the ladies' society and writing verses. You will have no time for thoughts of me, nor I of you. If you are good enough to write to me, Stanley, I shall not be good enough to answer you."

"Is Norris to be permitted to give us news of his master?" asked Wenlock.

"I shall send Norris to the Chase when I set forth on my adventures. I do not ask him to share my privations. He likes his comforts almost more than you barristers do."

"It seems to be a kind of pilgrimage or ascetic task on which you are embarking. Shall you walk barefoot?"

"No, I shall ride the grey."

"What does your sister think of this scheme?" asked Stanley.

"I have trained my sister to the perfection of womanly amiability. Everything I do is right."

"And Mrs. Watson?"

"Oh, she always thinks me a sadly wild gentleman. By the way, I shall write and tell *her* when I am coming to the Chase, because she says it gives her the spasms when I do not, and I do not like my old friend to have the spasms."

"We are not to be entirely bereft, then?"

"Knowing that the ordinary fate of such courageous characters as I is to be killed and eaten by the highwaymen of the Eastern Counties, I shall make a point of informing you by means of a special messenger, who shall also bring you a lock of my hair, which, being straw colour, you will at once recognize as a relic of the departed."

When Wenlock had left, the two friends sat on, talking.

"Come, good night," said Monkhouse at last, "till we meet again."

"I have a strange desire that you were not going," said Stanley.

"What a womanish desire, Stanley."

"Not so womanish, for you often travel with a large amount of gold on you, and you have been attacked more than once."

"Yes, but I have always come off victorious, and I am not afraid. The gentlemen of the road like people who are afraid of them. Still, I am not ungrateful for the affection that dictates your wish. You are as dear to me as a brother, Stanley, dearer far than that precious brother of mine. One should not presume to read the secrets of a woman's heart, but I believe if you could but summon courage to declare your love to my sister, we should one day be brothers indeed. Therefore whatever befalls me, you shall, if possible, have news of me!"

In the following February, Stanley, after hunting in Northamptonshire, was on his way to visit a friend at his old college—Trinity, Cambridge. He was riding alone over the level expanse of fenland in Cambridgeshire. His servant's horse had lost a shoe. There had been delay in repairing it, and Stanley determined to press on and leave the servant to follow, as the weather was threatening, and the inns in that neighbourhood notoriously bad. He was overtaken by a violent fall of snow. Landmarks were obliterated, and he missed his way; he found that he was off the road; the snow descended more heavily, and progress became difficult. Night came on apace, and a high wind arose. The horse was completely exhausted; he dismounted and led it. It seemed to Stanley that he had been battling in the darkness for many hours, when suddenly the faint flash of a light darted up and disappeared.

He pressed forward to the spot whence it came. It shone again, and the outline of a house became visible. It was the light of a small lamp carried past the window, and again it vanished. Now, however, Stanley had reached the house. He knocked long and loudly. At last the door opened a crack, and the carrier of the lamp spoke.

"What is it you were wanting?"

"I have missed my way, and the horse can go no further. Will you have the goodness to give me a bed for the night? I do not know at what house I am knocking, but I will reward you liberally."

"I can't let you in to-night. You must go on. I haven't a bed in the house to spare."

"Let me sleep on the floor. I shall be dead before morning if I stay in this snow. Take this."

Stanley held out two sovereigns. The man could see them gleam; the spectacle sweetened him.

"Well, sire," he said, "this here is an inn, but we're in a small way, and the ostler's gone to Barcombe, so if you'll excuse it, I'd best take the horse myself."

Stanley saw the horse properly attended to, and then entered the house. The landlord shut the door softly, and as softly opened another.

"Come in to the parlour, sir. It's chill now, but we'll light a fire for you, and make it comfortable."

"Don't trouble yourself. I will join the rest of the company, if it is agreeable to them."

"Asking your pardon, sir, I should say they was gentlemen that liked to keep themselves to themselves."

"Whatever is most convenient to you, then," said Stanley.

"Thank you, sir, and now I'll show you your bedroom, and don't you talk quite so loud, sir, if you'll excuse me, going up the stairs, for there's a party here already gone to bed that might not like to be disturbed."

"In bed at nine o'clock?"

"Yes, sir, perhaps he don't feel just the thing."

While the landlord was guiding Stanley stealthily towards the stairs, the door of the room opposite suddenly opened, and a man came out, also carrying a lamp. His face was red and gross, and he called out in an insolent voice:

"Hi, you there, who's that fellow you have with you?"

"It is just a poor traveller, sir, what had lost his way, and could not be denied, not such a night as this."

"Not by such a Christian as you, you mean to say, Jimmy."

"Softly, Mr. Kennett, sir."

"Mr. Kennett, you scoundrel," replied the man, swelling and purple with wrath. "*Dr.* Kennett. Now what did you swear not an hour ago, you ——"

"Aren't you forgetting something" said the landlord.

Kennett suddenly seemed to restrain himself, and turning to Stanley, he said: "The fact is, sir, I am a doctor, Dr. Kennett, and I am now giving my professional services to a gentleman in that room, and nobody hadn't better have nothing to do with him, for he is suffering from a putrid fever, putrid and contagious, that's what it is, if he don't want to be a villainous dead corpse, so don't you go putting your nose inside that door."

"Do you speak thus of the sufferer under your charge?" asked Stanley.

"The sufferer, sir, has everything he wants in this world, and whatever he has, he won't want it for long, I dare say."

Thus speaking Dr. Kennett walked to the end of the passage and began to sing.

"The man is drunk," said Stanley, turning to the landlord. "Is there no one here who can soothe the last moments? Let me visit him, if there is none else."

"I assure you, sir, there is no occasion. Dr. Kennett is very attentive."

It seemed vain to interfere further, and Stanley went to his room. He arrayed himself in some infamous garments,[1] provided by the landlord, and descended to the parlour, where a fire was lighted, and supper ay before him.

After supper he was abandoning himself to the pleasures of rum punch, when he was disturbed by a cry. Three times he heard it. The second cry was choked and feeble, the third still more choked and feeble. Then he could refrain no longer. He went out into the passage, and was in the act of opening the door of the room opposite, when a man he had not seen before laid his hand on his shoulder.

"Pardon me, sir," said the stranger, "that room is occupied by my patient, and I cannot permit him to be disturbed."

Stanley turned, and beheld a small, cadaverous man, with a bright roving eye.

"Allow me to present myself," said the stranger. "I am Dr. Marks."

"I beg your pardon, sir," said Stanley, "I had understood that a Dr. Kennett was in attendance."

"Dr. Kennett is in attendance also. Fortunately for our patient we were forced, as you were also, I surmise, to shelter here from the inclemency of the storm. The poor gentleman has met with an accident."

"An accident? I understood that Dr. Kennett mentioned a contagious fever."

---

[1] Infamous: unpleasant, disgraceful.

"Dr. Kennett doubtless referred to the fever induced by concussion; the blow was on the head. The word contagious is used perhaps too freely by some medical men. I should not myself describe it as contagious. The condition, I grieve to say, is critical. Absolute quiet is essential."

"I fear your patient is in pain. His cries were pitiful," said Stanley.

"They distressed your humane feeling, but happily they did not indicate peculiar suffering, for the patient is unconscious. It is just possible," continued the doctor with some hesitation, "though improbable in the highest degree, that there might be further cries. If the proximity of the patient is disagreeable to you, doubtless the landlord could give you another room. I believe there is no one but ourselves in the house."

"No, sir," said Stanley, "the landlord need not disturb himself. But if there are beds to spare, can you tell me why he would not at first admit me?"

"Dr. Kennett and I are to blame. Knowing the precarious condition of our patient, we implored him to admit no one. The bustle of arrival might have had serious effects."

"In that case," said Stanley, "I must tell you that your friend, Dr. Kennett, is not fit to attend on the patient. He is drunk, and he was hallooing just now at the top of his voice."

"His intoxication is very regrettable," said Dr. Marks, "but prey recollect in his justification that he had no expectation of exercising his profession here. At home I believe he is a day nurse to all the old ladies and gentlemen in his practice, and to their poodles as well. But we require our enjoyment like other people. On 364 days in the year he does not take a drop more than is needful, on the 365th he may sometimes exceed. But the patient will not be neglected, of that you may be certain; I shall be constantly at hand."

Stanley returned to the parlour. The punch was fragrant, and the fire burned bright; but often his thoughts turned to the sick man's chamber.

And now a cry rang out, far more piercing than the former ones, then a voice speaking loudly and rapidly; no words, however, were distinguishable. Then there was a noise of violent movements; they lasted perhaps a minute; then silence fell. Stanley knew not what to do. The disturbance seemed to him more than the unrest of delirium. He called out, "Dr. Marks, what is the matter? Can I be of any service?"

At the same moment Dr. Marks entered the parlour. His face was paler than before, and his dress was disordered and torn in one place.

"I am infinitely obliged to you," said he. "You can be of no service. You have been disturbed, I see, and it is not to be wondered at. That was a painful crisis, painful even to one like myself, inured to scenes of suffering. The poor wretch fought with me in his madness, but he is now at rest."

"Is he better?"

"That can hardly be hoped for. Even a doctor cannot foretell the precise moment of death; I do not, however, think that he will last out the night. You are going far to-morrow, sir?"

"I am on my way to Cambridge."

"You are a son of Cambridge, happy fellow. You are leaving early in the morning?"

"As early as possible."

"That is, if the weather permits," said the doctor. "I am on my way to Colchester, but my departure must depend on the condition of my good friend in the next room."

"You will forgive me," said Stanley; "in consideration of my early start, I will wish you good night already."

The presence of Dr. Marks was irksome to him, and he made his way upstairs. He was exhausted by his ride, and got into bed, but he could not sleep. His thoughts were continually of the unknown patient. He feared he knew not what. At length he leapt out of bed, dressed himself, and went down to the parlour, where the fire still burnt. He sat and waited, but he could not say why he waited. Blaming himself for his folly, he made up his mind to go upstairs again. He went out into the passage, when a voice came from the room opposite, "I am very near my end." He heard a moan, and then the words were repeated with profound sighing.

He opened the door. The room was dark, but by the light of his candle he saw a man stretched on a bed; the face was turned completely away. The breath came in heavy gasps. The sheets and the head also seemed stained with blood, but of this Stanley could not be sure, for hardly had he entered the room before a gust of air, rushing through a crack in the window-frame, extinguished the candle, and all was again dark.

"Forgive the intrusion of a stranger," said Stanley, "but I feared you were suffering. Can I be of any assistance to you? Let me summon Dr. Marks."

He could hear the figure turn in the bed towards him. In a strained and unnatural voice it said to him: "Who is he?"

Unnatural as it might be, the voice seemed in some strange manner familiar to him.

"Have not Dr. Marks and Dr. Kennett been in attendance on you since your accident?"

"I do not know," replied the man. He then said eagerly and very rapidly: "Listen to me. Where have you taken my letter?"

"What letter, my dear sir? I have no letter of yours."

The sick man spoke with still greater eagerness.

"That letter to him. Tell him, I implore you, that I am dying. I promised I would tell him."

"Tell whom? I entreat you tell me his name."

"I cannot remember it." He repeated, "I cannot remember it."

Stanley approached the bed, feeling his way, and laid his hand on the man's arm. It was shaking as in a palsy.

"My dear sir, compose yourself. My one desire is to be of service to you. Tell me what is your own name?"

"My own name," he said mournfully and wildly, "I cannot tell you." He closed his eyes.

The heavy breathing ceased. Stanley waited. Then he took the right hand in his own. It was already cold.

He let fall the hand, and groped his way back to the parlour as fast as possible. He could see the glass and bottle by the firelight. He poured out some rum and hastened back to the bedside, and endeavoured to force some drops down the stranger's throat. But it was in vain. When Stanley had abandoned hope of restoring him, he made his way out of the room, and seeing a light at the end of the passage, he repaired thither. He knocked at the door. There was no answer, though he heard the sound of cheerful voices within. He knocked again, and entered. The landlord and the two doctors were seated at cards. Dr. Kennett had advanced some degrees in intoxication, and gazed on him vacantly, as did the landlord. Dr. Marks, however, rose and advanced towards him.

"I shall be glad if you will come at once," said Stanley, "your patient requires your attendance. In fact, it is my belief that he is already dead."

"The patient dead?" said Dr. Marks gravely. "You have already seen him?"

"The patient dead?" said Dr. Kennett, whom this intelligence seemed to rouse from pleasant apathy. "Why I left him for dead two hours ago, and he rose again, and you left him for dead an hour ago, and he rose again, and half an hour ago in you came with "I've settled him," and up he hops like a cat with nine tails—is it tails I am talking of? I never knew such a fellow."

"Dr. Kennett," said Dr. Marks, turning on him a look of repulsion. "There is a limit which should not be exceeded even in liquor. You are disgracing your cloth, sir."

"Come at once, I entreat you," said Stanley, his thoughts intent on the patient.

"I can only assure you, sir," said Dr. Marks, as they walked down the passage, "that the abnormal condition of the atmosphere has affected Dr. Kennett. It is a well-attested fact that the presence of snow in the atmosphere, when combined with over-indulgence in alcohol, occasionally produces a disastrous confusion of the spirit."

Dr. Marks now entered the death chamber, and shut the door. Nothing more could be done, yet Stanley lingered, unwilling, for reasons he could not explain, to leave the lifeless, unfeeling corpse to the ministrations of Dr. Marks.

The doctor was not very long in the room.

"You were right in your conjecture," he said, when he came forth. "Life is extinct. The end was sudden. A copious discharge of blood occasioned it. The cause of that discharge is unknown. Nature has many mysteries, which she keeps secret from us. You observed the blood?"

"I fancied so, but my light went out, almost as I entered the room."

"Ah! Was the patient conscious before his death?"

"I do not think so. I mentioned your name and he did not recognize it. Do you know anything of him? Who was he?"

"He told me his name was Joseph Hooper, and that he came from London. I asked him these particulars, fearing the worst, but he had only a short period of consciousness after his accident. I could ascertain nothing further. In those few minutes his thanks were profuse for the little I had done for him. Such tokens of gratitude are flowers in the dusty high road of a doctor's existence. You had a special reason for your enquiries?"

"Hardly. Yet I have an idea, unfounded, I believe, that his voice was in some way familiar to me. His face was turned from me, and I could not see it. What manner of man was he?"

"Insignificant," said the doctor, "but for a cast in the left eye and a scar to the left cheek. Can I give you any further particulars?"

"No, sir. I am obliged to you. I have already trespassed on your time."

"I am sorry my information is so meagre."

"Nay, Mr. Joseph Hooper can be nothing to me, only the spectacle of the decease of a fellow creature with none to shed a tear of regret is shocking and unnatural."

"True," said the doctor. "Alas, poor mortality!"

An incomprehensible desire overmastered Stanley, and he said, "Dr. Marks, I should like to see the dead man's face."

You shall," replied Dr. Marks. "Not at this moment—you understand—it is better. I will summon you in half an hour."

Stanley waited in the parlour with impatience and restlessness. At length Dr. Marks entered. "Will you come with me," he said.

His lamp burnt rather dim, but it sufficed to show the deceased lying decently made ready. He wore a voluminous night-cap, which covered the whole of the head and neck, concealing the hair. It framed the ashen countenance. The features were finely chiselled; the eyebrows and lashes dark. It was the face of a stranger; yet either the dead man's beauty or the lamentable circumstances of his end affected Stanley almost to tears.

"I do not call that profile insignificant," he said.

"You are right, sir," said Dr. Marks, "and I was mistaken. Death sometimes lends a peculiar grandeur to what was of little count in life. I have seen many dead; I speak from experience."

Stanley was liable to the unreasoned impulses of the poetic character. Pity drew him now to lay a caressing hand in farewell upon the deserted corpse. He lightly touched the cold forehead. "Come away," said Dr. Marks, taking his arm. "The melancholy scene overcomes you. Come with me."

He gently impelled him towards the door; he turned and locked it.

"It would not be seemly," said he, "that there should be the possibility of riotous intrusion here. Your distress does you credit, sir, but it is the duty of a physician to steel himself against too much sensibility."

Although Dr. Marks had always spoken, and spoke now, with a perfect propriety of demeanour, he gave Stanley an unaccountable impression of not in his heart meaning what he said.

Now that the sick man has passed beyond the reach of human aid, Stanley's one desire was to leave the inn as soon as possible, for his aversion to the landlord, Dr. Kennett, and above all, to Dr. Marks, had increased twenty-fold. Marks had rejoined the landlord. Stanley went to his room, unbarred the shutters, and found that the snow had ceased to fall and a few stars were shining. His clothes had, he knew, been taken to some kitchen downstairs. After opening two doors in vain, Stanley found a room with a bright fire burning. His clothes hung on a chair at one side of it. At the other sat an old woman. From her meaningless singing, and the bottle and mug to which she constantly had resort, he gathered that she, in this house of debauchery, was also intoxicated. Stanley approached her, and asked for his clothes. She gave them to him, seized him by the arm, and said: "Is the poor gentleman dead yet?"

"He is dead."

"Dead is he? Then they've gone and locked that door, I'll be bound."

"Certainly the door is locked."

"Didn't I know it? It was just what they did the last time, and again a twelve month ago come Old Barcombe Fair. Begged and prayed of 'em I did not to lock it, but I might have cried to the dead. And Dr. Marks is such a kind gentleman, it ain't his way to refuse."

"But has Dr. Marks been here before?"

"Oh, that he have. Comes three or four times a tear, they does, on the way to see their good mothers at Colchester. 'I wouldn't miss seein' my mother,' Dr. Marks says, 'for the old lady looks to it.' Very feelin' he spoke, very free with his money too. Dr. Kennett ain't, and when I'm a nuss, and there's a corpse in the house, it do cut me to the heart not to lay them out."

"In this case Dr. Marks has already performed the last services."

"But I looked through the keyhole one morning early when they weren't up, and they hadn't washed the blood off."

"The blood? What in Heaven's name do you mean?"

"Why that poor creature what took his own life, which was a very wicked thing to do. 'I thought we *should* have saved him, nuss,' said Dr. Marks, always calls me nuss he does, so civil like, 'but it wasn't the will of Heaven.' "

"Do you mean to tell me that others have recently died in this house besides the man upstairs?"

"Well, folks has to die."

"How did they die?"

"That ain't my place to say nothink about. My sister was here afore me. She says to me, 'You gets your money reg'lar, and there are tips and no stint of beer,' but one went off in a nasty fever. 'Don't you go near him,' Dr. Kennett he says, 'if you don't want to catch it.' Ain't that the door I hear a'going? When they're off to bed, I goes and does what is right."

"Here," said Stanley, handing her money, "if occasion should arise that more should be done for the body of the gentleman upstairs, will you do it?"

"I don't know," he thought, "why I should distress myself. It makes no difference to that stranger now. Any why should I feel that this drunken hag is more tolerable than Marks?"

"Yes, poor thing," said she. "I'll do my best."

"Wait," said Stanley, "can you read?"

"I ain't a scholard, but my niece up in London, she can read."

"This is my address in London; 7 Fitzroy Square."

He handed her a card. "Will you remember it?"

"Fitzroy Square, why I was maid to a very high lady in Percy Street, twelve year, and my dear niece lives at Smithfield, and she say I am to live with her soon, because I'm gettin' old for service. I shan't stay here much longer, such goin's on as there are."

"Come to me in London, or send this card to me, and tell me where I may find you. I must speak to you again, but not now."

She promised. She gave him his clothes, and as he touched his coat, a small black stain appeared on the sleeve; he did not heed it. He groped his way to the stable by the faint starlight. He found his horse; he saddled and bridled it, and rode off as fast as possible. He felt he could have no peace of mind till he had left the inn with its detestable inmates far behind him. He rode some miles, but he was continually haunted by the melancholy face of the dead man, and his earnest oft-repeated words. He felt he could not be easy until he had discovered whether there were any papers on the body which might aid in delivering the message. He turned and, as he thought, rode back in the direction of the inn, but he was again overtaken by snow. Suddenly he was hurled forward with violence, and he knew no more. He had fallen into a disused pit, and there he was found several hours later almost dead from exposure. He was taken in and nursed for several weeks by a lady and gentleman in the neighbourhood and, when he was sufficiently recovered, he was removed to his father's house in London.

One of the first visitors he was permitted to see was his friend Wenlock. He at once poured forth a languid, yet agitated, narration of his adventures at the inn.

"Yet I am not clear, Wenlock, how I came there, nor how I got away. There was a room opposite, of which the door was constantly locked, and the cries that issued from it ring still in my ears."

Why does not Monkhouse come to see me?" he asked, some days later, with the fretfulness of convalescence.

"Monkhouse is still at the Chase."

"And Miss Monkhouse?" said Stanley. "I hope Miss Monkhouse is in good health?"

"Miss Monkhouse is not quite in her usual health. She has been solicitous for your welfare."

"I am sorry," said Stanley. "Miss Monkhouse's health is a matter of concern to all who have the honour of her acquaintance."

And he became stronger from that hour.

"Stanley," said Wenlock, one day. "The time has now come when you must hear bad news. Our friend Monkhouse was expected at the Chase in February. It is now the 13th of April, and he has not returned."

"But you know his eccentric habits," said Stanley. "He likes to return unexpectedly."

"He wrote to Mrs. Watson on February 16th saying he would be at the Chase in the following week, as he was expecting an important communication from his lawyer, which was to be sent to the Chase. He never came, and the lawyer at length wrote to his brother, as the letter required an immediate answer. Advertisements were inserted in the newspapers; rewards were offered; a competent lawyer engaged to trace him. But since the day he left the Welbys on February 27th, he has not been seen or heard of. We can only conjecture that, like you, he must have had some accident in the great snowstorm of February 20th and 21st and died from exposure."

Stanley covered his face with his hands, and remained silent for some moments.

"We have lost the best and truest of friends," he said. He paused. "How does she bear it?"

"Bravely, while there was still hope, but now she is sunk in grief."

"Can nothing more be done? Is the law in our enlightened age incapable of rendering assistance?"

"Do you not know that in our enlightened age, and I believe in all other enlightened ages, the law is only capable of providing a precarious living for myself and other worthy men?"

"How can you jest, Wenlock?"

"In sober earnest, can you not rest assured that I should leave no stone unturned? He did not take the route he spoke of to the

Welbys, for every inn on that road has been visited. The Welbys say he had a large sum of money with him when he started; it is possible that he may have been robbed. I was in Paris at the time, and you know Mr. Philip Monkhouse; he was, of course, more occupied with his palpitations than with the mere loss of a half-brother. Precious time was lost. The investigations were not begun till my return several weeks after his disappearance. His one night's sojourn would doubtless be already growing dim in the minds of the innkeepers. They might have given some clue, but it was then too late to find it."

"Of course, I know your ardour to trace him would be as keen as my own, and your wisdom far greater. I spoke in the bitterness of my soul. And now forgive me, I would rather be alone."

When next Stanley saw Wenlock, he said to him with agitation: "As I am a living man, the dead stranger at the inn was James Monkhouse."

"What makes you think so?"

"Did I not tell you the voice had a remarkable familiarity? It was his voice distorted by delirium. I cannot understand how I did not recognize it at the time."

"And the face, did you recognize the face?"

"The features, as I recall them, resembled James's features, but the eyebrows and lashes were black."

"James was a fair man."

"Yes, but you recollect the scar on his left cheek? I saw the scar."

"Other men might have scars on their left cheeks, but a fair man cannot become a dark man."

"I have been pondering that point the whole night. Could there not possibly have been some disguise?"

"What disguise? Why should Monkhouse, the most rational of men, paint his face?"

"Nevertheless, I believe that there are times when the mind receives a superior power of intuition. The face was the face of James."

"That faint resemblance of the voice—you observe you did not recognize it at the time—and the scar, are the sole indications?"

"No, not all. Last night I had a dream of singular vividness. I was in that room at the inn with the sick man. He spoke to me. It was the voice of Monkhouse. His words were 'Tell Stanley, I implore you, that I am dying.' I am now absolutely convinced."

"What do you propose to do under these circumstances?"

"I propose going down to Cambridgeshire immediately, when I shall visit the inn, and question the landlord and housekeeper. Would that I had spoken with them further then."

"What was the name of the inn, and where was it situated?"

"I do not know, but I shall not rest until I have discovered it."

"Then you will never rest, Stanley, for there is no such inn. Your spirit is naturally depressed by the death of our friend, and this has led to a recurrence of the fever, which we hoped had left you. Your agitated brain has added what is occupying it most to the airy edifice it had fabricated in delirium. I am not at all surprised that it was Monkhouse whom you met at the inn."

"As I am a living soul, a man died at the inn on the night of February 20th."

"The incident of a man dying at an inn attended by a drunken doctor is not in itself improbable, but there are some fanciful decorations added, hardly suited to this prosaic age."

"You think with Hamlet that the Devil,

'Out of my weakness and my melancholy,
As he is very potent with such spirits,
Abuses me to damn me.' "[2]

"I should never think anything with Hamlet, who was a whining fellow I cannot endure. At any rate defer your investigations till you are stronger. The dead cannot run away."

"There is no good in postponement; my mind is made up."

"Forgive me," said Wenlock gravely, "if I speak with the freedom of a truly attached friend. You are allowing a sickly fancy to usurp your reason. The dead lie under the bounteous protection of a good Providence. It is our duty not to yield to unmanly regret, but to give our minds to the business of life. Your exertions cannot bring Monkhouse back from the tomb."

"You forget that my desires are shared by another person."

"I do not, and you show yourself little fitted to be, as you desire, her dearest guide and protector, while you encourage her in the vainest of illusions."

"On the contrary, if I can set her mind at rest on this matter, I shall feel that I have done something to show myself less unworthy of her love."

Wenlock talked to his friend, till he hoped he had dissuaded him. But when he called the next afternoon, he found that Stanley had started for the country that very morning, leaving no directions or messages for him.

He went at once to the house of Stanley's rescuer. They searched the country, but could hear no news of him, till Wenlock

---

[2] Act 2, Scene 2. The Devil takes advantage of Hamlet's sadness, as he has influence over melancholy people, to trick him into damnation.

received a letter from Stanley's father saying that he had returned to London.

"My dear Stanley," said Wenlock, "I am relieved to see you again. I had begun to fear another drunken doctor had murdered *you*."

"I deserve your mockery," said Stanley. "You were right. I went on a wild-goose chase, I failed, I have returned. Let us say no more about it."

He was so dejected that his friend with all his efforts could not cheer him.

As they sat together one afternoon Stanley's servant entered with a dirty scrap of cardboard in his hand, which he brought to Stanley.

"The party that gave me this would not be denied, sir," said he. "She would have it you had bidden her come."

Stanley examined the card.

"Show her up immediately," said he.

"Begging your pardon, sir, she's a low, filthy creature, not fit for a gentleman to speak to."

"Nevertheless I will see her."

"Wenlock," said Stanley. "Here is a tangible figment of my imagination. This is my card, which I told you I gave to the woman at the inn."

Wenlock looked. "I grant this is your card," said he, "but I do not at present see occasion for granting anything else."

The old woman entered. She was covered with mud, and her face was bleeding. "I thought I should 'a been killed," she wailed, "stopping me in the street, knocking me over. 'There now,' he says. 'You can go where you like. Your teeth's drawed now,' he says."

"You have been hurt," said Stanley. "Sit down here, and rest before you speak further."

She was refreshed with meat and wine, and with the bottle by her side she stopped weeping, and was able to speak more briskly. "I *have* been treated crool. Turned out of the One Tree, and nearly met me death there. Didn't I hear Marks a-tellin' to Mr. Wally, tho' little he thought I heard him, but two days after you were gone."

"Mr. Wally?" said Wenlock. "Pray, who is Mr. Wally?"

"Why, Mr. Wally as keeps the One Tree; every fool knows that. 'Ah,' says Marks, 'the woman's been a-rifling Monkhouse's body.' "

"Stop," cried Wenlock, "whose body? Monkhouse's? Good God!"

"Monkhouse, that was the pore gentleman's name. I hear 'em say it to one another, afore ever he came into the house that night. Then Marks says such wicked words. 'Let her carcase lie in the lane with the rest of them.' Me to lie in that dark lane with never a prayer said over me. But I never told them I spoke to you, though they asked me time and again. 'If you come back here,' he says, 'I'll break every bone in your body.' And I come to London where my niece has a little shop, all the long, long way I come, and I kept the bit of cardboard, as if it had been me poor mother's Bible, and the chap what opened the door to me, he said I shouldn't see you, the swine! But I've got something for you, I have."

"What have you got?"

"Didn't you say I was to do me best for the poor gentleman, and didn't I go in, and take the ring off his finger and his watch and his seals, and the buckles off his shoes? and this very night they was took."

"Then you have nothing?"

"Nothink, but only this."

She gave Stanley a black pocket book with a silver clasp. He took it, and recognized a present he himself had made to Monkhouse in the preceding year.

"Wenlock," he said, "look at this."

"It is in truth Monkhouse's book. Let me question the woman further. My experience in extracting evidence may serve us now."

But his efforts were vain. Her volatile and enfeebled brain could not rest longer on the one topic.

"Think once again," said Wenlock. 'I have a golden guinea here. It shall be yours if you will tell me what was on the person of the man who died when Mr. Stanley was at the inn."

"Oh, if I could but show you the miniature of that dear lady what breathed her last at Cheapside, but there, I haven't a pick-up left in the world."

"Where did they bury that gentleman?"

"There's my poor niece will be expecting me back, and I like to keep respectable hours, seeing as I am a respectable person, so I'll bid you a good night, gentlemen."

"Let her go, Wenlock," said Stanley. "I have something of importance to show you."

He rang the bell.

"Tell Mrs. Leacock to do something for this poor creature."

Wenlock took the book and read the following.

"One Tree Inn, Feb. 20th.

> "Came S.E. 15 miles from Denham. Road vile; inns fair. I cannot rid myself of a singular depression of spirits, for which there is no cause. They should on the contrary be elevated by the excellent glass of port sent in to me by a fellow guest. I have a foreboding that I shall not see Stanley again. He had a

strange apprehension for my safety before my journey. Never was a man more truly blessed than I in his friendship. He was both son and brother to me. I have written a letter to be delivered to him in case we do not meet again."

Stanley closed the book and cried,

"Now, Wenlock, are you not convinced?"

"I am convinced. Much is yet unexplained, but how can I not be convinced? And by God, we will not rest till we get these scoundrels swinging on a gallows."

With the information at their disposal they went down to Cambridge to the house of Stanley's rescuer. He took them to Sir William Eveson, the squire of a village near and Justice of the Peace, and they laid their tale before him.

"They're a nasty lot over at Swinford," said he, when he had heard their tale, "and Wally at the One Tree Inn is a particular beauty. Dirty Whig property it is. They're small farmers and cottagers working their own land; that's always villainous farming. They have some queer tales of Wally, but it's a remote place, and we've never been able to get evidence, and they're all in with him at Swinford and share in the profits. But I've never heard of a Dr. Marks or a Dr. Kennett. I didn't think Wally flew higher than drovers."

It was decided that Wenlock and Stanley should, if possible, secure Wally and through him get hold of Marks and Kennett.

They reached the One Tree Inn, a forlorn and desolate house, standing in the middle of partially drained fenland. The door was opened by the landlord. They entered and asked for beer. He went to fetch it. While they waited Wenlock said, "I envy you the task of confronting that ruffian, but it is yours by right. I merely had commonsense and reason entirely on my side. *You* had enthusiasm and improbability; they are invincible. Your magnanimity is almost too far removed from the sinful nature of man. You have not yet triumphed over me. That you should have been so much wiser than I, who am always right, is very disturbing to my peace of mind."

Stanley smiled faintly. "I intend to triumph at my leisure," said he, "but now I am filled with apprehension that I shall bungle it, and let the scoundrel escape. I believe it would be wiser for you to speak."

"No, it is your due. Think that the bright eyes of Miranda are upon you, and you will not fail."

"It is for her sake that I am anxious."

"Think then that she would ten times rather that you should attempt it and fail, than that I should attempt it and succeed. Utter foolishness, but so it is."

When the landlord returned, Stanley fixed his eyes on him steadfastly and said.

"Mr. James Monkhouse was murdered in this house on February 20th. You and two others, Dr. Marks and Dr. Kennett, were guilty of his death."

The landlord changed colour, and answered in a shaking voice. "Not me, sir, no sir! I had no hand in it."

"We know a great deal," said Stanley. "You had better confess."

"I'm sure it was never me that was wishful they should die. Just take what you can and let them go. Time and again I've said it, and there weren't only the three; all the others was let go as peaceable as lambs. It's the Gospel truth I'm telling you, gentlemen."

"Tell us more Gospel truth," said Wenlock. "Who are these accomplices of yours?"

"It's Marks as laid the whole plot, gentlemen. The gentleman can tell you I never went near Mr. Monkhouse save to take him a glass of port wine, and to bury him respectable in the lane."

"If you want to continue your worthless life," said Wenlock, "I should advise you to assist us in getting hold of Marks and Kennett."

"Indeed, gentlemen, I'll do my very best. As to Dr. Marks, he sends me word that he and Kennett will be coming here next Thursday, for Cambridge Fair day, otherwise I ain't set eyes on them since that night you was here, Mr. Stanley, sir, if I may make so free with your name."

"Are you to be relied on? It shall be made worth your while."

"Indeed I am, sir. I'm sure it was always my wish to keep the house a decent house."

"You will now speak to Miss Monkhouse, Stanley," said Wenlock, when they had returned to London.

"I believe so, yet how should I presume so far?"

"We should none of us presume so far, but if none of us did that, the fairest of fair creatures would shed her sweetness unrequited. I believe you have a good prospect. I ventured yesterday to ridicule your little eccentricities, I assure you with the greatest tenderness, in her presence. The lady cast a glance of reproof upon me and said: 'My brother James had the highest possible opinion of Mr. Stanley, and he was always right.' You are a lucky dog, Stanley, luckier than some dogs, who deserve quite as much as you, and want just the same bone."

That same evening Stanley and Miss Monkhouse were betrothed.

Wenlock made all preparations for the arrest of Kennett and Marks. The next Thursday he and Stanley were waiting in the parlour of the One Tree Inn.

"You be ready," said the landlord to Wenlock, "when I send them in, and you'll get the pair of them as easy as mice in a trap."

"I confess to a feeling of excitement," said Wenlock as they sat and waited. "I want to see what manner of man the ingenious doctor is."

"If Marks and Kennett do not get wind of the thing," said Stanley.

"No, I think we have brought Wally to heel, and he will do his best for us."

An officer entered with three men. "Here we are, sir. I've brought six of my fellows, as they say this Marks is likely to be a bit of trouble. I've three others posted round the house. They won't escape us."

Half an hour later the landlord opened the door, and looked in. "You may expect them now any minute, gentlemen."

As he spoke, Dr. Marks came in, smiling.

The officer immediately advanced, saying, "I arrest you in the King's name for the murder of James Monkhouse and two others."

The guard seized his arms and he was secured. He did not struggle, nor did he turn any paler than his natural hue.

"I understand now," said he, "the affectionate agitation of my friend Wally. It was with the greatest difficulty I could escape his presence for a moment."

"Where is your accomplice?"

"My accomplice is in the room opposite, gentlemen, finishing an excellent glass of port. You will not be so inhuman as to grudge it to him, for to all appearances it will be his last. Poor Kennett is not in funds to provide himself with port in gaol."

Stanley and Wenlock saw Dr. Marks more than once. Wenlock asked him to acquaint them with the particulars of Monkhouse's death. His narration, related during several visits, is set down here.

"I shall be very glad to give you any information, gentlemen," he said, "and you must pardon me if I am sometimes prolix. To converse with such as you is a pleasure rarely obtainable in my profession. That is a deprivation to a man of breeding, and a man of breeding I once was. I and my lamented friend, Dr. Kennett—Kennett was not his name, and Marks is not mine, nor were he and I members of the medical profession—have been in the present line of business for several years. It is a profitable one, and attended with less risk and difficulties than is sometimes supposed. The simple device of fastening a rope across a road on a dark night has put hundreds of pounds in my pocket. The worthy drovers, who constitute the majority of our rustic prey, are sturdy fellows, but their strength is invariably surpassed by their stupidity. Our methods with them were as follows. Having unhorsed them by some expedient, Wally and Kennett would draw near, and in the confusion of setting them on their legs and leading them into the house to recover, they contrived to relieve them of the money they were carrying home from the fair. I came in later as the doctor, and relieved them still further, if the work had been left unfinished. I had studied medicine at one time, and was glad to plaster up their bruises. Carnage has never been any satisfaction to me. In the course of business it has been more than once necessary to take human life; I have always sincerely regretted it. A more prudent and hard-hearted scoundrel would have taken yours the night we met, Mr. Stanley, but I am anticipating. The One Tree Inn was not the only scene of my activity; we came only for Barcombe, Littlemere and Cambridge fairs. I had enterprises in London also, which demanded sagacity. Poor Kennett was invaluable in the rural districts, but often quite astray in the metropolis. To come to Mr. Monkhouse.

"I had been advised that he would be travelling on February 20th, with large sums upon him. We had people in our employ who kept us informed of what I might call suitable clients. It was solely on his account that Kennett and I came to the inn that day. The rope across the road was not suited to Mr. Monkhouse. With persons of standing I was in the habit of using a narcotic. Mr. Monkhouse arrived late in the evening. I had stored in the cellar some choice port. I am partial to port. I told Wally to take Mr. Monkhouse a glass. I put in sufficient grains of the drug to induce a lethargy, when we could rob him at our ease. I always preferred extracting the larger sums in person. I then distributed what I thought proper to my companions. I am ashamed to own I am an inveterate gambler, and though I have in my time acquired very large sums, I shall die a poor man. I allowed rather more than the usual time for the drug to work, before I visited Mr. Monkhouse. He was not as I expected asleep. He was lying on the bed, knitting his brow and muttering. The drug had taken an effect, but not that which I desired. He turned on me sharply and said, 'Who is there?' I said that I had heard him moving restlessly as I passed his door, and that being a physician, I had ventured to intrude to see whether I could be of assistance. Might I bring him a cordial, which I was sure would relieve him. He thanked me, and I brought and gave him another powerful dose of the narcotic. He then asked me to do him a favour. He gave me a letter addressed to yourself, and begged me to keep it until the next morning. If he himself had not then asked it back from me, I was immediately to send it to your address. Your friend was majestic looking beyond the ordinary beauty of man. I consider myself less rather than more susceptible to the passing doubts and sick fancies of mankind, but I was glad to be out of his presence. Even in his enfeebled condition I feared him. To drown my fear I joined my companions, and we abandoned ourselves to carousals. Wally had been given strict orders to admit no one.

"But I could not altogether master myself, and when I felt sure that the drug must have done its work, I sent Kennett to Mr. Monkhouse's room. As he came out with the money, he met you and Wally in the passage. We had more than once found it expedient to describe our clients as patients. It was Kennett's pride to parade as the Doctor. I let him have his way in the country, he was not much more ignorant than the genuine country practitioner. His 'Putrid' and 'Contagious' were swallowed with reverence by the yokels. You were less easily satisfied, nor do I think my clumsy explanation sufficed you. The excellent port must plead for me.

"When Kennett returned he said: 'He is like a log in there, and it is my belief it's more than the drug, he's dead.' I had not willed Mr. Monkhouse's death, but it was opportune.

"Then as we sat pleasantly at cards, with you disposed of in the parlour, what should we hear but that ill-timed cry which agitated you so much. Kennett's surmise had been incorrect. What the effect of the excessive dose of the narcotic might be I could not tell. I had sufficient acquaintance with medicine to know my complete ignorance.

"But I was aware that there might be dangerous consequences for us. The occasion was far too important for Kennett. I went in to your friend. He was plunging and groaning on the bed, and at first did not see me. When he did, he called out loudly, 'What have you done to me?' I feared the consequences. There was but one course open to me. I seized him by the throat. I had once amused myself with a voyage to China. The Chinese have a method of choking their victims so quickly that there is hardly time to cry out. I employed it then. When I felt certain the man must be dead, I left him. I met you at the door. I felt certain he must be dead, yet I listened for some sound within the room. All was silent. I rejoined the company. 'There is no doubt,' I said; 'I have settled him.' Yet, as you discovered, this time also Mr. Monkhouse was not dead. Never in my long experience have I known a spirit so loth to leave the body. He cried again. This time I took the carving knife; I ran to the room. With all his failing powers he fought with me. I had a severe struggle to unclasp his hands. I cut his throat, the blood spurted forth, and I fled. In my haste I omitted to lock the door. Whether my trembling hand had completed its work I knew not. He lingered on, as you are aware, for more than half an hour.

"When you asked to see the face, I perceived a delicate task before me. Your suspicions had already been roused. While you were at supper, I had examined the contents of your bag. I found nothing for myself worth risking discovery, but I observed that your name and address were the same as those on the letter Mr. Monkhouse had entrusted to me. If, which was possible, nay even probable, you recognized your friend, I should have been under the unfortunate necessity of choking you. I had studied painting amongst other things, and I was fond of dabbling with my colours during the tedious hours of waiting my profession continually demanded. I blackened the eyebrows and lashes of your friend to disguise him, and put Wally's great nightcap on his head. To hide the wound in the throat, I washed the blood. All had to be done in haste, to permit you as little time as possible to nourish your doubts. I felt a distaste in desecrating the maimed body of your friend, but at times necessity demands such tasks. The paint was still wet, when you touched the face: you smeared a stain on the forehead, but I held the lamp away from you, and in your agitation you observed nothing. At four o'clock next morning we rose; we made ready to carry the body to the lane, where the other victims lay. I was about to divest it of whatever articles of value might be upon it, when I observed that the signet ring was gone from the left hand. Someone had been before me. I knew what had occurred. There were two other members of the household besides Wally; the ostler, a morose fool, whom we sent off to Barcombe when we had business at the inn, and Betsy, the cook. I thought at first that she was completely engrossed by the pleasures of intoxication, but once, when we had to put a bullet through the head of an obstreperous farmer, she crept up at night and rifled his body. She hid her booty like a magpie; she had not the wits to sell it. If she had, I could easily have traced it. We had a second casualty; she somehow obtained possession of a lost key—she was as sly as the Devil—and again robbed the body. Still it seemed prudent not to get rid of her; we might have got worse in her place. Difficult facts would leak out in any case, and she was so crazy, no one would believe her.

"When Wally went to your room in the morning, Mr. Stanley, he found you were gone. Could Betsy have warned you? She vowed with tears that you had taken your clothes while she was asleep. I did not believe her. I saw her interference was becoming a menace. She would be safer under the sod. But feelings of humanity prevailed: drink would be terminating her career shortly without my intervention, and I dismissed her from the inn.

"Business brings me into close connection with a certain Jewish pawnbroker in the purlieus of London. A week ago I saw among his wares a signet ring bearing the inscription, 'James Monkhouse, with affectionate regard from William Stanley.' That ring you gave him I had already observed on the hand of your friend. On inquiring, the pawnbroker told me a drunken hag had brought it to hm for sale. She had promised to bring a brooch the next day. We watched the shop and tracked old Betsy. We pursued her to the miserable kennel she shared with her relations. We heard from them that she spoke continually of a rich gentleman who would make her fortune, for she had something to give him he would prize. We heard his name and address; yours, Mr. Stanley. Kennett waylaid her in the darkness, and forced her to disgorge her hoard. 'And here is everything I took,' said he on his return, 'a fortune for the witch, if she had but known it. No need for her to crawl in poverty.' I asked him if he had taken all. 'All but a little black book,' said he, 'she sobbed and cried and I left her that, as the good boy leaves the mother bird one egg.' 'Fool,' said I, 'go back and get it; that black book may be our ruin.' And so it proved, for that same night she had, as we discovered, gone to your rooms.

"Kennett had a doglike devotion to me and brandy punch, and had saved me in many a difficult situation by his mere muscular strength, but he was a fool who led me into more trouble than he saved me from. It was Goldsmith, I believe, who travelled through his friends' minds. I have travelled through Kennett's mind, and it is time we should part.

"Destiny has decreed that my hour is come also. A more prudent man would have left the country for a while in this stage of our affairs. But the prospects at the coming Cambridge Fair were unusually rosy, and I was in desperate need of money.

"I look back on my life with satisfaction. My day is over, and I am now going into night eternal—and perchance troubled. Farewell!"

Both Marks and Kennett were hung as murderers at the next Assizes.

And some recollection of all this the roan horse sees at twilight.

THE KIND ACTION OF MR. ROBINSON

We had been telling ghost stories, not an unusual occupation in these days of superstition or of psychic activity, whichever the reader pleases. The guests of the evening had left. I was paying a visit of a few days, and I and my host, Mr. Redmayne, a man of sixty-eight, sat and smoked our last pipes by the fire.

Our talk wandered in a desultory manner over various things, and then we harked back to the ghost stories we had heard.

"It's odd to me," said Mr. Redmayne, "that you younger men should attach any value to these things. We told ghost stories to amuse ourselves, work ourselves up into a happy condition of horrible fear, but there was an end of it. You are all hoping to find clues, apparently; clues to what, I can't quite make out. Anyhow, I'll show you something, and you can tell me what clue you find there."

Mr. Redmayne went to his desk, opened it, took out a small green leather pocket-book and a bundle of papers, and handed the pocket-book to me.

"Read out what's in it," he said, "there isn't very much."

There were only six entries, written in the excellent ink possessed by our forefathers. They were these:—

"Dec. 19th, 1780. Mr. Robinson lent me £500.

Dec. 18th, 1790. First reminder.

Dec. 18th, 1800. Second reminder. Voice of Mr. Robinson.

Dec. 18th, 1810. Third reminder. Appearance of Mr. Robinson in passage, his back towards me.

Dec. 18th, 1820. Fourth reminder. Appearance of Mr. Robinson in the passage, his face towards me.

Dec. 18th, 1830. Fifth reminder. Appearance of Mr. Robinson standing by my side.

May God Almighty help me!"

"Well, what do you say to that?"

"I don't quite know what I am expected to say. Is it automatic writing?"

"Oh no, none of that claptrap. These words were written by a Mr. Charles Marsden in his own person. I can vouch for his existence. My mother saw him once when she was a child, and his niece, Mrs. Field, was a special friend and also a cousin of my grandmother, my mother's mother. He showed that pocket-book to Mrs. Field and explained the contents, and at his death it came into her possession, and she gave it to my grandmother shortly before her death, with other personal things. She had no children, and her money was to go to a nephew in America she had never seen. As to the papers, it was only a few months ago when I was sorting out rubbish, the accumulation of more than a century, which ought to have been sorted out long before, that I came across them. I don't think my mother, or my grandmother either, knew of their existence; at any rate my mother never spoke of them. They are an explanation of the entries in the pocket-book; you shall look at them afterwards. Have you any further remarks to make about the pocket-book?"

"Only that I observe the first five entries are written in a good hand, and the last feebly. But, as there is an interval of fifty years between the first and last entry, this might be accounted for by old age."

"Yes, Marsden was a man of seventy-two when he wrote the last entry, and he died the next day. It's not really very late, and the story is not very long, so if you like to hear it, you shall."

I said I should like to hear it, and Mr. Redmayne proceeded:

"Marsden, you must know, was a taciturn solitary man in later life. My grandmother saw him occasionally between the years 1820 and 1830. He was always particularly courteous to her on account of her friendship with Mrs. Field, to whom he was attached. My grandmother heard some of what I am going to tell you from her. Mrs. Field was the child of Marsden's only sister. Mrs. Field married a soldier, and was wandering with him for several years in various parts of the world, so that after her marriage she did not see Marsden until he was an elderly man. He must have been sixty-two when she first went to stay with him. Her husband was then on active service.

"Marsden had been engaged in some shipping business, had made money, and had retired, and was now leading a somewhat desolate life in London, without friends, and with no special tastes or occupations, a commoner state of things I fancy than one imagines. A detestable existence." (My host had lived all his life in the country, and meant to die there.) "Marsden had been fond of his sister, and was therefore well disposed to Mrs. Field; but for the first few days of the visit he did not break through the cold reserve which was habitual to him. One morning he sent her a message begging her to excuse his presence at breakfast, as he was not well. Later in the day, he was better, and he joined her in the dining-room with that pocket-book in his hand. He made some unimportant remarks to her, and she noticed that he wandered restlessly about the room while she answered, evidently quite indifferent to what she was saying. At last she spoke to him—'Dear

Uncle, is there something the matter? Are you ill?' To which he replied, 'I hope so. I hope I am ill.'

"She was startled, and begged him to explain, and he said, 'I believe, Mary, it would be an immense relief to tell you all.' He then handed her the pocket-book, which contained all the entries you see but the last. She was as puzzled as yourself. She asked him again to explain, but he turned away his face and said, 'I cannot.' At last he recovered himself and said, 'You will wonder at me, but it is only that I am a little disturbed; disturbed in my digestion, I think. I am liable at intervals—intervals of ten years or so—to such disturbances, but they pass off, and it is all nothing.'

"He then pointed to the first entry and told her what follows. He did not show her the papers, which contain a record of his experiences. I think that, though he declared he would tell her all, he could not, when it came to the point; for the papers contain details which he never gave to Mrs. Field. I will read you what he wrote as the narrative proceeds.

"When Marsden was twenty-two, he was lively and foolish, and got into debt to a money-lender. The sum was £500, a large one for a young man with his own way to make. He was then only a clerk in a shipping office where he afterwards rose to be senior partner. Hs father was comfortably off, but by no means rich. On the 18th December, 1780, he journeyed from London by coach to Streatham, where his home was, to confess his difficulties to his parents, and ask their help. The father was a stern man. Charles began; the father became angry, Charles did not dare to finish, and when asked for the exact amount of his liabilities, he said £50. He had no other possible means of paying the debt, no relation to whom he could apply, no older friend. The money-lender was threatening to expose him. It was no use staying any longer at

Streatham. He felt he would rather meet disgrace in his lodgings in London. He declared that pressing business called him back to the office, and went to the inn to avoid further questions, two hours before the coach started. The coach, which passed through Streatham, came from the country, and was due at four o'clock. Marsden sat and waited before the coffee-room fire in a state of extreme dejection. He wavered between the alternatives of enlisting, working his way out to America, or putting a bullet through his brains. It was at this juncture that he had his interview with Mr. Robinson. Here is his memorandum on the subject:

> 'I had pondered over my misfortunes, and sought a way out so constantly, that I now could ponder no more. I may have fallen into a sort of trance of wretchedness, for I remember I was startled when I heard the clock strike 3.30. The early dusk of the winter afternoon was closing upon me, the room was only lighted by the flicker of the fire, when I became aware, how I know not, that there was someone behind me. I turned my chair, and at the same time a voice with which I was unfamiliar said, "Mr. Marsden." I saw a tall man in black clothes, with somewhat the appearance of a clergyman, only perhaps more handsomely dressed than is customary with them. He wore his own hair.[3] I did not observe this at the time, but I did later. He looked some years over thirty.
>
> ' "I am in great haste," said the stranger, "and have only a word to say. My name is Robinson. I know, do not inquire how, that you are in difficulties, and am happy to say that it

[3] Powdered wigs were the fashion for men during this time.

is in my power to relieve them." He handed me a packet. "Examine this at your leisure."

'My bewilderment was too great for surprise, and almost for speech. I faltered out that I could take nothing. In the first place, he was a stranger; in the next, I had no present hope of repaying him.

' "Do not let either of those difficulties deter you," he answered in his remarkably agreeable voice; "we will make this bargain; if in fifty years' time you are alive, and, which is less likely, I am alive, you shall meet me in this room, and at this hour, and pay me back. You need not trouble yourself with an I.O.U., for I myself will remind you from time to time."

'When Mr. Robinson said this he smiled. His countenance I thought in no way striking, but for his eyes. He had black lashes on the lids, and also under the eyes, which gave a curious glitter to them. This glitter seemed to become more piercing when he smiled. I believe it was to avoid his gaze that I turned my head aside. Being ashamed of my weakness, I looked back in an instant, and he was gone as secretly as he came. By chance at that moment my eye rested on the clock, and I saw that it was twenty-seven minutes to four; the interview had lasted three minutes.

'The packet lay on my knee. I opened it, and found that it contained five hundred pounds in bank notes. My astonishment, my unspeakable relief were so overwhelming that for a few seconds I could think of nothing, but when these sensations passed I was seized with a feeling of what I can only describe as horror. This communicated itself to my body. I think I had not less nor more than the courage of my fellow men, but I found myself shaking from head to foot. It was, I have no doubt, as a physician has told me, a sudden chill and derangement—in short such a state as is by no means unusual. In this disturbed and unreasonable condition I took the notes, and hastened from the room.

'The inn was a great rambling place, where much business was done. The coffee-room opened out of a long passage, which led straight from it to the front door. Another passage crossed it at right angles, leading to a door looking on to a stable-yard, and at the other end to the dining-room. I went first to the front door. I found the landlord, and begged him to tell me if he had seen a Mr. Robinson. The landlord knew nothing of such a person. I described him as minutely as possible, but in vain. I hurried to the stable-yard, and asked if Mr. Robinson had ordered posting horses. No trace was to be found of him there either. At the risk of losing the coach, I went all over the house, asking waiters and chambermaids, but again without success. My anxiety to return Mr. Robinson the notes was indescribable. This agitation ceased, however, as suddenly as it had arisen. My fears left me; I put the notes into my pocket, took my place on the coach, and returned to London. I showed the notes to a friend, Walker, who had at the time just finished his medical training, and consulted him. I at first concealed the unnatural fear which had seized me, feeling upon reflection that it was a hypochondriac condition which was best forgotten. Nevertheless it was with an indefinable sensation that I placed the notes in his hands, half expecting that he would say they were not bank notes at all. They were, however, correct in every particular. I then confided my dread to him. He laughed heartily, and said that if Mr. Robinson, or Mr. Smith either, would come by and offer him five hundred pounds, or if he cared, five thousand, he should be very happy to accept them without question. This eased my mind, and I came gradually to the conclusion that some rich eccentric person had wished to do good by stealth, and that I should be a fool to trouble myself further.

'I had, however, a great desire to thank my benefactor in person, and I caused the following announcement to be inserted in the papers:

> "Mr. M. would esteem it a particular favour if Mr. R. would communicate with him in remembrance of their meeting, December 19th, 3.30, Coach and Horses Inn, Streatham."

'This announcement appeared for several days, but without any result. Date of memorandum, Jan. 5th, 1781.'

"There the first record ends," said Mr. Redmayne.

I asked whether Mr. Robinson never gave any explanation of his strange behaviour.

"Never. Marsden never saw him again, though he imagined he did, as you shall hear. It was a queer affair, but I think Marsden's explanation was the right one. My idea is that until the Victorian era there were a number of people, gentry, in England, who prided themselves on being what used to be called 'Characters'; very odd, very bad-tempered, very prodigal, some special characteristic; and I think one of them was quite capable of stealing into an inn parlour, and rescuing an amiable young man from his difficulties (I have no doubt the difficulties were a subject of talk among grooms and waiters—grooms and waiters always know everything), stealing out again, and making a mystery just for his own personal satisfaction. Of course, Mr. Robinson may have been a little mad, or a great deal mad, but I don't think it's necessary to suppose him mad at all. There was no C.O.S. in those days,[4] you know, and the rich didn't save their money and buy baronetcies by building convalescent homes; the humanity and delicacy of that unenlightened age didn't require it. What they liked was to patronize poor deserving individuals. Read Cottle's 'Recollections of Coleridge'; why, wealthy men were perpetually coming forward and offering Coleridge an income. I like their way better than ours, but that's neither here nor there. I expect the glittering eye was a figment. As to the 'as much courage as most men' my opinion is that Marsden had considerably less. However, now we will go on with the story.

"Marsden got out of the money-lender's clutches, and apparently was never so foolish as to get into them again. Things prospered with him; he advanced in his business, and in the words of a letter of his I came across the other day—I fancy he rather prided himself on the choiceness of his style—he 'surrounded himself with a happy circle of friends, and threw himself into the pleasures of youth, as youth alone can,' and I expect forgot Mr. Robinson completely.

"We pass over the next ten years. Marsden was thirty-two when he was sent from his firm on business to Marseilles, in December of the year 1790. On the evening of the 18th he had been hospitably entertained by some French gentleman of his acquaintance, and I think very likely ate too freely of his host's excellent dinner. He left this record:

---

[4] Charity Organisation Society. It claimed to use 'scientific principles to root out scroungers and target relief where it was most needed'.

'Shortly after midnight I went to my room and must have slept an hour or two, when I woke with a start. My mind seemed intent on recollecting something, but for a few seconds I could not think what. I then found myself repeating these words; whether I had been dreaming them before I woke or what brought them into my head, I cannot say: "Mr. Marsden, remember December 19, 1830, forty years hence. This is the first time." The words though simple, created that exaggerated impression upon me which is the peculiar horror of nocturnal delusion; they recalled to me the episode of Mr. Robinson, which I had seldom thought of since, and thought of only with satisfaction as the beginning of my good fortune. They revived also that inexplicable feeling of fear, which I had experienced at the moment of Mr. Robinson's departure. I lay struggling with my disquiet for some hours. The light of day restored my composure. Nevertheless, I cannot explain by what impulse I made this short memorandum of the occurrence. Dec. 23, 1790.'

"You can see for yourself, Marsden even as a young man was morbid, and what one now calls neurotic. Besides these memoranda he had, you remember, made the entries in the green pocket-book, which he apparently reserved especially for incidents connected with Mr. Robinson."

"Did people look upon him as morbid, do you know?"

"I never heard that they did in early life. There are some jovial letters upstairs from his friend Walker, but the whole thing is past and gone so long, it's impossible to say. Well, now we pass on to the third entry.

"In the February of 1800 Marsden, being then nearly forty-two married a young lady of one-and-twenty. The marriage was happy, I believe, but it was short lived. They young lady died in December of the same year at the birth of her child, and the child died too.

"Marsden writes thus:

> 'On the night of December 18th, which preceded the funeral, I tossed in unspeakable anguish of spirit for many hours, the mortal remains of my beloved wife and her infant reposing in the adjoining chamber. The sufferings I had witnessed during her illness, and the prospect of the solitude which must henceforth be my portion, alternately occupied my mind, until I fell asleep. I woke at last, hearing these words, as I thought, close by my bed: "Mr. Marsden." I said, "Who is it?" There was no answer, but in a minute the voice continued, only now sounding more distant, "Mr. Marsden, remember, December 19, 1830, thirty years hence. This is the second time." I again called out, "Who is there?" Again there was no answer. I drew back the curtains, but the night was dark; therefore, though I had no shutters to my window, nothing could be seen through the surrounding blackness. I listened; no sound was to be heard but the falling of heavy rain. I sprang out of bed, groped my way to the door, opened it, and called out a third time, "Who is there?" There was still no answer. The servants, wearied out, were in deep sleep. I went back to bed. Incredible as it may appear, at that moment the death of my wife and child seemed nothing to me; my mind was entirely filled with what had just occurred. In particular I was oppressed with an insane desire to remember whether I had ever heard the voice before. It sounded familiar, but what it exactly reminded me of always eluded me. I believed I could not sleep

again, but Nature reasserted herself, and in the morning I had no thoughts but for the melancholy ceremony of interment. Dec. 31st, 1800.' "

"December 18th, 1800," said I. "That was the night before the twentieth anniversary of the meeting with Robinson, the first reminder being the tenth anniversary. Isn't that the case?"

"Yes, that was the case. At the same time you must remember the poor fellow was completely unhinged by what he had gone through, and the recurrence of a nightmare is not uncommon. In fact once you start a nightmare—I am glad to say I don't suffer from them—it is liable to recur like hay fever. The coincidence of the anniversary does not seem to have struck Marsden at the time, but it apparently did subsequently, as I will proceed to tell you.

"I think it was a remarkable coincidence, Redmayne."

"Oh, I grant you it was a remarkable coincidence, and it became much more of a coincidence later. So much for 1800. As far as one can ascertain now, it was after his wife's death that Marsden gradually got into a secluded way of life. I suppose he always had the tendency in him, only youth kept it at bay, and the liking for solitude usually gets stronger after forty. I don't imagine that the nightmares had much to do with it. He continued extremely energetic in the pursuit of business, and amassed money, what they called money then—our big grocers and drapers would think nothing of it—with much zeal.

"We pass on to 1810, when he was fifty-two. He kept a journal for part of that year, and there are two or three entries of interest.

"On November 1st, 1810, he writes:

'The thirtieth anniversary is now approaching. I have no grounds for apprehension, I can have no grounds, yet I cannot help feeling, though doubtless without reason that it would be in *every way* more comfortable if I could repay Mr. Robinson the five hundred pounds. I have seen my friend Walker from time to time, though his persistent joviality is somewhat repulsive to me; I believe it might be prudent to consult him on the subject.'

'Nov. 11th. I have seen Walker. He entirely agrees with me that it would be advisable to endeavour to repay Mr. Robinson. He himself will institute enquiries, using all possible discretion. It would be desirable not to offend Mr. Robinson.'

'Nov. 23rd. Walker came to visit me to-day with the happy intelligence that he had actually come across the traces of Mr. Robinson. He could not give me any particulars, as Mr. Robinson expressly desires that everything about him should be kept secret. Walker is arranging to pay the five hundred pounds, and he thinks the interest I am offering by no means too high.'

'Nov. 25th. All is arranged. Walker brought me Mr. Robinson's receipt this morning. I examined the signature of this mysterious being with that strange mixture of horror and gratitude with which I have regarded all connected with him. "And be sure you make no inquiries about the business," said Walker, "for that he particularly forbids. He is an eccentric creature, and we had better yield to his whims. He told me, by the way, that of course, as things now stand, your promised interview with him will not take place. He will have no further dealings with you." I asked if Walker was certain of that, and he said he could not be more certain. "And Mr.

Robinson is not angry with me?" "I think Robinson loves a mystery, but he is not so foolish as to be angry." My mind is now at rest. What my fears were I would not, I dare say, inquire, but I thank a merciful Providence that they were without foundation.'

"Then there is this further record:—

'On the evening of December 18th, 1810, I brought the transaction with Prevost Frères of Bordeaux to a satisfactory conclusion, and I retired to rest with a sense of a burden off my mind. I went to sleep, and I next recall hearing the clock in Percival Street strike four. I opened my eyes, and found to my surprise that there was a red light flickering near me, and on looking about I discovered that I was not in my room at all, and that I was opposite a bright fire. It shone on various objects, such as some plated candlesticks, an old-fashioned clock, two china figures, and on a coloured print of George III, which I seemed to remember having seen before, I did not know under what circumstances. There was some light besides the fire, twilight or moonlight. Turning my head from the fire I observed that the door, which was exactly opposite to the fireplace, stood open. It led into a long passage, which I could make out distinctly, though the light was faint. Another passage passed the door at right angles. As I looked, I recollected that this was the coffee-room of the Coach and Horses Inn at Streatham, which I had not revisited since 1780, thirty years ago. I now suddenly had the sensation that I was expecting someone to appear in the passage. This disturbed me, and I should have been relieved to shut the door, but seemed unable to do so. As I watched, the figure of a man in black came from the passage at the left of the door, turned with its back towards me, and went rapidly down the other passage, which as I remembered led to the front door of the inn. At the same time I heard the words I had already heard twice before, in 1790, and in 1800. "Mr. Marsden, remember December 19th, 1830, twenty years hence. This is the third time." On this occasion I distinctly recognised the voice as Mr. Robinson's. I was now troubled with anxiety to discover whether the figure was that of Mr. Robinson, whether it was the figure which had spoken, and in that case whether, while speaking, the figure had smiled. I felt that I *must* assure myself on this point at all costs. I sprang forward, and called very earnestly, as I thought, several times, "Mr. Robinson, turn round your head." The figure however made no sign that it was aware of me. It constantly receded before my view, walked to the end of the passage, and was gone. I believe I then woke up; what I imagined to be consciousness must in reality have been troubled sleep, for I found that I was out of bed, standing near the window, saying the words "Mr. Robinson" very loudly and rapidly. My nightgown was wringing with sweat. I experienced the same miserable perturbation which I particularized in my two former memoranda, but I trusted with the advent of the morning I should look on things with a more manly calm. Alas, the hopes I had formed after the repayment of the debt had proved to be entirely illusory. Unreasonable as it may appear, I could not rid myself of the possibility of something more than coincidence in the three experiences I have recorded. I recollected only too vividly the words of

Mr. Robinson, "You need not trouble yourself about an I.O.U., for I myself will remind you from time to time." Nor did the morning bring the hoped-for oblivion. My remembrance of the previous night had not been, as formerly, dissipated by sleep, and my feverish longing to see the face of the figure in black was hardly abated.

'I went to Walker and told him my experience of the preceding night. I saw that he looked embarrassed, and at last he said, "It may be better to explain to you that, as far as I am concerned, there is no such person as Mr. Robinson."

'I asked him his meaning.

' "I saw you were oppressed by the idea of the money," said he; "we physicians know that the mind and the body are dependent on one another. I thought that, by allowing the debt to Mr. Robinson to prey on you, your very fears would produce what you dreaded. I therefore concocted the story of the payment. Your thousand pounds is safely at your bank."

' "But the signature?" I said.

' "Oh, the signature was mine."

'I must have shewn more concern than I intended, for he continued, "Forgive me, I did what I hoped was for the best, but I was mistaken."

'I thanked him for his kindness. It would have been the act of a child to blame him. My hopes had been unreasonable, utterly unreasonable, and my disappointment was equally unreasonable; but I could with difficulty master the intolerable dread that I was now for ever in the power of Mr. Robinson.

'While despising myself for weakness, I determined to consult with another physician. I went accordingly to Dr. S., who had been recommended to me as a skilful practitioner. I

> explained my case with some hesitation, showing him the memoranda I had kept with the dates. He assured me that he had listened with much interest to what I had told him, and great was my relief when he added that my experiences were readily explainable by hypochondria, a disease well-known to physicians; that there was nothing alarming in what I described, and that change of scene and foreign travel was all that was needed to restore me to health. Dec. 24th, 1810.' "

"Begging the skilful Dr. S.'s pardon for questioning his diagnosis," I said, "I do *not* think hypochondria solves the problem. Nor does your theory of the eccentric Mr. Robinson. What did Mr. Robinson mean by 'I myself will remind you from time to time'? And then the reminding, what did that mean? There seems no reason why poor Marsden should have been disturbed on the particular night he was disturbed, no special anxiety for instance; he went to bed, as he himself says, in unusually good spirts."

"It's no good throwing the burden of explanation on me, Bartlett; I particularly declared that it was to be left to you. It's an odd story, but the one thing we really know about life is that it is very odd. Well, to continue.

"Marsden followed the doctor's advice and went abroad, and he kept a journal, and made the correct observations about St. Peter's and the Sistine Chapel, and he even was so much pleased with his observations that he revised them with the intention of printing some of them. However that scheme fell through. I should imagine all went well, and he forgot his fears. The only change I perceive during these years was that he gave large sums away to the Society for the Abolition of the Slave Trade and to the Church Missionary Society and other good works, and these words recur from time to time, 'I trust all is well. I think all must now be well.'

"Now we get to 1820. It was in December of that year, you remember, that his niece, Mrs. Field, first came to stay with him. It is evident that by that time the affair was again disturbing him, for on December 17th he writes:

> 'As the fortieth anniversary of my meeting with Mr. Robinson draws near, I cannot conceal from myself that, do what I will, I feel considerable apprehension, though I cannot say of what. Chapman' (that was his housekeeper) 'is an excellent creature; I am glad, too, that Mary is with me; but what support it would be to me if Walker were still living; we might have spent the night together in cards and conversation, as we have done in former times; or even Bates. Bates would have been better than to be alone. Both, alas, are no more. I wish I could again have consulted the excellent Dr. S., but he was an old man ten years ago, and is now gathered to his fathers. I believe it would be a satisfaction if Chapman would sit up with me, or if I could confide in Mary, but this is weakness.'

"Then we have the record two days later:

> 'On the night of December 18th I determined not to go to bed, so that it would be impossible for me to fall into the power of dreams. I established myself in my study beside the fire, a book on my knee, and a bottle of strong spirits by my side. I drank, I smoked, and read for several hours, feeling each hour, as it passed, that a danger had been averted. Hope and fear were mingled together, now one, now the other, struggling

for the mastery. The admonitions of Reason and Religion alike seemed nugatory in dispelling the agitation which oppressed me, though both were summoned to my aid. It came on me as no shock, but rather as dreadfully familiar, when I beheld Mr. Robinson advancing towards me along the passage of the inn. An instant before I had been in my own room, and I still, as far as I could ascertain, was sitting in my chair, yet I was also in the coffee-room. Though he appeared to me to be walking slowly, Mr. Robinson was upon me before I was aware, looking at me through the door. I had changed, I was now an old man of sixty-two, but he—though I saw his face distinctly only for an instant, I had time to observe it—had not changed at all. He was still a man entering the prime of life, exactly what he had been forty years before, only that I, being now old, thought him younger than he had then appeared. He wore his own black hair, without a tinge of grey, and there was no wrinkle on his face. He paused at the door, and said to me in an agreeable voice, "Mr. Marsden, remember December 19th, 1830, ten years hence. This is the fourth time." He smiled at me, turned down the passage to the left of the door, and disappeared. It seemed to me that this smile was what I had been waiting for and dreading *inexpressibly* for forty years. The limit of human endurance was now reached. I knew no more till next morning, when I found myself lying in bed in my own room. Chapman, awakened by my cry, had hastened to the spot, had seen me on the floor, and discovered that I was unconscious. January 14th, 1821.' "

"This is a very dreadful story, Redmayne."

"I don't know about dreadful. Marsden evidently drank more whisky than he was accustomed to; that was unfortunate, but hardly dreadful."

"I see from the last entry in the pocket-book that the terrible Robinson came and stood by his side. Do you know, Redmayne, I feel like Macbeth, 'We will proceed no further in this business.'[5] Whether, as Mr. Marsden says, I should have more manly calm in the morning, I can't say, but I don't like watching the torment of the wretched man."

"I will not answer you with Lady Macbeth's 'What beast was't then?', for I know I was the beast, and I'm sure I had no idea I was such an unfeeling beast. Times have changed. I and my brother were always asking for the story of Mr. Robinson. In fact my mother kept it as the greatest treat to soothe the anguish of toothache. It's true she had only heard a very imperfect version, and depended on what her memory retained of the account given her by my grandmother forty years before. Still, I confess, there was a sort of toughness and hardness of nerve about people in the generation that is gone, which you don't find nowadays. Not that my mother was a heartless woman, very far indeed from it. After all, you know, Bartlett, Marsden has been dead a hundred years, and if, as one longs for, memory continues beyond the grave, the recollection of his wretchedness must, one would suppose, have been softened; or if, on the other hand, memory does *not* continue, why, nothing of his earthly life can matter to him now. So if you can bear to hear the rest, you shall. Only perhaps I had better warn you, it is not a story with a happy ending."

"Very well; continue."

---

5 *Macbeth*: Act 1, Scene 7, when Macbeth stands up to Lady Macbeth and refuses to kill King Duncan.

"Marsden, as I said, told Mrs. Field the substance of what I have told you. She was a good deal agitated, and I think she insisted on his seeing another doctor, who said very much what the first doctor said. What else was there for him to do? However, Marsden was fidgety and upset for some weeks afterwards, and Mrs. Field persuaded him to come and stay with her for a visit. Then he calmed down and recovered his usual spirits. She wished to keep him with her, but he preferred to return to his old moping, solitary existence. She liked pleasant hospitality and the amenities of life, and he hated them. Before he left her, she implored him to stay, unless he felt himself completely restored.

" 'I *am* restored, Mary,' he said. He paused and then added, 'What I told you was merely the weakness of a disordered fancy. It should not have been revealed. A man with more fortitude would have said nothing.' Mrs. Field assured him that it should be to her as though it had never been.

"Mrs. Field told my grandmother that from that day for the next nine years Marsden never referred by a single word to Mr. Robinson; but whether the affair was ever in his thoughts she could not say; that it did not weigh on him unduly she felt pretty certain. In may, 1830, he, being now a man of seventy-two, left London and retired to his early home at Streatham, one of the pleasant houses with large cedar trees in their gardens of which there used to be so many round London. It and the Coach and Horses have made way for improvements now, of course, but I remember them very well. Marsden said he should like to end his days where his parents had ended theirs; and Mrs. Field, whose husband's regiment was at that time quartered at Windsor, used to visit him there as frequently as she could. He was gradually declining all that year, and it became clear that he was not much longer for this world. As the months went on, he began alluding to Mr. Robinson, and Mrs. Field at last came to the conclusion that that business preyed upon him more than he cared to own; and that it was in fact the prospect of their meeting which had made him anxious to come back to Streatham; but it was not easy with a man of his reserved nature to find out what he was thinking of. She tried to divert his thoughts, and she determined that at whatever cost she would be with him during the month of December.

"Marsden seems to have kept no journal or memorandum during these years, so that we have no record of 1830, except the entry in the pocket-book and what Mrs. Field told my grandmother after Marsden's death.

"Mrs. Field watched outside his room all the night of December 18th, but heard no sounds, and she concluded that, if he had received the final warning, it had given him no distress. But when she greeted him at breakfast, she was shocked at his appearance; she told my grandmother he had turned in the night from an old man to one on the last confines of old age. He said to her he hoped she would excuse his accompanying her on her drive that afternoon, as he would be occupied by important business at half-past three.

" 'I wonder if I could be any help to you in your business, Uncle,' said Mrs. Field.

" 'Thank you for your kindness, Mary, but you could be no help.'

" 'But how do you know, Uncle? Let me hear what the business is.'

" 'That is not possible for me to tell you,' said Marsden.

"His manner throughout breakfast was strange, restless and unsettled, and Mrs. Field felt so much anxiety that she resolved not to lose sight of him throughout the day. But soon after breakfast an express came from London, where her husband was staying for the night, saying that he had been seriously injured by a fall from his horse, and that she must go to him at once. She could not bear to leave the old man, but there was no help for it. She charged Chapman to keep continual watch over him; she explained to her that he might take it into his head to go to the Coach and Horses, but that he must by all means be kept at home.

"Chapman did her best, but about two o'clock he evaded her, and she saw him walking feebly but hurriedly down the road. It was snowing fast and bitterly cold, but he seemed to be unaware of it. She hastened after him and said, 'Excuse me, sir, but were you by any chance going to the Coach and Horses? for they've sent up special that you're not to go.'

"He looked at her, she told Mrs. Field afterwards, as if a great burden had been taken off his mind, and said, 'Indeed, is that really so?'

" 'As true as I stand here, sir,' answered Chapman.

" 'In that case I may return home,' he said, and went back with her.

" 'And you won't go out again, sir, will you?' said she. 'Because it's not fit for a gentleman like you to be out.'

" 'I shall go out if it is necessary,' he replied. 'But I think it will not be necessary.'

"She settled him comfortably by the study fire, and she made a pretext for looking on him more than once. At first he seemed reading happily, but the last time he was sitting looking fixedly into the fire. He turned and said rather severely, 'I am busy, and wish to be quiet.' She did not venture to come in again, till she brought the lighted candles, when she found the room was empty.

She ran all the way to the inn, though it was nearly a mile away and she was a stout woman.

" 'Yes,' the landlord said in answer to her question. The gentleman had come half an hour or more ago. He said he was expecting to meet a Mr. Robinson in the coffee-room, but that it would not be necessary to announce him, and he did not wish to be disturbed. 'I haven't heard whether Mr. Robinson has come, he's not a gentleman we're acquainted with, but I'll inquire. It was William took Mr. Marsden to the coffee-room.'

"Chapman pushed past the landlord into the coffee-room. I suppose you can guess what had happened. Marsden had been soothed for a time by her assurance; later the uneasiness had returned. He had made his way to the coffee-room, and there Chapman found him with his throat cut. His razor was lying by his side. He must have died at half-past three. The face was a good deal contorted.

"The waiter said no one had entered the coffee-room since he had shown Mr. Marsden in. 'Leastways,' he added upon reflection, 'I didn't see nobody; only I heard footsteps coming up the front passage, and the coffee-room door open and shut again, and then footsteps going down the passage, but when I looked out of my pantry, I couldn't see no one. The gentleman, if it was the gentleman, couldn't only have paid a very short call, for it struck half-past three, when he first went in, and it wasn't more than twenty-seven minutes to four when I head the door go again, for I happened to look at the clock at the time.'

"Mrs. Field did not find the last entry in the pocket-book till after Marsden's death. Both she and Chapman could not forgive themselves for what they considered negligence, but I don't think either was to blame."

"That's the end of the story?"

"That's the end of the story. Now, have you any theories?"

"None whatever."

"Chapman had. She was convinced that Mr. Robinson was the Devil, and I cannot help suspecting that this theory presented itself to Marsden also. In his misery a man may sometimes harbour the most inconceivable phantasms, hidden amongst the farthest recesses of his soul. Is there not a possible connection here, an explanation of those large contributions to the Missionary Society? Marsden died a poor man. You know how harsh and rigid they were in old days, and the Vicar refused to read the funeral service over the poor defenceless body. This nearly broke Chapman's heart, and she went to plead with him. I think the devotion that some women servants lavish on uninteresting masters and mistresses is one of the strangest things in our unaccountable human nature. Chapman looked on poor Marsden as a sort of nursling. I don't believe upper-class women, ladies, have that same power of devotion. I've got here the Vicar's letter to Mrs. Field, trying to ward off Chapman. It's rather amusing:

'Dear Madam,

> 'I regret that it will be quite impossible for me to reconsider my decision. I feel no good purpose would be served by receiving Mrs. Chapman again. Further discussion with one so wild in her opinions would hardly be seemly in my position as incumbent here. I have no doubt that, as you say, she discharges the duties of her humble sphere with zeal and fidelity, but you will agree with me that the vulgar and uneducated can be no judge of what is proper in the unhappy circumstances under consideration. To appear in the smallest

degree to condone the rash and shocking act by which your late uncle terminated his earthly career would be to aim a blow at the very foundations of religion and morality in this country.

'Your obedient servant,

RICHARD BLENKINSOP.'

"So Chapman had to go elsewhere. She found another spiritual practitioner, a Methodist—the Methodists then were less preposterous and sleek than they are now—and he pointed out the following to her.

" 'And it was given unto the Beast' (Mr. Robinson) 'to make war with the Saints' (Mr. Marsden) 'and to overcome them… Here is the patience and faith of the Saints.'[6] And again, 'The Devil is come… having great wrath, because he knoweth that he hath but a short time.'[7] Then Chapman was comforted. And if we are to have theories, and if we are prepared to call Marsden a Saint, I am not sure after all, that Chapman's theory is not as good, or as bad, as any other. The Spirit of Evil, not considered poetically as majestic like Milton's Satan, but prosaically as the quintessence of meanness, would, one might fancy, fasten on an entirely harmless person, and torment him to death."

"This opens up a very interesting vista for meditation, Redmayne."

"Well, meditate on it at your leisure in bed. It's actually two o'clock. Good night."

---

[6] Revelation 13:7 to 14:12.

[7] Revelation 12:12.

LETTERS FROM MANNINGFIELD

Miss Corbett's comments and inquiries about her friend's affairs are omitted from these letters.

Manningfield Vicarage,
June 5, 19—.

MY DEAREST HILDA

Do write to me as often as you can. I suppose I ought not to ask you, when I know how busy you are, but you have no idea how delightful it is getting your letters. As I told you, you are the first real friend I have had. In old days we were so complete in ourselves, Mother and Father, the three boys, my sister Muriel and I, I did not want anyone else. Then the boys went off abroad and Muriel married; she has been in India for years, and they're not well off, so she has only come home twice. Don't think I am unhappy; I love my life here, but just living all day with old people is a drain on one's vitality, and I sometimes long for a contemporary. I go and have a chat with Gladys in the pantry to freshen me up; not that she would like to be considered my contemporary; I expect I am draining *her* vitality. I don't seem to know how to make friends now; there is not much opportunity in the country, if one has not been to school or college. I had all the opportunities there were, tennis parties and so on; it must have been my own fault. I always take it for granted people will not want to be bothered to make friends with me; I know I have so little to say first of all. Then suddenly you appear and *insist* on being bothered with me. Even now I often feel you must think me distrait and indifferent, when all I am is shy. I could talk for hours on paper to you, only I am so afraid of boring you.

I am pleased that you want to know what my surroundings are like; I have not got any photographs, so I will try to tell you. Our house is not at all romantic; I wonder why you thought it was. It was built in 1880 of yellow brick, but the autumn mists, the sun, and the rain have made it rather a pretty brown by now, and all the creepers tumbling over it have got mixed up together. They oughtn't to be allowed to do it, but the garden can't be as tidy as I should like, because Father, who used to do a good deal, is a little pottery now; he likes going about with a spud, and you know "what the boys are nowadays", or perhaps you don't. I do the useful, and nothing is more sweet and inspiring, I think, than the vegetable garden, shining in the sun after a shower. I like the smell of the blackcurrant bushes, the mint, and the cabbages better than roses and lilies of the valley; and the frogs are so pleased, and hop about so gaily, and the birds whistle with satisfaction, and our tabby cat lies all his length on the gravel path, and lashes his tail, and gives silvery mews to call the birds to him, but they know what *that* means, and keep well out of reach.

I am afraid you would think our house very old-fashioned. Most of our furniture is what Mother and Father had as wedding presents, and a little is older still. We have mahogany, horsehair, chiffoniers with gold mirrors on the top; what gets described as the furniture of the most stick-in-the-mud lodgings. Fancy that, we have red rep curtains still, and no linoleum! Is there another house in England which has no linoleum? Mother and Father had a little outburst when they came here, and we have some Morris cretonnes,[8] and there are Mother's Kate Greenaway antimacassars with the colours almost washed away. They are historical now, I

[8] A heavy cotton fabric decorated with a William Morris design.

consider. There were many drawings of mine framed; I was thought artistic. I have sent all I can to the jumble sales, but some Mother cannot bear to part with, pencil heads of girls with very sad saucer eyes, done at my most sentimental stage. The little armchairs made for crinolines are very cosy. We have one on which Mother sat when Father proposed to her. She must have been so lovely. I asked her once what being lovely had felt like, and whether it was very horrid losing it as one got older, and Mother said, "I think it was comfortable not to have to wonder whether one was pretty, but I felt that it was quite right that it should go, and somebody else should have their turn!" That sentence is *so* like Mother. She is an invalid now, and her memory is not *quite* so good as it was, she gets confused, but she takes that loss equally calmly.

Can't you imagine our pictures? photographs of Switzerland and the Lakes and French Cathedrals, and—don't discard us—"The Gambler's Wife" and "Wedded."[9] I always thought, when I was a child, they must fall backwards, she is leaning against him so wallowingly.

My room is not so tidy as it should be, and it is very dull; there never seems time for my room; it is mostly snapshots of babies I think, and of the grandfathers and grandmothers of the village. That photograph I inveigled out of you is on the mantelpiece looking at me.

Does this give you an idea of what we are like?

Yours,

E. N. C.

---

[9] *The Gambler's Wife* is a painting by Marcus Stone (1885, oil on paper). *Wedded* is a painting by Lord Frederic Leighton (1882, oil on canvas).

Manningfield Vicarage,
August 19.

DEAREST HILDA

I meant to have answered your letter weeks ago, but we have been in a rush, what *you* would call a backwater; all our treats. The beautiful sea; I have had three treats there already and two more are coming. Then that will be over till next year. You asked about Father's books. I think you have got an erroneous impression into your head that we are intellectual. Perhaps Father is, but he does not read much now. He has sold all the books that were of any value—he wanted money for the roof of the church—and now he has just got the sediment. Some of it is rather past its prime. "The Clergyman's Friend. Affectionate Counsel to those about to take upon themselves the Pastoral Office," 1829; "Homely Addresses suitable for Intelligent Mechanics," 1841; "Intelligent," a little as if they were fox terriers, but the "Homely Addresses" are so hard and so dry to me, I do not feel my intelligence at all up to them. They had to work their minds in those days.

As to the "Affectionate Counsel," if the clergy round put its precepts into practice, I think they would lose the not very large congregations left to them. The precepts are so interfering. Sometimes I wish Father would get an up-to-date "Clergyman's Friend," though; there might be some comic anecdotes for him. His jokes at socials are not *very* good. I don't mean not witty; of course *that* doesn't matter; but somehow they don't seem to come home very readily. The vicar at Slingsby does his with a bounce, and the congregations there make one's mouth water. No one could work harder than Father; he takes endless pains with his sermons, but they are on the long side, and I think there is too much about the customs of the Jews. We are not dealing with intelligent mechanics nowadays.

Do you know what parish work is like? It is not particularly easy or encouraging. Perhaps Heaven thinks if it were we might have our heads turned; but sometimes I feel just a touch more success would be a help. Mr. Prior, the pillar of the Wesleyans, and I were talking over things. We agreed that Church and Chapel always get the salt of the village, and besides the salt, the old, the elderly, the plain, the dull, the failures, the feeble minded and the lunatics, but we are not so sure of the rest. If a girl wants to teach in the Sunday School, she is likely to be one who has not managed to pick up a boy, and that *may* be, but also may *not* be a qualification. Then there is that heavy sediment of both sexes, which saunters about and only wants to suck either a walking stick, or sweets, or a blade of grass. Occasionally one can persuade them to begin a thing, but never to stick to it. Our schoolmistress is very nice, but on the dull side, and unlucky. When the inspector came last time, she upset an inkpot, and lost the key of the cupboard, and he wasn't as nice about it as he might have been, perhaps, because he tripped over a hole in the mat. She plays the organ; she is not very musical. She's a trump really.[10] I train the choir; I am not at all musical. Our festival anthems! If we didn't have a tenor solo, Percy Sanger would go to the Wesleyans, and if we didn't have a bass solo, Mr. Dodds would go to the public house; so there can never be a soprano solo, though the girls have nicer voices and attend more regularly. When the men make mistakes, I say it is the girls. Everything *must* be sacrificed for the men, of course. I was laughing at this necessity with Gladys, and

---

[10] A trump: an admirable person.

she said in a motherly manner, "One must always treat men like children, I think." She ought to know; she has been engaged several times!

More about Manningfield next letter, as they say in "Home Chat."[11]

Your loving,
E. N. C.

Manningfield Vicarage,
Sept. 6.

MY DEAREST HILDA

You have a beguiling way of leading one on. I have never poured myself out like this before. You say you want to hear about Manningfield. Hilda, it *is* luxury to tell you about the village. I *adore* it. Now it is romantic, only I shall never be able to make you see it. There are beautiful, protecting elms, and old lanes that twist round and round because the deer made winding tracks for themselves in the old primeval forest. Then we have several what Mrs. Hawkins calls "old, ancient" cottages, with high, sloping, thick thatch roofs, built in a century when it seemed as if one might lavish any amount of time, love, money, labour and delight in the work. They stand round little bits of greens, near shady ponds. There is too an "old ancient" farmhouse, with a large quadrangle of black wooden barns, also thatched. In that yard are the most beautiful cart horses in the village; you should see them playing touch with one another in the meadow on Sunday. Of course voices are clamouring that the thatch must be replaced by corrugated iron, but our squire is an old lady dozing her last years away. She

[11] A weekly women's magazine which ran from 1895 to 1959.

half wakes up occasionally to have us to tea, and long may her doze last, for while she rules, nothing will change, and we still see her carriage and greys driving about the lanes.

Our church, St. Margaret's, is very magnificent. Our patron lady must feel degraded from her high estate when she sees the congregation, a small group of insects lost in the towering arches.

Our vicar's warden is a little gentle old man, a retired schoolmaster of days very far past. The only person he cannot bear is Cromwell's wicked general, who stabled his horses in St. Margaret's.[12] "When the Bishop came," said he, "he spoke very affably to me, and I saw he thought a great deal of the church. 'This is the finest church in the diocese,' he says, and I could read his mind like a book, though I daresay he thought it premature to speak. There's a talk of the diocese being divided, and I make no manner of doubt ours will be the Cathedral church. Ah, there are beauties it takes years to appreciate. It breaks my heart that none of the young ones care for it. But what do they care for but themselves?" Do you think the village girls and boys were ever addicted to architecture and archaeology, even in his young days? Dear old man! When you see our hamlet fast asleep, and seven miles from a station, you will smile to think of us as a Cathedral City, but I should like St. Margaret's to get up in the world again.

You asked me what we do in the evenings. We play bridge, old-fashioned bridge. I used to call no trumps automatically without looking at my hand, every evening, and I always won! That grew monotonous, so now I go misery to myself, and see how few tricks I can make. It is very difficult, even when I cheat. I cannot make them

---

[12] Various local legends claim that Oliver Cromwell and his men stabled horses in religious buildings throughout the country during the Civil War.

score, they are so unlucky. They are always revoking and trumping one another's tricks. But they like the game, and when Mother was tired one night, she said, "No, we must have our bridge, we mustn't let the child miss her game." So I see it is also a special treat for me!

Your loving,

E. N. C.

August 29.

MY DEAREST HILDA

Do you really like ghostly things? That is a new side to you. There is no proper ghost. The hall is not haunted. They have had no murders there, only dullness for years and years, and a fair amount of prosperity. Things have been seen and heard however in the village, and still are, but rarely now. The older generation were more susceptible. I wonder why? Do you think it has anything to do with compulsory education? There were some old people who had wonderful tales when I was a child; they would not frighten me with them then, but I heard them later. When I was fourteen or fifteen, I was told one or two things, but at that time I thought them silly, or was shocked by them. Looking back twenty-five or more years ago, I think I and the grown-up people round me were continually being shocked by something; now that there is far more to shock us, we seem to have given it up as a bad job.

You would have loved the village in our early days; you would not have wasted your opportunities as I did. I kept a journal for some years then. I was turning it over the other day. "It was very rainy, so we could not go out. I had two games of draughts, then I crocheted, and read 'The Talisman,'[13] and then I practised, then

[13] *The Talisman* by Sir Walter Scott, first published in 1825.

I wrote my journal till supper." Pages of it. Don't you think fourteen to sixteen is the poorest in imagination of any of the ages we have passed through? If only I had recorded some of the old people's sayings in their beautiful Elizabethan language, which is now dying so rapidly! There was something truly poetic about them. You laugh, and say I can cap any quotation, and I certainly do love poetry, but those old people possessed its essence. After the sixteen stage I felt a sort of awe of them. Mrs. Hicks and Mrs. Beasley are very good, they could not be more excellent, but I feel no awe whatever of them; if anything, they feel awe of me. Perhaps I am too old for awe, or the past may be transforming itself into too radiant colours, but I think not. I am just going to read "Nicholas Nickleby," so good night.

Your loving,

E. N. C.

Sept. 11.

MY DEAREST HILDA

I meant to have told you about our haunted spot, when I broke off the other day. We have that instead of a ghost. It is a narrow strip of green called Little Hollow, lying between two large fields. I loved it when I was a child, because the lords and ladies—I think they are such interesting flowers—grew so abundantly in the hedge. Nurse used to hurry through, and say I was a slowcoach. I heard later that the village people do not like it; they see things, though they can never agree what things. That is to say, the old people; the white shoe girls and their boys, when they come down on visits to their parents, walk through it unconcernedly. They have their own superstitions however, dreambooks and mascots, just as there might be in a suburb. I am not affected either, only I do not happen to go very often, as it is at the other end of the village. Yesterday I thought I would try and get some stories for you about it, so I have been paying a series of calls on the aged poor. I am amused that you think the State in its benevolence is taking all the duties of the vicars' daughters away; but I expect it will leave us the visiting of the people who have no one to visit them. If it does take that, I am sure it will not derive such satisfaction from it as we do.

I was unlucky yesterday, I could not extract much about little Hollow, only nods and shakes of the heads and glances round the room or up the chimney. It is better to go just after Christmas, when father's annual distribution of his old port, bought long ago, when he was rather rich—the port is a very particular reason why the village is attached to father—has warmed the imagination. Miss Porter however told me something you will like. I often go and see her and her sister. Life has left them behind, and they are forgotten almost as if they were dead. Then they are chapel, and dressmakers, and above the ordinary village run, which is a mistake, if you live in a village. Miss Porter said she saw the Devil one evening in Little Hollow. "He was standing by the dead tree there like a great bat. Black wings he had as plain as I see you. He took and pinched me, and my poor side was black and blue all down. I cried out, and suddenly an angel came. Rather like a young lady I should describe him, with a white dress, cut low in the neck, the skirt draped, and beautiful white wings like a swan. That was enough; Satan never troubled me again." So now you know how an angel appears to a dressmaker. When you come, if ever that wonderful time arrives, you really must pay Miss Porter a visit. I am sure you have never met anyone before who has had an interview with the Devil. She does not talk about it much apparently; for her sister told me, when she mentioned it to their minister, he pooh-poohed the whole affair. He has got about as far as the rationalizing 'nineties you see, and she is still just at the beginning of the nineteenth century. Her feelings were very much hurt. I know how nice you will be to her, and I will ask her to tell it to you.

Your loving,

E. N. CORBETT.

Sept. 21.

DEAREST HILDA

To think you were here yesterday morning. I must write you a Collins to thank you for coming this abominable journey just for three days;[14] it was good of you. It must have been a strange shock to our bedroom walls to hear conversation going on up to two o'clock in the morning.

I am very glad you saw the Miss Porters, but it was a pity Miss Harriet was so shy about the Devil. I do hope she did not think I meant to show her off to you; I don't think she can have. Anyhow they were deeply gratified by your call, for I saw them this afternoon, and they were singing your praises. I ought to have explained to you about the younger, Miss Lizzie. I meant you to have sat by Miss Harriet, but the chairs got wrong somehow. We had such a rush afterwards for the train, I had no time. She is a little paralyzed, which makes her words, not her mind, hard to understand, unless one is used to her. She has spent all her life from eighteen onwards, nursing invalid relations, so now she is an invalid herself. She would not for an instant complain of her lot, but it has given her an unusually blank past to look back on, and

14 A 'Collins' is a letter of gratitude for hospitality.

that story she was telling you is her only story; it is regarded as the great romantic incident of her life. I saw you were getting a little bewildered. It was only that as a child she and her sister, when on a visit to their uncle, Lady Martindale's coachman, were summoned to amuse Lady Martindale's little grandchildren, who had colds. And when Miss Leonora in rose-coloured muslin with coral beads and Miss Rose in blue with a tiny turquoise locket—that was where you cast me a look of despair—were going down to dessert, Miss Leonora gave Harriet a doll, saying, "You may have that, I don't want it any more," and Miss Rose kissed Lizzie and said, "I want you to have my dolly, because I love you." It is a tale so oft repeated that I now know it by heart, and am quite fond of it. Excuse me, Mrs. Hawkins to see me in the dining-room. No more chance to-day.

Yours,

E. N. C.

Sept. 27.

MY DEAREST HILDA

I really have got some rather odd things to tell you in this letter. Three days ago I saw Miss Lizzie Porter. She looked unusually bright and animated and a little excited. It seems she had hobbled out in the sun the evening after our call, and reached Little Hollow, which is quite near their cottage. She often goes there in spite of the general prejudice and the encounter with the Devil. She says she saw just in front of her a little creature, shaped like a human being, but only as tall as a cock and dressed in green. "It was laughing and smiling at me, and oh, its hair! There, well, I never have seen such hair, so silky and as flaxen as silver, it put me in mind of Miss Rosie, why it might have been Miss Rosie, only it was so small. And would you believe me, Miss Corbett, it called out at me, quite clear, 'Come here.' There it was, and the next minute it wasn't there. I came back all of a tremble. Oh, it *did* put me in mind of Miss Rosie. I was thinking of her all the evening. She married, Lady George Carr she was, and then she died when her baby was born. Poor Miss Leonora, she lived to be an old maid, it is what comes of being too proud." (That I suppose is why I am an old maid; too proud.) She said she felt in such a flutter. "How it did laugh, that little creetur. I'm goin' out the next fine evening. But if you wouldn't mind, don't say anything to Harriet, for she don't like it."

She came up quite close to me, when she said this, and it seemed to me that her remarkably innocent face took on a partly sly, partly vacant expression. This gave me a slight turn against her, and I moved away. It was the first time I had heard her utter a syllable, which was not in submissive agreement with Miss Harriet.

Now are you not interested in Miss Rosie with the silver hair? I am, I believe. I really believe she must be a fairy. What else can she be? I have always thought it most reasonable that there should be fairies, and longed to see them. And if there are, Little Hollow is cut out for them; it is so cosy, much more suited to them than to ghosts or devils. But it is odd that Miss Lizzie Porter of all people should be vouchsafed a sight of one. Still, we do not know the laws which govern fairies; she may be most suitable.

Miss Harriet came to see me in the evening. I found, as I might have guessed, that she was very unhappy. She thought Miss Lizzie's adventure, if it was anything, was a wile of her old adversary, to which her sister had yielded. "My poor mother, what she would have said. I'm glad she's spared the shame. I spoke to Lizzie about her. But she takes no notice; just goes talk, talk, talking fit to talk your head off. In a general way she's not one for talking, she often doesn't speak more than once or twice the whole evening, but last night, though I spoke quite sharp to her, I couldn't stop her."

I think it's most excusable to be excited under the circumstances, only Miss Harriet likes to be in the foreground. I believe she is a shade jealous.

I saw Mrs. Hawkins in the afternoon—Mrs. Hawkins is our veteran, eighty-five and highly respected—and found that Miss Porter's adventure had already been repeated to her. She is always hostile to the Miss Porters, and expressed herself thus.

"So she says she's seen a girl the size of a cock, does she, same as some folks calls a fairy? Poor, silly creetur. Why there ain't no such thing, any child could tell her that, and if there was, it ain't nothing to be proud of. My dear mother, that's what she said: 'We know better now,' she says. 'People was very ignorant when I was young.' There was a person come from Devonshire, Silly Sally they called her, that's when *I* was a child. She says her father tell her he seed one, and he says: 'Once is enough, don't you go for to see 'em again, it ain't lucky. They're artful. Once they see you, they likes to call after you, but don't you turn round your head, for you may live to repent it.' A young fellow, what he knew, he turned round his head, and he broke his leg falling off a tree the very next day. So I don't know what Lizzie Porter has to be so set up about. There was a rhyme Silly Sally used to say:

'Should'st thou a faity see,
He' (or it might be 'she', there's both sorts) 'will kindly smile on thee.
That which thou lovest best
Into thy mind shall come
All the long way home.

The nest time thou goest that way
Run fast, make no delay.
He will call after thee.
Be sure thou dost not turn, for he
Lies in wait to harm thee
All the long way home.'

And I daresay, when all's said and done, that's truer nor what she thinks it is. Of course Little Hollow ain't a place I cares about, never have done. Old Mr. Matthews, he used to say: 'Ah, that's a funny place, that is. No place for a Christian soul what goes to church reg'lar, after dark,' he says. Them rampaging children, they goes through Little Hollow as bold as a lion, but pore things, what do they know? And the Porters," satirically, "of course they're Chapel, perhaps they're different, and them pore creeturs what are fond of dressin' up in Church and Roman in their ways, *they* must meet what they wish to meet."

My envelope won't take any more sheets, so good-bye.

E. N. C.

Oct. 1.

DEAREST HILDA

I feel rather troubled about Miss Lizzie. This afternoon Miss Harriet called again, still more unhappy, and it certainly is not only jealousy. She said Lizzie had gone out again to the Hollow, when her back was turned. She came back crying and confused. Miss Harriet made out with some difficulty that Lizzie had heard a voice calling after her, she had turned round, and she declared she saw the little figure nodding at her. Then she somehow lost her way, and was an hour before she reached home. She seemed very low all the evening, and would have no supper, and "spoke to me quite abruptly. That's not her way at all, she's such a contented soul." Miss Harriet felt so worried, she asked Dr. Close to call. He came, but after the usual medical fashion of dealing with the working classes, would say nothing at all. Prudent and possibly necessary, but rather unkind, isn't it? I said I would question him, if I got the chance, and asked if Miss Porter thought a visit from me would be cheering. She thought it would; I am generally a favourite with Miss Lizzie. But when I went, Miss Lizzie would not pay much attention to me. She sat with her face turned, looking out of the window, and sighed now and then. Her sister and I did our best to beguile her into talk, and she would say a word or two; but soon her eyes would be turning to the window again, and her face became empty of everything but a feeble sort of sadness. I felt that hateful, unreasonable irritation one has, when people cannot be well when one wants them to be well; I had tried so hard, and Miss Harriet was so anxious, but she did not rouse herself even to say good-bye.

Miss Lizzie's condition makes me think of that word they have in Scotland—rather a terrible word—"Fey." Do you think she is fairy struck?

The doctor came to the vicarage next morning to see cook, so I broached the subject of Miss Lizzie.

"Oh, yes," said he, "I should say it's senile decay starting. I've been expecting it for some time. It often begins with hallucinations."

I said it seemed a very harmless hallucination, but I could not help thinking of her strangeness.

"They are harmless at first," said he, "but sometimes people get worried and restless with them, and make themselves a nuisance. If she does, we shall have to send her off to the infirmary. That other old thing isn't capable of looking after her."

Poor dear little mouse-like Miss Lizzie. If this is to be the end of her more than blameless life, I shall feel the world cruel; but then no doubt it is cruel.

I tried to explain to Miss Harriet that Miss Lizzie might be suffering from a hallucination, but she would not own that there could be a hallucination about a fairy: she knew there might be about some things. I don't suppose she has harboured a new thought for about forty-five years—she is now seventy-eight—and when she had them, I imagine she dispensed them to the company, never received them from others. Good-bye.

E. N. C.

Oct. 1, *evening*

MY DEAREST HILDA

I know you have already had one letter to-day, but I cannot help it, you must put up with another, for I have a most queer thing to tell you, quite after your own heart.

About six o'clock to-day I was walking through Little Hollow, when *I*, prosaic *I*, saw Miss Porter's fairy—I will not call it a devil, anything less like a devil you cannot imagine—standing on a small log. It was beautifully made, and its little hands were as delicate as a mouse's claws. It had on a black crested feathery cap, which made it look like a handsome bird. The way it strutted up and down was bird-like also, and it kept turning its head about perking, as if it was delighted with its own graces and self-importance. Sometimes it whistled, sometimes it sang, and sometimes it danced a sort of swaggering dance, changing from each abruptly. The song it came back to was always the same. The note was clear and thrilling, without any expression whatsoever. Then it took off its hat, and I saw the bright hair Miss Lizzie spoke of. It had a silver comb, and combed its locks, which were almost as bushy as a fox's brush, only with the sun shining through, they looked the colour of sovereigns, not in the least flaxen. With the hat off I thought the fairy like a boy rather than like the lovely Miss Rose, the sort of fairy boy just my own age—my brothers were older—I used to long for when I was a child. I never wanted a girl. I wanted a fairy prince of my own. Then he laughed so heartily that I, who am not much given to laughing, laughed too. Oh, it was *delightful.* He turned to me, and gave me a most inviting smile. Then he looked over his shoulder, called out "I'm coming"—I heard the words quite plainly—hopped off the log as a bird hops, and was gone.

I was so thrilled I felt I must sit down and think a minute, and immediately I had the sensation most vividly that I was back at six years old. I was in the garden; it was the half-hour before sunset, the time of day I used to think fairies *must* come out. I constantly used to run away from the boys and Mother, to be alone at that time of day, because I thought the fairies might be shy of more than me. But I never found them. I was always sent to bed a minute too soon. I have lost almost all that side now, though I believe I was an imaginative child, but that one thing I have kept; a passion for fairies, and even a secret hope that they are somewhere to be found. I could see the grass and the sunlight so extraordinarily bright, much brighter than they have ever been since, or I suppose than they ever really were. It was so strange; all the thirty-five odd years seemed blotted out. I remembered—no, not remembered—I really was living for the moment in the time when one always skipped and ran everywhere, never walked, and I knew about hiding under the laurels, where there was room for nothing but me. Beloved childhood, it was the best time of one's life. I felt in a trance, I had not thought of all this for years. I fancied I sat there for hours, and after all, with so much meditation, the whole event had not lasted more than five minutes.

There now, what do you think of this for an excitement? You can't beat this in London, my love. I have been writing my letter all evening, but I feel so excited I can't sit down steadily to it. Father is out, I ought to be upstairs ministering to Mother, but one cannot always be ministering, and I must enjoy myself alone for once.

Excuse me, Hilda, I must do a little more wandering. I am in such tearing spirits, I feel I want to climb the cedar, or dance a Bacchanalian dance with the gardener, or something really sensible. We had a gypsy *faux pas* some way back, you know, that's where my eyes came from, only we don't talk about it, and I think my ancestress has got into me to-night. I must go to the Hollow to-morrow and see what I can see. I shall be sure to let you know at once what I have to report.

E. N. C.

Oct. 25.

DEAREST HILDA

I know I promised to write before. Your letter of this morning with No. 1 still unanswered rouses me from my lethargy. There isn't very much to say, and I am not sure that I am particularly anxious to say it. However I must keep to my compact. I told you I had a ridiculous craving to go to the Hollow again. So when six o'clock came the next day—it was pouring—off I set. Not that anyone who lives in the country is so idiotic as to mind rain, still I think this was silly. I can see I really was in the condition old nurse used to describe as "You'll come to a cry." When I got to Little Hollow my excitement fizzled out and I felt apprehensive. Everything looked so moist, black and decaying. There is a trickle there almost too small to be called a brook, it had swollen with the rain. "It crossed my path as unexpected as a serpent comes… So pretty, yet so spiteful."[15] It was *just* like that. I went squashing into it, and disturbed several things. I think they were only bits of sticks and leaves, but it seemed as if I were in the midst of a swarm of glossy black slugs. Ugh! Or I wonder if there really are snakes in the Hollow, I am certain I saw one wriggling yesterday. I walked on faster than usual, when I heard a little rustle behind me, then a distinct pitter-patter, then a faint but clear sound, then a voice lower than a whisper. I thought it said, "Turn round." I daresay it did not. I longed to turn round, though I could not endure the thought of what I might see. Mother, who is Highland, told me once she had that feeling —steps following her, and she must, and yet she must not, look behind. I did not wait for more. I put my hands to my ears and I ran till I was out of the Hollow. Now, you think of that jingle of Mrs. Hawkins. Wasn't it *extraordinarily* like it?

> "The nest time thou goest that way
> He will call after thee."

I suppose it is utterly absurd, but I am thankful I did not turn, for he "lies in wait to harm thee." I really do not know what I think, it is so inexplicable. I felt extremely confused, when I got out of the Hollow, as if I had come to from a fainting fit. I do not in the least wonder Miss Lizzie lost her way, and I was very frightened. Then the fright turned into extreme ennui, and general loathing of life, and my life in particular. Do you know that fear and ennui are connected? I

---

[15] From 'Childe Roland to the Dark Tower Came', a narrative poem by Robert Browning, first published in 1855.

found out that, when I was a child, and I am not sure that ennui —abysmal ennui—is not worse than fear. I have never felt so wretched in my life. I was too wretched to go home, and just wandered about in the rain, cursing my sad fate. After all I have had a very dreary life, my fun was short and over long ago. I consider Mrs. Hawkins' rhyme is *most* apt, for "That which I loved best into my mind did come all the long way home." As I told you, I was thinking of nothing else. Miss Porter you see thought of her Miss Rosie. It's odd we should both agree in having had our happiness packed into those early fleeting years. Neither of us had a romance to look back on. The only person who ever proposed to me was more than unromantic, and I longed for someone as romantic as Cyrano de Bergerac. And it's not only romance one misses. Life goes by, occupied with little fiddling duties, too small to be dignified by the name of work. Look at Mrs. Jardine at the Archdeacon's tennis party, so rude, and smart, and vulgar, and cold hearted, and so bursting with well being, with her devoted husband, and two perfect babies, and three neighbouring squires who find her an inspiration, not to mention five pekinese, which she finds most satisfying of all. I think Miss Lizzie and I do deserve a crumb or two off her floor. You with your overflowing life can't picture what mine is.

I came back wringing wet to our dark shabby house; I wish those great sprawling chestnuts were cut down. I was very late: it really was "All the long way home." Poor dear Mother and Father were so agitated. Father was standing out in the rain without his hat, and Mother literally could not get out a consecutive word. Father kissed me, and blundered against my corn, and I felt their agitation was so aggravating I could have screamed.

I cut out bridge to-night; I said I had a headache and must go to bed, but I can't sleep, so I am writing to you. I have been passing a horrible hour, hating my life and hating them. Old age is a morass which has almost engulfed them and is beginning to suck me in too, and it is an octopus, for wherever I go there are its tentacles, Mrs. Hawkins, and the Porters, and Aunt Ada and dozens of others, all lying in wait, catching one. Old age saps not merely the bodily strength and the mental—that is bearable, though the concentration on tiny futile trifles is very wearisome—but it saps the heart. Love and feeling die, and what is left cares only that it may eat, drink and be warm. I am chained to those husks, and cannot get free. Muriel and the boys escaped, they left me to the chains, and forgot me, though Muriel and I had been everything to one another. I suppose there are thousands of these dying homes in England, from which the bright flame of life has been carried to form new homes, and the poor little flicker goes on in the socket, waiting, almost without the energy to become extinct. That's an allegory of us. It doesn't seem worth while sleeping—what is there to sleep for?—but I can't inflict more on you. What a scrawl. I'm so sorry. I shall be better soon presumably, but at present, as you see, the salt is gone, if there was any salt.

E. N. C.

Oct. 27.

MY DEAREST HILDA

Your true friend's letter makes me most deeply ashamed of myself. *Please* burn mine. I was mad, that's the only explanation I can give you. I really laugh when I think I was abusing our venerable chestnut trees, the pride of the whole parish. I think it was just autumn. Dear autumn is the best of all the seasons, but it is so terrible, full of death and corruption. Each time as it comes round, I feel that there are some days which are almost more than I can bear. The

Russians, you know, commit suicide for joy that the spring has come. If I ever did anything so enterprising, it would be to escape from the majesticness of autumn. If you ask, was Miss Lizzie's episode simply autumn also, I own at once that I am entirely out of my depth.

It is good of you to offer to visit, but you must not think of it. Much as I should love to have you, I know you cannot really spare the time. I am glad to say I have come to my senses; the clouds are entirely dispersed. I recall all my idiocy, and will simply say, what I have very often thought, that if ever a person was cut out to be a clergyman's daughter in a remote village it is me (bother I, I can't say I), who enjoy country things and people, silence, solitude, and reading; so it is particularly well arranged that it should be my lot, and not yours, who would loathe it.

I went through the Hollow to-day; I own I had put off doing it. It was just as it always was, and I felt neither elated nor melancholy. I went on a sad errand. Miss Lizzie Porter is dead. She missed her footing, fell downstairs, and broke her neck; she was killed on the spot. I feel glad for her. If senile decay really was coming on, of course it is far happier, and even if it was not, I know she would not be sorry to join her invalids. I had not seen her since she sat apart at the window. I had a shrinking from the sight of her, and in my cowardice I yielded and never went near her, and now it is too late. So you need never call me "devoted" in visiting again.

Miss Harriet said, "She looks lovely, you'll like to see her. I had a nice bit put by, and I'm giving her a beautiful funeral. This last week she's been as quiet as a lamb, just like old times. She said to me only the night before she didn't seem to have a care in the world. I think she'd a touch of influenza, when I came to see you about her. The doctor says there's been a nasty germ going about."

So that cloud has gone too.

Mrs. Hawkins is nodding very significantly. There is a kind of primitive hardness about some of these old people, which is rather repellent. I have noticed it more than once. She thinks Miss Porter's death a fulfilment and confirmation of her distrust of fairies. If it is, I and her poem do not agree what "harming" is. I do rather wonder this however. If I had turned round my head, should I have fallen down stairs, and broken my neck? What say you?

Your loving,

E. N. C.

I must tell you about Mother and Father. All their solicitude for my headache, the inquiries, port wine, Bovril, arrowroot and sal volatile made my load of guilt almost more than I could bear.[16] Father is often silent at meals, but at lunch he made unusual efforts to talk about his old Cambridge days. Then he said, "There is a little proposal your mother wants to make to you, which I think is a very wise one." He always has considered everything Mother proposed very wise, and she has always considered everything he proposed very wise; they think one another perfect. You cannot imagine how sweet it is. Theirs is one of the real romantic Victorian marriages. The boys and Muriel have very nice, happy, sensible marriages, but they don't compare with Mother's and Father's. Yet I have never felt out of it; they always seemed to want me in with them too.

I went upstairs and found Mother flushed, and looking lovely. Often her utterance is a little thick and confused, but to-day she spoke in her own beautiful clear voice; it gave me such a pang when she first began to lose it. I could see she was bracing herself to make

16 Sal volatile: a solution of ammonium carbonate in alcohol, used as smelling salts.

an unusual effort. She said, "Father and I have been consulting together" (that was always the way from childhood she told us of any arrangement) "and we feel you are wanting a little change, you work so hard, dear, and if your nice friend Hilda could go with you perhaps to Switzerland I am sure Cousin Agnes could come and be with us. We want you to have a good holiday, so here is that little brooch Father gave me. I think you could get something for it, for it was most extravagant of him to buy it."

I couldn't speak for a minute. I hugged her and I know the tears were pouring down my cheeks. I could feel hers also. She said, "I never forget the sacrifice you made for me, love, I think of it often and often." It was so absurd, because I would so much rather be what I am than married to Mr. Higgins at Blackburn. When he proposed it was just after Muriel's wedding, and I felt rather left out, and I wanted children, and I did contemplate it, but I never got engaged, and then Mother fell ill, and I couldn't leave home, so luckily I was saved. Well, I did manage to get out that I didn't want a holiday, having already had a particularly nice one with you this year, and that certainly she must never sell Father's brooch, but we agreed that I should have a little old ring of hers as a symbol that I was happily married to her and Father and the village, for better or worse, in sickness an in health, till Death us do part.

I could not say what I wanted, though, so I say it to you to relieve my mind: that if old age is sometimes pitiful and dismal, sometimes on the other hand it is in old age that the soul seems to rise to maturity. Its best is not till then, yes, even the more the outward man decayeth, and even though the battle against weakness is always a losing battle.

Your loving,

E. N. C.

October 29.

DEAREST HILDA

I wonder if that wicked little sprit took it into his head that he would "bless this house," as the dear fairies did in The Midsummer Night's Dream. I have three things to tell you which are heartening to my spirits.

1. I called on Mrs. Northcote; excellent but usually grumpy. She said to me, "What's this about your all leaving and going to London?" (Who shall say how she picked up that tale?) " 'Well,' I said, 'they'll make a poor exchange, for they're well liked here, every one of them, whatever Mrs. Downs *did* say.' " I wonder what Mrs. Downs *did* say. Mrs. Northcote would tell me in two ticks, but I mustn't ask. When she heard we were not leaving, I think she would have liked to recall her words, but she was too honest, and she even added grudgingly. "Everyone speaks well of you." We shall feed on the compliment for weeks; we don't get too many.

2. Mr. Higgins wrote this morning to ask if I were still free, as his affections have never swerved! I cannot help feeling that he must be rather lethargic not to have roused himself to write before, and perhaps still more lethargic not to think of anyone else, but still to be eighteen years remembered is not so bad.

3. Muriel is coming home for six months with the two children, and will leave them for us to bring up at the Vicarage. I am so *happy* I don't know what to do.

Your loving,

E. N. C.

TALES OF WIDOW WEEKS

The village of Manningfield is remote and, being remote, still retains a primitive simplicity. It has no picture theatres within several miles, so it must provide its own amusement, and it inherits from past generations some strange sources of animation within itself. These sources are drying up; each decade there are fewer. Let us look at them while we may, and accompany Miss Corbett the Vicar's daughter on her visit to Mrs. Hawkins.

Mrs. Hawkins, the patriarch of Manningfield and eighty-five years of age, is suffering from the rheumatism, and has on this late end of a September afternoon sent her great-grandson up to the vicarage to invite Miss Corbett to step in and have tea with her.

Miss Corbett put on her hat gladly, but as she knocked at the cottage door, her heart quailed, for surely Mrs. Hawkins' cottage is the stuffiest in England. The bad smells of many generations seemed to hover over it. Miss Corbett had at various times presented Mrs. Hawkins with peat, pot-pourri, and e*au de cologne* to allay them, but Mrs. Hawkins, "don't hold with none of them queer smells," and things went on as before.

Miss Corbett carefully chose a plain wooden chair.

"Won't you please to sit by the fire, miss?"

"Thank you, Mrs. Hawkins, it is very nice here."

"But I've put the armchair all ready for you, miss."

"Thank you, really this is so *very*..."

"And I've put that cushion, what my mother used to have when her poor dear back was bad."

Miss Corbett privately thought the armchair and that cushion the great source and origin of the smells, but they must not be avoided any longer.

"And here's your cup of tea, miss; it's nice and strong."

It was indeed, but tea is clean, and so is the cup with pretty roses and forget-me-nots on it; dust doesn't count. It is the cake and bread and butter; but they say burning is a purifying process, and Miss Corbett ate three cakes. Now all that could be criticized in the afternoon was over, and she abandoned herself to unalloyed enjoyment.

They wandered over a variety of subjects; at length they landed on mice.

"I never could abide mice," says Mrs. Hawkins.

"They are so mischievous, aren't they?" said Miss Corbett.

"It ain't that; it's what they've got inside of them."

"Nice plum cake, you mean," said Miss Corbett, making her little joke, "which we ought to be eating instead of them."

"It weren't no plum cake I was thinking of. No, it was *them*."

"Them, what?"

"Why, the sperrits."

"The sperrits, Mrs. Hawkins?"

"Yes, witches' sperrits. Imps."

"Oh, really. What are they?"

"Nobody rightly knows what they are, and nobody don't ought to know, and it's no good asking me. But I can tell you a tale about them, as true a tale as ever I sat here. You're one of them as likes to hear my old tales, so I'll tell you."

"*Please* do!"

"There was an elderly man, my mother knew, a Mr. Laver. He was a very still quiet man in his habits, just did his work, and went to the public-house regular, and never did no harm. He had an aunt, Widow Weeks she went by the name of. I daresay she might be my age. He give her half a crown a week, and the best of everything out of his garden she had. Oh, he was very different from some what I know. Nobody don't give me half a crown, and as to vegetables, why they only give me one dish of peas out of the garden all last summer, they did, yis, and I give everyone of 'em a card at Christmas, everyone; but then, it would be better for me if I was in my——" The conversation must be quickly turned, and Miss Corbett cried:

"Was Widow Weeks a nice old lady?" A silly question perhaps, but it was successful.

"That's all as how people may think. What I know is Mr. Laver and his wife was very good to her, and this is how she served them. Mrs. Laver, she spoke hasty about Widow Weeks one day, and she said, 'I can't abide that there dirty old woman always coming about my place.' She spoke without thinking, and she turned round, and there was Widow Weeks behind her. Mrs. Weeks, oh, she *did* give a look, won'erful great eyes she had, and a beard, and she says, 'There's one thing nobody mayn't say, and that is that I'm a dirty woman. Everybody knows I washed myself every Saturday night, and them that tell lies don't come to no good, and that you'll find.'

"Mrs. Laver, she did all she could to pacify her, but no, it wasn't no good. Then it began; first their bees wouldn't swarm, and there was no honey; then their pig got sick, then their youngest boy had boils, then Mrs. Laver's face swelled out like a marrer. Mr. Laver, he went to Widow Weeks, and spoke very respectful, and he says, 'If Patty said anything to upset you by accident, she's sure she never meant it, and will you accept of a pound of tea and a dozen eggs? And it was a great disappointment,' he says, 'not to have no honey to give you this year, and my wife's face it's swelled up, you never see such a size, and if you could give her a few words to say to take it away, she would take it kind!' "

"A few words to say, Mrs. Hawkins?"

"Yes, a spell, like."

"Oh, did Widow Weeks know spells?"

"Of course she did."

"Yes, I see. Please go on."

Mrs. Hawkins does not care for interruptions, but it is well to get things clear.

" 'I'll do more than give her a few words to say,' says Widow Weeks, and she goes upstairs, and back she comes with a box. 'You give her that,' she says, 'and tell her to be sure to open it in the dark, and see if that won't make her better, but don't let her open it in daylight nor yet in candlelight, it won't do her any good. Give her my kind love, and tell her bygones shall be bygones. I'm a-goin' to the workhouse next week, where I shall be well looked after, but I should like her to have my box.'

"So he took the box home to his wife, and he tells her not to open it till after dark, and she says to her youngest boy, the one that had the boils, 'Now don't you touch that box,' and he says, 'I won't, Mother.' But after a time, when she was out of the room, he goes and he takes up the box, and he heard something a-movin' inside. And when his mother came back, he says, 'Mother, there's a something moving in that there box.' 'No, there isn't, you naughty boy,' says she, and she took the box and she opened the lid a little way, and oh, she did give a holler. She wouldn't say what she see inside, but she said to her little boy, 'Run to Mrs. Prout' (that was a neighbour, a very respectable person she was) 'and ask her to step in.' And Mrs. Prout came and she says, 'Why, pore thing, you've got the 'sterics,' and Mrs. Laver says, 'Oh, that box, Mrs Prout!' 'Why, what's the matter with the box, Mrs. Laver?' 'Mrs. Prout, I couldn't tell you, I couldn't tell you, if you ask me till next Christmas.'

"Then Mrs. Prout she opened the box, and whatever Mrs. Laver saw, I can tell you what Mrs. Prout saw, and what do you think it was? Why, three *mice*. Yes, three mice. Oh, Widow Weeks, she *was* a spiteful woman."

"Why, were those three mice spirits?"

"To be sure they was, her imps they was. If you get a witch's imps about the house you'll never have no more luck. They're such nasty things to get rid of."

Widow Weeks was a witch, then? I hadn't quite realized that."

"Ain't I said so? And she had her sperrits same as other people. I've never heard of no witch without her sperrits, nor don't expect to. Kept them in mice, she did. Some has them in pigs; I've heard of them in ducks; they have them in goats frequent."

"Yes, now I quite understand. And what happened after that?"

"Mrs. Prout, she shut the box up again, and she says 'Don't be upset, Mrs. Laver, and be thankful I come when I did, and tell Tim' (the little boy was Tim) 'to get a pail of cold water'; for there's two things the sperrits can't bear, that's fire and cold water. So after all no harm was done. But Mrs. Laver said to my mother, 'To think I should give she a pound of tea and twelve eggs, when eggs are so scarce, and then she should serve me like that.'

"Mr. Laver he went to ask Widow Weeks what she meant by it. But when he came to her door, he said he felt all of a shudder.

" 'You didn't ought to have sent them mice, Aunt,' says he.

" 'How did Patty know it was mice?'

" 'Why, Aunt, she see them.'

" 'And how could she see them if she opened the box in the dark?'

" 'I don't think it was rightly dark, Aunt.'

" 'If Patty don't do as she's bid, she won't never get well, and you can go home and tell her so.' "

"Did you ever see Widow Weeks yourself, Mrs. Hawkins?"

"I often see her when I was a child. She knew my mother well. Yes, she played my mother a nasty trick too."

"Do tell me about that."

"There was a Mr. Bidwell in Cayley." (Cayley was a little town not so very far from Manningfield.) "He killed a pig, same as Mr. Saunders might have done. My mother, she was in Cayley, on a Saturday it was, doing her shopping. 'Oh,' says Mr. Bidwell, 'I've killed a pig,' he says, 'would you like the pluck? You shall have it and welcome.' "

"The pluck?"

"Yes, pig's inn'ards; take 'em and fry 'em in a drop of sherry wine, and a spoonful of brown sugar, as my good aunt that kept the Crown used to do 'em, and Queen Mary on her throne wouldn't scorn 'em. But there's nobody does them like that now, and nobody thinks of me."

"Well, Mrs. Hawkins, so Mr. Bidwell gave your mother the pluck?"

"Yes, he often give it to her. She was a widow, my mother; she was poor, but she was very well thought of.

" 'I'm sure I'm very much obliged,' says my mother, 'for there's nothing I fancies more.'

"So she took the pluck, she did, and she went home. She was a-cooking it before the fire, when Mrs. Prout, Mrs. Prout what I told you of just now, our next-door neighbour she was, she comes in all out of breath.

" 'Oh, dear,' she says, 'let me fetch my breath, and then I'll tell you.'

"So soon as she could speak, she says, 'Take and put that there tom cat of yours on the fire.'

" 'Oh, Mrs. Prout,' says my mother, 'whatever are you talking of? I don't think you know what you're saying.'

" 'Yes, I do, Mrs. Tower, and don't you argue, for you've no time to lose.'

" 'Put the poor dumb cat on the fire is a thing I never *will* do,' says my mother. 'Give the creatures the stick, when they misbehave, same as you would a child, say I, but always be kind to them.'

" 'Oh, Mrs. Tower, you don't know what's a-goin' to happen to you. I was in with Mr. Bidwell, and he was a-tellin' me he'd give you the pluck, and then who should come in but Widow Weeks. "Oh, Mr. Bidwell," she says, "you've been a-killin' a pig." No one hadn't told her, but know it she did. "Will you let me have the pluck? I do get the crave for a bit of the pluck for my supper." "Well, Mrs. Weeks," says Mr. Bidwell, "I'm sorry, but that you can't have, for I've given it away already." "I know," she says, "it's them Towerses," she says, "always gets everything." Yes, she says that, and though no one ain't said a word of it being you; and then Mrs. Weeks began, and oh, she did say things of you.' Yes, Mrs. Prout told 'em to my mother, but it wasn't what I should care to repeat to a lady like you, miss, I couldn't do it."

Mrs. Hawkins wished to repeat them and Miss Corbett to hear them, but there are duties incumbent on the position of daughter of the vicar.

"No, it is much better to forget them. Then what happened after that, Mrs. Hawkins?"

"Mrs. Prout she says, 'Widow Weeks give a nasty look, and she says, "I'll make Towerses sorry they ever was born." After that I came along as fast as I could,' says Mrs. Prout, 'for I know she'll play you a mischievous trick. She's very artful. So now you understand, Mrs. Tower, what I mean about the cat.' "

"Ah, he was a won'erful fine cat, just three white hairs on his forehead, and all the rest black. A quiet cat he was in general, sat before the fire and drank his milk like a baby, but when the wind set up a-blowing, he kept jumping up and down the chairs, a-wagging his tail and crying to go out."

"It's funny," said Miss Corbett sympathetically, how excited animals get sometimes; in the snow, for instance."

"Ah, it was funny, too. We'd open the door and off he'd go. And where do you think he went to? Why, off to Widow Weeks to be sure."

"Used she to feed him?"

"She may have, and she may not, but she kept her sperrit inside of him."

"But I thought you said she kept them in mice?"

"So she did, but that wasn't all she had. Why she may have had hundreds; kept some in this and some in that, she did, and certain it is she kept one in our tom. Still, my mother was wonderful fond of that cat. A good cat, he was, sat up so pretty for his milk."

"But surely your mother didn't have him put on the fire?"

"No, she went next door, and she asked the young man, a very civil young chap he was, to kill poor Tom. So he says, 'I will, and I shall do it with a feeling heart, though I am in the butchering.' When the cat was dead, they took it and they put it before the fire, 'and mind you don't let in get done too quickly,' says Mrs. Prout. 'Do it slowly, it's always best, and oh, Mrs.

Tower,' she says, 'do stick a pin in near the heart, for she's a wicked creetur.'

" 'You know best,' says my mother. She wasn't a very knowin' woman, my mother, but a better soul never lived, so she stuck a pin in, but she wouldn't put it near the heart.

" 'Now I must get home,' says Mrs. Prout, 'but *whatever* you do, Mrs. Tower,' says she, 'don't you take that cat off the fire, not if she goes down on her knees to you.'

"Mrs. Prout hadn't been gone not five minutes, when in comes Widow Weeks at the door. 'Oh, Mrs. Tower,' says she, 'let me set down on that chair, I'm took with the faints.'

" 'So you shall, ma'am,' says my mother. She was always afraid of the widow.

"I was a little thing at the time, maybe seven, maybe eight, but my mother's often told me how I ups and says, 'Why's that old woman cut her face?'

" 'Oh,' says Mrs. Weeks, 'that was a bramble caught me, as I was coming along the road.'

"So I says, you know what children are with their back answers, 'There ain't no brambles in Febbervery.'

" 'No,' she says, 'what was I a-saying of? It was a nail in the wall.'

" 'Let me give you some ointment for it,' says my mother. 'It's a dreadful place you've got.'

" 'Oh, no, there's nothing the matter with that,' says Widow Weeks.

"Well, you may believe me, and you may not, but that there wound she had on her face was just where my mother stuck the pin in the cat's body."

Miss Corbett did not dare to express anything so bold as doubts, with Mrs. Hawkins' piercing eyes fixed on her.

"Then Mrs. Weeks says, 'Oh, Mrs. Towers, there's such a smell of burning here,' she says, 'couldn't you take off what's before the fire? I'm afraid it'll be burnt to a cinder!'

" 'Thank you, I'm sure,' says my mother, 'but it's right that should be cookin' slowly.'

" 'Mrs. Tower, ma'am, if you'll take my advice, you won't let that go on burnin'.'

" 'You mind your own business, Mrs. Weeks, and I'll mind mine.'

" 'If ever we may have had a word or two, or I may have spoken sharp behind your back, no harm was ever meant, you know that, don't you, Mrs. Tower?'

"My mother said nothing.

" 'Oh, ma'am, I do beg and pray of you take that there off the fire, it's burning the heart out of my body.'

"Still my mother said nothing.

" 'Oh dear, Mrs. Tower, if I go down on my knees, will you take that there cat off the fire?'

"My mother used to tell me how all this time Widow Weeks kept a-heaving and a-sighing, the blood coming out of the place on her face, and as to the sweat—if a lady like you won't think me rude—why it was a-pouring off her like rain. Yes, she *did* strive and pray, and she turned terrible white, as white as your hand, miss; so my mother says, 'We're all sinful creatures, Mrs. Weeks, and I am no better than anyone else, I won't judge you,' and she took the cat off the fire. And there right away was the widow as gay as you please, and that place on her face, why you couldn't see there'd ever been one, and off she skipped out at the door with never a word of thank you. 'I don't grudge it, no I don't grudge it,' said my mother afterwards, 'but she might have said thank you.'

" 'Oh, Mrs. Tower,' says Mrs. Prout next morning, 'you didn't do what I told you, and you're a foolish woman. If you'd left that there cat on the fire, she'd have melted away, and we should never have been troubled again.' "

"But why, Mrs. Hawkins? Do you mean because the spirit would have been burnt up?"

"That's what I can't tell you" (rather testily) "and what's more, nobody can't tell you. All I know is that if that cat had been burnt up, that very minute Widow Weeks would have died. It's happened time and again; time and again it's happened, it has."

It required some courage to ask another impertinent question, but Miss Corbett's conscientious mind could not bear to be puzzled.

"But, Mrs. Hawkins, what I don't *quite* see is, why didn't Widow Weeks die, if she had to die, when the cat was first killed?"

"I tells a tale, as my pore mother told it to me," was the severe reply. "It mayn't be good enough for some folks; they may like to listen to Mrs. Bowley's tales about the gentry she met London way, all what they said to her, and every word of them true." With a withering quiver of her head.

"Some may like those stories, but I like your mother's, as you know very well, Mrs. Hawkins."

"Do you, my dear," with an ancient wily smile of pleased content, not too much of a smile, for fear Miss Corbett, being young, should become set up; the young are so easily set up. Then, jumping swiftly back to Widow Weeks, "Of course what they say is 'always burn it *slowly,* if you want 'em to die'; killin' ain't much good, if you don't burn 'em *slowly.*"

The whole idea was so complicated that Miss Corbett had to give it up, and go on to something else.

"I hope Widow Weeks was grateful to your mother?"

"Yes, I must say she was always civil to my mother after that; but Mrs. Prout, well, she didn't have no apples what was worth anything on her trees that year, and my mother, just next door, had beautiful apples, beautiful. Ah, it's better not to cross 'em, not if you can help it."

"Widow Weeks must have been an awful woman, Mrs. Hawkins, and Mrs. Prout, too. I think Mrs. Prout was the worst, for after all Widow Weeks didn't try to murder anybody."

"No, miss, Mrs. Prout was a very hard-working woman, a better woman at the mangle never lived; I've often heard my mother say so; only she and Widow Weeks never was good friends. As to Widow Weeks, well, of course, it's best to keep out of the way of a witch, but my mother used to say 'Remember there's good in *everybody*,' and Mr. Laver often said she behaved very handsome to him before she died.

"It was the Christmas two years after she sent the mice to Mrs. Laver. They went to see her reg'lar in the House, and nobody didn't mention the sperrits, and they always brought her a bit of something, because she fretted in the workhouse, and besides you never knew what she might be doing next. It was Christmas Day, very cold it was. Mr. Laver went by himself; Mrs. Laver she was poorly with her chest. Mrs. Weeks, she seemed feeble first of all, her bed was so far away from the fire, but he made her a nice cup of tea with a nice drop of something hot in it, and it cheered her up like.

" 'James,' she says, 'you won't see me no more. I shall be dead come 28th of this month, Thursday that'll be.'

" 'You think so, Aunt?'

" 'Yes, my mother she died the 28th of December, thirty-seven years ago, and my husband the 28th of December, twenty-three years ago, and I should like to die that day same as them, so I means to.'

" 'Well, Aunt, you've had a long life.'

" 'Yes, and I've been a good woman and tried to live quiet with my neighbours, though there's been them that wouldn't let me. I should like to be at peace before I go, and I forgive all what's behaved wrong to me. Mrs. Prout, well she's dead' (she died sudden that summer) 'and I won't say anything against her, now she's dead, only this I will say—she was cut off at fifty-two in the prime of her years, and I'm eighty-six, come Old Christmas Day,[17] only I shall be dead before then, and there's many would say it looked like a judgement on she, and I shouldn't be the one to gainsay it. You can tell Patty I forgive her for saying I was a dirty woman; that cut me to the heart, for a clean person I always have been, but Patty's a poor ignorant woman, and a foreigner' (she came from Broadfield, that's fifteen miles away, you know, miss), 'and you couldn't expect her to know better. It was quite right and proper she should have the face-ache, and that Tim should have the boils, but I'm sorry I sent her them mice, and so you tell her.'

" 'They was thrown straight into cold water, Aunt, so don't worry yourself about that.'

" 'And there's another thing, James. I've often said I should harnt you when I was gone, but I won't. I mean to lie quiet in my grave and not take no notice of you. I often think there's my husband will be glad to have me alongside him, it will be company for him now his pore dear soul's gone to Heaven.'

---

[17] 6th January. When the Julian calendar was abandoned in favour of the Gregorian, 25th December according to the former became 6th January according to latter, this date then being referred to as 'Old Christmas'.

" 'Thank you kindly, Aunt, I'm sure. I own the thought of it's often right upset me, to think of you a-walkin', and poor Patty she's felt it, wakes up in the night about it, she has. It'll be a burden off my mind.'

" 'Well, God bless you, James, and your poor wife too, and don't you nor her trouble to come again. I don't want nobody by me when I go. Oh, and, James, there's a little thing or two I have in my box that you and Patty might like, only Nurse won't let me have my box by my bed, because she's so spiteful; so you can't have them till I'm dead, else you should have them now. There's a brooch and my poor husband's snuff-box. Come up Friday or Saturday and ask for it.'

" 'I can't come before Sunday, Aunt, but I'll come then, thank you.'

" 'Good-bye, James.'

" 'Good-bye, Aunt.' "

"And did she die on the 28th, Mrs. Hawkins?"

"Oh yes, she said she'd die then, and she did, in her sleep; went off quite quiet early in the morning."

Miss Corbett wanted to hear more, but the church bell was ringing for the Wednesday evening service, and if she were not there, the congregation would be diminished by fifty, perhaps by a hundred, per cent. She bade good-bye and hastened out.

She could not help being glad Widow Weeks had given that distinct promise that she would lie quiet and take no notice; otherwise, as she walked past her grave—the Weekses were all buried near together—Miss Corbett could almost have suspected that the widow was "harnting" her. She had an odd feeling she had never had before. Then too the twinkling stars illuminated faintly some dark shapes, which seemed like bending figures advancing towards her, and her mind saw plainly the won'erful great eyes and the beard. Altogether it was pleasant to get into the lighted church.

What amazing childishness these old people were content to live in! Miss Corbett thought about it all the way to London, where she went next day. There she sat in the tube, and walked up the moving staircase, and saw the sky signs and advertisements, and passed an hour or two amid the wiggle-woggle and other pastimes at the White City.[18] It seemed as if London's one object was to provide us with great toys, and, blocking everything else out, to limit all thoughts, desires, and aspirations to last week, to-day and next week. As she came back in the train, she wondered which was the more childish, the past generation or the present?

---

[18] The wiggle-woggle was a sloping funfair ride at the Japan-British Exhibition of 1910. Passengers travelled down it, zig-zag fashion, in what looked like oversized buckets.

FIFTEEN CHARLOTTE STREET

It was the evening of a day at the end of March many years ago. The elements were disturbed, and a fierce wind had arisen. The rain was falling heavily in Tottenham Court Road, but this did not seem to diminish the countless stream of people, ever meeting one another and ever passing one another. One among the stream suddenly by chance stood still, and found a man waiting for him, as it were, upon the pavement. The first, with his mild and amiable aspect, might have been some respectable labourer. The other fixed upon him his restless, searching, and vigilant eye, and spoke thus: "You are in some difficulty, I think. Can I help you?"

"It's this address," said the mild man, speaking in a rustic accent. "I've asked more than one, but they don't seem to understand me."

"They talk in the vile accent of London," said the other, whose voice and bearing were those of a gentleman, "and you I hear speak the pure Saxon dialect of East Anglia. Tell me the address."

The countryman told it him.

"Is anyone expecting you there?"

"Not to say expecting me, he isn't."

"This address is miles away from here," said the gentleman kindly. "It is getting late, and the weather is so desperate. Come to my house for the night."

"Shan't I be taking you in before your time, sir?"

"Not at all, Mr.—. What is your name?"

"Dence, sir."

"Mr. Dence. My business is now done. My name is Morell. Let us come."

During their walk Mr. Morell encouraged the countryman to speak freely to him. He had come to London in search of work, and Mr. Morell promised to exert himself in his behalf. They stopped at 15 Charlotte Street, an old, narrow house, whose windows were unlighted. The door was opened by a man-servant.

"Smee will take every care of you," said Mr. Morell. "He is an excellent fellow, but I must warn you that he is stone deaf."

Dence was given dry clothing, and then was taken to the dining-room for supper.

He found that there were other guests besides himself; a negro, an old man, and an Italian. Dence refreshed and cheered by the warmth, lights, food and excellent beer, was ready for good fellowship, but both the old man and the negro seemed sunk in apathy. The old man now and again gazed about him furtively; and the negro, having speedily devoured his food, kept his eyes, which had in them the distant and wild expression of an animal unspoilt by contact with man, fixed for ever upon vacancy. The Italian, a youth of about nineteen, talked incessantly, but his utterance was so rapid that Dence could not understand him. The subject of his conversation seemed to be the benevolence of Mr. Morell, his charity to strangers and to the poor. "He goes out night after night into the street to help them," said he. None of the three paid any attention to the other; each might have been in solitude.

After supper, Smee took Dence into another room.

"Mr. Morell will be with you in a moment," said he. He shut the door and left him.

The room was hung with crimson curtains, and the light cast by the lamp, deeply shaded in red, was faint and confused. At first the softness of the cushions on which he seated himself, and the warmth of the rosy fire, were soothing and agreeable; but as minute after minute passed by, his fancy conjured up serious and unreasonable forebodings. It seemed to him that he must have waited a whole evening, when a voice close to him made him start, and almost cry out.

"I hope you are refreshed after your fatigues, Mr. Dence."

Mr. Morell had entered without his knowledge.

"I don't know how to thank you, sir," said Dence, half stammering.

"Don't thank me for that," said Mr. Morell. "I think, however, I can be of some service to you. Give me your hand and let me feel your pulse. I am a doctor, and I am not altogether pleased with your appearance."

Mr. Dence felt an unaccountable shock, as if his heart ceased beating for a moment, when Mr. Morell gently took his hand and said: "Would you be so good as to look at me."

He held it for so long that Dence became anxious.

"I'm not very ill, sir, am I?" said he.

"I do not like to alarm you unnecessarily," said the doctor, "but I should be more satisfied if I could sound you. The quickness of your pulse may come from quite unimportant causes; on the other hand it may indicate something serious. Would you oblige me by lying on the sofa."

Dence did as he was bid.

"The light is in your eyes," said the doctor. "I will move it."

"Don't, sir," said the poor man, fearing he knew not what.

"Do not be afraid. This instrument I have in my hand will not hurt you. It is only for testing the heart. Fix your eyes on me."

The man did so, and the longer he looked the brighter shone the eyes of Mr. Morell in the darkness. They might have stared at one another for about five minutes, when the doctor, bringing his face suddenly close to the patient, said in a low, clear whisper: "You are now coming upstairs with me. What happens there is a secret, which no one must ever know."

"What is to happen to me, sir?" said Dence.

"That you will see," replied the doctor. This he said with his eves gleaming, so that the man began to quail. He wished to turn his face away, but he seemed powerless.

"We will come now," said Mr. Morell.

"Let me out, sir," said Dence. "Do, for the love of God, let me out."

"Into the rain?" said the doctor, still with his eyes upon him. "I would not let out a dog on such a night as this."

"Let me go, I don't care where I go, if only I don't go upstairs."

Mr. Morell laid his hand on Dence's shoulder, and lightly impelled him forward.

They went together to the third floor and into a long room, softly lighted with clusters of candles. The walls were hung with mirrors, interspersed with purple, black and amber curtains of the richest velvet. The air was heavy with delightful perfumes; prominent among them was incense. There were two fireplaces; in one ordinary coal was burning; in the other logs of various kinds, which emitted blue, green and iridescent flames. There was at one end an image in black marble, a copy probably from some primitive sculpture. The figure was seated; its hands lay on its knees. The smile on its face, inscrutable, wild and despairing, was unsuited to our comfortable London, and carried the mind back to another world altogether, the world of Babylon or Assyria. The number of mirrors increased and confused the reflections, so that it seemed to the bewildered senses of the countryman that the room was filled with a multitude of people. In reality there was no one but himself and Mr. Morell. Mr. Morell shut the door, and gazed upon him with a smile. The clock at the same moment struck the hour of midnight.

Mr. Dence's relations were concerned to receive no news of him for three months after his journey to London. At the end of that period he returned to them. It seemed he had not met with the success that he had expected. He had obtained several situations, but had been discharged from each owing to incompetency and lack of the necessary physical strength. This was the more surprising as, up to the time of leaving the village, he had been reckoned sturdy and industrious. The young man seemed now in a state of nervous and physical collapse. The explanation he offered was too confused to throw much light on his condition. He said a gentleman had taken him to his house the night of his arrival in London; that he had been hospitably entertained, and that he had stayed with him; but how long he could not remember, nor could he relate anything which had happened while he was there. He knew nothing more until he found himself walking in a quiet street, which was entirely unknown to him. He had walked till he came to a large thoroughfare: he observed the name, Blackfriars Road. Then again he remembered nothing, till he woke in the ward of a great London Infirmary. Here he had stayed until he was discharged as cured.

The village doctor, Dr. Arleigh, who was more enlightened than the ordinary country practitioner, listened to the narrative with interest. Though overwhelmed with work, he had found time to make some study of nervous diseases.

"The first thing to be done," said he, "is to write to the Infirmary, and to get the report of the doctor there."

An answer came saying that James Dence had been admitted on March 30th at 3 a.m. He had been brought there by a policeman.

He was suffering severely from collapse, produced by some shock, aggravated probably by alcoholic poisoning. He had been discharged on April 10th.

"So the patient's story has a certain confirmation," said Dr. Arleigh to his friend, Mr. Weir, a London physician, who was staying with him at the time.

"Alcoholic poisoning is a flight of the imagination, but we do not expect great accuracy in our medical brethren in infirmaries."

He again examined Dence, and gradually drew from him a description of all that had occurred until his entrance into Mr. Morell's upper chamber at midnight.

"You tell me you went to London on the 25th of March. Where were you, when you met the gentleman?"

"That I couldn't tell you, sir. It was miles away from my brother's address, that I know. The gentleman told me so."

"Can you remember nothing at all of the street where you met the gentleman?"

"Yes, sir, now you ask me I remember the name of the Street was Tottenham—Tottenham Court. I remember that, for Tottenham was my poor mother's name."

"That is something at any rate. Can you tell me anything about the gentleman?"

Dence began to tremble.

"You are perfectly safe here," said Dr. Arleigh, "and I believe it will be a comfort to you in the end to tell me what is frightening you."

"He had a very saller skin, and his eyes was screwed up, sir. Every night it seems as if he was looking at me still."

"Yes, that uncomfortable sensation will pass as you get stronger. His name was Morell, you say?"

"Yes, sir. A doctor he was. He told me that."

"A doctor? In that case, we shall soon trace him."

No Dr. Morell however was to be found in the Medical Directory.

"Dence's story is curious, don't you think so, Weir?" said Dr. Arleigh to his friend that evening. "Either this is all an illusion, in which case he has a decidedly richer imagination than I had given him credit for—you should hear his description of a negro, a foreign gentleman and crimson curtains—or he really has had a queer experience. But if it is an illusion induced by some drug, why was he drugged? Evidently he was not robbed. His own clothes, which they had taken away, were returned to him, and also the little money he had in his pocket."

"You say he was in a perfectly normal condition when he went to London?"

"Perfectly. I have known him all his life. He is a good, slow-witted creature. I should like to be acquainted with Mr. Morell that I might set Dence's troubled soul at rest. I shall be in London in September for my usual holiday. What do you bet I come across him?"

"A thousand pounds that you don't. If Mr. Morell is like all sensible people, he will be out of town."

"It is the only month I have to spare however."

"Do you mean that you are going night after night to stand in Tottenham Court Road, waiting for Mr. Morell?"

"You must remember that the foreign gentleman declared that Mr. Morell went out constantly to befriend strangers. I may meet him."

"My dear Arleigh, you always were a little mad."

"I am quite reasonable enough to know that the scheme is utterly wild."

"Well, I shall be only a few miles out of town in September. Let me know when you come up, and count upon me if I can help in any way."

Accordingly, in September Dr. Arleigh took lodgings in the region of Tottenham Court Road, and amused himself, in the intervals of research at a laboratory, in hunting for Mr. Morell. He consulted a detective; he inserted a discreetly worded advertisement in the papers; but without result. He also waited night after night for several hours in Tottenham Court Road, but he never saw Mr. Morell.

The month's holiday that the doctor had permitted himself was nearly over. It was the 25th of September; he was to return home on the morrow. The equinoctial winds were rending the poor London trees, and the rain fell heavily. At a few minutes past seven, Dr. Arleigh was walking in one of the streets behind Tottenham Court Road on his way back to his lodgings, when he saw a thin man coming towards him. The head, he observed, was turned in a strange manner over the right shoulder. The eyes were half closed, the mouth drawn down, and the expression was one of dejection, if not of despair. The singularity of the pose first attracted Dr. Arleigh's attention, then the profound melancholy, and then the certainty that the face was formerly familiar to him. Looking back into the past to recollect whose the face might be, he did not notice where he was going; the man, equally absorbed in his recollections, almost fell against him. Both apologised, and the man, rousing himself, said with a melancholy smile: "My mind just now is occupied, very much occupied. That must be my excuse."

"Why, Curran," said Dr. Arleigh, "is that you? How long is it since we met? Not since student days, twenty-five years ago, I believe."

"I am glad to see you, Arleigh, more glad than I can say. I am on my way home; come back and dine with me. I live not two minutes away."

"I shall be delighted. I am in lodgings near. Let me just go back and tell them that I shall be out, and I will join you."

"Don't leave me, my dear fellow. Come with me at once. Whatever you do, don't leave me."

"The remarkable fervour of the plea surprised the doctor. Observing which, Mr. Curran added: "The fact is I am not very well; nothing at all serious, but I am not very well."

"You do not look well."

"Oh, but it is very trifling. You will come with me now?"

"Certainly I will."

They set off together.

"You would not object to walking on the right side of me rather than the left?" said Mr. Curran. "I have a particular reason for desiring it."

"Of course not."

"Thank you."

They walked on a pace or two.

"I don't know why I should conceal the reason from you," said Mr. Curran. "I am deaf of the left ear."

Dr. Arleigh observed that Mr. Curran kept his face turned in the same strange manner during their walk, though the reason now might be his desire of facing his companion. As he conversed, he smiled and looked more animated, but his eyes preserved their expression of dejection.

They reached the house, 15 Charlotte Street, in a few minutes.

They sat down to an excellent dinner. Mr. Curran threw off his depression and became gay and talkative. He signed to the butler to bring more wine. The butler bent down and said something in a low voice, to which Mr. Curran responded. Dr. Arleigh noticed that the butler was standing at his left side.

"Why in that case," thought Dr. Arleigh, "should Curran go out of his way to tell me he is deaf?"

After dinner they retired to a small parlour, where the ruddy glow of lamp and fire cheerfully illuminated the crimson draperies. It seemed to Dr. Arleigh that the room was familiar to him: he had a feeling, which was almost oppressive, that he had been there before. It was filled with books, which Mr. Curran showed with delight. His stock of subjects was the strangest Arleigh had ever seen, ranging from mesmerism to the ancient religions of the East and the Devil worshippers of Africa.

"You have a curious taste in literature, Curran."

"Have I?" said Mr. Curran. "Each one has his own, I suppose."

They had much to talk of. Arleigh, though a middle-aged man, had retained a youthful zest for knowledge, while Curran showed himself to be an omnivorous reader.

Mr. Curran, who had been a year or two junior to Dr. Arleigh, told him that, before he had finished his medical course, an uncle had left him a considerable sum of money. The prospect of private practice had always been distasteful to him; he did not continue his training, but read, studied, and wrote, and travelled wherever the spirit led him.

"It is strange, Arleigh, do you not think so? How this modern generation is content to buy and sell and trouble itself with elections, taxes, philanthropic societies, marrying, and so forth, when, separated from us by a veil, which in some parts is thin as gossamer so that the beautiful and dreadful light beyond is apparent, there is a realm of bliss, of woe, of powers and faculties far transcending what we know of here."

"Such a realm there is, no doubt. A doctor has cause to know it. In madness and delirium he sees glimpses, which make him thank Heaven that he does not see more."

"That is true. But what a trivial world this is in which we are confined. I sometimes stand in Tottenham Court Road, and see the streams go by. What small, mean, silly and bovine faces one beholds. Thousands upon thousands day after day. One might take two or three here and there, anywhere in the stream, and, if it chanced that they should never come back, they are so ineffectual, so superfluous, no one would miss them. They are like raindrops falling in the ocean, or caterpillars dying in the summer."

They were talking in this strain, when Mr. Curran suddenly started, and said in a voice of entreaty: "Do not speak to me, do not speak to me."

At the same time his face, already so pale, assumed the pallor of a corpse. He seized Dr. Arleigh's arm in fear, and his fear communicated itself to his companion in the form of a strange repulsion against Mr. Curran. Dr. Arleigh shook off the detaining hand, and stood up.

"Let me hold you, Arleigh,' cried Mr. Curran. "Let me hold you. The touch of your warm hand supports me."

Ashamed of his impulse Dr. Arleigh took the shaking fingers in his own.

"My dear fellow," he said, "put both your hands in mine. Lean against me. I will keep my arm round you." They remained thus for a minute.

"Curran," said Dr. Arleigh gently, "let me move for a moment to get you some brandy. Tell me where it is, or let me ring for your man."

"No, no," said the other pressing against him. "Do not let go of me. Brandy is utterly useless. I shall be well in a few minutes."

They sat in silence. At length Mr. Curran relinquished his grasp and pulled himself erect. Hie eyes opened, the expression of fear had left them, and his cheeks returned to their usual tint.

"Arleigh," said he, "how am I to apologise to you? I am liable to these seizures. I am deeply ashamed, but I confess to you I am absolutely unable to withstand them. I strive against them, how desperately no one can tell but myself. In those moments I pass through indescribable anguish. Tell me, did you hear no voice?"

"Nothing."

"No, I suppose not. I shrink from speaking, yet I cannot express to you what a relief it would be to me to tell you all. I am so utterly alone. Old friends have deserted me, or I them. I have many pleasant acquaintances, but all are now out of town, and of what avail would they be, if they were here? We were friends long ago. Will you have pity on me, and listen?"

"My dear Curran, I will do everything I can for you. Very likely what is oppressing you comes from some simple bodily cause."

"Thank you, Arleigh. For the past three years I have been troubled with depression. There was a sudden death in the house, which shocked me very much, and lately this depression has been aggravated by hallucinations and appearances. I have seen the figure of a small, fair boy. He was with me in the road when I met you, always on my left side, and a voice, a deep and terrible voice, speaks to me with an awful distinctiveness, repeating continually: 'Shall I not visit for these things? saith the Lord.'[19]

---

[19] Meaning: 'Shall I not punish them for these things?' Jeremiah 5:9

For what things? I have done nothing. Why should that be said continually to me? My dear Arleigh, for the love of God, tell me why?"

"For no reason. As you know very well, these hallucinations are directly contrary to reason, probability, or past experience."

"That is true, but one wonders—perhaps—does the Lord visit for these things, Arleigh?"

"I have had little time in my life for reflection on serious matters," answered Dr. Arleigh. "I have had my work to do. I do not presume to give you counsel, but have not all sinned, and is not forgiveness promised to all who repent?"

> "Try what repentance can: what can it not?
> Yet what can it, when one cannot repent?"[20]

said Mr. Curran. "No one but the man himself knows what lies hidden in his heart."

"Why do you not consult some clergyman? He could guide you with more authority than I."

"No, no, that is impossible."

"Then would it be a relief to you to tell me what is troubling you? Is there some past folly, some error, whose consequence you dread?" "The poor fellow is a prey to some fixed idea," the doctor thought to himself.

"Many follies, and worse than follies. I have not given enough to the poor. I have spoken impatiently to my servants. I have been idle and procrastinating. I have given way to anger. I have been spendthrift."

---

20 William Shakespeare, *Hamlet*: Act 3, Scene 3.

"So have we all, that is to say, all who have had any money to spend. I never had, and I never shall have."

"There might be other things also," said Curran, speaking with hesitation. "I believe, I am certain, I was not always kind to those younger than myself at school. One boy, a fair boy, who was delicate. Might he not possibly desire retribution?"

"I was a delicate boy once," said Dr. Arleigh, "though I don't look it now, and there was a bigger boy who used to kick my chilblains to make me cry. But I bear him no grudge; he was not a bad fellow in his way. I don't suppose your victim thinks any more of it than I do."

"He is dead," said Mr. Curran, "he died when he was twelve."

"Then there is all the less likelihood that he is remembering it against you now."

"You may be right," said Curran. "I hope you are right."

"I am sure of it. Put all that out of your mind. Now that I am here, let me ask you a few questions and examine you."

The examination made it evident that there was advanced disease of the heart, which was bound to terminate life in a year or two, possibly within a still shorter period. Agitation such as had been suffered that evening might cause instant death.

"You don't think me very ill? not dying?" inquired Mr. Curran anxiously.

"Who can say when death will come? I may be dead before you."

"I *cannot* die," said Mr. Curran, with a peculiar emphasis, which Dr. Arleigh did not forget for many years. "Not yet. I must have time to repent. It is not too late."

"Much lies in your hands," said Dr. Arleigh, and he advised his patient to rest and seek change and gentle unstimulating companionship.

"I have been away already three times this summer," returned Mr. Curran, "but each time I have been driven back. I am better here."

"Well, get away from this room and your diabolical books, then."

Mr. Curran gave Dr. Arleigh a strange look, saying: "Why do you call them diabolical?"

"Because they are," said Dr. Arleigh, laughing. "Now let me write you a prescription."

While he was writing, the clock struck ten.

"You will excuse me," said Mr. Curran, starting up. "I have an engagement at ten. I had no idea it was so late. I regret extremely, Arleigh, that I must drive you away and go out. Infinite thanks to you for all your goodness to me."

"I will call and see you again," said Dr. Arleigh.

"Yes, indeed, come again."

"It is raining very heavily," said Dr. Arleigh.

"It is," returned Mr. Curran, "and the equinoctial winds are up."

"I like them," said Dr. Arleigh, "I like their friendly howls, but should you expose yourself on such a night as this? It is not very wise."

"It may be a mere fancy of mine," said Curran, "but I seem to derive distinct benefit from a short ramble on a stormy night; it soothes me, I believe."

His eyes rested on Dr. Arleigh, but it was evident his thoughts were at work elsewhere. Something pleased him, for his eyes began to glisten.

"I must not linger now," said he. "Forgive my haste. Good-bye, good-bye."

He walked towards the door, then stopped. An idea appeared to strike him; a small smile played for an instant round his mouth; he turned and came back.

"Come to-morrow night, Arleigh," said he.

"The morning is better for me," answered Dr. Arleigh. "I am returning to the country in the afternoon."

"Put off your return," said Mr. Curran. "Let me beg you to put of your return, if it is possible. I have a pressing engagement to-morrow, which will occupy the whole day, yet I would not miss another visit from you for the world. There is something healing and salutary in your presence. Do not deny me."

"Of course I will come. What time will suit you?"

"Half-past ten, and dearest Arleigh, whatever you do, do not fail me."

The exaggerated affection displayed by Mr. Curran seemed to Dr. Arleigh another indication of his friend's morbid and unhealthy condition. This weighed on him so much that he wrote at once to Dr. Weir, asking him if possible to come to London the next day.

"You don't mean to say I have lost my bet," said Dr. Weir, as they sat in his house in Harley Street. "I am not to pay you a thousand pounds?"

"Oh no, the laugh is all on your side in that matter. It is only that I met an old friend of ours, Curran—you remember Curran?"

"I remember him, but he was not a friend of mine. I never hated but one man in my life, and that was Curran. He was callous, utterly callous."

"He was callous, but I believe it was only a relic of the ugly side of boyhood, lasting on too late. It does, you know, sometimes, and then the man outgrows it and becomes a decent member of society. Anyhow, you must extend your pity to him now, for he needs it, poor fellow."

Having explained the circumstances, Arleigh continued: "I want to put him into your care. Hearts being your province, you will be able to suggest alleviations. I can do almost nothing for him. I only have to-day. I must be back to-morrow. My locum is screaming to be off. I have promised to call on him this evening; he is engaged in the day. Will you come with me?"

"What time? A man is dining with me at my club to-night."

"Half-past ten."

"Then as soon as I can get rid of my man, I will join you at Curran's."

At the appointed time, Dr. Arleigh went to Charlotte Street. While he was knocking at the door, Mr. Curran himself came up behind him.

"I am delighted to see you, Arleigh," he said. "Come in, come in."

"Weir is joining us later," said Dr. Arleigh. "You remember Weir? He is a great man now, and I want him to look at you. I think he can help you. How are you?"

"Better, far better. I am a different man to-day. I was in a wretched state last night. Let us forget it. It is very good of you and Weir. I shall be delighted to see him. When is he coming, did you say?"

"A friend is dining with him at his club. He will come on from there."

"When?" repeated Mr. Curran. "In half an hour, should you think?"

"He will come as soon as he can."

"Exactly. Forgive me for a moment. I will tell my servant to be prepared for him."

They went into the red parlour and, though the light was dim as before, Dr. Arleigh could see that Mr. Curran did look in sober fact a different man. He seemed taller and more commanding.

There was, besides, a bright flush of excitement on his pale cheek; his sunken eyes were wide open and the pupils dilated. They sat down facing one another, the light falling on Mr. Curran's face. After some enquiries of Dr. Arleigh's doings since he left College, Mr. Curran began to talk to him softly and charmingly of his own travels in the East; of the reposeful life there, of basking in gardens of cypresses, of the Persian music, some of which he sang in a somnolent monotonous voice. All this time his eyes were fixed on Dr. Arleigh and Dr. Arleigh's on him. As they gazed, it seemed to Dr. Arleigh that Mr. Curran's eyes grew larger and brighter, far larger and far brighter. Mr. Curran himself seemed to shoot up to a height above the natural height of man. While he talked, he put his hand now and then very softly on Dr. Arleigh's shoulder, and stroked his arm down to the elbow, as if he were stroking an animal. Dr. Arleigh found that the acuteness of his senses had become suddenly intensified, so that this light touch sent a shudder through him, pleasing and almost excruciating. The low gentle voice also penetrated his whole being, and the eyes pierced into his defenceless brain like knives.

"What the devil are you doing, Curran?" said he. "Take your hand off my arm."

Though the room was hotter than a greenhouse, he turned cold as he spoke, and his teeth began to chatter.

"I am doing nothing to you, my dear Arleigh," said Mr. Curran in crooning tones, continuing to caress him. "Nothing, nothing. Do not take your eyes from me. It is a pleasure for us old friends to look into one another's eyes. Is not that so?"

Dr. Arleigh would have given ten years of his life to turn away his face, for it seemed to him that long, long ago, he had either read or heard that Mr. Curran was not always to be trusted, and that to look at him was to put oneself in his power. While his senses appeared stimulated to extraordinary vigour, other faculties, such as the reason and the will, were growing numb and incapable of action. He could not rouse himself to make the effort necessary to turn his head. Struggling against this lethargy, he endeavoured to speak. He began: "Curran, take—will you? ——" but something seemed to paralyse his utterance, and in an instant also the idea of what he was about to say, and then even the desire to speak, had slipped from him.

"Arleigh," whispered Mr. Curran, putting his face close to his, "we are now going upstairs. Whatever you see you are not to interfere with, nor are you ever to reveal it."

In spite of the confusion and sloth which had overcome him, Dr. Arleigh was able to follow Mr. Curran with perfect ease. Mr. Curran with the agility of a youth, sped into the passage, and up the stairs. Dr. Arleigh felt certain that they would come to a long room on an upper floor, lighted with candles, and that there some disaster would befall him. He was as sure of this as he was of his own identity. The idea did not trouble him, but there was a doubt, which lay on his mind.

"Stop," he said to Curran, as they were on the stairs. "Who are you? Is your name Morell?"

"No, Arleigh," said the other, turning round, and lightly stroking him on the face. "My name is Curran, your old friend Curran."

The room they entered was, as Dr. Arleigh anticipated, lighted with candles. The heavy scents were almost overpowering. An Italian youth was swinging a censer, and a blind man was seated by the fire.

When Mr. Curran had closed the door, he turned and looked at Dr. Arleigh. His glance was malicious in the extreme; it chilled Dr. Arleigh's blood.

"The cause of the overmastering fear one pities so much in the insane has often puzzled me," he used to say afterwards, "but I once experienced myself what unbridled terror is, and since then I understand."

Dr. Arleigh now heard a cry; whether he himself uttered it, or it came from some one else, he could not tell; and a voice came from the man by the fire.

"Spare me, Mr. Morell, remember I am blind."

It seemed to Dr. Arleigh that immediately after, or long after—he could not say which—someone, he believed Mr. Curran, approached him. He put his hands before his face; he heard another cry, and also voices. The cry, he thought, rose to a scream. It continued so agonizing that it seemed to him it was prolonged beyond the limits of human endurance. Then he lost consciousness.

He opened his eyes, and found himself in bed, with Dr. Weir standing beside him. "That's right, Arleigh," said Dr. Weir. "Don't disturb yourself. Shut your eyes and go to sleep."

Dr. Arleigh stayed with Dr. Weir in Harley Street until he was completely restored, and, while he was there, each related to the other their adventures of the preceding night.

"I called at 15 Charlotte Street, as we had arranged," said Dr. Weir. "The servant who opened the door said that Curran was engaged and could see no one. I told him I came by appointment, but he still refused admittance. At the same moment, a loud cry from the room upstairs struck my ear, and the sound of someone falling. I pushed past the butler, telling him I was a doctor. I rushed to the top of the house. I found the door open, and the body of a man lying across the threshold. It was Curran. He was dead, but life was quite warm. I gathered with some difficulty from the Italian, who was in a very bewildered state, that it was Curran who had cried out. Something suddenly had frightened him excessively, the Italian did not know what. He went to the door, and had just time to open it, before he fell, when he must have instantly expired. I was alarmed to see that you were lying on the ground unconscious. I soon found, however, that there was nothing seriously wrong. I took you to a room downstairs, but as long as you were in the house you remained confused, and unable to account for yourself. I had an odd night's work. The Italian, the blind man, the butler and the cook, seemed almost as incapacitated as yourself, and I had to make the necessary arrangements unassisted. It was a great relief to get myself and you out of the house. I felt suffocated there both in mind and body. Do you realize that that upper room had no windows, and was reeking with musk, incense, and other horrid stinks? Most unwholesome. It was padded too, and, but for the accident of Curran opening the door, I should never have heard his scream. That is the end of my story; and now tell me, Arleigh, does not something very surprising occur to you?"

"I have seen, heard, and suffered so many surprising things in the last few hours, that I do not think one thing has struck me more than another."

"Have you not been reminded of anything?"

"That red room of Curran's seemed familiar, too familiar; but my recollection of the evening is so confused. Still, I believe its familiarity was one of my last waking thoughts before I completely succumbed."

"Perhaps you will understand why it was familiar, when I tell you that the Italian spoke to me of your late friend as Morell."

"No, really! Wait! Let me think. Yes, I see, I understand. Many mysterious things are now explained. What an ass I was not to discover it sooner. So Dence had not a creative imagination after all, and I am afraid I must trouble you for a thousand pounds.'

Many hours of conversation were required before their surprise and excitement could be adequately expressed.

It was not necessary to hold an inquest, as death was clearly due to natural causes. Advertisements were put in the papers, asking relations of Mr. Curran to communicate with a solicitor, but no answers were received.

The blind man and the Italian recovered in a few days what equilibrium they had. The Italian said he was a waiter; that one night some months ago, how long he could not exactly say, Mr. Curran had seen him at a restaurant. He had been persuaded to come to his house for the evening, and had stayed there ever since. At first he spoke in the warmest tones of Mr. Curran; but as days passed, he would shake his head, and say that he himself had seen sights in that upper room which must not be described. The blind man, who begged in the streets and was given to drink, had been brought to the house by Mr. Curran on the night before his death. He could remember nothing of what happened but thought this the most dreadful place he had ever seen. He and the Italian were both disposed of satisfactorily.

Mr. Curran's affairs were found in good order. He had a large balance at the bank. He left no will. The tradesmen spoke of him as an excellent customer, and the servants as a good master, who gave little trouble and paid their wages regularly. He was constantly absent from Charlotte Street and they knew nothing of his pursuits. It seemed as if there could rarely have existed a being so entirely solitary and isolated as Mr. Curran. His death was greeted by eulogies in English and foreign papers; his erudition and the elegance of his writing were particularly mentioned. The butler, who declared that Mr. Curran had promised him and his wife large legacies, revealed some curious habits of his master, but it was clear he could tell very little. It was only when searching among his papers that Dr. Arleigh discovered a record of Mr. Curran's inner thoughts and feelings. These threw light on much that had hitherto been inexplicable. Dr. Arleigh read his friend some extracts from Mr. Curran's narrative, which are appended here.

RECORD OF MY EXPERIENCES

"The possession of leisure, of money, and of perhaps a rather uncommon curiosity, has enabled me to enquire with a certain measure of success into matters which have been in general avoided.

"I had long pondered upon the government of the universe, and I came to the conclusion that, while there is an over-ruling Principle, it is not beneficent, but, on the contrary, actively malignant.

"This conclusion at first filled me with unutterable horror; there were periods when I could only lie in my bed, while convulsive spasms shook my frame. Gladly would I have sought death, but the dread of what might await me held me back.

"I do not know when the idea presented itself to my mind that, following the example of the religious in every age, I should endeavour to propitiate my deity, that is to say, to propitiate Evil. For this purpose I studied with the utmost eagerness all the conclusions arrived at by the ancient world. Even the most primitive and superstitious beliefs had something to teach me. All religious rites are on the same level as drugs. They are some of the keys we possess, which open the doors admitting us to communication with the unseen. Much of what I read was repulsive to me. But habit broadens the judgement.

"At school I had tormented those younger than myself. At an early age I developed powers of hypnotism, and had by their aid reduced many boys to the last extremities of terror. My studies showed me that the use of those powers might prove an important means of communication between me and the Power I was anxious to propitiate. By hypnotic aid I could for instance suggest remorse for a crime which the victim never committed; dread of a disaster which will never come; or a more elementary terror can be induced by the suggestion, 'What may a man find when he looks at his own face in the glass?' Indeed, human peace of mind rests on the frailest foundations. I have reduced one of my fellow creatures to the farthest limits of anguish by these simple words, 'You do not know what time it is, nor where you are.' One could then observe what the religious aptly term a lost soul.

"One evening, while I was meditating what means I should employ, I suddenly saw a form rise up before me. It was the figure of a man. I thought the dress and face familiar. I asked it, trembling: "Who are you?'

"It answered me: 'You know who I am.' It seemed that it was my voice, answering my voice. I looked at it more closely. It was myself I saw before me. My sensations were indescribable. Yet why should I fear myself, whose impotence I could read as a book?

"I spoke again. 'Tell me what I am to do.'

" 'Follow the dictates of your heart by night at the equinox, particularly when the wind is high and the rain is falling.'

" 'What are the dictates of my heart?'

> " 'Why do you ask? You know them.'
>
> "I longed to question further; the form had vanished. My intentions were now confirmed."

"Then Curran relates how he established himself in Charlotte Street," said Dr. Arleigh. "I skip that. He gave out that he was a doctor who took charge of mental cases. He has a characteristic sentence about his servants. He says:

> "I knew a man who had cheated me. He was both afraid of me and indebted to me. I engaged him as butler and his wife as cook. By a simple combination of drugs and hypnotic suggestion I was able to render them both stone deaf. This made them more suitable to my purpose, and by continually assuring them that I should leave money to them in my will, which, as I took care to say, I had not yet made, I gave them an unwearied interest in my prosperity."

Now we continue with the narrative.

> "I set about to secure a victim. It was without much difficulty that in our wealthy and well-ordered Metropolis I found a tramp feeble in mind and body. To bring him under my control was however less simple than I had anticipated. I was in an unusual condition of doubt and agitation; my whole future peace and good seemed to depend on the success of my experiment, and it was long ere I could calm myself sufficiently to hypnotize him. But in the end all was happily accomplished.
>
> "I was soon aware of a wondrous enlargement of my faculties. It resembled that induced by morphia, but far exceeded

anything I have experienced from the use of that most powerful drug. It recalled the state described by Milton—

> 'Opener mine eyes,
> Dim erst, dilated spirits, ampler heart,
> And growing up to Godhead.'[21]

Nor did I observe the expected depression attendant on exhilaration. I continued my studies with a new zest. I published a work of considerable importance, which brought me recognition from the most celebrated men of science in Europe.

"At the next equinox, I was again able to carry out my design. On this occasion I beguiled a Pole. From henceforth I periodically performed the ritual. Each time the expansion of my faculties became more amazing. I felt an assurance of boundless increase. The growth of my hypnotic powers which, whenever I chose to exert them, gave me a complete ascendancy, seemed to me an earnest of the sovereignty I should enjoy in the future, not merely over weak, dying humanity, but over enfranchised spirits in distant spheres of being.

"I found, as time passed on, the friends I had associated with ceased to visit me. I did not know why: I felt no regret, for I had ample compensations.

"I early saw the utility of having someone about the house who might be employed as a decoy duck to the subjects of experiment. I depicted myself in glowing colours to the duck, when hypnotized, and he would pour himself out in my praise to all comers. He was also serviceable in keeping the upper

---

[21] From *Paradise Lost* by John Milton, published in 1667.

room in order. Here the rites were performed. I never allowed the servants to enter it. A recurrence of hypnotic trances wears out the system, and after each assistant had served his turn, I disposed of him.

"Nothing could have worked more smoothly than all my arrangements. But at the end of five years an unfortunate accident occurred. The danger attending my experiments had always been before me. It was my endeavour, while making my oblation worthy of acceptance, not to risk detection by producing too great a derangement of the delicate human organism. Now, however, there was a miscalculation as to the vitality of one of the subjects, and he succumbed under the experiments. I had already decided that there should be no concealment in the event of such an accident. I immediately secured medical assistance, notified the death, and aided the authorities by every means in my power; but there is no doubt that, though definite proof was wanting, suspicions, which had more than once been aroused in the past, were strengthened in a high degree. This almost disposed me to leave Charlotte Street, but the associations of Tottenham Court Road had endeared themselves to me, and I remained.

"The circumstances had no doubt been extremely distressing, and from that date I trace the physical deterioration, which soon after declared itself in me.

"On the evening of the funeral, which I had arranged, while sparing no expense, should be quiet and suitable, I was sitting in my study, when I saw a light flickering round me, and then, standing by my chair, the appearance of a very small, fair boy. I knew it at once. When I was at school there had been a child whom it had been my special delight to torment. He was ill, and was taken away suddenly before the term was over. He bade farewell to each. When he came to me, he put his hand behind his back, and said: 'I shan't say good-bye to you. I forgive all the others, but I shall never forgive you; if I was dying I should not forgive you.' I laughed, and in the holidays he died. The figure was looking at me. Only the disturbed state of my nerves could account for my unreasonable terror at the sight. I fled to my bedroom. I locked myself in. I changed my study, but unavailingly; I left the house. Then I left London and travelled, and from that time I was never free from apprehension. Custom did not stale my terror, nothing allays such terror, alas! It increased. The appearance of the child showed itself to me at the rarest intervals. Once it spoke, whispering in a voice as frail and thin as air: 'Spare me, Curran.' Oh, the unutterable horror of that moment. I, who had conceived myself the superior of powers transcending the comprehension of our mortal nature, I quailed, as an infant might quail, and at what? At the reflection, the mere, pale, embodied memory, of the feeblest of mankind.

"I returned to Charlotte Street, shaken in mind and body, clinging like a child to what was familiar. I consulted a doctor. I knew his opinion from his questions. He advised me most earnestly to give up all drugs, and told me I had made myself an old man at forty-seven.

"As my exhilaration had been greater than normal, so was my abasement far, far greater. And now a new terror was added, a voice uttering words full of foreboding. The safety, in which I thought I had secured myself, seemed to slip from me. Death, I knew, was fast approaching, and after death, as my disordered fancy clamorously reiterated, judgement. I could not but recall the long, long forgotten words of Matthew —'One of these little ones.'[22] Many and many of these little ones, the weak, the utterly friendless, I had made my sport. I cherished but one hope, that, if someone of more consequence than they could be presented to the Evil One, my danger might be averted. It was a vain and childish hope, since I now questioned the efficacy of evil. At other times, I cherished the illusion of rapid, but fundamental, repentance."

"Here it ends, Weir, but a sentence has been added which is dated September 26th, the night he died, you know. 'I am not forgotten—on the contrary, I am singularly blessed; Arleigh is coming to-night.' "

"Well, I congratulate you on your friend," said Dr. Weir. "I think I showed more discrimination. There wouldn't have been much left of you, if he had had his way."

"And I was sorry for the animal, and held his hands and comforted him. Crazy, malignant, pitiable wretch."

"Do you know these words?" said Dr. Weir. "I learnt them when I was a boy, and I think they aptly describe Curran.

" 'For while he supposed himself to be hid in his secret sins, noises sounded about him, and sad visions appeared unto him. No power of the fire might give him light, neither could the bright flames of the star endure to lighten that horrible night. Only there appeared unto him a fire kindled of itself, very dreadful. For being much terrified, he thought the things which

---

[22] 'But whoso shall offend one of these little ones which believe in me, it were better for him that a millstone were hanged about his neck, and that he were drowned in the depth of the sea.' Matthew 18:6.

he saw were worse than the things he saw not. Over him was spread a heavy night, an image of that darkness which should afterwards receive him.' "[23]

[23] Paraphrasing Wisdom of Solomon 17:3-6

THE UNQUIET GRAVE

Two women were sitting over the fire in a new villa parlour, a little, nooky room with small casement windows, looking out on a neat garden, a pergola, and a crazy pavement path. Beyond the garden were other bright red and stucco villas. One could fancy them at their most characteristic on long June afternoons, with sidecars at the rustic gates and young couples, who might have been to the Slade or a Socialist Summer School, running in and out of the front doors.[24] For this neighbourhood was artistic, intellectual, and domesticated, and all was like a poster of Metroland.[25] Only to-day the weather did not fit the crude little scene, for the rain was pouring down, and the wind came crashing round the corners, threatening to carry any unwary open casement window away to the other end of the world.

"I love it," said Mrs. Breton, a weather-beaten elderly lady, sniffing at the wind as though it were a perfume. "It makes one sure there is something beyond this puny, cabined, cribbed, confined South, and I feel back in the North again."

"Yet you've been a Southerner most of your life," said the other lady.

"Yes, Fate compelled me; but not for the most important years. I never left the fells till I married at twenty-seven."

---

24 Slade School of Fine Art.

25 A term coined in 1915, referring to the housing estates built to the north-west of London in the early part of the 20th century and served by the Metropolitan Railway.

"Tom, did you hear that? Emily says her most important years were spent without you."

Tom, the elderly husband, who was finishing a letter, looked up and laughed.

"Tom has all the right feelings about the fells," said his wife, and the two exchanged a pleasant glance together.

"Yes," said he, "and observe, while it's she who does the rhapsodizing, it's I who go out and walk in the wind, as I propose to do at this moment. Anything for the post, either of you?"

"Put that new scarf on I gave you, dear," said Mrs. Breton. "I don't care if it *does* throttle you."

"I'll tell you what a day like this reminds me of," said she, when the two women were alone; "the old nursery at home, with a real north country fire and a real north country tea; the wind and the burn outside both roaring as loudly as they know how; old Nannie gone down to the kitchen, and my dear mother sitting in the rocking-chair, telling us stories. She used to tell stories wonderfully; no one ever had her gift; and she told them to us long past nursery days, for some of them were not nursery stories, they were too tragic.

"My mother was a woman born and bred on the fells, and she married late, and was already an old women when we were grown ups, so that her tales went far back. She remembered the north, when it was more as the Brontës wrote of it, a time that is long gone by. Nature can't be tamed, but I think the people have become as smug and tame as they are here."

"Tell me some of the stories, Emily."

"No, I'm no story-teller."

"Oh, you are; I've heard some, and there's your own wind to inspire you, and you're sitting on a rocking-chair, and I'm sure the cakes we had yesterday were as good as any they can make in the north country, so we shall be able to imagine your mother in the nursery."

Mrs. Breton smiled, and looked into the fire. Then she said she remembered one story.

"Not really a story, but one tragic incident: and if you like you shall have that.

"When my mother was a girl, her father was a clergyman in the fells, and Peters, the gardener and sexton, a south country man who had come with her father to the north, used to tell her the tale.

"There was a very lovely Ellen Braithwaite, and *how* beautiful some of those fell girls are, so noble and stately. She was the daughter of a prosperous farmer. Of all her admirers there was one she fancied, a young Thorny, the son of a squire of an old family rapidly going down in the world; a very handsome youth, the best rider and shot in the district, but idle and spendthrift. Her father was entirely against the marriage, and she would not take him without her father's consent. One day another lover, whom she hated, tried to molest her. Thorny came up and attacked him. They struggled, and in the struggle the man was killed.

" 'Well, now,' he said. 'I always hoped I might have a chance with you in the end, but this will do for me. I shall be hanged if they catch me, so good-bye.'

" 'But women are queer, as you know very well yourself, Miss,' Peters was wont to remark to my mother, and the fact that Thorny had lost everything made Ellen sure, so she told her sister afterwards, that he was the love of her heart. She threw herself into his arms and kissed him, and said to him that, wherever he went and whatever happened to him, she would be true to him. So it was settled he should get out of the country as fast as possible, but that he should come for her as soon as he could marry her, or, if it were not possible for him to come to her, she would leave her father's house, and go to him.

"Thorny got away safely, and she told her father what she had decided. He was furious with her, but nothing could change her resolution, and she refused all other offers of marriage.

"A year passed, two years, and still no word. Then she became ill. The North was a terrible place for consumption in those days; in that pure lovely air of the fells she began to fade. She got worse and worse, and it became evident that she was pining away for love. At last her father gave her two letters from Thorny, which he had intercepted, declaring his unalterable love for her, and imploring her to write to him one word. He had enlisted, and the last letter was from Ireland; but it was some months old and, though she wrote immediately, her letter was returned to her. Advertisements were put in the papers, begging him to let them know his whereabouts, for now, too late, the father was alarmed. But there was no answer.

"She grew very weak, and one day she spoke to the doctor. 'Tell me the truth,' she said. 'I want only the truth. Am I dying?'

"He knew she was dying, but he said she would be better when the summer came; the autumn and winter were a trying period in the north. 'You must keep cheerful. Don't indulge in depressing thoughts. You have relatives in London. Could you not arrange to pass the winter with them?'

" 'No, no, no,' she cried. 'I would not leave here, not for one single day.'

"She desired most ardently to live, and she would not take to her bed. She never spoke of Thorny to anyone.

"Once at midnight her sister, who slept in the same room next to her, heard her speaking at the open window. 'You have forgotten me. Oh, I cannot, cannot, cannot bear it. Oh, come to me, come to me. I cannot rest without you.'

"Her sister opened the door and went in.

" 'Ellen,' she said, 'what are you doing? Whom are you speaking to?'

"Ellen gave a strange look and she answered: 'No one.'

" 'Come back to bed, Ellen. You are in a fever; you are burning.'

"She allowed her sister to lead her back to her bed.

" 'You are thinking of Thorny,' said the sister. 'He is either dead or he has forgotten you. You should put him out of your head.'

"Ellen made no answer.

"After this she got rapidly worse, but she would not give up hopes of Thorny, and the very moment before she died, she raised herself violently in bed, stretched out her hands to her sister, and gasped, 'Is this death? I cannot die. You must not let me die. I must wait till he comes back,' and fell back dead.

"It was bitter winter weather in December, the shortest day of the year, when they buried her. On the afternoon following there was a second funeral of an old parishioner. Peters was covering the grave, next to that other new grave, the mourners had all gone home, and the twilight was falling.

"Suddenly he heard quite plainly, 'as plain as I hear you speak, Miss,' he used to say to my mother, a sound that made his blood run cold, a sigh from the grave where Ellen's body lay.

"There was no one in the churchyard, and there were no houses round it. The church stood in the midst of the fells, there was not even a shepherd's hut near, and the vicarage was half a mile away. I have seen the little church and the churchyard; you cannot imagine anything more desolate. Oh, those winter dusks in the North. Far as the eye can see, grey sky and grey, grey hills, with some distant trees sombre and dark, and the forlorn cry of those northern birds that rejoice in solitude. My mind's eye sees it so well, and my heart loves it so dearly. The wind was blowing high; even in the summer it never ceases moaning in that spot; but clear above the wind Peters said he could hear the sigh, the strangest unearthly sound that ever was. It came again, and yet again. Then he heard a low, thin, sweet voice speaking. 'Oh, I cannot, cannot, cannot rest.'

"That was more dreadful still, the old man used to say. 'I would have laid down my spade, and gone home as fast as I could, but that it was my duty to finish my work.'

"Just then a man opened the gate and came up to Peters. He said in an agitated voice, 'Where does she lie?'

" 'Who may you be speaking of, sir?'

" 'There's only one in the world for me. They told me in the village I was too late. Night and day I travelled to be with her, but I was too late.'

" 'Oh, Mr. Thorny, Sir, is that you? This is a sad day for you, for here she lies at your feet.'

" 'At my feet, do you say?' said he. He knelt down and kissed the damp, cold grave.

" 'Three weeks ago she called me. I woke up one night, and I heard her voice. There never was a voice like hers. She called to me, 'You have forgotten me. I cannot, cannot, cannot bear it. Come to me. I cannot rest without you.' I had enlisted, and they'd promoted me; I was an officer and I'd saved money. I was coming back to claim her, but when I heard her voice, I deserted—they'll put a bullet through me, if they find me—and off I came before dawn, and I travelled night and day, and I'm too late.'

"He flung himself on the ground and wept.

"My mother used to finish the story in Peter's words.

" 'You'd better be coming home with me,' I said to him. 'It's getting dark, and she's past all help now. You can do her no good by staying here.'

" 'Yes, I can,' said he starting up. 'And you are to help me. Get a crowbar, while I uncover the grave.'

" 'A crowbar, Sir?'

" 'Yes, I *must* see her face.'

" 'No, Sir, that's contrary to my duty. Once a grave is filled, it's against my duty, or any man's, to tamper with it.'

" 'Look here,' said he, taking some bank notes out of his pocket-book. 'Here's fifty pounds; here's more if you want it. Tell me what the figure is.'

" 'No, Sir,' said I, 'I don't want your money, but I must do my duty.'

" 'No,' he said earnestly, 'don't speak to me of duty. I must see her, for I have a word to say to her.'

"Then I spoke to him as solemnly as I could, and said, 'Don't seek to see her face. She was very sickly and sunken before the end, and she's now been four days dead. Leave her to lie in peace.'

"He had been a fierce, wild young man, but now the tears poured down his cheeks, and he cried to me, 'Oh, for the love of God, help me to see her again.'

"I remembered the sighs from the grave, and the voice I heard, and I thought it should not lie at my door to keep them two parted. So I fetched my tools—it was I that had made the coffin—and we undug the earth. It was a large grave; her coffin lay beside her mother's. We got the coffin up; then I did my best and we wrenched the lid off. Just before I said once again to him, 'Be advised by me, Sir. It's better not,' but he shook his head.

"When he saw her body, he gave what they call in Scripture 'an exceedingly bitter cry'—I've heard your papa read it of a Sunday—and he calls out: 'O Christ, that *can't* be her.' I touched him and said, 'Come away, Sir. You have seen enough.' But he shook me off, and he stooped down, and put his face to hers, and he kissed her. Ah, there was a kiss, you would have thought he could never part from her, and I heard him speak to her. I had only heard him in general when he was jolly with his friends, or speaking harshly to the labourers; he was a hard master; but now his voice might have been a mother talking to a child.

"He said to her, 'My own fair beloved one, I have made all the haste I could. Did you not know I would come to thee? I would never, never be untrue to thee.' Then he got up, and he looked quite happy. 'Thee,' he said. That seemed very strange to me when I first came North, so very plain. Those were very touching words to my mind, and it showed what some say, that the north country people have no hearts, isn't correct. They may be very ignorant and backward, very superstitious I should call them, but they have their feelings like the rest of us.

"Then he said to me, 'Let us nail up the coffin, and put it back in its place. She'll rest quietly now, and so shall I, till we meet on the Resurrection Day.' Night had come on some time ago, but there was a moon and I had my lantern, so I could see him plain. His eyes looked very bright and glittering, but I didn't notice anything specially strange about him. Only after he said good-bye, and thanked me—I remember his words 'I can never forget what you've done for me,' quite rational they were—he went away singing. I took my way home, and I never saw him again. But a few days after he was found wandering on the fells, and he did not know where he was, or what he was doing. He was arrested for the murder of the man he had killed, and he was hanged. But he never took any notice, and kept on saying up to the last, 'This is my wedding to-day, and I must be merry, for I have kissed my bride, and she's waiting for me.'

"It would have seemed just that those two should have lain side by side in their graves; but, as you know, Miss, one who has been hung on a gallows may not be buried in consecrated ground, and I was uneasy, when I went to the churchyard, lest the voice I told you of might be speaking again. But no, she had had her fill, and was content, and the poor corpse has lain still and quiet ever since.

"Whenever my mother told the story, she used to sing that verse of the old ballad, the most moving of all the old ballads I think.

" 'My time be short, my time be long,
To-morrow or to-day,
May Christ in Heaven take all my soul,
But I'll kiss your lips of clay.'[26]

My mother used to sing so sweetly right up to the last. My dear mother!"

She was silent for a moment, musing into the fire. She suddenly looked very old, and her companion felt a faint sensation of uneasiness, mingled with awe, and did not like to disturb the scene. Just for an instant it seemed to her that the clouds of triviality rolled by, and the little suburb was no longer here. She fancied

---

[26] 'The Unquiet Grave', or 'Cold Blows the Wind', is an English folk ballad (collected by Francis James Child in 1868 as Child Ballad number 78). According to Cecil J. Sharp and Charles L. Marson in *Folk Songs from Somerset* (1904), it was so great a favourite with Somerset singers that at least 'seventeen different tunes and variants' existed at the beginning of the twentieth century.

she saw something generally concealed, which nevertheless goes on unchanging from generation to generation. But perhaps she was mistaken, for then the door opened, and a ruddy, hairy face appeared.

"That you, Tom?" Mrs. Breton said gaily, coming to herself. "And you've got the paper. Now we can see who is right about the acrostic." And the strange melancholy past, shy of the lighthearted present, sank back into oblivion.

CHRISTMAS NIGHT AT ALMIRA

It was November now and the days were drawing in. They sat round the fire waiting for their tea, which should have been at four, and the clock had struck a quarter past.

"How short the days are getting," said elderly Mrs. Wallington, knitting busily.

"I wonder how you can see," said Mrs. Tracy, who had passed from elderly to old. "I find it very difficult to read my paper."

Someone might have turned on the light, but Mr. Haynes, the proprietor of the boarding house he had named Almira, did that when he brought in the tea. It was better to leave it to him, or he might be vexed.

"I never need the light," said Mrs. Wallington. "I can knit just as well in the dark. I've knitted, I was going to say, hundreds of socks in the War. These are for my boy in Rhodesia; my boy in the north has a wife to do them for him."

"My boy in Rhodesia; my boy in the north." The boarding-house heard a great deal about them. Mrs. Tracy only had a son-in-law; "My son-in-law in town, I think I mentioned him, he's getting on so well." Miss Malden, stout pleasant and middle-aged, who by reason of her spinsterhood had no son, talked of nephews; "My nephew in the Air Force; my nephew, who's a Master at Westminster." They also were getting on exceptionally well. The ladies did not talk of their own uninteresting sex, which carried no prestige; though a niece or daughter might be the stronger say, the dearer, more intimate companion. But the most wonderful son was Mrs. Gwynne's; she was an old lady with touzled hair, sitting on the sofa in a brown golf coat. She had a clear-cut profile, and there was something noble in the carriage of her head, and in the magnanimous curve of her lips.

"I've knitted my boy's socks from the day he was born," said she, "and I knit them now for him; and those stockings men are so fond of with very elaborate patterns. I knit all of those for him."

She smiled, and her face looked young. One could see what she was in the 'seventies; a lovely girl, gentle and dashing, sweet and spirited.

Nobody answered her, but Mrs. Wallington's needles clicked. She said later to Mrs. Tracy: "I wonder when Mrs. Gwynne knits those socks; never in the drawing-room, I know *that*."

"Christmas will be upon us before we know where we are," said Miss Malden, starting something new.

"Yes," said Mrs. Tracy, "I see they have the King and Queen's private greeting cards in the paper to-day. What a lovely one Her Majesty's is, and the Prince of Wales's too."

"I love that boy," said Mrs. Gwynne, smiling again. "He's such a sport." They talked about him, and from him passed to cricket and last season's matches and averages. The church clock struck the half-hour.

"It is too bad of Mr. Haynes. I think someone *ought* to speak to him. Perhaps you would, Mrs. Wallington, as you've been here the longest."

"Wouldn't it be almost better if you did, Mrs. Tracy? You've been here so often."

"Oh, I couldn't. When I had my own house, it was so different. My husband always said I was wonderful in keeping the maids up to their work. If one passes things over, they take advantage. You never should let those people presume."

"Yes," said Mrs. Gwynne "and what is he after all? Just a butler. He was with the Deans at Leyton Mount, and the Deans were nothing; he was an ironmonger. They bought the place from Sir George Saville, such a delightful man; he was a great friend of my father's."

Mr. Haynes came in; he began deliberately making room for tea, moving a palm, three aspidistras, *Hotels of England*, *Lady Cathcart's Crime*, *The Jest Book*, *One Thousand Humorous Anecdotes*, and the inkstand.

"I wonder if it's rather late," said Mrs. Wallington, tentatively to the drawing-room.

Mr. Haynes' back looked unrepentant.

"The clock on the mantelpiece has stopped," said he.

"Oh, I know it has, but I thought I heard the church clock."

"They always keep the church clock fast," snubbingly.

"It was so nice and cosy when we had tea at four." Mrs. Wallington pleaded.

"You can't expect things to be exactly as they are in the summer. There's much more to do in the winter, with the fires and the short days, it makes a lot of work."

"I know it does," said Mrs. Gwynne obsequiously; a change from the truculent speech of five minutes ago.

Mrs. Franklin, a younger lady than the rest, somewhere near thirty-five, came in with a little girl. She moved in the latest manner and her silhouette was a picture from *Vogue*.

"Good afternoon, everybody," said she condescendingly. "I'm stony,[27] and expiring for tea. Is it awfully stood?"[28]

---

[27] Entirely without money.

[28] Over-steeped.

"It's only just come in," said Mrs. Tracy, bowing before what was young and smart; "let me give you a nice cup. Don't get up; you're tired I know."

"Oh no, please," said Mrs. Franklin. "Oh, thanks so awfully. I've been having the most hectic time. People here play such appalling high stakes, and my cards have been wicked."

"You poor dear, what a shame," from Mrs. Tracy.

Everyone present more than disliked Sunday bridge, they resented even the mention of it, but the *Vogue* silhouette cowed them.

Mrs. Franklin continued; "Really one can't afford it, only it's so unsporting not to play, but when your banker writes and points out things, you know what it is."

She told her tale very distinctly.

"Yes," said Mrs. Gwynne. "But I wonder if it isn't better to say something about those high stakes. It wants some cheek," smiling her sweet smile, "but my husband—he rowed in the 'Varsity boat; I think I told you—he used to say: 'If only a lad will speak out, if there's anything he disapproves of, he'll often help the others, who haven't got the pluck. He may be laughed at at the time, but they do not forget it.' "

She delivered her husband's little speech very charmingly; he became an attractive hero in a play, saying something noble to the audience. It gave Miss Malden courage to say she thought so too.

The little girl Letty sat in silence. She had passed most of her life in boarding-houses. She was to be sent to a convent school, cheap, when money could be extracted from the absentee Mr. Franklin. Her ill-tempered mother, too selfish even to spoil her, had turned her into something still and quiet, but when a friendly voice spoke to her, she sprang to life. She was tall, thin and pale, and her short socks and very short jade green frock made her look taller, thinner and paler. Once her hair was silky, but bobbing gave it a kind of lank hardness. It was tied with a black bow on the top of her head, and the ends stood up like horns. The wistful eyes underneath were out of keeping. Her get-up was the smartest thing in children's modes that season; it was suited to a more bouncing prosperous little girl. The boarding-house liked her, while disparaging her thin legs, but most of the fleeting guests had hearts too much occupied with daughters, nieces or grandchildren to have room to spare for her. Mrs. Gwynne, whose heart had empty places, loved her.

She turned to Letty now, and said, "Well, lady fair, how's yourself? Come and give me a kiss."

"Shall I be too heavy?"

"No, indeed, kiddies like you are never too heavy."

"Are you going to sing any more nice songs like you did last night?" asked Letty.

The old lady gladly consented. She burst into snatches of old comic songs she could not remember, and sentimental ballads of eighty years ago. She made nonsense of the words and mistakes in the tunes. Her voice cracked in the high notes, and burst out like thunder in the low notes, yet all was done with a captivating playful grace and broken by melodious girlish laughter.

Some of the songs were what might have been called naughty in her youth; she sang them with innocent mirth, and Letty laughed as merrily as she. They were received with mixed feelings by the audience; Mrs. Wallington read her book emphatically; Mrs. Franklin despised these poor efforts, she required something hotter.

"Oh, Mrs. Gwynne," said she, "Please don't trouble yourself for Letty; you'll get so hoarse. No, Letty, you mustn't bother Mrs. Gwynne like that, come over here."

"Oh, don't tell her to go," said Mrs. Gwynne "it's such a pleasure to me. I do so love wee girlies, and they never bring my grand-daughter to see me, never. It's very——" her voice trembled, but she struggled on. "Cheerio, one must have grit. That's the important thing, isn't it, Letty?"

Mrs. Franklin was like the cuckoo, and often deposited her fledgling with other people. Of all nests she preferred Mrs. Gwynne's; there was an overflowing welcome there, and it was seldom inconvenient for Mrs. Gwynne to have a visitor, though it was sometimes.

Mrs. Gwynne's long unoccupied hours were irresponsible as a child's; they were broken only by meals. She had no grown-up serious amusements; she did not play any games, not even patience, she read nothing but the picture papers; she did not sew, or crochet, or knit, not even comforters for deep-sea fisherman on the largest needles. She did not care for shopping, dressing, "the pictures," going to church, or seeing the doctor. She wrote no long letters to friends or relations, so she could expect no long interesting letters in return. Her son was her one correspondent; from him she received rare scanty scraps. She seldom paid a call, and still more seldom had a caller. The round of tea-parties went on regardless of her.

She would have liked to ride skittish horses, to take long country walks, to dig in the garden, to play with dogs and cats. Age and fate denied her these pleasures; boarding-houses put their feet down on pets. All she was permitted were the birds that flew past her window. She spent long hours wiling them into confidence. This was her solid occupation; her relaxations were dozing on the sofa at half-past ten in the morning, at five, at any unchartered hour, and talking to all listeners she could lay hands on. If the attention of grown-up guests flagged, the little girl's never did, for Mrs. Gwynne's mental age, as psychologists say, was seven, the same as Letty's.

The wind of time had blown the little company together at Almira; soon it would blow again, and disperse them. Mrs. Wallington was there for her health; next month she would return to the dignity of a flat of her own. Miss Malden was winding up the affairs of an aunt, who had died three doors off. She was busy hastening to and fro; she also would go back to real life, her sister, and a cosy circle at Blackheath. Mrs. Gwynne, Mrs. Tracy and Mrs. Franklin roamed from boarding-house to boarding-house year in year out.

When tea was cleared away, they slept, knitted, read the Sunday papers they had already read, talked again of the days drawing in, or the approach of Christmas.

"I shall be going to evensong at St. Michael's," said Miss Malden, "I think you said you would like to come, Mrs. Gwynne."

"Yes but not such a damp night as this, I couldn't venture. The doctor wouldn't hear of it."

"Oh, I'm having a taxi there and back," said Miss Malden coaxingly, "so it will be quite comfortable, I'm rather rheumatic this evening."

"I think I won't. I've got no change at all, nothing but a pound, and it makes it so awkward, when the bag comes round."

"I've got plenty. I could easily lend you——"

"Oh, I shouldn't care to borrow for that sort of purpose."

She had something else to do that night. She got up and told Mrs. Wallington she was going to wash her handkerchiefs. "I always like to do that on Sunday. Mrs. Haynes gives me a nice jug of hot water, and with Lux it's easily managed, isn't it? I really like to keep to that rule better than going to evening church, don't you? I'm not very fond of evening church. I like going at eleven o'clock. Don't you think it nicer?"

Mrs. Wallington grunted, and Mrs. Gwynne went out of the room. She was drowsy when she came back, and not inclined to talk to anyone.

Mrs. Tracy in Mrs. Gwynne's absence poured out a long, long story of her iniquities. Mrs. Wallington, who was reading an American book, deep but chatty, *Cash Values in Spiritual Life*, again gave grunts in reply.

A few days later Mrs. Gwynne had a letter. "Mrs. Wallington, good news," she cried joyfully, as she came into the drawing-room. "My boy's coming for Christmas, and he's bringing Barbara. She's going to her mother, says she's ill; she's no more ill than I am—Lorna's always been so unkind to me, jealous of me, because my boy loves me so much. Oh, Miss Malden," as Miss Malden opened the door, "my boy's coming, and he's bringing Barbara. Letty darling," as the little girl ran in, "I've got such a lovely Christmas treat for you, a dear little baby friend is coming here for a week. She's four years old."

"Four years old and how much?" said Letty.

"Four years and five months." Letty pranced in the air. "She has violet eyes," went on Mrs. Gwynne "and golden curls, just like mine were. My hair was bright gold, brighter than sovereigns, and my eyes were deep, deep blue. Dear old Sir George said to my father when I was sixteen—my hair still down my back, below my knees. 'By Jove, that's a child that will break many hearts.' "

"And did you?" said the little girl, puzzled. No one else paid much attention.

"I'm afraid I did," with gentle mournful dignity. "I was very young and spoilt, everyone petted me, and I trifled with men's hearts.

It's a thing no girl should do. Remember that, dear, you must never trifle with love. There was a young man, very handsome, dark; dark men always liked me. When he offered, I could not take him. I loved him, but not as we should love the man who is to share one's life. "Oh, Millicent, my darling,' he said, 'my heart is broken.' And he mounted his black Arab, Sultan, and galloped away, and his head was dashed against a tree, and he fell, and he never spoke again."

A keen observer—but no keen observer was there—might have seen, as the narrative proceeded, that the light in Mrs. Gwynne's eyes was not quite sane.

"That's a nice story," said Letty. She liked all stories. "It's like a lovely one Mummy read me in the *Grand Magazine*, only he had a chestnut horse. I should like to hear more about the black Arab. Did he have a long tail?"

"I'm sorry, Mrs. Gwynne," said Mrs. Tracy, "I think that's my *Daily Mail* you're sitting on. Might I have it, please?"

"Those wonderful stories, *always* about herself," said sensible Mrs. Wallington, when Mrs. Gwynne was gone.

"And such nonsense," said Mrs. Tracy jealously. "Of course I could tell a number of things. I was very much admired. There was a man at Southsea—Are you going out, Miss Malden?"

Miss Malden's conscience allowed her to escape the young man at Southsea.

But Mrs. Gwynne's stories were not all nonsense. There had been seeds, and from them her stories sprang to the sky like Jack's beanstalk. Once she had been courted, admired, loved. She had kept a jolly, generous, merry house where she entertained, not merely the amusing, but the bores; and now both the amusing and the bores had forsaken her. She put on a flimsy cloak to hide her nakedness, but it did not hide it either from herself or from the world.

None of the other boarders were so fortunate as to expect a son for Christmas, and they wearied of Mrs. Gwynne's transports. But in a week the son wrote again: he could only come from Christmas Eve till Boxing Day.

"It's what he said last time," she said to Miss Malden, "and in the end he never came at all. Do you think it means—Oh, it can't mean—he won't come this year either? Read it, and see what you think."

Miss Malden was sending presents off to her nephews and nieces. "Oh, *of course* he'll come," said she. "You see he says 'Expect me without fail.' " But she thought, if she was a mother with one treasured son, she would have liked a different letter from the one she read. "Dear Mum. There's a fearful rush on, we're humming at last. This will keep me in town till Christmas Eve. Expect me then without fail. Yours in haste, Phil."

A tear slowly trickled down Mrs. Gwynne's face. Miss Malden took her hand and said, "It's not like you to be desponding, Mrs. Gwynne. You're the one who cheers us all up."

"I do try not to grizzle,"[29] she answered humbly, gulping back her tears, "but sometimes it's very hard not to think it would be better if one was out of the way, but I know I mustn't say that. You're so lucky to have sisters, I envy you. They don't fail one, and I think," she hesitated, "sometimes sons do."

She retired to her room. Outside the door some hours after she heard Letty crying and Mrs. Franklin saying, "Never mind, go and tell her." There was a knock and Letty came in, still sobbing.

---

[29] To cry or complain.

"What is it, darling child?" said Mrs. Gwynne.

"I got you some chrysanthemums, I saved up my money, and a nasty dog bit at them and spoilt them."

"Never mind," said Mrs. Gwynne, "I love them just as much. Some other friends have given me some flowers, my friends are very kind to me, but I think these are the sweetest of all, because a dear sweet little girl gave them to me, whom I love very much."

She said this with such graciousness and dignity, that Letty said, "May I call you another name? Will you mind? I think you're a Queen, and I do love you."

"Do you, dear little Letty? and I love you. It's very, very sweet to love and be loved, it's the most precious thing in the world, and when we get to my age, there is nobody who loves us very much and, though we *love* to love just as much as ever, there's nobody who wants it. So I thank you, dear, and prize your love very much."

The little girl threw her arms round the old lady's neck.

"What a funny smell," said she.

"Yes, it is a funny smell, isn't it? I wasn't very well, and my medicine has a funny smell. Now let's put the flowers in water. There's a vase there on the left hand of the chest of drawers."

"I can only find this," said Letty, bringing a bottle.

"Yes, that's my medicine."

"Isn't it a big bottle? I remember Daddy had it too, when I said good night to him. He had just that funny smell."

"Now put it back. I told you the left, and you went to the right. I thought an old lady like you knew her right hand from her left. And there's something else you must get me. Do you see that blue box on the little table? Will you bring it here? There, that's for you. It was my own, when I was a little girl like you, and I want you to have it."

"For me. I think it's the nicest thing in your room. I looked all round, when you sent me to get your bag that day."

"And now you must open it. There's something for Mummy in it."

Letty opened the box, and her face fell.

"But it's only an envelope. Do you think Mummy will like that?"

"Yes, but it's a fairy envelope, and when you've gone to bed, Mummy can change it into anything she wants. Only it's a secret, and you must give it to Mummy when you're quite alone. If you tell, the envelope will fly away." Letty listened enthralled. They talked a little longer.

"Is that you?" asked Letty, pointing to a lovely water-colour portrait, the only beauty to redeem the dull, untidy bedroom.

"Yes, that was me at seventeen."

"But it isn't golden hair," said the little girl, puzzled. "It's brown."

"It's what, dear?"

"It's brown."

"Oh yes, my hair was brown, deep nut brown."

"I think nut brown's even nicer than golden," said Letty, for everything about Mrs. Gwynne was perfect.

"I had lovely hair," said Mrs. Gwynne. "An artist saw me, and asked my father's permission to paint me, I was so beautiful. But beauty is not everything, you must remember that. I expect Miss Malden" (Miss Malden was extremely plain) "has had *numbers* of offers, she is so good and kind, many more for instance than Mrs. Tracy, though I daresay *she* was pretty in a dolly style." She spoke as a connoisseur.

There came a knock at the door.

"I'm so sorry," said Mrs. Franklin, "Letty must go to her dancing. I'm afraid you're not well," she added, coming further into the room. "Is there anything I can do?"

"No, nothing, thank you," said Mrs. Gwynne, "I was a little tired, and I had a headache, and I've been asleep. I'm much better now."

"There she was, poor old thing," said Mrs. Franklin later, "in the most awfully dilapidated condition with her hair like a furze bush,[30] and a most ominous odour. Is she in the habit of——?"

"They say Westmead wouldn't keep her," said Mrs. Wallington, pursing her lips, "and really sometimes she is very——"

"I wonder if it's safe to let Letty be with her so much. There might be an accident or something."

"Oh, do leave her Letty," said Miss Malden. "She seems so fond of her."

"Letty's taken the most *enormous* passion for her," said Mrs. Franklin laughing.

When she opened the fairy envelope, she grew pink with satisfaction. "She really is the—I wonder if one can," she said. One *could*, and did.

The whole of Christmas Eve Mrs. Gwynne was worrying people with "My son and Barbara." "As if no one else had grandchildren," said Mrs. Wallington, who had seven. She was running up and down stairs to visit Barbara's room. She prepared the most expensive Christmas tree money could buy, all hung about with presents, hidden away in the basement.

"There's the taxi," she cried for the tenth time. A good-looking, spruce man jumped out. "Well, Mum, how are you? Barbara

30 Another name for gorse.

has a bit of a cold, so Lorna thinks she's better at home. They send their love and all sorts of good wishes, and I've got some parcels somewhere for Granny."

He talked on rapidly, perhaps fearing an outburst.

"I think Lorna might have telegraphed," said Mrs. Gwynne. "Then I needn't have—She never does think of my—But I've got you, dearest boy, and I'm very very thankful to have you." He consented to a prolonged embrace.

She did not care for Lorna's elaborate powder puff and fancy box; "I've not come to powdering my face yet, whatever the girls may do"; but she laughed with joy at Barbara's woolly lamb, "for dear Granny with love and xxxxx."

He did not talk much to her at dinner and, after he had smoked by himself for a long time, he went up and sat by Mrs. Franklin in the drawing-room, and told his funny stories to her. His mother did not complain.

"Phil never could resist a pretty women," said she, "and I'm glad he should have somebody so smart and jolly to talk to. He can't resist a pretty face, and then he goes and marries *such* a plain girl."

"Well, Mum, you keep early hours, I know," said he. "I mustn't keep you up. I want to have you fit for our Christmas dinner to-morrow." She laughed, touched and gratified. He opened the door for her, saw her upstairs, and went off to a dance hall.

She did not see much of him on Christmas Day; he said he had business letters he must write, and a man he must meet. At lunch he was kind, and laughed and joked with her. This excited her, and he wished she would not talk so much. He escaped downstairs and said to Mr. Haynes; "I say, I can't stick a cat party,[31] I shall get back to town by the evening train. Isn't there one about 8.45? Order me a taxi for half-past, will you. Have you the telephone here?"

He had a walk in the afternoon; "I must get some country air, you know, Mum."

To console herself she called Letty into her room, and said she was a witch, and would turn herself into whatever Letty liked. She was a cat, a dog, a cock, a parrot and Punch in Punch and Judy. Letty screamed with childish laughter.

The noises made Mrs. Tracy's Christmas visitor give lady-like winces. "She seems very uplifted to-day," sighed the visitor.

"We do have lovely times together, don't we?" said Letty.

"Don't we?" echoed Mrs. Gwynne gaily.

"I'm most awfully sorry, Mum," said Phil, "but Roberts has had me up on the phone, and they want me to get back to-night. It's a big thing, which I mustn't miss, so I shall have to be off by half-past eight. I shall have time for a jolly dinner with you before I go."

"Do they do business on Christmas Day?"

"No, not generally. This is a very special thing. It's private really, so I can't tell you."

But he was not sure whether he had bamboozled her, for she said quietly, "I daresay things have changed; in father's time, there was no business on Christmas Day or Boxing Day."

"Ah, things have speeded up a bit," said he; he felt his colour changing, and avoided her gaze.

"Have you got room for these parcels for Barbara?" she asked. "I want her to have them at once."

---

31 A party consisting only of women.

"Well no, dear. It seems to me you've bought the whole of Harrods, and I've only got a suit case."

"Never mind," said she. "I'll post them to her."

"You mustn't be depressed," he said. "I'll come again, as soon as I can."

"Yes, it isn't like me, is it?"

"I got the champagne from London for you," said she at dinner. "It's the brand you like."

"I'm rather off champagne, as a matter of fact," said he nervously. "Let's have some lemonade."

"I got it specially for you," said she tearfully. "I shall be so dreadfully disappointed. Do have some dear."

"Very well," said he. "Just one glass. It doesn't suit me particularly well now."

"I'll have one too, or just half a glass. I never take anything, as you know. I don't like it even for medicine. Whisky suits some people, Mrs. Wallington for instance, but it never suits me."

He sipped the excellent champagne with relish, and did not take much notice of her. Suddenly he realized she was talking confusedly. She had drunk two glasses, and was pouring out a third.

"Now look here, Mother," he said firmly, "you mustn't have any more, you've had quite enough already."

But she was too quick for him, and drank the third glass. Her loud vulgar singing, her laughter, her shouts made Mrs. Wallington's decorous Christmas party ready to sink to the floor. Letty burst into sobs of terror.

"I say," said Mr. Gwynne, "Take the child out. Don't let her see it."

She was trying to get at more champagne, fighting with him, screaming and abusing him. "Just come and help me, will you," said he to Mr. Haynes, and the two men carried her to her bedroom. Miss Malden followed them, and asked if she could help him.

"It's awfully good of you. Yes, I believe she has some tabloids somewhere which quiet her down. Can you get them, while I hold her?"

"I think I know where to find them. I gave them to her once, when she was ill."

"I suppose you know, then. You've seen it?"

"Oh, never like this."

"If only I'd stood out about that champagne. By Jove! I ought to be starting. It's deuced awkward leaving her like this. I suppose Haynes will be getting restive and turn her out. I never thought he would have kept her after last year. These places always turn her out in the end. She'll have to pay a lot more, and so I shall tell her. She's a mother to be proud of, isn't she?", as Mrs. Gwynne turned over, and began snoring drowsily.

"Oh, don't say that," said Miss Malden, "she's so devoted to you."

"I know she is," said he, ashamed of himself. "Much more than I deserve."

Miss Malden undressed and washed her, and put her decently to bed.

It was not till two o'clock in the morning that Mrs. Gwynne woke from her lethargy. At first she could not remember what had happened; when it came back to her, she determined what she would do.

She was cold, ice cold, chilled to the bone, and neither the gas fire nor the old fur coat, nor the cup of tea she made herself could bring any warmth to her. This time she did not fortify herself with brandy. Her fingers were so stiff they could hardly do what she wanted. Yet there were various tasks she must perform, before she could lie down and rest. When she had washed and dressed herself in her smartest nightgown, she did her hair as the boarding-house had never yet seen it, or rather she tried, for she felt shattered, so that she could hardly stand. She went to a drawer, and took out stamps, and stamped all the parcels for Barbara, and the costly brooch she was sending Lorna.

She rummaged in her untidy trunk, she found a leather case, packed it up, and put on the parcel "For Letty." She would have liked to add some message of love, but she had so little strength, and there was something more important she must write. This was a short note to her son. She framed the letters as clearly and neatly as she could. Then she took a pill box, swallowed some pills, got into bed, and cried herself to sleep.

When Mrs. Haynes came in in the morning primed by outraged Mrs. Tracy and Mrs. Wallington, to tell Mrs. Gwynne she must leave that day, she found the old lady was still asleep. From that sleep she never woke, for it was the sleep of death.

The son came down at once to settle her affairs. He saw the note which was left for him.

"My own darling boy. How I disgraced you yesterday, you the only treasure I have in the world. What can I say to you? The shame of it has broken my heart. I have tried hard, you don't know how hard, but I have been so lonely. You don't want me, now you are married, and I don't think you love me very much. I know dear Lorna is a good wife, and loves you truly. Give her my love, and kiss my little Barbara. You shall never be troubled with me any more, and then I hope you will forgive me. Your loving mother."

He asked if he might speak to Miss Malden.

"Did you have any idea? Did she say anything?" he asked.

"No, she seemed as if she was asleep, when I came in to her at half-past seven; and I thought she had better have her sleep out, I wouldn't disturb her."

He asked her to read the letter, and she handed it back to him with tears in her eyes.

"I suppose she wasn't responsible for the moment," said he; "temporarily insane, they call it."

"No, I don't think she was that," said Miss Malden.

"She was an awfully good mother to me, when I was a kid," he said. "But my father failed, you know, and then there was the shock of his death, and she got overstrained. Also I played the fool at College, etcetera, and that worried her. She had an illness, and after it this kind of thing began. She'd just tipple a little on the quiet for months, and then there would be a row."

"Why didn't you come and see her oftener?" said Miss Malden. "She wanted you so much."

"Yes, I ought to have come down, and looked after her, but you see my wife and she didn't hit it off. My wife didn't like her little ways, I don't know anybody that did, and she was afraid for the kid. Then she was jealous; they both were. If only I'd brought Barbara down yesterday, but my wife was jealous about her too."

Letty spent her Christmas tips on a bouquet of hothouse roses.

"She goes on that she must go into the room," said Mrs. Franklin to Miss Malden, "And she'd awfully highly strung, just like me, and I know she'll have a nightmare. What am I to do?"

"Shall I take her?" said Miss Malden. She wished to erase the dreadful picture of the Christmas dinner.

"I wish you would. I'm not up to that sort of thing. Did I show you those pearls Mrs. Gwynne left her? Downs says they're

A.1. One must say that for her, she was a wonderfully generous old thing."

Now that they were relieved of her presence, nobody grudged her expensive flowers. Mis Malden arranged them in the room.

"Would you like to come and see her with me?" she whispered to Letty.

Letty nodded very seriously.

"She was very ill and now she's quite peaceful."

They went in, and there lay Mrs. Gwynne very serenely. Now she looked indeed a stately Queen.

"Shall we put the roses here?" said Miss Malden laying them on her breast.

"May I kiss her, do you think?" said Letty.

She put her arms round the cold face. The chill touch made her realize her friend had gone for ever. She burst into tears and would not be comforted.

Mrs. Gwynne had been unwanted, but many are not really wanted, especially when they outlive old ties and old friends. She was much more than unwanted. Her death was a great relief to her surroundings, above all to her beloved son. But at the last, most cheerless stage in the journey of life a companion had been granted her, who loved her as ardently as she had been loved in her days of triumph, and mourned her with fidelity.

IN THE 'BUS

The 'bus was bumping along its hour's route. This gave the two girls, seated in the front seat, just the time they wanted for a talk; a talk on the part of the pretty, sickly energetic girl, a listen on the part of her stout and heavy companion and the ever-changing audience.

"Smell my flowers, Rene," said the heavy girl. "Lovely."

"No thank you, can't stand any flowers now, brings back my operation and dear Ward C. IV."

"Didn't they treat you nice? I shouldn't mind being back at St. Bridget's."

"Yes, you were medical. Of course you can only speak as you find. I daresay it was all right at C. IV. When I first came in, and saw the table with masses of flowers, and Sister smiling at me, I thought it was going to be so nice. Sister was like that girl's face on the *Grand* last week,[32] lovely, and her cheeks—she never wanted a lip-stick. Some of the nurses did. I could see them at it when Sister wasn't there. I heard her say once: 'All these people with their finger-aches, and their back-aches, and their tummy-aches—I've never had an ache in my life.' *I* thought it was a crude way of speaking. She came up so nice to me that first day. 'Oh,' I thought, 'I *shall* love you.' I said to her, silly fool I was: 'You won't grumble at me, Sister, will you? I feel so frightened.' Wish I'd cut my tongue out."

---

32 *The Grand Magazine*, a British periodical published monthly from February 1905 to April 1940.

"Did they hurt you much?"

"Of course they have to, and you hear the screaming; it goes on all night and most of the day. Sometimes it's when they're under anaesthetics, sometimes it isn't. You hear it all the twenty-four hours you're waiting for them to cut you up, and you think 'I'm in next.' I didn't care a bit when I went down to the theatre, though, I felt as calm as I do this minute. I just thought, I hope they'll give Mum my things all right, if I don't come out of it.

"The doctors were ever so kind. One said: 'You'll have rather a hard time for four days, but it will be well worth it.' I don't know what well worth it is, it depends what you call worth, however it's done now.

"The next thing you know clearly is that everything about you hurts so that you feel as if you're mad. You don't care for anything or anybody. I didn't care whether Sister smiled then; just when I didn't want it, I think she did. Then you come to yourself and you feel you would like a little bit of comfort. I lay and cried, I couldn't stop myself, quiet you know, I didn't want any of them to hear. There was the woman that scrubbed the floors—didn't the nurses look down on her, and keep her at it too? She says to me: 'Yes, do cry my girl, it'll do you good. I can't get used to it. Every time a poor soul goes into the theatre, I think, "Ah, what she'll be feelin' next mornin'?" and them dressed up bits of nurses don't turn a hair.'

"My lady came to see me as soon as I was allowed to see anyone. You should have seen her talking to Sister, that dear old bonnet of hers all on one side as usual, same as if Sister was Cook or me. I could hear her just as if she was the Royal Family. 'My housemaid has a very delicate digestion, nurse,' she says, 'and she wants very careful feeding. I am bringing her some jelly, which my doctor thinks would be of benefit, and I am sure you will take great care of her.'

"So Sister answered in her best voice—nurses talk rather nice when they try, they practice it before the glass, I think—'We will take every care of Irene.' Cheek, I wasn't Irene to her, only to *my* nurse, what I'll tell you about presently. Wasn't she wild, though, at anyone calling her nurse? Then my lady comes up to me ever so pleased. 'I'm glad you've got such a nice nurse,' says she, 'so kind and sympathetic.' Just like ladies; talk soft soap to them, and they swallow anything. I always say they have no more sense than children.

"When she'd gone, Sister called out to Nurse: 'What price skivs?'[33] So poor skivs can't be let alone even in a hospital. Nurse says: 'Charley's Aunt isn't in it.' I thought of telling them they were quite out of it, but I didn't want to enter into an argument, I would not demean myself, besides, it hurt me talking. I did rather wish she'd put on her best bonnet, not that it's a great improvement, but I don't care, and I laughed to think Sister was so wild.

"I was feeling a little better, and I was looking forward to my jelly for my tea, Cook's a rare one at jellies. Nurse brought my tea, and it was a pink jelly, mine was yellow. I wasn't surprised, and I didn't say anything, only when she was clearing tea away, I said: 'I like pink jelly made of powder you get at the grocer's better than yellow jelly made at home, don't you, Nurse?' She said: 'I can't bear jellies at any time,' and was off like a shot. When my lady came next, she said: 'And did you like your jelly?' 'Ever so much, thank you,' I said. 'That's right,' says she, nodding and smiling, 'for I've brought some more.' I wasn't going to make a fuss.

---

33 Skivs (also skivvy), a female domestic servant.

“There was a fat woman with her hair all dyed, very well to do. She was got up to kill if you like. Sable coat, real of course—it was the height of summer—bronze shoes, those very exaggerated heels, and her hair—she hadn’t quite settled whether it was bobbed or Grecian, with a bit of ribbon, that loud jade green shade. That’s the sort they like. *Her* visitors might stay on till ten o’clock at night. You should have seen the flowers her—well, we’ll call him her husband—brought her. Those great roses tied up with satin you get at a florist’s.

“Those blasted roses! ‘Oh, the roses,’ says Sister, ‘you haven’t given the poor darlings a drop of water, Nurse. No, certainly not, you really can’t have anything to drink now, you must wait for tea.’ That was to me. I could lie and wish I was a rose.

“The dresser, that’s what they call the one that dresses the wounds, she was a terror. She used to come along down the ward singing all the latest songs, putting the screen round the bed. Then the poor soul who had the screen knew what was coming and trembled. Oh, she was rough. ‘I’m the quickest dresser in the whole hospital,’ she said. ‘I can get round the ward with five minutes to spare some days; once I had ten.’

“One morning I never shall forget. There was an elderly party in the bed next to me; Nurse was taking out her stitches. Oh, how she screamed, you never heard anything like it. Nurse hadn’t put the screen round her properly, and I could see her face. She had a jolly round face, and I shouldn’t have known it. She looked like a poor dog I saw when some boys were chivvying it.[34] Then sister came along in her war-paint and stormed: ‘You dare to make all that row, Number 16,’ she says, ‘you ought to be

[34] Chivvying: hunting or hounding.

ashamed of yourself. Why, you don't know what pain is. Stop it this minute.' She was just like a barmaid out of a public,[35] and her accent—talk about Cockney, you should have heard her.

"But the old party couldn't stop, she didn't know what she was doing. Nurse went on taking out the stitches all the while, as if the poor thing was a piece of wood. When she came to do me, I kept my mouth shut tight, and put my hands over it, and held my breath, and lay quite still. 'Well, you are a plucky girl, I must say,' said Nurse. 'Oh, she was afraid I should grumble at her if she called out,' said Sister. Spiteful cat. I wouldn't let her see I cared, whatever they did to me.

"The old lady in the next bed, she lay and gasped and moaned, and she couldn't eat anything. They'd scared her so, it sent her temperature up.

"There was a very common girl in the bed the other side of her, real slum she was, and I heard her say: 'Tell Doctor about it to-morrow, mate, don't put up with them treating you so.' But she didn't take a bit of notice, she just said over and over again: 'I've got three more stitches to come out, and I don't know how ever I can bear it.' She kept on saying it all night.

"Next morning Nurse comes along as fresh as a daisy. I was thinking of the old lady, and I wasn't feeling over-bright. 'Oh,' says Nurse, 'you do look a misery.'

" 'Don't know that I've seen anything here yet to make me feel very merry.'

" 'Oh, you'd never make a nurse,' says she. 'One must always be cheerful with the patients. I used to feel things first of all, hurting people and that, but I don't think anything of it now. It

---

35 Public house.

wouldn't help them, and it wouldn't help me. You've just got to take no notice.'

" 'I'm not so sure that I'm so struck with being a nurse as I used to be,' I said.

" 'Oh, I like it, particularly Nursing Home work. I did that before I came here. Why, the presents! A patient gave me a *crepe de Chine* nighty with masses of cerise chiffon; it cost pounds. And the rides in people's private cars. Oh, it's a lovely life.'

"When the doctor came to the old lady's bed, there was Sister smiling on us as if we were all baby princesses, and her voice, it was like butter.

" 'Mrs. Jennings had her stitches out yesterday, and is getting on very naicely. Appetite good, and a very good night.'

"That common girl, Doris, I told you of, she was up and dressed, she was going that day. She up and says: 'Oh, Sister, you are a story. She never ate a crumb all yesterday, and she didn't sleep a wink.'

"I nearly jumped out of my skin. You're all supposed to be like dead corpses when the doctor comes in, you mayn't move an eyelid, nurses and all. There's a nurse planted down in the middle of the ward, just to run and open the door to him when he's done. He's a kind of god to everyone except the Sister. Sister turned away when Doris spoke, so I could see her face, and she *did* get red, and then she went white.

"Doctor said very quietly: 'We know quite well you think you're telling the truth, but after operations some people get hallucinations. Next case. What is the report here?'

"After Doris left that morning, Sister sang out loud to Nurse for us all to hear: 'I always think, when those common girls are gone, it leaves the ward so much sweeter somehow.'

"The old party left before me, and there was a girl came, such a little mite; she was sixteen, but she looked less. She was so nervous, poor kiddy, and the doctor was so rough, rougher than the dresser even. Sister could be ever so gentle when she liked; she was a splendid nurse. I thought doctor treated us all as if we were a lot of cows.

"The morning doctor was to examine Annie, that girl next to me, her hand shook so she spilt all her tea at breakfast, thinking of it.

" 'Gracious, do pull yourself together,' says Nurse. 'A great girl like you.'

" 'I'm sorry, Nurse,' she said, 'I can't help it. I'm so frightened.'

" 'That kind of thing makes me sick,' said Nurse. 'Clean sheet all for nothing.'

"When the doctor came, I saw her shaking all over. Oh, I did pray he wouldn't hurt her, I've never prayed so hard. He was talking with Sister. They were rather sweet on one another, you could see by the way they looked at one another and laughed. He stood with one of his feet resting on the iron bar at the bottom of her bed, and made his jokes with Sister.

" 'Have you heard the latest about Clotty and Matron?' he said. Clotty was a silly name they called one of the doctors. 'Matron did tick him off.'

"Then he went on. I didn't understand a bit of what it was all about, and they laughed to split themselves. You can guess what Annie felt waiting there.

"At last he said: 'Great Scot, it's late, and I've a footer practice at two.[36] Report on Number 16, please, becoming solemn all of a minute. 'I shan't examine her to-day. Number 17.'

---

[36] Footer: football.

"Oh, I was glad. She wasn't very brave, poor kiddy, but everybody can't be brave, and they all said she'd had an awful operation.

"Annie did love 'my nurse.' We all did. We used to call her sunshine, because the ward seemed a different place when she was in. 'My nurse' used to ask her a new riddle every time she went off night duty. 'And you've got to find out the answer by the time I come on again, or I shall report you to Matron.' That made a bit of fun for her. Oh, she was *lovely*." A dreamy expression came into the bright quizzical eyes. "She wasn't pretty—red hair and red eyebrows, it did seem a pity. I seem to run to red hair, my friend has red hair."

"Then you've got another; it was a dark one I saw."

"Oh, yes, that was Percy. I gave him the chuck months ago. Stan's the present one, he's in the motoring. She was on night duty part of the time, and she said to me: 'I think everyone's so brave here, much braver than I was when I had an operation.'

"That's the way I like to hear them talk. Once she kissed me. I was very down one night and I was crying, and she said, 'Is it very bad? It's not like you to break down.'

" 'I don't know,' I said, 'it's just that I'm silly, and I haven't had a letter I was expecting.' That was Stan; it came next morning.

"She gave me such a nice kiss. 'I'm so sorry,' she says.

" 'That's more than the others are,' I said.

" 'No, no, that's nonsense,' she says. 'We all care. My mother made me promise to give up nursing if ever I found I couldn't feel, but it's not come to that yet.'

"That's the time I said she might call me Rene, but I never said so to Sister. Of course she was *quite* different to the others, though she might say they cared—not common. I'm crocheting her some of my mats, that lovely bird pattern what I did for you. She'll like it ever so.

"They weren't so bad when I was going. Nurse says, 'Well, I must say, Miss West, you never gave a bit of trouble.' And of course I didn't.

"I sent them fifteen shillings. I put on the envelope—now what was it I put? 'From a patient who thinks, if you get as much as she is giving from everybody and care as little for them, you will be doing well.' Then I thought of my one, and scratched out 'and care as little for them,' and it ran better.

"When I came home, and there was my dear old Mum and the aspidistra, and old Tabby on my lap, it seemed so homely. And there was sausages for tea, and she had sent peaches from the house, our hothouse ones, and I was to know the house didn't seem right without me, and no wonder, when you think of Edie—you know what young girls are nowadays, no thought of anything but swank—well, I cried for joy, till I couldn't cry any longer. But I should like to meet Sister and say to her just very quiet and dignified—Now then, we get out here, mate, good thing somebody was keeping a look-out."

So the 'bus could never hear what was to be said to Sister.

MOTHER AND DAUGHTER

Seagate was preparing for the Easter rush.

"What are you doing with your chronics?" said dejected Miss Dendy of Strathcona to bouncing Mrs. Pack of the Nookery. They were sitting in Mrs. Pack's private room, strewn with old *Eves* and *Gollywogs*. "I think I shall chuck mine," she sighed. "I'm fed up with grousers all winter.[37] But then after all you only get grousers again."

"Chuck," "fed up," "grousers," those words seemed out of place on such spiritless lips, but even Miss Dendy, though slow on the uptake, knew we must all talk slang now.

"Oh, I'm keeping my chronics," said Mrs. Pack. "Chronics" was her word, borrowed by Miss Dendy. "I thought of giving Miss Robins the hoof,[38] you can't call that kind of poverty-stricken female a good 'ad.' Elsie" (the housemaid) "tells me her undies are one mass of darns. But I'm too good natured, that's a fact. Besides that room never gets a scrap of sun, it's a box room really, and people always kick at it. As for grousing, I never allow it. When Mr. Selby came, I said from the first: 'If you're going to early every Sunday'—he's rather High—'you can't expect tea before breakfast, it's not provided Sundays,' and he never said a word. And Mrs. Fairholme's always very bright, so quick at all those brainy Sunday crosswords, and she's asked to tea by all the nicest people, and her shoes are always the latest—I like that, so really I can't complain."

---

[37] Grouser: someone who habitually complains or grumbles.

[38] Give the hoof: throw out.

Strathcona was next door to the Nookery, so that Miss Dendy could run in daily to be snubbed. Eastcote was on Strathcona's other side, and held itself aloof. It catered for an exclusive circle of clergymen's daughters and serious officers' widows.

"Such a stuffy crowd," said Mrs. Pack jealously. "Twiddling their thumbs, and talking about sales of work, and Miss Fraser and that airified parlourmaid of hers spoil them so, taking them up hot drinks at night. Sickening."

There were three harmless chronics who tried to make the Nookery their home. All had seen better days. Small, meek Miss Robins was brought so low that it was a treat to sit in Mrs. Pack's private room and laugh at her jokes. They were propitiatory laughs. She shook when she must tell Mrs. Pack she had had an accident, and with her unsteady hand she was always breaking and spilling.

Mr. Selby was a mild old gentleman of eighty, now left alone in life. He had lived adored in his country parish for thirty years, and had hoped when he came to Seagate he might still be a little use to the Church. He offered his services to the vicar of St. Andrew's. He preached one or two sermons that had once been well liked. He took a Bible incident and discussed the habits of the Jews and the original Hebrew. "And now what lesson can we derive for ourselves? I think three points arise." But by the second, the coughing and rustling to look at wrist watches were so insistent that his quiet voice was smothered. The efficient vicar saw it would not do. Ten bright minutes on "The Church and the League of Nations' were all his congregation could swallow. So Mr. Selby confined himself to putting in the occasional little word at the Nookery. Mrs. Pack told him sharply she could not be bothered with that sort of thing, but Elsie thought him a sweet old gentleman, and said it reminded her of Sunday School. His eyes began to fail him; he could no longer read the Greek of his affection; in time his English was curtailed too. He fell back on bridge, when there were sufficient ladies who liked the game. Men were unusual at the Nookery. Bridge he played earnestly; recklessness grieved him, especially Mrs. Fairholme's recklessness.

"To go no trumps with not a single ace or king in your hand!" said he; his spectacles looked almost stern.

"I know," said she. "It was very wrong, but I thought you must have one or two, and then we should have done so well. I've always taken risks in life, and I've always lived to repent them, and now, dear partner, I'm repenting hard."

But Mr. Selby's chief occupation was musing, roaming slowly about the front, or sitting over Mrs. Pack's small fire. They were small fires when there were only chronics. At other times: "Oh, put on more coal than *that*, Mr. Selby, I love a jolly blaze." Often he could not go out. He had a bad chill once at the Nookery and heard Mrs. Pack proclaim: "If only people would try and realize the endless bother illness is, the trays they *will* have carried up, then perhaps they would rouse themselves a bit."

He thought with envy of Eastcote and Miss Fraser, even of Strathcona and Miss Dendy, but he had no spring to make the move. He sometimes looked forward to the last move, when he should trouble Mrs. Pack no more, but there must be some carrying up of trays before it was accomplished. He trembled, and kept himself as well as he could.

Little Mrs. Fairholme, the third chronic, was still elegant at sixty-five, her eye still blue, her mouth still dimpling at a joke, though at the Nookery few jokes came her way but Mrs. Pack's. She took pleasure in gently teasing Mr. Selby, and he loved to be teased, though not about bridge; there he was adamant. Sometimes she teased Miss Robins; this was rapture to Miss Robins, but all that dear Mrs. Fairholme did was rapture to Miss Robins.

Mrs. Fairholme, like Mr. Selby, hankered after Eastcote, and the hot drinks she was often too tired to make, and Granger, its spoiling parlourmaid. Hot drinks were to be had at the Nookery; Miss Robins would have thankfully made them every night. But she *would* use her own spirit and cocoa, a reckless sacrifice to her idol, and the idol could rarely allow the treat. There was Elsie too, but she expected payment: a monologue while she stood half in half out of the door, leaning against the handle.

"Oh, my big toe, Mrs. Fairholme, my corn. I went to Lake's. Some like Wall's better, but his medicine's so pale, it's nothing but water. Lake's are ever so dark, one was almost black. He gave me a bottle, it didn't do me a lot of good. Then I went to Boots, they gave me a powder. Then my friend said to me: 'Oh, Elsie,' she said, 'do try Jallup's lightning cure, Dad's asthma's a lot better since he took it… Now my corn—" and so on like a recurring decimal.

It was not only for hot drinks Mrs. Fairholme longed for Eastcote. It sometimes troubled her that, struggle as she might, each week she sank deeper in a slough of tiredness. Cordial Miss Fraser's "*Now* we shall get you better" might give her confidence. But she must not leave her comrades at the Nookery. Her glance sometimes quelled Mrs. Pack, she could not imagine why. Without her they would be defenceless.

"I've a nice crowd coming to-day," said Mrs. Pack to Miss Dendy.

The rush was now upon them. It showed itself in Miss Dendy's hair, a cross between a bob and a shingle. Agitation made her like a gollywog left out in the rain. "A nice crowd" meant flappers with their boys, cocktails, film-star gossip, naughty stories, people who wore their bathing clothes in the front garden, and made such a noise that Eastcote visitors hurried past and murmured: "How disgusting." The dream in its entirety was never realized; the favourites preferred the big hotels. Sometimes fat little girls in scanty frocks raised hopes as they walked up the path, but they turned out to be mothers of families, trying with middle-aged dad to pretend they were seventeen.

Most of the guests at Strathcona and the Nookery were old and elderly ladies, with gossip not of film-stars but of operations. Their stories "What my own doctor said" and "What the specialist said" were unrelieved by any touch of naughtiness.

"And I'm expecting four or five men," said Mrs. Pack.

"I've only two," said Miss Dendy. "I'm thankful, I don't like gentlemen."

"Oh, I love them," cried Mrs. Pack, "just a hen party gets so narrow. But of course they come more where there's a married woman. One knows their little ways. How they do love a bit of chipping."[39]

Miss Dendy had no gift for chipping.

"Who do you think I'm letting my best front to?" asked Mrs. Pack. "You'll never guess. Mrs Fairholme for her daughter and a friend. She was uncertain about their coming, so I put the price up, but she's paying it like a lamb. I said, chaffing her: 'As you're so rolling, I think you can fork out a bit more for your own room.' She said: 'I should like my daughter and her friend to have the best you've got,' and turned a bit pink. She doesn't really care about chaff, she's quite a little duchess when she likes."

"It's all right, Mr. Selby," said Mrs. Fairholme, "Helen and Linda are coming. I heard this morning for certain."

---

[39] Cheeky or imprudent banter.

"I'm very glad you should have a daughter with you for the Easter Feast," said he. "What a great joy it must be to have a daughter."

"It is, yes, it is. But I'm a tiny but dreading their coming. You'll think it absurd of me, but I feel so shy of Helen's friend, and I'm shy of Helen too. The time comes, you know, when one loses the children."

"Surely a mother doesn't lose a daughter. Don't they say 'My son is my son till he gets him a wife, but my daughter's my daughter all her life'?"

"Sometimes I think one loses one's daughter more. Perhaps she will be my daughter again when she gets her a husband; marriage opens one's eyes to so much; or perhaps it may be later still after I'm gone. We used to be so close to one another. I don't think all that love can be really lost, do you? I simply adored her. They say mothers generally feel more about the boys. I adored them too, but I was silly about her, and now——" she broke off. "She got into a different set, and it was much better for her to live with them. Of course the birds must leave the nest some time, the daughter birds as well as the son birds, and I was a drag on her. Only, if I *could* see her a little oftener. But she's absorbed in her work, so she can't come very much. Sometimes I feel I've lost her more than my boy Gilbert in India. I must try and be like the mother in Stevenson's poem who saw her sons out in the world and was well content,[40] but then I'm not very content with her work; she's an organizer for the Labour Party."

---

40 'It Is Not Yours, O Mother, To Complain' by Robert Louis Stevenson.

"The Labour Party!" said he, his spectacles gleaming at her with wild horror.

"Yes, I knew you wouldn't like it either. But she thinks it's the only way to help the world; she's got a tremendous sense of right."

"Couldn't you say a word?" said he. "Just to show her how mistaken——"

"Say a word. It's evident you don't know much about daughters. She'd be more likely to say a word to me. Besides she's so much cleverer than I am. She has her father's brains. It's hard on a clever daughter to have a stupid mother. One's husband doesn't mind one being rather stupid, but daughters have a much higher standard. But you're to fall in love with her, Mr. Selby, though she is Labour, so I tell you she's nearly perfection—that's the opinion of an entirely impartial mother."

"I'm sure I shall fall in love with her, if you tell me to do so."

"I think you will, for she's very good looking. I've noticed rather a weakness for pretty people before now."

"You choose to say you're not clever," said he. "I don't know—I should have thought—and cleverness is such a small thing, but at any rate, let me say she gets her good looks from her mother."

"No, she doesn't," she laughed. "They're her father's, not mine. Though I don't mind owning," she smiled, "I was very pretty once. It's so long ago, I don't think it matters saying it, do you?"

When she smiled, her blue eyes, still very bright, sparkled anew, and the beauty, in which she had never been much interested, came back to her. It warmed her laugh and smile, and the chill of age relaxed its hold.

After lunch there is an idle moment, when the men—Mrs. Pack's had dwindled down to two—the precious men, stand and look out of the window, wondering what they shall do next. To-day the Nookery men were refreshed by the sight of a large, expensive car drawing up at the gate. It broke the ice, and at once each could tell the other, "That's the sort I like for touring," as though its counterpart was in his possession at home.

Out stepped two tall girls; their well-cut tweeds and low commanding voices sent Mrs. Pack hastening with smiles to welcome them.

"We're very sorry to be so late, mummy," said Helen, the tallest, kissing Mrs. Fairholme. "This is Linda, and she must explain."

Linda greeted Mrs. Fairholme in a welcoming, a caressing, almost deferential manner. Was it a little gushing? But what a harsh word for making life run easily. It relaxed that shyness Mrs. Fairholme had spoken of, a shyness which always beset her in spite of the charm and beauty which would have made others certain of success.

"I'm most terribly, terribly sorry," said the pleasant Linda. "This is a new car, and she got into a wicked temper at starting, but she's promised never to do it again. Do say you'll forgive her. I'm looking forward tremendously to taking you to Chichester and the New Forest and nice places, if you'll trust yourself to me. Helen says she thinks you haven't seen them."

"What a lovely prospect," said Mrs. Fairholme untruthfully; motors made her head ache.

"We've had lunch," said Helen, "so as soon as ever you're ready to start we shall be, and it ought to be rather soon, for we've arranged a wonderful route for you and there's a lot to get in. What sumptuous apartments you're taking us to, Mummy. We're going to loll in the lap of luxury."

"And what heavenly tulips," said Linda.

"Do you remember those tulips, Helen," said Mrs. Fairholme, "in your little garden at Richmond? I got them on purpose."

"At Richmond, were they there? I don't think I remember."

"Was that the garden Helen has hanging over the mantelpiece?" said Linda. "You sitting with a black pom. I knew you from the picture in a moment."

"No, that's flattery I can't swallow," said Mrs. Fairholme, tingling with delight that Helen cared to have her photograph. "It must be thirty years old, when we wore trailing skirts and picture hats, and I can assure you we all thought we looked very nice. I didn't know you'd got that old thing, Helen."

"Yes, I can't think why it wanders about with me," said Helen. "I keep forgetting to throw it away."

"I've always been asking Helen for a photograph of you," said Mrs. Fairholme, turning to Linda, the delight in her heart fading, "or at ay rate to tell me something about you, but all I could get was: 'Linda is tall and I believe her eyes are blue. I don't think there's anything more to say.' "

"And even that's wrong," said Linda, opening her lazy eyes, "for they're not blue, they're inferior dirty yellow."

"Perhaps you can make Helen's letters more expansive," said Mrs. Fairholme.

"No, I can't. She writes the worst letters in the world."

"I'm sorry," said Helen. "I can't do with letters. I can remember the day when I used to write screeds, but really life's too short for them. Mother, if it suits you, I really think we ought to be starting now, we've got so much to get in."

"Yes of course, I'm ready whenever you like. This is a great excitement for me. I don't get taken out by grand ladies in a motor car every day. Helen, come and tell me if any of my hats are good enough. I must try and live up to the car."

When they were alone, she clasped her fondly, whispering:

"It's so lovely to have you, darling." The hug she received in return almost satisfied her hunger.

At first sight Helen and Linda were alike, both tall and both smart, but they had hardly anything in common.

Helen at thirty-five, with glowing cheeks and earnest yet rather unfeeling brown eyes, looked in face and figure like a handsome young man. She had the zest of an undergraduate, but none of an undergraduate's doubt and self-consciousness. She was sure of herself and her views. If only Victorian ideas and institutions could be changed, the world would rapidly improve. She was too busy to perceive that they were already gone. How many there were like her before the War. Such people are instruments in the hands of that mysterious spirit of the generations to make progress impossible.

But Helen preserved all the old Victorian sense of right and wrong. She cared for goodness as much as her mother did, though they might differ sometimes as to what was good. She had been more than once sought in marriage, but she said with sincerity she had no time for men. Tributes to her good looks were nothing to her, she had no vanity. She dressed well, because all she did, she did well. Her relaxation was her women friends. Her craze just now was driving Linda's motor.

Pretty and charming Linda was the grand-daughter of a business man who had been made a peer, and she had the languor of the third generation of success. She was several years younger than Helen, but she looked more than her age, for she had been given everything, and surfeit had worn her out. She had zest for nothing, above all none of Helen's zest in helping the world. She did not believe in right and wrong, not even in social and anti-social. She looked quizzically at life, her amusement tempered by the natural sweetness of her disposition. She was exploring various paths, and just now it was the path of Labour.

"But I never quite know where I am with you," said Helen, who cared for Linda more than Linda cared for her.

"I'll drive, shall I?" said Linda, as they got into the motor. "Do you care to sit in front, Mrs. Fairholme? or I expect you would rather be with Helen at the back."

"You'd better go in front, mother," said Helen. "I shall have to be looking at the map, so there really is no point in sitting together."

"Still I think I will sit by Helen," said Mrs. Fairholme. "Then I can look at her. I haven't had the chance for such a long time."

"You're to look at something much more interesting than me, mother. Linda, if you sprint a little, I thin we ought to be able to get in that Norman church Sylvia told us about."

As they drove, Helen with her map glanced at the rushing landscape, discussed, examined, and hazarded short cuts. They whizzed and bounded. In the stream of other cars they dashed past lanes, downs, shops, woods, tea-rooms, high roads, sea fronts, thatched cottages, concrete improvements, lonely farms, bungalows with pink roofs, country seats in parks, gaudy filling stations, garages with motor hoardings, and sweet, tall, twisting hedgerows, decked with pale early leafage. The motor cast its strange diabolic spell on Helen. They must go faster still.

Fervent motorists will know why she wanted to see Sylvia's church. "Oh, there we are. We haven't time to go in. Mother, look, you're missing it. Mother, *dear*, you're in a dream. She's not worthy to be taken the gorgeous round. She's missing everything."

Her eyes shone brilliant with excitement, she did not heed her mother by her side, she wanted no company but her map.

"She wants no company but her map." Mrs. Fairholme's thoughts, teased to restlessness by the vibration of the car, always came back to that. She had counted the hours to a long leisurely talk, when she would say much to Helen and hear still more, and they might find that lost clue she had been seeking in vain. It was a cruel disappointment that these short precious hours of the visit should be wasted thus. But she told herself many times, she must have the common sense to face facts. Motoring was a symbol of Helen's life. Things passed so fast they could only be of concern at the instant; there was no time to look back. During the active working years, full to the brim, what place could there be for memory? And was not that as it should be? Old age, when work is done, is the time for remembrance. It would be a misuse of youth and prime to dwell much on the past. Now that their lives had separated, she was a part of Helen's past, called but rarely into her immediate present. She recollected those fully working years in her own life; had she not been equally unmindful? She remembered—how long it was since she had thought of it—a speech of old Aunt Dora, which had been repeated to her; Aunt Dora, who did her best to fill the place of the mother they lost. "I really came to Richmond to be near dear Millicent, but I hardly ever seem to see her, and it's lonely sometimes, but I know how busy she is." And her own answer: "I should have thought I was always seeing her, but she seems to think I have nothing to do but potter after her."

She wished Aunt Dora could return to earth for a moment. She would explain that she now shared that lot of loneliness. Life had paid her back, and broken her of impatience. "And how sane life is," she thought, with the laugh with which she usually met her troubles.

"Here we are," cried Helen, rousing Mrs. Fairholme from her musings. "We've done it under two and a half, Linda, with five minutes to spare. I was rather anxious just about Harrington. Now tea, don't you think, Mother?"

"Tea's my business," said Mrs. Fairholme. "You must find the place, dears. All I stipulate is it must be the best."

"What news of Gilbert, mother?" asked Helen as they ate their scones. "He never writes. I think I'm considered too lost to all decency. I retaliate and don't write often to him, so I've no right to complain."

"They're camping near Agra just now, making a tour of the district. Vera's revelling in it."

"She would be. They must adore doing the pro-consul and pro-consuless, condescending to the inferior races."

"He asks sometimes if you're still at your nefarious tricks undermining the British Empire."

"And what do you say?"

"I say I think your bark's worse than your bite."

They all laughed, and Linda said:

"I wonder whether that's not rather a severe remark underneath."

"Of course it is. I hope you give Gilbert a scratch too sometimes, mother, to show him he isn't quite as important as he thinks."

"Well, sometimes I say I think there are different ways in which one can help the world."

"That's the last thing he'd agree to," said Helen.

"These two children have always sparred," said Mrs. Fairholme to Linda. "I used to say to them: 'You're both right, and you're both wrong.' Perhaps I think it's the same now. But they never would own that; they both agreed then, the only time they ever did. I must tease a little," she said half timidly to Helen. "It's excitement. I'm so excited at having you at last."

They were sitting in Mrs. Fairholme's room before dinner, when a feeble tap came at the door.

"I won't stay one moment," said Miss Robins. "I know you're busy. I only wanted to tell you old Miss Dawson called this afternoon. She was so sorry to miss you. She sent her fond love and she has left the Armenian embroidery. I've put it on your table."

"Thank you, dear, very much," said Mrs. Fairholme. "Come in a moment. This is my daughter Helen, and her friend Miss Mallows."

"How lovely that your mother should have you for Easter," said Miss Robins. She repeated this thought in various forms, and withdrew.

"Wherever Mother goes," said Helen, "she always collects that sort of adorer, a small species of weazels, very meek with their hair hanging all over their faces. They simply cling like leeches. You really ought not to allow it, Mother."

"I'm sure Miss Robins is very harmless, Helen."

"No, she's not. She's a blot on the landscape; such people ought not to exist. I'm thankful to say they won't, once this generation's gone. We shall eliminate that type; we shall give women more self-respect."

"Perhaps you may," said her mother, "but I always feel, but for the grace of God there goes Millicent Fairholme, or very likely, there by the grace of God will go Millicent Fairholme. I'm so short, I might easily be a weazel. You're tall, you won't, and one might be something much worse. Miss Robins always is doing kind things for me."

"Don't think me horrid, Mummy," said Helen, screwing up her face amusingly, "but I do hope I may escape having kind things done for me by Miss Robins."

"What would you like to do after dinner?" said Mrs. Fairholme later at dessert.

"I know Linda wants to study the manners and customs of the nation," said Helen. "She's never been inside a boarding-house. The great spectacle of the day is breakfast, and I expect she'll be too slack to appear then. They have their noses buried in the *Daily Sketch*.[41] Possibly one, greatly daring, has a *Daily Mail*. I call them the Daily Sketchers."

"Still I think you'll find the Daily Sketchers made of flesh and blood almost as though they were members of the Labour Party," said Mrs. Fairholme.

"Now I'm being crushed," said Helen, pinching her mother. "Because I'm unkind. Unkind was a great word with Mother when I was small."

"I mean to be very kind," said Linda, "particularly to that old clergyman who comes out of George Eliot, the one who spoke to us before dinner. May we talk to him?"

"Mr. Selby!" said Mrs. Fairholme. "Oh, will you two play bridge with him? Helen's bridge will be such a treat to him."

"It will be a thrill for me," said Linda. "We're all enlightened agnostics at home; we say clergymen in inverted commas, because when you say clergyman it must be a scream."

Mrs. Fairholme laughed politely, but though she liked a joke, she never understood irony.

Capable Helen played bridge as well as she did everything else, and she and Mr. Selby carried all before them.

"But you had *very* bad cards," said Mr. Selby, beaming with

---

[41] A British weekly journal, primarily a society magazine with high pictorial content, that ran from February 1893 to June 1959.

triumph. "I must thank my partner for a very delightful evening," turning to Helen, "and if she *could* impart some of her prudence to her dear mother! But I'm afraid your mother has too much confidence in the benevolence of mankind and the kindness of fate, and it is not always justified."

"If I trust in your benevolence, I make a great mistake," said Mrs. Fairholme with a smile, which had made many captives. Yet she had not meant to make them; she hated flirting.

"You are very severe to-nigt," said he benevolently. "Your mother looks a different creature now you are here, Miss Fairholme. You must come oftener, and cheer her up."

"I'm very rushed all the winter," said Helen, "but I mean to make time to run down. Now I shall carry her off to bed, I'm sure she ought to keep early hours. We shall have to start early to-morrow, you know, Mother."

"I'm afraid I couldn't start very early, Helen," said Mrs. Fairholme as they said good night. "You remember it's Good Friday, and church won't be over till eleven."

"Couldn't we cut church?" said Helen. "It seems such a pity to waste the weather. Of course Linda and I are coming with you on Sunday."

"I shouldn't like to miss Good Friday," said Mrs. Fairholme. "You two go without me; I shall have you all the evening."

"Oh no, of course that wouldn't do," said Helen. "We must just start later, only I wanted Linda to see as much as she could."

"Don't let anyone start early for me," said Linda. "I know Helen could sit in a car throughout eternity, but I'm not made that way."

"You're not to motor your mother to death," she said later, as she brushed her long, unfashionable hair in Helen's room; she had more independence of mind than is usual in her generation. "And your mother's such a darling, she's so gay. I think it must be jolly to be sixty, and sit and smile at life, particularly when one has such an alluring smile as hers."

"Yes, Mother's a darling, everyone thinks so. But you can't really think it right simply looking on and smiling. It seems to me terrible, drifting on year after year, as she and all these people do; just games and puzzles and Miss Dawson's Armenian embroidery, and muddling-puddling with old women in hospitals, which is rather worse than nothing. They never take sides in any of the great questions, they never think, and Mother's perfectly satisfied with it all, that's what amazes me."

"Oh, when one's that age, one has a right to a little relaxation."

"Not till one's bedridden, and Mother's quite fit, now she's living here. We used to be very close to one another, but her outlook makes such a barrier. I know she wants me to talk more to her, but I simply feel I've got nothing to say. I'm so thankful there's the car, so that we can't get time for talking."

"I thought there were all sorts of jolly little rubbishy things one could talk about with one's mother. I lost mine quite early, you know."

"Yes, but mother wants me to pour out my heart as we used to do."

"If I had a mother she might have what views she liked; I don't care a damn about views," said Linda with post-war indifference.

"But one's views are one's life."

"Oh *no*, Helen"

"Then what is life?"

"Ask me another. Chaos, I should imagine, and one must hold on to people's hands, or one gets lost."

The next day they drove and drove in the car as before, and Mrs. Fairholme came back sick in mind and body.

"Mother," said Helen after dinner, "I'm so sorry, but I can't manage bridge to-night. That nice little housemaid's been telling me about her young man; he's been turned off.[42] It's one of those wretched cases of victimization we want to take action about, and it's so difficult to get evidence because people are afraid to speak out. Evidently the local branch of his Union don't mean to do anything, it's scandalous. I'll write to the Central Office, and get them to move. I think I'll call on the Secretary here, Elsie's given me the address. I shall just have time before the post goes. I feel it's such a shame," she went on. "Here am I, born with all the chances through no virtue of my own, and then there's a man like Bert, who's born with nothing. One can't destroy inequality, worse luck, but one can do something to make things a little less desperately unfair."

Now there was no want of feeling in her handsome eyes. Mrs. Fairholme was lost in rueful admiration, it was curtailing more of her all too meagre evenings; how few there were! But knowing Elsie's Bert, she had some sympathy also for Bert's employer, a small struggling builder.

"We had such a jolly party last night," cried Miss Dendy, rushing in in a moment of lull to make her boast to Mrs. Pack. "One gentleman brought his gramophone in the car, and another one had his banjo, and they sat out in the garden after dinner till ever so late, singing songs out of "She's my Girl." They seemed a wee bit too gay for me, but I think one ought to *try* and be broadminded. Eastcote sent round twice to complain."

---

[42] Dismissed from his employment.

Miss Dendy was Wesleyan by origin, and she would have been very happy taking class at Sunday School, as her mother had done before her, if only the spirit of the times had allowed it. But to-day Miss Dendy had struck the wrong note.

"That sounds rather trippery to me," said Mrs. Pack in her most refined tones.[43] "We kept early hours. Mrs. Fairholme's daughter is here and her friend, the Honourable Miss Mallows. Did I tell you she's Lord Rushden's daughter? I've always said there was something distinguished about Mrs. Fairholme. They had to make an early start. They've been taking Mrs. Fairholme out in the Rolls. It really is a lovely car, just that mousy shade I'm so fond of. I've got the Purdons again; he's in the ladies' shoe line, very well off, such nice people. He's very high—not a scrap of meat on Friday."[44]

A sorrowful murmuring from Miss Dendy.

"We had bridge last night, two tables. Miss Mallows plays with Mr. Selby; he loves his game of bridge, dear old man."

The lounge of the Nookery was furnished on lines advised by "Eve" and other experts.[45] The note was austerity. Grey paper, grey walls, white paint, black cushions, brownish drab curtains, on each wall one single picture in a black frame, no ornaments on the black chimneypiece, black ash trays, one aspidistra in a corner and three pale tulips in a plain white glass vase. Mrs. Pack thought it a beastly hole, and he own private room was very different, but such is the law of fashion that, on seeing the lounge,

---

[43] Trippery: like a noisy, vulgar tripper (tourist).

[44] High church, giving great emphasis to ritual.

[45] *Eve: The Lady's Pictorial*, a magazine established in 1926, later merging with *Britannia* to become *Britannia and Eve* in 1929.

visitors often exclaimed: "How cosy." The chairs were large, so that even the fattest man might wallow in them. Small men and ladies became quite lost, and had the greatest difficulty in getting out of them.

The dining-room was allowed to be more cheerful. There was a brilliant orange paper and pictures of comic incidents of golf.

One may be sure that Miss Dendy had everything wrong. Pink, red, blue, green and yellow all mixed up in the drawing-room, numbers of china ornaments, and even, poor thing, some woolly mats! While her dining-room had a blackish brown paper and a linoleum to simulate a parquet floor.

On Saturday evening Mrs. Pack's guests were assembled in the lounge; the two married couples, a spinster, Helen and Linda, Mrs. Fairholme and Mr. Selby. Other ladies were busy upstairs over little bits of laundry, that invaluable boarding-house resource.

Helen suddenly saw a friend enter the room, an elderly-young man with a *New Leader* sticking out of his pocket.[46]

"There's Mr. Richards, Linda," said she. "How unexpected and how convenient. I can ask him about Elsie's young man."

"Oh," said Linda, "I hoped I was having a rest from that type. Mr. Selby's going to teach me the Spider. Patience is *the* most fascinating pursuit. I definitely mean to join the Daily Sketchers."

"What a chance to meet you here," said Helen, going across to Mr. Richards.

In men as husbands she felt no interest, but she preferred their company.

---

[46] *New Leader* was a British socialist newspaper. Originally named *The Miner* when it was launched in 1887, it ceased circulation in 1986 (at which time it was called *Labour Leader*).

"I have a cousin of sorts, a Miss Robins," said Mr. Richards, "and my people asked me to look her up. I might say, what a chance to meet *you* here."

"My mother lives here, and I'm staying till Tuesday for my sins."

Elsie came up with Miss Robbins' fervent apologies; she had gone to bed with a bad headache, and could see no one.

"I rather expected that," said he. "I've never been forgiven because I had one of the Soviet people to lunch, such a charming fellow. My cousin in the army, on the other hand, who massacred hundreds of Germans, is an angel. The world's a funny place, and the mild, bloodthirsty spinster's one of the funniest things in it."

He did Miss Robins injustice. She would have liked to have seen her young man cousin, even a red young man.

"Well, I must go," said he rising.

"No, sit down again," said Helen. "I want to ask you about a case of victimization."

Bert dealt with, Mr. Richards looked round the room. "These strongholds of reaction are so amazing," said he, "but even here things are beginning to move. I heard someone say yesterday 'Good Friday, that's a funny name if you come to think of it.' The Christian tradition is losing ground very rapidly. Twenty years ago everyone would have known the origin of Good Friday. I should say in another twenty-five the Christian doctrine of resurrection and immortality will have ceased to count. Of course there'll always be a few individuals here and there, the natural mystics who can't quite exist without that sort of thing. It's strange to think one's mother and father were *almost* certain, and one's grandfather and grandmother absolutely certain that, when one was dead, one was going to sing hymns to God the

Father for ever and ever. It was a cruel affliction for God the Father, but that did not trouble them."

"I suppose they were certain, because they wanted to survive so much," said Helen. "But if one believes in progress, I can't really see that one much wants anything else."

"Yes, but can you wonder they wanted something else? I remember when I was a child staying at my grandmother's and groping one's way about the house with bedroom candles. Now at least they did have a decent light in Heaven. The Lord is the light thereof, you remember, which I suppose would mean at least a hundred candle-power."

Helen laughed, though a joke never interested her.

"You mustn't talk so loud," said she. "You're shocking their susceptibilities, you know."

"It's good for them," said he. "They want a little fresh air to get rid of the Victorian fogginess. Of course one's grandparents thought it right to keep the world a disagreeable place. They hated science because science might make it more comfortable, and that might weaken people's faith, which is of course exactly what has happened. Eric Watson gave a remarkable lecture the other day showing the biological impossibilities of survival."

Helen wished his high-pitched voice were not so penetrating. She stole a glance at her mother's face, but the look she saw there made her turn hastily away.

Mr. Richards' talk displeased others. Mr. and Mrs. Purdon, for instance, listened in High Anglican disgust. Mr. Barker, who attended church, garden, dog and golf permitting, felt uncomfortable if conversation ever took a turn outside the humorous; his wife was knitting for a bazaar. All felt too shy to speak, but Mr. Selby. Linda saw him throw aside the ace of hearts they had been awaiting, and look across at Mr. Richards. His lips moved for a moment, and she thought what an old pale little face it was.

"I beg your pardon," said he in his gentlest voice, "but until recently I tried to keep abreast of what is written in Germany and elsewhere on the subject of the survival of the soul after death, and I think the views of the biologist you mention are not universally held. For instance, there is—" he hesitated—"I was going to say that for instance——" he stopped again, and Linda could hear him panting. "There is I know—I can't quite remember——"

He flushed purple, and a look of distress, almost of anguish, came into his eyes.

"I think I know what you mean," said Linda. "Isn't it that German biologist who says that the present tendency in science is towards religion, not against it, as it was sixty years ago? I read an article about it lately. It's funny scientific people never seem to agree, do they? What on earth was his name? You'd know it in a minute," turning to Mr. Richards, "because it was—I can't remember, but it's two syllables, I think. We must go on with our game, Mr. Selby. I shall expire if we don't get an ace of hearts. Oh, *there* it is," she deftly rescued it, "we're saved. Thank God."

He wished she had not said "Thank God," but he smiled on her gratefully; the strained look left him and he recovered his speech. "Two years ago I should have got hold of the article you mention," said he, "but alas, my German days are over. Are you a student of theology?"

"Not exactly," said she with a serious smile befitting the subject, "I just roam about, reading all sorts of things."

Meanwhile Mrs. Pack had come into the room. She had not at first gathered the drift of the conversation, but now she called out:

"Oh, let's get off religion whatever we do, and it isn't even Sunday. Turn on the loud speaker, Mr. Purdon, will you? You're nearest. 9.30. It ought to be the Gnomes by now, and we shall have a bit of fun."

"I'm afraid I've shed rather a bombshell," Mr. Richards whispered. "But I won't throw any more. No Gnomes for me. Farewell."

Helen followed her mother into her room that night.

"Mummy," she said, "I'm so frightfully sorry you heard what Mr. Richards said just now. I ought to have stopped him, but he's rather a gas-bag once he begins."

"But I can't understand, Helen," said Mrs. Fairholme. "You seemed to agree, and you were laughing."

"Yes, one had to, he expected me to laugh. People joke in that way now, and it doesn't mean very much. And he doesn't only mock, he takes things very seriously indeed."

"But you aren't like him, dearest; you haven't lost your faith?"

"Yes, I suppose I have. I don't believe in what we used to be taught. I'm not a Christian."

"You don't believe, but how can we live without believing?"

"I do believe in a sort of spirit of progress."

"When did you lose your faith, Helen?"

"I don't know; gradually, I think. I found people round me didn't believe, and I suppose one naturally goes with one's generation. Yours had faith, I know."

"Don't you think you'll ever meet George and Father again?"

Helen shook her head.

"Poor child," said Mrs. Fairholme. "How terrible for you."

"I don't know, Mother. I felt it at first, but it doesn't seem to make much difference now."

"But don't you long for them?"

"No, I've put all that part of my life behind me. I don't think it's any use brooding over the past. I just live in the present."

"I can't understand that you shouldn't care."

"I don't think I want another life. This one's good enough for me; it's so rich and full."

"But the time comes, you know, when the rich, full years are over."

"Yes, but why should one anticipate?"

She stood looking down on her mother, invulnerable in her strength, her clear, empty eyes unseeing of all but the immediate present, so at home in this world that she seemed to exclude the possibility of any other.

Mrs. Fairholme walked to the window. She stood with her back to Helen, gazing out; she could see the crudely lighted esplanade, with the quiet, murmuring Good Friday crowds, for the English, as ever, take their pleasures sadly, streaming endlessly up and down. For them also had Christ suffered, died and risen in vain?

Helen went up to her and took her hand.

"Darling Mummy," she said gently, "I'm so terribly sorry it hurts your feelings so much. I'd been wondering for a long time if I'd better tell you, it seemed so insincere keeping it back, but I do wish I hadn't."

"It doesn't hurt my feelings," said Mrs. Fairholme. She withdrew her hand. "It's not that, but it grieves me, it grieves me terribly."

"I'm desperately sorry, dear, but one can't stop progress, you know. The old ideas have to go, however beautiful they may have been."

Mrs. Fairholme did not answer, and she still did not turn round.

"But why did you mean to come to church with me?" she said at last.

"Linda and I thought it would please you, Mother."

"It was kind of you both to think of me, but I would rather you did not come."

The tone was low, the voice gentle, but they made Helen feel, as they sometimes could, that she was a child once more, her mother grown up and very wise, even formidable.

They were again silent, but Helen broke the pause: "Perhaps I'd better say good night now."

She put her arms round Mrs. Fairholme, and said, "Won't you look at me?" and Mrs. Fairholme felt that she was trembling. She cried out: "How thin you are, Mother."

Mrs. Fairholme turned, and gave Helen one of her peculiarly sweet smiles. "That means your arms haven't been near mine for a long time, and I do love to have them. I'm fattening, darling, and very well indeed. I was bitter, dearest Helen, and you must forgive me. This has been a shock to me, but it is much better to have it said, and it is my want of faith that makes it bitter. Good night, dear, God bless you. You are His child, whatever you believe."

Helen went to Linda's room to fetch her map and guide book. Linda was already in bed. She was tireless at dances and night clubs, but when she had an evening to herself, she was fond of curling up among the pillows to read a detective thriller, a French novel, or philosophy, as the mood might take her, or if the mood took her to do nothing, to do nothing. Now she lay blinking and smiling lazily to herself, her face framed by her dark reddish hair, of which she was very proud.

"You look rather in the dumps, my child," she said to Helen.

"It's so miserable," said Helen. "Mother's terribly upset about Richards' conversation. I knew she cared about religion, but I didn't know she would care like that. I suppose I ought to have known. I remember it seemed everything to me at college."

"Why didn't you stop Richards? I can't imagine how you could let him go on tormenting Mr. Selby. Mr. Selby's poor little hands were trembling so. It makes me feel shaky all over when old people's feelings are hurt."

"But don't you think old people ought to know the truth?"

"Oh, I've never cared much about the truth. Besides, what is truth? I'm sure someone else said that. Who was it? I know Mr. Richards thinks whatever he thinks becomes the truth because he thinks it, but I should feel just the other way. Why, he believes in progress. I'd heard of progress, but I never met anybody in the flesh who believed in it. I thought it was quite given up. Just think a minute. If there were progress, how could people shingle,[47] which makes everyone look so frightful, except you—not to mention the War?"

"But there must be progress," said Helen earnestly. "How can one live without progress? If there isn't, you knock the bottom out of things. Why should one do anything?"

"One needn't."

"I couldn't exist doing nothing; it wouldn't be life."

"No, so I expect it's as well to have a hypothesis that there's progress, it keeps people busy."

"But, Linda," persisted Helen, "I'm sure what Mr. Richards thinks is the general opinion of scientific people."

"Except of my German professor, of course," said Linda with her teasing smile. "Did you hear Mr. Selby ask if I was a student of theology? And the professor's name, I must think of a name for him."

---

47 The shingle was a popular hairstyle in the 1920s.

"You don't mean you were making it up?"

Linda nodded. "Richards was being so didactic I couldn't bear it, and I read something in a magazine the other day, which came in handy."

"I call that *really* unprincipled, Linda."

"Yes, but you know I haven't got any principles. It was amusing to see Mr. Richards pondering, wasn't it? I wish Mrs. Pack hadn't butted in with the Gnomes, 'though it wasn't even Sunday'—I liked that touch—and then one really had to come to Mr. Selby's rescue."

"I do wish you were serious sometimes."

"Well, I will be. When I saw the look on Mr. Selby's face, just before he spoke to Mr. Richards—I can't explain, but I suddenly felt quite poor and small. I think there's more in heaven and earth than is dreamed of in our philosophy, and he knows something about it, and we know nothing. And scientific people could talk till they were blue in the face, it would just be irrelevant. I daresay I shall forget it all to-morrow, but on the other hand I don't think I shall." She was ashamed of feeling too much and said: "This is getting almost portentous, let's go to roost. Good night."

It was long before Helen could follow her example. She went to her room and stood at the window, looking out, like her mother, upon the distant crowds. She did not quite know what she wanted for them and the world. But if Linda were right, and there was no progress? She felt suddenly left behind, one of the old generation with her views discarded, the views she had thought immutable, as she had discarded her mother's. Must the spirit of the new generation be always alien? She shuddered. She had not felt the inexorable instability of life since George died in the War. A veil fell from her eyes, and she understood her mother. Does not a moment come in most lives when the children see their parents, whom they thought remote, as one of themselves, standing by their side, though that moment may come too late, when the grave lies between them?

Helen remembered that she and her mother used the same words; "How could one live without believing?" "How could one live without progress?" She would go to her mother and say: "If life is without hope for both of us, let's try and comfort one another." She looked at her watch. It was past one. She, who had never thought, had been thinking for three hours at the window. She could not disturb her mother now, and there was the morning's route still to prepare. Once back at her map, all seemed solid again. She went to bed, and slept the hearty sleep of perfect health. She woke to find a letter asking for her immediate help at an election. Not a moment must be lost. The prospect fitted the hour. All else was excluded.

"I'm so sorry, Mummy," said she, "I'm afraid we ought to get off as soon as we can. The election's going to be a very close thing, if we do it at all. But as soon as the rush is over, I'll come down again, and have the two days I'm missing and something over."

Her eyes sparkled. Mrs. Fairholme saw she was hasting to be gone. There was a rush of telegrams, of telephoning and counter-telephoning, packing and early breakfast, and Helen forgot the words she had meant to say. There were many affectionate kisses, hilariousness, and: "You're to look much fatter when I come next time, or I shall be seriously annoyed."

Mrs. Fairholme waved gaily also, and kissed her hand, till the car was out of sight. Then she went upstairs and cried. After a while she knocked at Mr. Selby's door.

"Will you come with me to the cemetery this afternoon?" said she. "I could not go on Saturday. It is the first Easter I have missed, and it is so lonely to-day."

"I should like to come with you," he said. "We went together last year, you remember."

There had been some balmy shiny showers, which made even half-past two poetic, that dull prosaic hour.

Mr. Selby moved slowly now, but at length they escaped the sea front, the visitors, the waste paper, the charabancs, and shouting cyclists. They walked through meadows, and the primroses in the hedges, the happy conversation of birds, the calm clouds resting so peacefully in the blue heavens, preached to them sweetly of the Resurrection. But they preached in vain to Mrs. Fairholme. She longed for the dead who seemed for ever gone. She longed for the living Gilbert, passed out of her life away in India, and Helen, from whom she had just parted, farthest away of all. Mr. Selby was musing of past happiness, and they walked almost in silence.

At length she could not restrain the tears. He roused himself from a dream, and in his eyes there were tears also.

"How one longs for their bodily presence," said he. "But we must not sorrow without hope, at Easter above all."

"I try not to," she said. "But it made me so wretched when Helen and that Mr. Richards spoke as if none of the younger generation believed. You'll think me miserably weak, but it seems to shake my faith. I ought to have said something, but I couldn't when it was Helen's friend. I wanted to thank you for speaking as you did."

"But I said nothing. I often lose my words now, just when I most want to be clear. It's a trial. At two o'clock this morning I had it all pat, just when it was no good to anybody. But don't think the world has ceased to believe, it never can. There was Miss Mallows for instance. How interesting that was about the German biologist, although she could not give us any very exact details. I feel she is carrying on the lamp, and she is such a *very* nice-looking girl."

"Yes, perhaps Linda will bring Helen back to faith. I do feel Helen's unbelief so bitterly, Mr. Selby. Give me some Easter message, my soul aches for it."

"*Sursum Corda, Christus resurrexit*," said he.[48] "That was my father's greeting to us all on Easter morning."

"You must translate that for me. I'm not a paragon of learning as you all were." He did so, and she said: "It cheers me to think that we can say what they have been saying for hundreds and hundreds of years."

"And it will be said for hundreds of years more," said he. "Thou are the same, and Thy years do not fail."[49]

"It is my hope," she said, "but sometimes it gets dim. And as life goes on, *how* one thirsts after it. One's own lights go out, one isn't wanted any more. In old days so many people seemed to want me. Now one's elderly, very lazy, dull and stupid. I liked so much what I heard in a sermon; the Holy Spirit is never elderly. It was rather too familiar, but that's the way nowadays. And my life's so useless, so trivial, just helping old ladies like myself muddling over their crosswords, only they really are even stupider, and *oh*, how tired one gets of it." She laughed youthfully.

"You useless!" said he. "You who make sunshine wherever you are. Now I can speak with experience in the matter of uselessness.

48 'Lift up your hearts, Christ is risen.'

49 Meaning: you will live forever. Hebrews 1:12

Nothing is left me but to be as little trouble as I can, and alas, I *am* a trouble; Mrs. Pack makes me know I am, a terrible cumberer of the ground. But even there," said he, his words halting with emotion, "His right hand shall lead me. It fortifies me to know that at the end of life, as in youth and middle age, our portion is allotted us, and one task is still left—to accept it with readiness." A look almost of glory irradiated his face. Of that look on aged faces, one can but say: "Mine eyes dazzle."[50] It is a witness to divine grace withheld from youth and prime, and granted only to old age.

"You make me feel so ashamed of myself," cried Mrs. Fairholme, "and so proud of you." She laid her hand impulsively on his sleeve. Her warm praising had always flattered, because it came from the heart, and Mr. Selby had reached that stage in life when praise seldom came his way.

"That's actually four o'clock striking," said she. "We shall be late for tea. No, you're not to hurry, it's very bad for you. We'll support one another under Mrs. Pack's reprimands, and I'll make you some tea in my room. Now the Rolls Royce has gone, I shall be scolded again. For those three days I was perfection. When I reminded her of clean towels, I only got smiles."

Mrs. Fairholme was right; the culprits were received with black looks.

"It seems a funny thing," said Mrs. Pack, "that when one has tea at four o'clock entirely for the visitors' comfort, they persist in coming in at any odd time. You can't have any more. It's all washed up and cleared away half an hour ago. There's Kate out

---

[50] From *The Duchess of Malfi* (published 1623), the tragedy by English dramatist John Webster.

and Phyllis with a bad finger. You seem to suppose one pair of hands can do everything."

Mrs. Pack had been vexed. In happier days she would have wreaked it on the servants. Now they gave back as good as they got, particularly Phyllis, aged fourteen and a half.

"Mother says she wouldn't stand it, if she was me. Mother says you're not there to be put upon, and if I don't give satisfaction I'd better leave, she says, there's lots of nice places better than a common boarding-house."

Phyllis received almost the same consideration as the Honourable Miss Mallows.

The cause of vexation was this. There was war between Eastcote and the Nookery, all the keener because Miss Fraser did not seem to realize there was war at all. But Mrs. Pack and Ivy, the Eastcote parlour-maid, who preferred to be called Granger, were old and tried foes. Granger modelled herself on a lady-like widow, one of the Eastcote boarders. She hung her head prettily a little to one side, and her manner with visitors was a mixture of refinement and solicitude. She had her reward in Mrs. Fraser's red book: "*Such* a happy little visit, thanks to all at dear Eastcote!" or in the more exalted vein of poetry:

"How sweet is the lot of the stranger
With Eastcote, Miss Fraser and Granger."

Mrs. Pack met Granger that Easter afternoon, and could not resist crowing.

"I suppose you've been pretty busy with the Easter rush," said she. "We're so packed, I say sardines aren't in it."

"We're always busy," replied Granger in a soft voice, "but we don't go in for a special rush at Easter. Really I should hardly know if it was Easter, except for hot cross buns and the lovely Easter hymns. We know a number of people have to take their holiday at Easter, but Miss Fraser really likes rather a different class of visitor."

She glided away. Mrs. Pack had to go back, bottle her anger, and wreathe her face in tea-time smiles. It was a comfort there were the chronics to trample on.

Mrs. Fairholme listened to the storm with a small, interested smile, which rather hampered Mrs. Pack's style.

"Now that's over," said she, "let's come and have nursery tea; I've got some guava jelly. Mr. Selby, you must ask Elsie for milk and bread and butter, because she never can refuse you anything, and I'll ask Miss Robins to come and join us, and we'll keep our Easter feast."

The weeks passed, the months passed, and Helen was always coming, and she did not come. The work was so important, so all-absorbing. How could she be spared? In the autumn there was a general election.

"I'm so rushed," she wrote, "I don't know when I can get away. So only a p.c. to say I'm looking forward to some quiet later, and will run down for a week-end. At any rate book me a room for Christmas." But there was a new friend, Monica; for Linda left the Labour Party, married an earl, and went triumphantly to India in the Vice-regal retinue; and Monica persuaded Helen to join a winter sports party at Montana. She had been working too hard, it would be wrong not to have a holiday. "So I'll get my Christmas week in February, Mum. I'll write reams from Montana." But she had not a moment, for she ski-ed all day and danced half the night. She sent postcards of bob-sleighs and skating experts.

There was an epidemic of influenza that Christmas, and among the sick were Mr. Selby and Mrs. Fairholme. He, stricken in years and longing to depart, recovered, but Mrs. Fairholme died. The news reached Helen in the midst of an uproarious breakfast, all shouting plans for the day. As middle-aged people trying to be schoolboys, they made a point of shouting. There were two telegrams; one, which had been delayed, summoned Helen home, the other announced the death. Helen turned cold and hardly knew what she read. She heard herself say: "Come to my room, Monica."

"My dearest girl," said Monica taking her arm. "I'm simply too sorry for words. Now what can I do? If I settle up and you pack, I think you'll do the express. You've got half an hour."

Helen nodded; in that half hour she thought of the race against time. She enjoyed finishing with five minutes to spare.

"Of course, poor dear, it's a terrible shock," said Monica to the party. "But I don't fancy they meant so frightfully much to one another."

When Helen called at the nursing home, they were so full and busy that Matron at first confused Mrs. Fairholme with a Mrs. Battersby. When she realized whom they were talking of, she said: "But your mother must have been going downhill for months, she was so fallen away. She was at the Nookery, wasn't she? I've heard that's rather tough. Eastcote is much nicer. There really is very little to tell you. From the first your mother was very drowsy and hardly said anything. When we spoke of sending for you, she shook her head and said 'No, no,' and Nurse wasn't sure if she understood. It was sudden at the last, but I never had much hope."

Helen heard and answered in a trance; words had no meaning; and Matron said later to Sister: "What a hard woman. People say nurses are hard, but we can't hope to rival relations."

"And Mrs. Fairholme was such a dear," said Sister, "one *had* to be fond of her."

"You would like to see your mother," said Matron, and led the way upstairs.

Helen looked, but it seemed the sweet, laughing Mrs. Fairholme had escaped the form stretched on the bed; her place was taken by a stranger, stately, solemn and terrible. It was hard to believe what she kissed had ever been her mother. She left the room with her heart like a stone.

She went to the Nookery, where Mrs. Pack received her with sobs both heartfelt and conventional.

"I quite miss her," said Mrs. Pack. "We all do, she was always so bright. One thing I was simply thankful for, I got her away to the nursing home when I did. I thought at the time it would be serious, and anything of that sort happening in a boarding-house is so bad. Sets people against it; it's unreasonable, but so it is. She hadn't been well for a long time. I said, 'I shall write to Miss Fairholme,' and she always said you were not to be worried. I said I should do it that day she went to the home, and she said, 'No I want her to have a nice holiday, she needs it.' You oughtn't to have put her off, twice you did it, and it was very awkward for me. She fretted: she cried when you put her off that last time. She thought I didn't hear, but I listened at the door, and I heard her say: 'It means nothing to her.' Your friend the Honourable Miss Mallows used to send her lovely flowers till she went abroad. Miss Robins and I were only saying this morning what a wreath she would have sent for to-morrow. Mr. Selby does feel it; it's turned him quite dotty, and they won't take cases like that in a nursing home, and as I tell him, I can't be running after him all day. The doctor says he'll pick up with the warmer weather, but I say there's all the worst part of the winter to come. Of course if you can get on with the packing to-day, Miss Fairholme, I shall be glad. I've let the room to Miss Child from Strathcona; she wasn't comfortable there, it's too rough; and she's coming in at once. I'll look in later, if I can give you a hand."

At last she was gone, and Helen was alone in the room, shabby, dark, and mean. To Mr. Selby and Miss Robins it was a shrine of peace. A few trifles of Mrs. Fairholme's lay about, and some of her sweetness pervaded them still. Many belonged to Helen's childhood, some were her presents. There was a china spaniel she had bought with the eager earnestness of eleven, and the handsome carved box she had sent from Montana a fortnight ago, as a compensation for the disappointment. As she looked, a dim sense came to her that the mother who had treasured these trifles was gone, and would never return. But she must not delay her packing. If she hurried, she might escape Mrs. Pack's visit of assistance.

The task would not be difficult. Mrs. Fairholme's possessions were few. She had sold everything which could turn into money to help Gilbert with his wife's two costly operations. The sale had been a landmark: she felt it cut her off not only from the old days of home and marriage, but from her life, almost from her identity as mother. She allowed herself but one luxury, her old letters and photographs.

There was no time to spare, but Helen lingered over the old photographs, George, Gilbert, her mother, her father, perhaps above all herself; the faces looked out at her from the past, and the years fell away. There was a group taken when she was eighteen; it recalled a Christmas scene she had forgotten. They had sung, danced, acted, and laughed, and she said: "I don't believe there's anything better than this in the world." Her reserved father put his hand on her mother's shoulder; she could see the look that passed between them. He said: "I don't think there's anything better either, but all of you will find one thing better still, that's your own homes, when you start them; but when you do, don't forget the old one." It was the Christmas he died, and she had forgotten, she had not thought of home for years.

Then came the letters, piles of them, tied up and dated; Mrs. Fairholme was always methodical.

She had laughed at her: "You're a regular mid-Victorian hoarder. Look at those masses, and you'll never read one."

"Yes I do," said Mrs. Fairholme, "I often take out a bundle when I'm lonely, and then I feel you're all round me still."

She saw the piles, so large at school and college, dwindle in later years to short, dull letters written at committees or in trains as she went to important meetings. Sometimes she would interrupt an engrossing discussion with: "I'm afraid I must just dash this off."

She was sorry Gilbert's recent piles were scanty too.

"I'm going to make a stand," Vera had said, "we shan't be absorbed by in-laws."

Helen recalled her last comment: "The last thing I should wish is to absorb Vera, she's Anglo-Indian to her finger tips!" The retort satisfied her. But she wished that, of the two children left her mother, one at least had written the long letters they knew she loved.

Here, surrounded by objects her mother had touched only a week ago, it came home to her at last that she was dead. With that realization, things to which she had been blind became clear. She could have come to Seagate any or every week; the obstacle had been herself. It seemed as if there had been a barrier between them on the Easter visit, and for months and years before, a miserable earthborn cloud which severed them; her preoccupation with her own pursuits, her dread of being behind the times. Looking back, it seemed she had searched for points of difference she might criticise, she had almost taken pleasure that they were apart. There had been that moment at Easter when the cloud had broken, but alas, she had let it pass, she had said nothing. Death sometimes shows us to one another as we really are. She knew now there need never have been a barrier, that all the time she loved her mother better than anyone in the world.

"I mean nothing to her," they were some of the last words her mother had spoken. She might live to be ninety, but time could not efface them. "Oh, Mother, Mother, Mother," she cried, "if I could tell you." She felt she would give all the years she had to live of this life, which she had said sufficed her, for one fragment of immortality. But she knew there was no immortality, that dream had been abandoned.

Against all reason something within her cried that her mother would not let even death come between them, the love which had always enfolded her must be going on. For an instant she had an exquisite sensation of being back in childhood, holding her mother's hand, it was gone as suddenly as it came. In an agony of realization she faced the facts before her; that love would never be hers any more. She might search through the universe, but all that was left of her mother was a cold statue on a bed, soon to fall to corruption.

The indescribable anguish of that hour was at length relieved by tears.

"I just happened to be passing the door," said Mrs. Pack gloatingly to Miss Dendy, "and she was sobbing so that I thought she'd break a blood vessel."

"Poor Mrs. Fairholme," said Miss Dendy, "she'd be very pleased about it."

"I was thinking," said Mrs. Pack, "shall I take her a cup of tea, or shall I send Elsie with it, or shall I just call through the door 'would you like a cup of tea'?"

"I think I should leave her," said Miss Robins.

"It seems rather unkind," said Mrs. Pack. "And crying like that's really dangerous."

"Yes, but I think I should leave her," said Miss Robins with unusual firmness.

An hour later there came a knock at Miss Robbins' door. Helen entered as faultlessly trim, as coldly composed as usual. One who observed, but Miss Robins never observed, might have seen a different look in her heavy eyes, a look of seeking for what she never found: that look remained with her.

"May I come in for one moment?" said Helen.

"Oh do, oh please, yes," said Miss Robins more confusedly than ever. She remembered what Mrs. Pack had heard, and felt as if she were eavesdropping.

"I wanted you to have this little remembrance of my mother," said Helen. "I know you were fond of her." She gave Miss Robins a garnet brooch Mrs. Fairholme had often worn.

"Oh, Miss Fairholme—how very very—your darling mother—"

She could not continue, she gulped back her sobs. She tried not to fret dear Mrs. Fairholme's daughter by noisy laments.

"And would you give this book to Mr. Selby, please? I wanted to see him, but Mrs. Pack says he isn't well. Good-bye, and thank you very much for all you did for her; she said you were so good to her."

She bent forward, and she, who hated kissing, gave Miss Robins in expiation the kiss she had sometimes denied her mother. It was so unexpected that in her confusion Miss Robins jerked some of her hanging ends of hair into Helen's face. How exactly like her; they *never* have any hairpins. But she endured it and did not shorten her kiss. Henceforth when Mrs. Pack and Miss Dendy discussed Helen's heartlessness, as they became fond of doing, Miss Robins took courage, and spoke in her defence.

The popular vicar took the funeral service. Mr. Selby, shrunk into a very bent old man past almost everything, faltered the blessing at the end.

"Really," said the Vicar later, "One wondered if poor Selby would get through it, but he was so keen to do it, it seemed inhuman to refuse him."

The majestic words of consolation meant nothing to Helen, but Mr. Selby's trembling accents stirred something dormant in her for many years.

She spoke to him after the service. "I wanted to thank you," she said, stretching out her hand.

He shrank back. "I really do not know who——"

"Don't you remember me? I'm her daughter, Helen Fairholme."

"I'm afraid I have not the pleasure of——"

"You must remember me," she said earnestly. "We played bridge together."

Recollection came dimly into his face.

"Is it Miss Fairholme?" he said. "I am sorry; my memory is not what it was."

"I know you believe I shall see her again," said she. "Oh, Mr. Selby, do help me. I think you might give me faith." She caught his hand, but he detached himself.

"I could not. I must—you must excuse me," he stammered feebly, and gave her a glance that was almost hostile. He turned and shuffled as quickly as he could down the path.

To be the channel of grace to Helen would have consoled him in that terrible hour. But it was too late, the task was beyond him now. The farewell blessing at his beloved friend's grave had spent all his failing strength. His thoughts, his words were astray. There was nothing but incoherent, nameless fears and misery.

He was not left forlorn. A widowed niece returned from Canada and made a home for him and comforted him.

For may months Helen felt everything the shadow of a shadow; after a while, however, her zest returned and life went on as before. But within there was a change. The memory of her mother was constantly with her, and sometimes the bitterness of regret was more than she could bear. But there were times, and as the years passed they became more frequent, when the thought of her was sweet and consoling, and she felt that somehow they were united and understood one another at last. With this thought there came, she knew not why, an expansion of the spirit, when she could say with the psalmist: "They shall perish, but Thou remainest."[51] So that Mrs. Fairholme might rest in peace, for she had gained her desire.

---

[51] Psalm 102:26.

INNOCENTS' DAY

The alarm woke Miss Perrin at half-past six. It was Christmas Day, and she was going to early service. She opened her window, peered into the darkness, heard the rain dripping, and went sadly back to bed. She could not go out in the wet, she must think of her health, not because it was precious to someone, but because she was poor, and nearly sixty, and knew by experience nothing is more expensive than bronchitis.

At 8 o'clock dawn broke, and dull light struggled through the window of her bed sitting-room at the Residential Hostel for Professional Women. Hers was a small, high room, looking out into a deep well, surrounded by black red brick walls. The light always had to struggle there. To-day the struggle was too much for it, and it died. She turned on the electric light in the ceiling. Darkness and black walls were nothing to the electric light. It leapt forth at once, and exposed the ugliness of the room. Nothing was old, and all was soiled and shabby save Miss Perrin's shelf of favourite books, her Wordsworth, Browning, Ruskin and Carlyle.

She went downstairs to hostel breakfast. On her way they told her she was wanted on the telephone.

"Is that you, Perks?" came a jolly voice. "It's too bad to bother you so early. Happy Christmas, and many of them, at least not many like this. What a day! I'm so dreadfully sorry, but George and Billy have gone and got mumps, bless their hearts, so all our Christmas do's are off. Isn't it too bad? Yes, I'll let you know how we go on, and you must come the minute we're out of quarantine."

She was very, very much disappointed. She was a teacher by profession, and felt herself still capable of work, though head mistresses knew she was too old. She had lately come to live forlornly in London. She had been invited to spend Christmas with a favourite former pupil, the joyous mother of five boys. She had counted the days to sharing Christmas with children, to looking on at merriment.

"Might I speak to you, Miss Dart?" said she to the secretary with the Eton crop.[52]

"Oh, happy Christmas, Miss Perrin," said Miss Dart officially.

"I only wanted to tell you," she said apologetically, "that I shall be in to dinner and supper."

"Oh, really, I wish you could have let me know beforehand. Didn't you see the notice? It makes it so much easier for the staff; of course they all want to get off for Christmas. I'm afraid it's absolutely nothing but cold to-night."

"I'm very sorry," said Miss Perrin. "They've just started mumps, so they've had to put me off at a moment's notice."

"Dear, yes, how unfortunate. Did you want me, Miss Hardy?"

Miss Dart liked active residents under forty, doing work that showed in the world; social, political, journalistic. "One wants to eliminate the decayed governess type," said she.

It was now ten o'clock, and the day decided it would turn into night. There was no fog, but the sky was dark brown, and black rain was dripping down the gutter. She must give up morning church too. She sat in her bedroom by the grate, and tried to think the central heating was a fire. She read the Christmas service. "His name shall be called Wonderful, Counsellor, the mighty God,

---

52 A very short, slicked-down, cropped hairstyle for women.

the Everlasting Father, the prince of Peace."[53] She felt a tear roll down her cheek. Was she really so foolish as to cry because she was missing the Christmas tree?

"In the Beginning was the Word, and the Word was with God, and the Word was God."[54] Her thoughts turned to Christmas long ago. They were all so excited with the stockings, they could not walk to church, they must skip. She was holding her father's hand, and made him run too. On their way they almost quarrelled over their favourite hymns, "While Shepherds watched," "Christmas awake." Gilbert was there; he did not mean much to her now, he was a prosperous business man in Liverpool. And Edith, she did not get on very well with Edith, she disliked her husband. And Lancy—he was dead.

"And there went forth a decree from Caesar Augustus that all the world should be taxed."[55] Once she could hear those words without tears, because they began what seemed then the most touching story ever written. Now she shed tears, because they moved her no more. She put her Bible and Prayer Book away and took out Wordsworth. She read Tintern Abbey. But she could no longer respond to the poet's serenity; her mind was numb, she felt with a pang that this was growing old.

There was a knock, and a smart much made-up girl, whom the hostel called Pam, walked into the room. Her low-necked, sleeveless, orange frock came well above her knees.

"Hullo," cried she, "I see you've cut saying prayers in church.

---

53 Isaiah 9:6.

54 John 1:1.

55 Luke 2:1.

You'll go to Hell, won't you, and *how* lucky you'll be—the one thing to-day is to frizzle. The furnace being out of order, as ever, I've got the shudders."

"Of course you're shivering, if you wear a dress like that in mid winter," replied Miss Perrin.

"I thought you must rise to that. I hoped Hell would do it, but you don't rise as you did. Now I've told you many times that the *more* you wear the colder you are. It's been scientifically proved. I say," breaking off erratically, "what freaks you read—Bible, Prayer Book, Wordsworth. How deadly, and I want cheering. Picture it: I'm going to a family party where we shall prance round a Christmas tree with small kids and sing 'Once in royal David's City.' Why, because someone chose to be born in a manger should we have to go on singing about it nineteen hundred years afterwards?"

"Does Christmas mean nothing at all to you then?"

"Oh, much worse than nothing," she replied gaily. "I have a religious complex. Carols depress me to the depths, and wherever you go you hear carols. Apparently they depress you, for you don't seem very gay either, my fair one." She said this kindly.

"You'll think me very absurd," said Miss Perrin, "but I'm disappointed because I'm not going to prance round a Christmas tree with small kids."

"Yes, you see you've got to second childhood, and I daresay that is really the best time of life. Now I've got something to buck you up." She unwrapped a very décolleté doll,[56] dressed as a ballet girl. "She was the most depraved doll I could find. It's so good for you to be shocked." She tickled Miss Perrin under the

---

[56] Décolleté: having a low-cut neck-line.

chin. "No, but I have got something *really* bucking. Here's your mail. Eight, you lucky beggar; I've only got four."

As a conscientious schoolmistress and good church-woman, Miss Perrin shivered at such talk, but misery makes strange bedfellows. Pam was her crumb of comfort in the hostel. Though much sought after, she alone found time to come and be pleasant to one so mossy.[57]

Miss Perrin opened her envelopes. They contained remembrances from steady old friends, who had been sending the same robins and kittens for thirty years. But there was one letter in a large, decided hand, which made her heart leap; she kept it to the last.

"29 Felix Street, S.W.

"My dear old Ethel,

"You know, I hope, that Wednesday is Innocent's Day. Do you remember more than fifty years ago my father used to say, 'It's Innocents' Day, let's ask the little Perrins and Fanny Fleet to come to tea'? I'm afraid Edith is too far to get at, but I'm asking dear Fanny, she's living in London now, and as you've been so delightful as to settle fairly near us, you must come too. Four o'clock sharp. If you can get 'bus 22, and make it stop at the dullest road you see, that will be Felix Street, which is ours, and we're half-way down.

"I know I'm a pig to write so seldom, but I really scarcely get a moment, and I don't change, but am as always your faithful and affectionate

"NELL."

---

57 Old-fashioned, dull, old.

Ethel and Edith Perrin, the doctor's daughters, Fanny Fleet, the vicar's daughter, Rosa and Eleanor Danvers, the squire's daughters, had all been children together in Lawton. Ethel had been fond of Fanny and Rosa, but Eleanor she had adored and, though life had parted them for years, she adored her still. As she walked down Felix Street next Wednesday, she overtook a stout heavy women, trudging along with difficulty.

"Fanny," she cried.

"Is that you, Ethel?" said Fanny, now the widow, Mrs. Bentley, "Nell told me she was asking you. I hobble along very slowly, I'm so rheumatic, also stout. I wonder you recognized me. You're lucky to have gone thin. Well, it's very nice to be meeting you again after all these years."

"I've often wondered about you. It was no good writing, for you never answered my letters."

"You don't get much time in the Bush. Now the children are all dispersed, I've come back to lay my bones in England. Have you seen Rosa and Nell?"

"Not for seventeen years, I think. I was in a remote school in Ireland, and I never came back to England all that time."

"Then I'd better warn you. Rosa's speech is affected, she had a queer sort of attack, and her mind too a little. I suppose you knew Colonel Danvers speculated, and he had to sell Lawton, and lost almost all their money as well as his own, so they're in lodgings. You remember Eric, the youngest brother? he lived close to us in New South Wales."

They were shown into a dull lodging-house parlour. The picture above the mantelpiece, one of the few relics from Lawton, shone out from its meanness. It was a portrait of the two Danvers at seventeen and twenty in the 'eighties. The sisters stood arm-in-arm smiling sweetly at life. Their smile was so disarming it seemed as if life must be kind to them. But it was pitiless, and struck them hard.

They had large fringes coming down over their large blue eyes, soft hats with feathers, worn at the back of the head, blue velvet frocks to match their eyes, with ruffles and gold lockets, little bustles and tapered waists. Miss Perrin well remembered the pretty frocks and the delight at the new gold lockets. As she took her thoughts back, one of the sitters came into the room.

"You two darling people," cried Nell kissing them. "How wonderful it is to get you both together again."

Her dark hair had turned grey, her blue eyes were faded, her cheek had paled; she looked as if a lifetime of rest would not sweep away her wanness. Miss Perrin could have wept to see such a ruin of her loveliness, but for her Nell still had the fascination which had brought her to subjection fifty years ago.

"Fancy our not being on the doorstep to bring you up," said Nell. "But Rosa slept badly; she was excited at the thought of the party. Will you come to her now? She is longing to see you. She's rather difficult to understand, but she loves to talk."

The fire flickered brightly in the bedroom, and the candles threw interesting shadows on the walls. By this light the visitors saw the poor invalid on the bed, her face a little twisted, and every attraction gone.

"Here they are, dear one," said Nell, "and this is nurse, or Nanna as we call her; Mrs. Bentley, Miss Perrin. Now, Rosa, you and Nanna must entertain the guests, while Mrs. Bone and I get tea."

Nanna and the landlady were under the same spell as Miss Perrin. Nell had exactly the right shade of manner for each; just as she used to have for the retinue at Lawton. The tea was charming; there were crackers, and an iced cake. It had "A Happy Christmas to Fanny, Ethel, Rosa, Nell and Nanna" in pink letters with silver stars and fairies.

"I made that," said Miss Danvers, "so please like it." She interpreted Rosa's uncouth murmurings, and when they were incomprehensible, she laughed cheerfully, and made the invalid laugh too.

When tea was over and cleared away, they blew out the lights, and sat in the red firelight. Miss Danvers went out and came back with a miniature Christmas tree hung with little candles and the bright balls and tinsel they had all loved in childhood. On the tree there were five tiny dolls.

"There's a settler with a kangaroo for Fanny," said Nell, "and a don in a cap and gown with books for Ethel, and a lady dressed for a drawing-room for Rosa, because we always have to read her the Court Intelligence first thing,[58] Mrs. Gamp for Nanna,[59] for obvious reasons, and that's me in a riding habit, because I always was mad on hunting, and I'm quite as mad still, when I get the chance."

The dolls were made with exquisite finish.

"I suppose they're all the work of your ten fingers, Nell," said Fanny Bentley. "You always were such a needlewoman."

"Yes, I was a clever creature, and it comes in handy here. Now let's have a carol to end up with, or it won't be really Christmas."

The thin elderly voices, singing harshly, huskily and sweetly, touched young, happy Nanna. "It was perfectly pathetic to hear the old dears," she wrote to the man she was marrying next year.

When the carol was finished, the singers did not speak for some moments. Each was thinking: Ethel of the child she once

---

[58] Press reports of the activities of the criminal courts.

[59] Sairey (Sarah) Gamp, the Cockney nurse-midwife from Charles Dickens's novel *Martin Chuzzlewit.*

was, long, long lost and gone; Nell of the children she had so much desired and never had; Fanny of the children who had been her all, now well content without her.

"After all this excitement you must rest, Rosa," said Nell, "I'll take these two into the parlour."

They sat round the fire; she leant back wearily in her chair, as if it was a relief to rest from the burden of gaiety.

Sometimes in the jog-trot of life comes a week, a day, an afternoon, lit up with some special sweetness, which sets it apart, and makes it treasured in the memory. The humble Christmas tree would be such a remembrance to Miss Perrin.

"You don't know what a treat you've given me," she said to Miss Danvers. "I wept because I thought I wasn't going to have a tree."

"I'm so glad you liked it. Nanna and I are babies, and love Christmas trees, and I wanted Rosa particularly to have one this year, for it may be the last she can enjoy. She'll gradually get worse, and lately it seems to me the progress has been quicker. Poor Rosa," she whispered to herself.

"What dreadful changes you've had," said Fanny, "and it was all so prosperous when I went to Australia. I thought you were going to be a marchioness."

"I used to think of marriage, but I aimed too high. I don't mean I was waiting for a prince of the blood, but I thought you mustn't marry unless you were carried off your feet by an overwhelming passion, and I never was. I daresay it wasn't in me, and I believe I might have marred very happily just on good, respectable love."

"Mine was the other way," said Fanny. "I thought something short of love would do, I wanted badly to get away from home just then, but it didn't work."

"But you had the children," said Nell.

"Yes, and they were wonderful years, but they're very short, they don't last."

"But don't you think the children come back?" said Nell taking Fanny's hand. "I believe they will, and you've had them. What would some of us have given to have had them?"

"Thank you, I must just go on and hope," said Mrs. Bentley. "Now tell me about Rosa. I thought she was going to marry Major French."

"Yes, but things went wrong; he didn't behave well. But sometimes I wonder, if she was to be ill like this, whether it was better she didn't marry. A husband would have loved her as much, but he would have found this illness very frazzling; men do. Now little Ethel," turning to Miss Perrin, as if she were still the little girl of seven, while Nell and Fanny were nine and ten. "We've been telling secrets of our lives, and you sit by silent and think the more."

"I always liked listening to you and Fanny," said Miss Perrin.

"But what's happened to you? You were going to be Head of Newnham."

"Yes, everything seemed possible at eighteen. I don't think anything happened to me. But I know I've regretted I spent so much time on study. Perhaps I've been unlucky, but being intellectual cuts you off; people don't want it. I used to think books could take the place of home and love, but they can't; you can suck books very dry."

"Still I'm grateful to books," said Nell. "*The Woman in White* has brought me through sometimes, when things seemed getting rather much."

"Oh, the dear old *Woman in White*," said Fanny. "Do you remember your mother reading it to us on Saturday afternoons?"

They laughed over the recollection. Then Miss Danvers said almost solemnly:

"Life's been very different for all of us from what we expected."

"It's been very hard for all of us," said Mrs. Bentley, sighing heavily, "particularly for Rosa."

"And as one gets older, it seems to get harder still," said Miss Perrin. " 'The best is yet yo be' is quite untrue."

"But dear Fanny and Ethel," said Nell. "This is Christmas time, I won't let you be so sad." She spoke playfully, but with earnestness.

"But does Christmas really mean anything to you still?" said Miss Perrin. "When one was a child of course——"

Miss Danvers had always talked without reserve. The country doctor's daughter, living in a less outspoken circle, sometimes wondered at her. But of one thing the squire's daughter never spoke, her own religious beliefs.

At first she did not answer, and when she did speak, she turned her head away, and the words came out with difficulty.

"When you're a child, you love it all, but it's quite unreal, because you know nothing. Now I'm old, it means much, much more, because I've been through more, and feel more."

"How do you mean exactly"

"I can't explain. But isn't there a poem 'Love came down at Christmas'?[60] only I like to think it's 'comes' not 'came.' "

"Say some more, Nell, you don't know how hungry I am."

"My dear child, I would in an instant if I could, but I *can't*. I have endless thoughts, but I have no words, you know I never have. Besides there aren't any, except the carol we used to sing at

60 The poem by Christina Rossetti, first published in *Time Flies: A Reading Diary* in 1885.

Lawton." She sang with a strong Gloucestershire accent:

> " 'The King of all Kings to this world being brought,
> Small store of fine linen to wrap Him was sought.
> But when she had swaddled her young Son so sweet,
> Within an ox manger she laid Him to sleep' "[61]

"That was my favourite verse. Can't you hear Ben Mathers? He was always so *concerned* at the small store of fine linen." She would say no more. Ethel felt herself gently silenced. She was reminded of their childhood, when she had sometimes been put in her place by the quelling dignity of the little beauty.

The door opened, and Nanna looked in. "Miss Danvers, could you come please?"

"All right, Nanna. I'm so sorry, dears, she sometimes gets a little difficult, and then it's better for Nanna to have someone. It's done me so much good, being all four together again. Do come often and cheer us up. Will you let yourselves out? Mind that nasty turn on the stairs." She gave a hand to each and kissed them.

The two friends walked along the shining road. It had stopped raining, and the long streams of light reflected from the small shop windows made the dull little street bright and homely.

"What pluck Nell has," said Fanny. "It makes one ashamed of one's grousing."

"Yes," said Ethel, "and didn't you love what she said about Christmas? I had come to think it was only fun for Children. But I see just to be jolly children again is only a small part of it."

---

[61] From the folk-carol 'The Virgin Unspotted'.

"Yes, but the children's fun is very sweet," said Fanny uncomprehending.

"I know, but I wonder if sometimes people aren't so loaded with presents and fun, and warm with love, that there is no room for Him in the fun. What Nell said makes me feel He comes especially to those who are in trouble, and perhaps to people like me too, who are not in trouble, but just stupid and lonely. So that at Christmas He setteth the solitary in families."[62]

"I always liked to hear you holding forth," said Mrs. Bentley, "though you were slow in getting under way," and then with motherly encouragement: "I think what you say is very nice. But," breaking off, "there's your 22 over there: you must run, child, if you want to catch it."

---

[62] He places the lonely in families. Psalm 68:6

A SEASON AT THE SCEPTRE

Tea was over in the lodgings, and now they were looking at photographs. The rouge on Vere's worn and agreeable face had only been half arranged, and powder lay all over her shoulders.

"I know *you* don't mind," she said to the dressy friend, Nita Elphick. "As to George he doesn't know whether I've touched up my face or not."

The dressy friend did not mind and George grinned. George and Vere were together in a West End engagement at last, and now, safe in port, could afford to be shabby on Sundays; Nita, struggling outside, must still be smart.

Vere and Nita discussed the photographs. George listened—he seldom talked—and thought how clever they both were.

Nearly all the photographs had one trait in common; the sitters were resolutely doing something to impress the public. But one of them, wrapped in tissue paper and tied with mauve ribbon, was quite apart from the rest. It was not that the girl was better looking—the standard of appearance was very high—though the pose of her head on her shoulders was exquisite, and her features of superior delicacy. It was not that she was more refined, though there was a kind of inborn distinction which drew one to her. It was the expression, the trustful, half-brooding tenderness in the eyes. She was smiling to herself; she seemed occupied with sweet secret thoughts, not concerned with managers.

"I say," said Nita. "She's not a pro."

"Yes, she was."

"Fancy. I've never seen one a bit like her."

She put the photograph down, and took it up again.

"I love that portrait," said she. "I expect she was an amateur, and gave it up. What's she doing now?"

"She's dead," said Vere.

"Is she? Hard luck."

"George loved her. You used to say she was the truest lady on God's earth, didn't you, George dear?"

"So she was," said George; he had been fidgeting nervously ever since Nita had taken up the photograph. "I say, Vere, you and Elphick won't mind, but I think I'll go out for a bit of a turn. Might go to Church perhaps."

"Yes, do; that'll be nice," said the motherly Vere.

"George was awfully keen on her," she continued, as the front door slammed, "he can't bear to speak of her even now; he's so tender hearted. But I've never, never known anything so sad as it was, Elphick."

"Tell me," said Nita. "I remember your thrilling tales of old. You tell me things as if they happened yesterday. Now, once they're over with me, I never think of anything again."

"I daresay I shall howl," said Vere, "but don't mind if I do."

This was the tale she told.

"It was when I was walking on at the Sceptre; Mervyn's season with "The Unknown Idol." That was the time I thought walks on in town might help you. I was feeling pretty cheap, it was so sickening being a chorister again, and there were all those West End girls in their expensive furs, either ignoring you, or saying 'Good morning,' so that you would rather they hadn't. And she came up and spoke to me, not in their swanky accent; but so prettily—of course I know mine's Cockney—and she asked me where she ought to stand, and I hoped she was a pauper like me.

"We did some movements that were rather complicated; she couldn't manage them, and I helped her. She *was* an amateur, if you like, had never been behind in her life, but she wasn't a bit like one—they're so airified and gracified. She was more helpless and innocent than you can imagine anyone could be. She lived down in the country, and she'd never had to do anything for herself, she couldn't even darn her stockings. Anybody could take her in. Our dresser, Lizzie, lost ten shillings Saturday night as usual. Of course Queen—one of the girls called her Queen, because of the way she held her head, and it stuck to her; her real name was Violet Heron—well, of course Queen gave Lizzie the ten shillings. I told her afterwards what an old trick it was, and she said, 'I'm sure people aren't like that.' She had no push in her, she used to take the worst place or the worst anything. So she was often late and got into hot water with Vesey, but that never seemed to trouble her. She was always giving the girls things, but she didn't spend enough on herself. I said to her, 'You mustn't dress so quiet, like a High School teacher. And your lovely hair, you don't make half what you might of it.' She said, 'Don't I?' and laughed.

"I said, 'You ought to make people look at you on and off the stage. I should love you in cerise.' But she went on with her old tweed coat and skirt.

"She said, 'I don't know that I want people to look at me.'

"I said, 'Then what the dickens did you go on the stage for?'

"She said, 'Just to act. I love to get in a room by myself and act. I never *could* be Juliet, but when I'm alone I can imagine what it's like.'

"Of course she ought never to have gone on the stage. If the stage were something different to what it is, and she had been quite different to what she was, it might have been all right. Not but that she could act, mind you. We used to study parts together. George used to come up too, that was how it began with George and me, and she used to make me cry buckets full.

"We had rather more Shakespeare than I wanted, but it suited George down to the ground. He revels in Shakespeare, only being short, he never seemed to get on in it. There was a bit in Juliet she loved, I can hear her say it now:

" 'My bounty is as boundless as the sea,
My love as deep; the more I give to thee,
The more I have, for both are infinite.'

"How her eyes shone, her beautiful eyes.

"I said, 'It's tall talk though, isn't it?' I think myself there is a lot of tall talk in Shakespeare.

"She said, 'I think I could feel like that.' Then she smiled to herself, such a sweet smile, and said, 'I'm sure I could.'

"We used to sit in the dressing-room, we had such long waits. One day she quite forgot herself, and went out and marched down the passage and ran into Danby. He was listening, and he was so jolly, and clapped his hands and said, 'That's great!' There was a common girl we called Barney, and she said, 'That's a good wheeze running into Danby by accident, so that we can show off how brainy we are, only I haven't the brass to try it myself.' You know what an artist Danby is, he was quite a big pot even then. He was such a gentleman, made me take his chair once in the green room, when I had a toothache. I know men do talk to the new girls, but he talked to the new boys, and they hardly ever do *that*, do they? Not but what he always kept up his dignity. He often talked to Queen. He used to ask how she'd take certain parts, and what she thought of some of the toffs. When it came to criticizing Horner in Hamlet, I thought it was going too far, but she never took in how they all must have their boots licked. Barney was the one for that, she was always oiling up to the big parts, putting bunches of violets in their way, and running their errands for them when their dresses weren't handy. It doesn't pay. Cynthia Bawn used to smile her eternal smile ever so sweetly, but smiles don't lead you far. One day Queen was ill and couldn't come, and Danby said to me, 'Where's your friend?' Then he went on, 'You know we, who are getting old, are looking anxiously about among the young ones to see who is going to carry on the torch. Some of you ought to do pretty well. You'll make a useful actress, so stick to it.' (I was bucked when he said that.) 'But I hope great things of that child. She has the unknown quality x—don't they talk about x in algebra?—which makes the actor. Now the thing she's got to do is to develop it. You girls so often think you can float to the top on suppers. I don't think they ever get you to the top, they certainly will never keep you there. We're a lazy lot, and we let the public expect too little of us. Art is a severe mistress, and what she wants is real hard work. Enthusiasm won't take its place. Miss Heron's got enthusiasm, but I'm not sure she's got application.'

"I asked him if I might write down what he said, because I knew Queen would want to hear. So he said 'All right, Boswell, you make me feel quite embarrassed.'—Those brainy men say silly things sometimes.—I came across the paper only the other day, so that's how I remember.

"I told Queen, and she laughed with joy. But I think he was wrong about suppers myself. If George could have asked the critics to champagne lunches, he might have had a theatre of his own by now; the talent was there all right. She seemed to take to me, I don't know why, for some of the girls were swells, or thought they were, and I fell in love with her the first minute I saw her. She never talked much in the dressing-room. She used to learn Shakespeare to herself. Of course with most girls that would be swank, but it wasn't with her. She took it to rehearsals sometimes, and Tommy Pease, he was rather a jolly boy, used to say, 'At it again. Now my motto is, "Blast the blooming bard." '

"The other girls liked her, you couldn't help it, but they used to laugh at her a lot. Our dressing-room wasn't at all bad for talk, but for Barney. I don't think Queen generally understood what she meant, but one day Barney talked really hot stuff, and Queen turned quite white. So one of our girls said to Barney, 'You've quite upset the poor Queen, and she's not to be upset, so don't do it again,' so she didn't. But Queen never took any notice of Barney after it, she used to look through Barney as if she wasn't there.

"She was so lovely, but the men didn't go after her much, she was too good for them. Of course there were always three or four round Barney, she was great sport, she was more revue style, eccentric dancing. Mervyn used to come behind pretty often, and I noticed he sometimes said a word to Queen, and didn't every eye in the company notice it too?

"Mervyn was one of those smart men, and he was still very handsome then. He had such an easy, pleasant way with girls; of course he knew so much about them, and he never said anything anybody could mind, like Vesey did.

"Queen told one one day Mervyn had seen her acting, and had asked her to come and walk on. That was how she got to the Sceptre. You know what Mervyn is, so I guessed what he was after—she didn't—and I just said, 'I wouldn't tell the other girls. There's so much talking round in a company.'

"We had a newcomer in our dressing-room, a married woman, Elise Marshall. She was rather loud in her talk, so I asked her not because of Queen.

" 'Rot,' she said. 'If she's on the stage, she'd better begin to know something about it.'

"She talked about Mervyn one day; she said, 'Some people are down on Mervyn, and I daresay he isn't a saint, and drops you like a hot coal. Mrs. M. would see to it if he didn't. But he often gives a girl a chance she'd have to wait years for, and now my husband's dead, and I've got to work again, he's done something for me, which is more than anyone else has.'

"That very evening Queen told me Mervyn had asked her how she liked the part of Daphne. He said, 'I seem to see you in it. I daresay we shall be able to fit you in somehow on tour.' It was a small part, but it was good. Queen was wild with joy. She said, 'Daphne's the part I want to play,' and she went on as if she was mad.

"I wasn't quite so mad myself, because I didn't see Mervyn risking even Daphne on tour without getting something for it. And he wasn't.

"Queen said to me quite coolly after the show one night, 'Mr. Mervyn has asked me to go and stay with him at Brighton next week-end. Isn't it odd of him? I don't know him a bit. But I can't go because I'm going to my aunt.'

"I was struck dumb, I thought she was so different. I asked her, 'Do you mean you'd go then, Queen?'

" 'No, I don't know that I would,' said she. 'It would be so much nicer if I knew Mrs. Mervyn. I shall feel so shy of both of them. I wish he'd asked you too.'

"She had no more idea what he meant than a baby. I nearly laughed. I thought I'd better tell her. I couldn't see her face because it was dark, besides I looked the other way. She just said, 'I see.' Not a word more.

"I didn't like to ask her anything. You couldn't talk to her as you do other girls. Of course she was quite a cut above us all. They used to say in the dressing-room her father was related to some earl. I don't know about that, but she *was* different. If she didn't like anything you said, she'd go into herself and get quite silent, and I can tell you felt squashed. I was always a little afraid of her in a way.

"I wasn't much of a chattermug, knew too much about a dressing-room for that, but when Cis Darrell and I were talking about Queen, I couldn't help mentioning the long week-end, and Cis laughed till she cried.

" 'The only thing is to take her to a *crèche* immediately,' said Cis. 'It isn't safe to let her go about this wicked world.'

"Cis gave me her word faithfully she wouldn't tell a soul, and all the dressing-room was talking about it next day.

"One of them said to Queen, 'Congrats, you lucky beast.' Queen said, 'Why? It isn't my birthday.'

" 'Oh, rats,' said Barney. 'Tell us about your glad rags for Brighton.'[63]

"You should have heard Queen say, 'I have no intention of going to Brighton.' Then she opened her book and began reading.

"I said to Queen afterwards I was very sorry I had let it out.

" 'It doesn't matter,' said she.

"Then I said, 'They'll all think you quite mad.'

---

63 Glad rags: best clothes.

"She said, 'You don't. You wouldn't go.'

"I said I didn't know, he hadn't asked me, but I was jolly glad she wasn't going.

"Elise Marshall joined us then, and she said, 'You're the only girl in the whole crowd who's really keen on acting. Of course they say they love their Art, but they wouldn't work for their Art to save their lives. How I loathe a stage crowd, always have. I wouldn't be here an hour, if I had the brains for anything else. Here's a chance for you, which you're damned lucky to get. You're not a man's girl, anyone can see, and you don't make the best of yourself off the stage, though you're so much more beautiful than any of them. Remember an actress's years for making good are very few, though there's time enough once she's arrived. As for the right and wrong I don't pretend to know, but the stage isn't a blooming vicarage. And I can tell you this: all those Bernhardts and people you're so mad about would never have let a little petty scruple stand in the way of their art. If Vere has been backing you up about not going, I shall call it cattish. She'd jump at it herself.'

"And that was exactly true. I'd been thinking it was hard that, when George and I wanted the money so much—we were just engaged on rather less than two-pence a year—she *should* get the chance, and I was glad she was missing it.

"Marshall went on at Queen, till it was time for the coming show. 'You realize, I suppose,' said she, 'you haven't the smallest chance of Daphne without it.'

" 'But Mr. Mervyn says I shall have it.'

" 'My dear kid, when you want to catch a fish, you have a bait, don't you?'

"But Marshall couldn't get anything out of Queen except, 'I couldn't.'

"Another time Marshall said, 'It seems to me so ridiculous a girl thinking herself so important. It's not a matter of life and death. I remember two or three rather jolly little times at Eastbourne with Mervyn, and then there weren't any more, and no tears were shed by anybody. I had a run of quite a good part, though I shan't relate my life's story and all my brilliant successes after the fashion of most middle-aged choristers.'

"Of course people said afterwards Mervyn added a little on to Marshall's screw in consideration of her chats with Queen,[64] but I don't think Marshall was that sort.

"At last she said, 'You're the most obstinate little cuss, and I wash my hands of you.'

"What she said about cattish wounded me ever so, and I talked to Queen too, till I was tired. I went on for weeks. Mervyn used to talk to Queen, but not too often, he was very quiet, never a bit familiar.

"Suddenly one night she said to me, 'I'm going to Brighton next Saturday.'

"I didn't know what made her yield, I didn't ask her. I said, 'Are you?' I couldn't say any more. It was what I'd been urging, and I felt so down, I went and cried. I wanted her to be high above us all. I was unhappy about her, and I know that made me fly out, and we had a sort of row, and I hardly saw anything of her all that week. She went with Cis and Marshall.

"Barney said to me, 'What do you think Marshall says about you? "I really thought Vere had a large heart, but those proletariat girls from the provinces *have* to be petty and jealous." And I asked one of the boys what proletariat means, and it means common.'

---

64 Screw: wages, salary.

"I hadn't expected Queen would throw me over, but Cis and Marshall were both rather toffs compared to me, and Marshall took no end of trouble rigging Queen out.

"Queen quite changed that week. She talked without ceasing, and kept us in fits in the dressing-room, I never knew she was a comedian, but she wasn't our Queen.

"Of course everyone knew about Brighton. I wouldn't tell George, but you may be sure someone else did. He never said a word about it.

"Then people began oiling. Cynthia Bawn came up all graciousness one night, she'd never seemed to see Queen before, and she said, 'That brooch of yours makes me feel simply wicked, Miss Heron. I know I shall steal it. I'm perfectly mad on old paste.'

"She expected Queen to fall prostate, but Queen answered as if Cynthia had been anyone.

"Another night Lizzie broke Queen's crown, as she was putting it on.

" 'Never mind,' said Queen, smiling graciously upon us as calm as you please, with the sequins pouring down. 'I don't think it'll show.'

" 'How we roared; it was Queen all over.

" 'Oh,' says Lizzie in a frantic state, 'whatever will Mr. Vesey say? He never misses anything.'

" 'Give me a needle and thread,' said Barney. 'I'll do it,' and before you could have thought it possible she mended it. Barney never put herself out for anyone, unless there was a reason, and out it came. 'There you are, old dear, and when you're number oneing with Daphne, don't forget your Barney.'

Queen said thank you to Barney, as if she was mud in the road, never a smile.

"Cis said afterwards, 'I'm going to pass you on a bit of advice I had about the stage. "Never make a friend, and never make an enemy." Don't talk to Barney like that. People will simply say you've got too big for your boots.'

" 'I think Barney's repulsive,' said Queen.

" 'Oh, of course she's a worm, and talks smuts, but that's no concern of yours. Besides you can get worse than Barney. I was with a tip top West End crowd once; these people think this is West End, but Mervyn's quite provincial. We had society girls, one with a title they said, and Oxford students, not a bit like this lot, and I thought they were decadent, and their everlasting talk about their passions made me sick.'

"But Queen went on being just as freezing to Barney.

"I've often thought of that week, the precious time I wasted seeing so little of her. I felt so miserable I couldn't wish her good luck, when she went off on the Saturday morning. She *did* look smart—Marshall had such taste—and *so* lovely. Her last words to me were, 'See you at the show on Monday.'

"On Sunday evening George and I were talking in my digs, when a ring came, and it was Queen. I shouldn't have recognized her for the same girl.

" 'Why, whatever's the matter?' I said. She didn't answer.

" 'You're seedy, ducky, aren't you?'

" 'Oh, no,' said she. 'Not at all.'

"George saw something was up, and was off like a shot, but she wouldn't say a word more when we were alone. I said she must go to bed, and I would bring her some tea. She just shook her head, and sat looking at nothing, but she did drink the tea. I felt her hand. Oh, it was cold, but she snatched it away from me.

" 'Come along into my bed,' I said.

" 'Oh no,' she said. 'Certainly not. But if you'll let me, I should like to stay here to-night. May I sleep on the sofa?'

" 'That awful bony sofa,' I said, 'you can't sleep on that. Do come.'

" 'No,' she said quite sharply, 'I've told you I'd rather not. But don't stay up for me. I'm perfectly all right.'

"There seemed like a wall of ice between us. Next morning she said, 'I don't forget what you were last night, only never ask me anything, will you, or speak of it to me.'

"When we got into the dressing-room, I saw Barney was bursting with joy. 'Oh,' she said, 'I met Hastings in the Strand, and she said, "Have you heard the latest? I was down at Brighton yesterday, and I met Mervyn, and he said 'My dear girl, I've got the hump. My week-end's been a hoar frost, and I want a tonic. What ever am I to do?' " '

"I'd seen Hastings; awfully loud and awfully smart. I knew she'd enjoy it, she was an old flame of Mervyn's.

"The girls all looked at Queen. She went on making-up as if she hadn't heard, but I could see her hand trembling.

" 'Bobby says it's the best scream out,' said Barney. 'As for Hunter—you know how dry Hunter is—' At first I couldn't speak to stop Barney, but I was just beginning 'Of all the beastly,' when Cis Darrell gave me a kick, and said 'Why is life always a burden on Monday? Barney, play the giddy goat, and give us Vesey, then I may feel brighter.'

"Cis came up to Queen walking home, and said, 'Don't mind them. It doesn't really matter a bit, if it was a frost. It's a compliment. Mervyn's nothing, only rich and handsome. His mind is just about the size of a button. Remember what Danby thinks of you, and feel jolly proud.'

"Queen said, 'Thank you awfully, Cis. It's not what they think, it's what I think of myself for going.'

" 'Oh, repentance,' said Cis, 'I've no use for that. Life's too short.'

"George told me all the boys were buzzing about it. He said, 'You know what a shrinking, sensitive thing a woman is. The stage is the beastliest muck for girls.'

"I don't know that sensitive and shrinking were the words for Barney, or Marshall either, if you come to that. They aren't the words for many of us, but I liked George to think it.

"The boys changed in their manner to Queen. Hunter, he was odious; he came up to Queen in the wings one night, and said with a low bow, 'I'm quite aware that this isn't correct for court circles, but the Prime Minister being out of town, I can't send my invites through him. Will my gracious Liege deign to come to supper, Mervyn included or not, according to taste?'

"Queen gave him a look straight in his face, then she turned and walked away, and he didn't try it on again. But I was standing near her, and she was shaking all over.

"George was there too, and he went and told Hunter to leave Queen alone, and Hunter said out loud so that everybody should hear, 'Truly grieved, but I had no idea Queen was your tart, thought it was the Gov.' And that's what they call a West End actor. George waited for Hunter outside and punched his head, only he had to be careful where, so that it wouldn't show, because of Vesey. Hunter was rich, and whiskies and sodas flowed from him, and Vesey never refused a whisky.

"It wasn't only the boys that changed to Queen, they all did. It was like wolves in a pack. I heard Cynthia Bawn say very distinctly in her nasty, mincing voice; 'The sole topic of conversation in this Company seems to be Miss Heron. I'm afraid I've never been able to take the smallest interest in novices. Oh, please don't move'; that was to Queen. 'Well, perhaps you *have* chosen rather a conspicuous position.'

"Lizzie said to her, 'Now Queenie, or whatever you call yourself, get out of my way do.' Fancy a dresser, there to wait on us, daring to call her Queenie. But Queen just said she was sorry, and never put her in her place. I told her she ought not to let Lizzie presume. She said, 'I didn't notice her.'

"She was very proud, but in a way she cared much less than I should have done for all the slights. I think she felt Barney and the crew so far below her. Still she did feel it. She went into herself, and hardly talked to people. She didn't cheer up a bit, and I could see how both Cis and Marshall got fed up with her. 'Let her buck up,' said Cis, and not go about like a dying duck, asking for pity.'

"I arranged she should come and share my digs. It was no use her fretting by herself, and she often would sit for half an hour together just looking at the fire.

"I didn't know what to do for her; when I said anything, it always seemed the wrong thing. Once I said, 'George and I don't think a bit the worse of you,' and she winced, as if I'd hit her. Another time I took her hand, and she said, 'No, don't. I'm not a subject for petting.' So I just had to leave her to herself.

"She gave me all the things she got for Brighton. I said I couldn't take them. 'Those lovely things, and you looked such a dream in them.' She stamped her foot, and said, 'You *are* to have them, otherwise I shall burn them.' And of course they did come in jolly handy.

"Mervyn never talked to her now, and naturally there wasn't a word more about Daphne. Vesey was beastly to her, now he knew Mervyn was off her, and she was more absent and kept making mistakes; she even missed an exit.

"One day Vesey was talking in the green room about success. 'I've had twenty years' experience,' said he, 'and girls may have x's or y's, or the whole alphabet if they like' (that was a hit at Danby I knew, he and Danby hated one another) 'but there are three things *I* want to know about an actress. Can she come up to time? Can she wear her clothes? Can she do what she's told? *Really* what she's told mind you, not what she chooses to think she's told. If she can, then I can get her through her part, and she can have all the kudos. And if she can't, I've no use for her. But then I'm not highbrow, so I don't think that if a chorister has been four months in a show, and mulls her exits at the end of it, she's going to be a star.'

"Of course that was meant for Queen.

" 'I wonder if Vesey was right,' Queen said to me.

"I said, 'There's something in it, I should think,' I thought it was best to rouse her.

" 'It seems a death knell,' said she. 'I had hoped absurdly much, I know. I never thought the stage would be like this, Vere.'

" 'There are much worse companies than this I can tell you. Look at Cis and Marshall, for Marshall is superior, if she is loud, not to mention Danby and several of the men.'

" 'Oh, I didn't mean that. I think Cis and Marshall are splendid, and everyone's been awfully good to me.'

"Of course I didn't think they had, but slights seemed to slide off her. I said, 'What did you think the stage would be like?'

" 'Heaven,' said she, and laughed.

"Cis said to me one day, 'Do make Queen go out and see people more. There's a woman coming to tea with me to-morrow, brainy, but quite jolly, she'd suit Queen, and it isn't a party, only her.'

"I never have been extra keen on theatrical tea parties. One gets a bit fed up with everybody trying their hardest to play the giddy goat. Queen used to sit and smile and look sweet, but she always said they made he feel shy, and she didn't know what to say. I didn't know if she'd want to go to Cis, but she did.

"Of course we got talking about big pots, and how they were getting on. The friend, Miss Lennox, said, 'Ruth Arundale has a little Jew running her. Isn't that beastly?'

" 'Is it?' said Cis. 'Most people have their little Jews.'

" 'That's what's so sickening,' said Miss Lennox, 'Taking it for granted. People do the same about business and politics, take it for granted you *must* be unscrupulous.' 'Now don't get excited, my child,' said Cis' she was always very cool. 'I don't know about politics and care less, but I do know about the stage.'

" 'But it's not true,' said Miss Lennox. 'There are hundreds and hundreds of actresses who aren't that.'

" 'Yes, I know. There's you, for instance,' said Cis, 'only we don't all happen to have invaluable husbands who can run us.'

"I didn't know what Queen would feel, but when we came out, she said; 'I do like Miss Lennox, it was like coming out of a tunnel into daylight to hear her talk.'

"I asked her what she meant, and she said such a queer thing that only she would say. 'I see it's only I that am rotten, not the stage.'

"There was a new girl came, one of those dark, flashy, foreign-looking girls, and Mervyn used to talk to her, as he did to Queen.

"The run was coming to an end, and they were settling the crowd that was to go on tour. There were a lot of small parts, and all we choristers were wild to know if they would take us. It was Vesey who settled them mostly, and some of the big parts too. Mervyn was so slack.

"That new girl, Dulcie Wantage, came prancing up one day. 'I've got Daphne in No. 2, girls,' she sang out, 'Mervyn says it's private, but I can't help that. The lamb says he saw me in the part from the first.'

"We all felt jolly sick. She'd only been in the company a week, and none of us were keen on her. No one congratulated her but Queen. She went up to her and said so sweetly, 'It's splendid, Miss Wantage.' She really meant it too. She said to me afterwards, 'Miss Wantage will make a much better Daphne than I should have done.'

"George and I got taken, only small parts, but we were to be together. We'd hung on late in the season on the chance of getting something bigger with Mervyn, and it was too late for other shops.

"Queen didn't get anything at all. I was awfully afraid after what Vesey said about mulling exits.

"We were waiting in a queue outside the office, each one going in and hearing her fate.

"Well, Queen,' calls out Barney. 'What's the report?'

"Queen looked at Barney, and said, so that we could all hear, 'Nothing.'

"Barney understood all right, but she said, just to down Queen, 'What do you mean?'

" 'I'm not going on tour.'

" 'Shame,' said Barney, beaming all over. She had got quite a good part.

"Queen told me afterwards Vesey said Mervyn was sorry he had overlooked her, and she needn't worry, he'd see about it.

" 'Why didn't you tell the girls that, instead of letting Barney crow?'

" 'I don't think he meant it,' said Queen; she'd learnt a thing or two during the run. 'And I don't care if they do crow.'

"When George heard Queen was out of everything, he went straight off and spent all his week's screw on roses for her. I was awfully glad, but I did grudge the money a little. It meant he only had bread and cocoa for nights, and that wasn't good for him, he never has been a bit strong. George thought more of her in a way than what he did of me. I didn't mind, he was quite right. It wasn't love, it was different, it was something more.

"She said to me, 'George is a darling, Vere, but I *hate* taking those roses.'

" 'He can't bear your having such a rough time.'

" 'If I have, I've brought it entirely on myself. How could I have gone, oh, how *could* I have gone to Brighton? It was what Marshall said about losing Daphne and petty scruples, but in my heart I never once considered it was fair to get on like that. To think that dear beautiful acting should be contaminated like that. I knew what you thought of me; you thought just what I thought of myself. That's why I wouldn't come near you. And I used to look down on Barney, but Barney never sank to that.'

" 'No,' said I. 'But wouldn't Barney have given her eyes to have the chance? But Mervyn would draw the line at revue hacks. Barney was Vesey's discovery.'

"She'd have hated what I said if she'd heard me, but she wasn't listening. She went on, 'The one thing I can bear to think of is that I didn't get the part.'

"I'd never thought of it in that way before, but then I've never found managers worrying *me* to go away week-ends with them, so the occasion hasn't arisen. Of course I've had fellows after me, but some men would go after a lamp post.

"I had hoped, when Vesey wouldn't take Queen, Danby would have done something for her, but he seemed to have dropped her. People said he'd lost a lot of money gambling, and had to give up going into management, as he'd meant to do. Anyhow he looked awfully glum, and wouldn't say a word. I thought it just like men; make a fuss of you when they're in the mood, and chuck you when they're in another mood.

"That same night, after Queen talked about Brighton, Barney lost her brooch, and promptly went into hysterics.

" 'Oh, dry up,' said Cis. 'I'm nothing but nerves to-night, and your yowls give me the pip.'

"Still she couldn't have come on without a brooch, Vesey would have turned her down. We none of us were too keen on lending brooches to Barney, because the things you lent to Barney you never saw again; it really wasn't fair to the dressing-room to have an outsider like Barney in it. Then Queen took off that paste brooch Cynthia Bawn had admired, and said to Barney, 'Have this, won't you?'

"I knew what was in her mind, but I wasn't surprised when Barney said, 'Yes, you think it's worth while to oil up to me now, but I can tell you you're a damned sight too late, my lady.'

"Queen didn't seem to resent what Barney said. She said to her, 'I'm not oiling, though it's quite natural you should think so. But don't have the brooch, if you'd rather not.'

"Queen had heavy, sleepy eyelids, very large, though they were lovely, and she had a way of lifting them slowly when she opened her eyes. Her movements were slow, they came in so useful for classical parts. She didn't lift her eyebrows often, but it gave her a proud look, though it was sweet too—I simply can't describe it—but it made you feel you couldn't take liberties with her. Barney had got a better part than any of us on tour and Queen had got nothing, and Barney crumpled up, and said, 'You're an awfully quaint girl. Didn't somebody say you were a clergyman's daughter? I expect that's why it is. I don't mind if I do have the brooch, thanks ever so.' And you may be sure she lost it, and I saw her wearing it on the sly afterwards. But I wished Queen hadn't given it to her, because all the girls thought she *was* oiling. You could never make them understand, not that I would ever have let out what Queen had said to me.

"On Sunday Queen said she was going down home, and would be back on Monday. She lived somewhere near Bristol, and was devoted to her mother. That was all I knew about her. It seemed awful extravagance to me to go all that way for one night when the run would be over soon, and she could get a nice long holiday in the country if she liked, and so I told her, but she said, 'I can't stand it any longer.' She'd never said a word of complaint before, but it made me see how she'd felt it all. She didn't come back on Monday. She telegraphed to say her mother was dead.

" 'Jolly convenient sometimes,' said Hunter, 'I buried my mother regularly every Derby Day for years, when I was in an office.'

"She looked dreadful the evening she came back. I went and kissed her; she didn't take any notice, but she said even before she sat down, 'Vere, I must tell you everything.' I was sure it was going to be something horrible. I said, 'Tell me to-morrow, you're so tired.' She shook her head, and said, 'I killed mother, Vere. I told her, and the shock killed her. I've always told her everything. She was very ill, and the doctor had said any shock would kill her. I had no idea. She wouldn't have me told. The look she gave, that last look; it's always before my eyes. Father couldn't bear to see me in the house. He will never be able to forgive me, and I shall never go home again.'

"I pulled her face down against mine; her cheek was burning hot. If only she'd been like other girls and would cry. I begged her not to keep it in. She laughed and said, 'One cries for happiness. How can I cry now?' She could cry so beautifully, when she was acting, but I never saw her cry in real life, except once.

"I tried to soothe her. I said, 'I don't think you quite know what you're saying. No wonder with all you've been through.'

" 'Oh yes,' she said, 'I know quite well.' She talked on, going over and over it again. I can't remember all she said. First I tried to get her off it; then I thought she'd better work it off. All the while I didn't know whether she'd got hold of some illusion. I remember her saying, 'If only one could be dead, and it was all over.' She said it twice. She was rather abnormal, and I was frightened of being with her, and I left her and went to bed. I hated myself for it.

"I went back to her. I didn't know what might happen if I left her alone. She was sitting with her head in her hands. I don't think she'd noticed I'd gone. I implored her to come to bed, she wouldn't stir. The only way to get her to come was to go to bed myself. I lay and listened for her. At last she came.

"She didn't sleep for hours. When she did I heard her calling 'Mother' over and over again, but when she was awake she lay quite still. I was so anxious, I only slept when the light was coming on. I thought she would be worn out in the morning, but on the contrary she was up very early. She came and stood by my bed. I was hardly awake. She looked flushed, but she seemed better, and spoke in her usual voice.

" 'I think you felt anxious about me last night, Vere, but you needn't, for I shall be all right. I've been going over everything, and I think I've come to a conclusion. You see Mother's gone, and someone else has gone, it's all gone except you and work.'

" 'You mustn't forget George, Queen.'

" 'No, I mean George as well when I say you. I've made up my mind about my life. I'm going to work as hard as I can. I may get on. Hard work does get you on. Look at Dorothy Ellis and Miss Macintyre, everyone says it's only hard work with them. Don't suppose I shall ever forget all that's happened, not one instant of it, but I don't mean to dwell on the thought, or I shall go mad. Cis was quite right, I ought to have bucked up. I mean to be careful about being punctual, and about dress, and not to let myself dream as I did. I was very idiotic. I don't wonder Vesey didn't want me. So will you come with me to the agent you spoke of?'

"It was a great burden off my mind to hear her talk so calmly. We went to the agent's, but she seemed so dreamy, she'd have missed her chance of seeing him if it hadn't been for me.

"Next day I was busy rehearsing for the tour, we were starting very soon, and I left her to go to another agent's by herself. When it was dinner time, she hadn't come in. When it was time to go to the theatre, she hadn't come in. I had to go without her, and she never turned up. She didn't come to our digs until ever so late, and she didn't seem quite to know what she'd been doing. I smoothed it over with Vesey somehow, but I did worry at the thought of leaving her alone in London. I asked her to come on the tour with me, travelling private of course, then I could look after her, but she just said no, she must find work. 'I don't mean to dangle on to you and George and be a burden.' She was always obstinate, and now you couldn't move her at all. I'd have chucked the tour if I could, but I simply couldn't afford it.

"It was the day after the end of the run, and in the evening she got a letter from Danby, saying he had been talking about her to Lancelot Willis, and she was to go round to him at The Cambridge next morning. He ended up so nicely; 'Your foot's on the first step of the ladder and I'm sure you'll make good.' I thought she'd be ever so pleased, but she didn't seem to take it in.

"I screamed for joy; it was a great deal Danby writing like that. 'Here's a real bit of luck at last.'

"She only said, 'Yes, I suppose it is.'

"I felt almost angry with her. I said, 'Do be a little glad, just for my sake.'

"She said, 'I don't know about being glad, I don't think it would do any company much good for me to be in it. I'm not fit for them.'

" 'Whatever do you mean, Queen?'

" 'I have a sort of feeling I was only meant to bring harm to everybody.'

"I turned quite cold, it was such a mad thing to say. I said to her, 'I think it's very wrong of you, a girl who has been brought up like what you have, to say anything so wicked. It's silly too.'

" 'What should I do without you, Queen?'

" 'You've got George, you'd soon forget me. I don't think anyone wants me.'

"Then I shook her, and said she must take all that back. And at last I made her laugh, and she cheered up, and we talked about Danby's letter, and she seemed quite pleased. Then she kept shutting her eyes, and I asked if she was tired.

"She said, 'Yes, I haven't slept for nights.'

" 'Go to bed now.'

" 'Yes, I will.'

"She put her arms around me, and held me as if she couldn't let go.

" 'My own darling, darling friend,' she said, and the tears came pouring down her cheeks. 'No one else would have done what you've done for me; I've stored it all up in my heart for ever.'

"I thought they were such sweet words, and they were almost the last she ever said to me.

"I said, 'I haven't done anything, but I would, if I could. If I could only give you a good night, that would be something.'

" 'I think I shall sleep to-night,' she said.

" 'If you don't, I'll come and read to you. Leave your door open, and call if you want me.'

" 'No, don't come in, I shall be all right.'

"Perhaps it was only thinking of it afterwards, but it struck me she said it rather peculiarly. Still I had no idea what was in her mind. Perhaps you can guess what happened to the darling girl. I knocked at nine, she didn't answer, and I was so glad to think she was getting a good sleep at last. At ten I went in, for there wasn't much time for breakfast and getting off to The Cambridge. She looked so peaceful I didn't know what it was first of all. I called to her, and shook her, and she didn't move. I rushed for the landlady, and she tore for the doctor. He came at once, but he said it had all been over hours ago. She'd got some stuff from the chemist."

Vere stopped. "I shall be all right in a minute. Excuse my hanky. I can't tell you about that awful morning, but she'd left a letter for me. In it she said 'I mean to go on if I can, but if it's too much, you'll know that, if I'd lived to a hundred, I never could have loved you enough.'

"She enclosed a letter to a man I'd never heard her mention. She didn't talk about boys like the rest of us. She said he'd written proposing to her after her mother's death, and she'd refused him, and that in this letter she told him she loved him, and why she'd refused him.

"He called the very day she died. He had come straight to her, as soon as he could, after he got her answer. He only had two hours to spare, he had to get back. I don't know how I told him. He just said, 'Where is she?' And I gave him the letter, and he went in and shut the door. I waited to the last moment, then I had to tell him he must go. I went in, and he was kneeling by the bed, and had her in his arms.

"It's all years and years ago, and I remember it as if it was yesterday. There was never anyone in the least like her."

"It's all so awfully old fashioned," said Nita. She wiped her eyes, and reflected. "No one would mind like that nowadays. But I'm glad you told me. I don't think I'll stay to supper."

The tears softened her rather hard face, younger and handsomer than Vere's.

"They say you ought to have the hide of a rhinoceros for the stage, don't they? Sometimes I think there's too much rhinoceros about me. There was rather a beastly thing I was contemplating, but I rather think——" She took up Queen's photograph, looked at it again and went out of the room.

THE LOUNGE AT THE ROYAL

A violent September wind and rain were dashing themselves against the windows. This made the inhabitants of the lounge feel all the more comfortable. The lounge "tastefully furnished with the most up-to-date arrangements has a very artistic and homelike appearance." So ran the booklet of the hotel.

The hotel was not on the coast, because it wanted to have an exclusive clientele, and that is becoming more difficult to secure at the sea now that everybody goes there. So a healthy situation inland was selected. In deciding to be exclusive the hotel must give up being amusing.

The guests were dull, elderly, or feminine, and usually all three. There were some old ladies in the lounge now. They wore grey toupées, low necks, large bead necklaces, short skirts, coloured stockings and sports coats; they looked frightful. One had a cap and shawl and looked very nice. Besides this, she had the distinction of being great aunt to Sylvia, the youngest and prettiest person present. They all thought Sylvia charming; they did not find her formidable as they found most girls, and she seemed almost as pleased to play bridge with them as they to play bridge with her. The only other girl, Hilda Watford, older, thinner, smaller, sadder, dowdier, recognised her charms. She was a high school mistress in a third-rate town. She imagined Sylvia led a life of receiving homage.

In every circle there are those who set the tone. Here it was the two Miss Carlyons, both over fifty. They were clad in irreproachable tweeds; they seldom demeaned themselves to show the lounge anything more interesting. They lived in Kensington.

They spoke little of themselves and their affairs, but from the words "in the country," "with my brother," it had been discovered there was a "place" in the family. They owed their position to their charmingness, which alternated with an icy, kind civility. To set the tone was an achievement for a spinster; that is usually the province of the married. Everyone desired a word, above all a confidence, from them, and many were the strokes lavished on the invalid Miss Carlyon's horrid fat terrier, as a means of worming into intimacy. Miss Carlyon would give a tepid smile, saying: "Yes, he's rather a sweet thing."

Lovely, demure Mrs. Lacey, a widow, was particularly assiduous. She might have been jealous that her own pretty, tedious, amiable little girl was unnoticed. Mrs. Lacey hadn't always been so demure, she had come to rehabilitate, and she *could* not dress dowdily enough to match the rest.

The two husbands of the elderly ladies counted for very little, handing tea and telling anecdotes. The silent bachelor counted even less. There was a young man also, a son, handsome, with a motor bicycle. His mother, proud that he was spending his holiday with her, should have had the Miss Carlyons' place, but she was so insignificant she was always forgotten. He was now by Sylvia's side. They were talking too intently to see the benevolent glances bestowed on them. The hope of a love affair animated the whole house. Such things were uncommon there. The Wiltshire down the road, with its rowdy week-ends, had so many love affairs it was sick of them.

Tea was coming in, and the usual topics were being discussed. "What a miserable day. I do hope it will be better weather for my nephew when he comes on Saturday." For if the actual men present were unimportant, the potential men talked about gave prestige to the speaker. "He is so busy. They all turn to him for everything at the office."

"That is just the same with my son-in-law. He always——"

"My nephew is such a clever man. He was from quite a small boy. It has just been one scholarship after another."

"The schoolmaster told my son-in-law's father——"

"My nephew was delicate, which made it all the more remarkable. They thought they would have lost him as a child."

"Really, indeed. Now my son-in-law——"

"But I am thankful to say he is quite strong now, except his digestion occasionally. He has to be a little careful. I shall have to ask Mrs. Long; now the mutton to-day was really *hard*, more than tough."

"Yes," said the other, definitely giving up on the son-in-law. "And it was a nice joint. It is that she doesn't manage her over."

"And the plates," said Mr. Gibson, "the plates were stone cold to-day. If she can't warm her plates, the things *must* get cold."

"Altogether I thought we were rather badly treated," said Miss Carlyon, "stewed bunny. One draws the line at stewed bunny."

"You're quite right, Miss Carlyon," said Mr. Gibson, "and they don't give us enough joints. We ought to get the best English meat for the price they charge. Don't you think so too?" he said to Miss Watford, liking to bring in everyone. "And the helpings are so small, so very small, for a man after a hard morning's golf."

"I hadn't noticed," said Miss Watford. "I think the food's very nice." Her answer was meant to be unfriendly.

"And if only the linen was better kept. There was a darn in my serviette, I should be sorry to say how large. They should cut off the parts where it has worn thin, and use the rest for tray cloths. That's what we always do."

"I don't think I mind darned napkins, if I can get enough to eat," said Miss Carlyon, "but sometimes I can't."

"Talking of joints," said Mr. Gibson, he was still at that part of the conversation, "reminds me of a story I heard of two Scotchmen in Paris."

All laughed, especially his wife. The laughter made Mrs. Lacey rashly forget herself. "Paris makes me think of a naughty little rhyme I know, but *rather* a nice one. 'There was a young girl who said—' "

"Oh, please," broke in Miss Carlyon, "I can't do with naughty rhymes or naughty anything. I never can see the point."

It had been wondered whether Mrs. Lacey's lovely rose colour was her own. This could now be proved, for it immediately became much deeper. Miss Carlyon with the hard excluding spirit of aristocracy was glad to have drowned her.

But she was up again like a jack-in-the-box, she had often been snubbed before, and now looking at the couple in the far corner she leant towards Miss Carlyon and said, "They're going it pretty strong, aren't they? I think I shall have to see about the banns for them."

This was an assumption of intimacy which again was amiss.

"They? Who? Oh, Glen you mean," said Miss Carlyon. "I'm afraid I'm the last person to notice that sort of thing. I wonder if Kate has forgotten our tea."

Mrs. Lacey could seldom see a young man unmoved. She had overtaken Mr. Glen in the road one day and had shown him a merrier side. Miss Carlyon, walking by with her sister, had seen her pass and heard her laugh. She said in low clear tones: "It's as if a horde of chorus girls had come down upon us."

The young man had received her advances with the coldness of an Englishman and public school man.

Tea came in. Kate, the formidable head waitress, brought it.

"It's rather weak, Kate," said Miss Carlyon. "I think we shall want some more."

Mrs. Lacey would not have dared ask. Servants always patronized her and often bullied her, they never obeyed her.

The handing round of tea began. Mrs. Lacey and Mr. Gibson, battling to give Miss Carlyon hers, collided against each other. The tea spilt over Miss Carlyon's homespun.

"Oh, let me; how appallingly idiotic of me!" Mrs. Lacey was on her knees in an instant, mopping up the tea with her flimsy handkerchief.

"Oh, no, please, no. This old thing has had many a worse adventure than a drop of tea on it." ("House parties. A day on the moors with the guns," was in the minds of all.) "And must expect many more. You mustn't spoil that wonderful transparent affair of yours, Mrs. Lacey."

Mrs. Lacey knew she was wearing the wrong frock.

"Shall we come out?" said the young man to Sylvia. "Do you mind rain? I don't think it's raining much. There's something I wanted to say. One can't talk here."

She could see that his eyes were brighter than usual. She felt something was going to happen. She did not own to herself what. But as she came downstairs with her hat and coat on, she stopped to look out of window at the very ugly garden. "I love rain," she said to herself, with her thoughts not on rain.

She turned and met Miss Carlyon coming up.

"Excuse me," said Miss Carlyon, patting Sylvia's shoulder. She had snubbed Mrs. Lacey, because as she put it, "I loathe spoiling those things by mauling them about." "I know I'm previous, but I think he's a lucky man. You'll get so tired of hearing that, so I mean to be the first in the field."

Sylvia blushed, laughed, said: "But there isn't——" Squeezed Miss Carlyon's hand, and ran downstairs.

During their six weeks' intercourse she had thought of him continually. He was the first young man she had known intimately. There happened to be no marriageable men in her neighbourhood, nor in their poor and busy household was it possible to entertain the most exigent section of the community, the young bachelors. It was a matter of congratulation to the great aunt that it was she who had caught such a rarity as a young man—to old and elderly spinsters young men are generally a rarity—and she and Mrs. Glen had settled every detail of the match many a morning in the lounge when Sylvia was out.

Sylvia had settled no details. She had a dream of a small house somewhere near London, of a small room—she could see it getting dark, and lighted only by the fire. She could fancy him sitting there by her side. In that house he should never say he was so dull nobody could want him.

They did not talk much. The wind was blowing hard. Sometimes it came in violent gusts, and she was nearly driven back. He caught her hand; it thrilled her to feel his hand on hers. But he did not say the something he had come out to say. The noise of the wind made him shy, and both felt there was a certain luxury in delay. He knew that when he was with her he had a wonderful feeling of expansion, of entire well-being and satisfaction. The various girls, not many, who had attracted him before seemed trivial compared to her.

Now the rain was stopping. The sun came out. They looked at a sweet heathery expanse with a pleasing sylvan prospect beyond it. It was perhaps too reminiscent of pretty bits in watercolours, seen so often that the picture-gazer has become blasé. The wildness was perhaps too tame and cared for, the solitude too liable to be disturbed by rich motors. Yet the scene was impressing itself more on Sylvia than she knew, for at any minute of her after life she could recall it.

Meanwhile most of the women were writing letters in the lounge; the husbands did not feel there was anyone they wanted to write to. We might read one or two of the letters.

This is Miss Carlyon to her married sister:

"Dearest Millicent,

"Here we are at the Royal again, but I doubt whether it will be possible to come another year. The Longs do their best, I know, to stem the flood, but the proletariat is upon one everywhere. I used to like some of our suburban fellow guests—you remember the Powells from Wimbledon. How thankful one would be if it was Wimbledon now. It's Hornsey and Acton suddenly become extremely rich and appallingly respectable. They ooze new electrical devices. We have got one questionable character here and she is more boring than the respectable. The bridge is what Ralph would call Bumble-puppy, and the men's trousers are to match.[65] They make me feel even gladder than usual I haven't got a husband. Everyone is dreadfully kind. Frances says she *literally* will be killed with kindness, and she wants you to think of some new appropriate answer to '*How* are you to-day?'

"I am quite sure the further one gets down, the kinder people are, my tongue is getting so tired of saying 'Thank you.'

---

65 Played unskilfully or without regard for rules, or ignoring time-honoured conventions.

"We have one of the spectacled, teachery tribe, and she finds us all rather a trial. She wants us to improve our minds discussing books, and some of us have no minds to improve, and some of us want to keep what minds we have to ourselves. So now we are given up as hopeless and left to our frivolity.

"There's such a sweet thing in girls here. There's quite a satisfactory young man, too, and they're getting very much involved. He's not quite good enough, but then you know to my mind they rarely are, and he has a nice straight back.

"Dawes has been in a good temper the whole time. She and cook are the fastest friends, and Frances hasn't had her hair once pulled out by the roots.

"Your affect. sister,

"L. CARLYON."

Then Mrs. Gibson:

"You will be glad to hear we really have struck oil, as Dad says. The hotel is small, really quite like a private house, a very good class and *such* nice people. There are two Miss Carlyons who seem thorough gentlewomen; I fancy they are related to Viscount Carlyon.

"The rooms are rather cold, that is the worst of it, and my old chest trouble has been threatening me. But, as Dad says, it's the organization that is wanting, and the heating arrangements are so old fashioned. The staff is nice, so respectful, but as I say to Dad, a housemaid more on our floor would make all the difference. Not whole time, she might help Cook downstairs as well.

"I spoke to Mrs. Long one day about the laundry and she said to me, 'I'm so glad you mentioned it, Mrs. Gibson, but you know what the staff is nowadays, nothing but outings.' I wanted to tell you about some lovely runs we have had in the car, but I see it is getting late, so with fond love, etc."

Here is Miss Watford's:

"You said you wanted to hear, though holiday letters are always the same. This will strike out a new line however, for I've sprained my ankle and have to lie up. Edith doesn't mind, this country is new to her, and she really likes herself as company much better than anyone else. She will pick me up again when I'm ready. Meanwhile, I've read all my books and loathe the sight of a patience card. The people here don't like me, and I don't like them. They grumble the whole day long about everything. There are two rather bluish-blood ones, members of the governing class. I tried to talk about books, I was so tired of myself. You should have seen the scorn of the governing class when I mentioned Anatole France. But when we play golf we talk about that, so why mayn't we when we read?

"I'm the youngest but two here. There's a handsome young man, and a girl, rather pretty. I'm not generally susceptible, unfortunately I do seem to like the young man, and he likes that girl. I feel it's unfair she should be pretty and I am not, though of course it would be as unfair if I were pretty and she not.

"Next term is getting close, it is the forerunner of the next and the next and the next until I die or retire. Still things might be worse. There's an importunate widow here and they snub her too. I expect she feels it odd to be in the same boat with someone who wears glasses."

Mrs. Lacey also wrote to a female friend:

"Well, old bean, here I am, getting respectable. It's an awfully tough job, you try it. No you couldn't, you'd never stick it. I make howlers by the dozen. Once I said my husband was in the Navy (he's dead you understand, but I had him, Captain Lacey), and once on the Stock Exchange, and those cattish women wouldn't let it drop. I perspired with horror and had to go and wipe myself down. My poor face simply screams for powder, but they're catty about powder too, and seem to like grease, so there you are. I don't know if I shall ever understand them. First of all I thought if you were only dowdy enough, you would be right, but there's much more than that. It's funny when you're as pretty as I am that I shouldn't count. There's an old thing here would like to be gay and giddy on the Q.T., so that the wife shouldn't see, but I'm not taking any. I want the kiddy to have a nice cosy rich home, and I think if I'm careful Johnson will come to the scratch, and I dare say I shall fit into it after a time anyhow, and I'm a bit tired of racketing! There's a nice girl here just getting engaged. It's awfully sweet seeing it, particularly as you aren't here to say sweet things. Pip. Pip."

But the watched pot of the engagement was not yet boiling. As Rex and Sylvia walked along, a girl came up to them.

"Can you tell me if I'm anywhere near Basingstoke?" said she. "I've done the most crazy thing, I've lost my map; I left it behind at a pub I suppose, and I'm simply miles out of my way, aren't I?"

Rex entered into the matter with zest. She *was* miles out of her way.

"What makes it so maddening," the girl went on, "is that there is something wrong with my motor bike. Is there a good place for repairs here?"

"Rather," said Rex. "I don't know if I could help you. If it isn't very complicated, perhaps I might. May I have a look at it?"

By the time he had looked at it, the first gong was ringing for dinner at the Royal. It was settled quickly that she must come and spend the night there.

"It's full, but I'm sure we can wangle a room for you somehow," said he.

"If the worse comes to the worse," said Sylvia, "there's a bed in my room. You could have that."

They turned towards the Royal, the girl talking mostly to Sylvia.

At dinner she was placed next to Rex. She talked and laughed with him incessantly; the senior guests thought too much. They had plenty of silence themselves in which to study her. She was squat, brown, with a wide mouth, sharp nose, black bobbed hair and slits of brown eyes, decorated with horn-rimmed glasses. She wore a strange fancy-dress kind of jumper, and large beads. After dinner she sat down by Rex, securing one of the two best chairs; she leaned close to him, almost over him, as she talked in a loud drawl, stretching her wide mouth still wider and showing her ("what I must own," said Miss Carlyon) beautiful teeth.

Sylvia wouldn't disappoint her aunt of her bridge.

"Do you play, Miss Lasky?" said Mrs. Gibson; she was always the one to get hold of new people's names and make first advances.

"I should love it," said Miss Lasky, "but I can't tell the difference between clubs and spades; it's so tiresome of me."

This answer made Mrs. Gibson, who unlike Miss Carlyon thought a good deal of the Royal bridge, turn rather red.

Miss Lasky lighted a cigar and turned her chair away from everyone, managing to cut Rex and herself off from the rest of the room. As the dull game proceeded Sylvia's thoughts wandered sometimes. She wondered what they were talking about; something amusing, she heard him laughing.

They hadn't talked and laughed much more than half an hour when Lilith said: "It's almost stuffy with niceness here, isn't it? Do you think we could come and see after my motor bike?"

"Rather," said he. "They've got electric light in the garage. Let's come now."

They went out. Looking after the motor bike took a considerable time, for the lounge had long been deserted when they returned.

"What a shame, they've let the fire out," cried Lilith. "I was going to say coffee. I think half-past eleven is the best hour in the twenty-four for coffee. I'll make you some sometime, and you shall see."

Later he reflected how easy and jolly she was, saying anything that came into her head, whereas girls were often affected. From these wise thoughts he turned to Sylvia, and then to sleep.

Less lenient opinions had been expressed while Lilith and he were in the garage.

"What an excruciating young woman," said Miss Carlyon. "I don't mix much with people of that age, except nephews and nieces, and I'm thankful to say they're not at all like that. But is she typical?"

"Such a very plain girl," said Mrs. Gibson. "And, oh dear, what a dead set she made at poor Mr. Glen. Mrs. Glen, I do think your son is to be congratulated on his patience; he was a marvel."

"Yes," said Mrs. Glen. "Rex would never at all like that sort of girl."

"Some girls are so frantic for notice, and it's such a mistake; men hate that sort of thing. It isn't the plainness. Men will always be rather weak about a pretty face, and we can't blame them, but plain girls make just as good marriages. But she's so more than plain, repulsive." Still pretty, thrice married, with five proposals and a broken-off engagement to her credit, Mrs. Oxenford could speak authoritatively.

"And her lip salve. It's such common stuff, like what those Continental girls use," said Mrs. Lacey.

"Lip salve," said Miss Carlyon kindly. "Dear me, the cup of her iniquity seems quite full. What a comfort she's only staying till to-morrow."

Such kind of talk made the two men present very uncomfortable. They thought how spiteful women were about one another, and stole off to the smoking-room, though the fire never burnt so well there.

"Now they've demolished her utterly," said Miss Watford to Sylvia. "However, I daresay she'll survive it."

"Do you think she's nicer than that?" said Sylvia.

"No, she's as bad, only they don't dislike her because she's bad, but because she's different from themselves."

Her aunt was not well that night. Sylvia sat up with her. The night passed quickly. Her thoughts circled round the something that he was going to say. It would be said to-morrow. By to-morrow night perhaps her whole life would be changed. The night was not long enough to become familiar with the idea. She was glad it hadn't been said to-day. She felt she wouldn't have missed the anticipation.

In the morning she felt shy of going down and meeting him. She thought with Portia:

> "Scant this excess.
> I felt too much thy blessing: make it less!"[66]

Her shyness was wasted; he was not in the dining-room. She was in a hurry to give her aunt breakfast, and went quickly upstairs again. Her aunt required attention for some time; it was not till eleven that she again descended to find the full hurly-burly of the morning was in progress. Papers were being read, letters written, two men were talking about a Kodak, someone expressed an intention of going out. He was not to be seen. The kind and garrulous inquiries of unemployed people detained her for some minutes. Then Miss Carlyon said:

"Hasn't he finished mending her motor bike *yet*? They began early enough."

"Oh yes," was the answer, "I heard them say they were going to take it a turn down the road to see how it ran."

She wrote a letter. She could see the turn in to the garage from the lounge window, but the motor bike came not. Not did it come all the afternoon, nor all the evening.

Mrs. Glen had been trained not to feel anxiety at any delay in a motor, but she could not restrain a very fervent "At *last*" when the couple arrived at ten. The Royal was just going to bed; the Wiltshire was beginning to warm up its jazz.

---

[66] From Shakespeare's *The Merchant of Venice*, Act III - Scene II.

"We had the most topping, topping run," cried the high voice of Miss Lasky. Rex's voice chimed in: "It was simply gorgeous."

Sylvia looked at them both. The ugly Miss Lasky was not ugly; they had all been mistaken. No one with such bright eyes—she had discarded her spectacles—could be ugly. She had never seen Rex so lively, almost so excited.

Her aunt was again indisposed; this night the hours passed more slowly.

She came down to breakfast. "No," she said to Mrs. Gibson, her aunt was not quite so well.

"We're going to have another day of it. I am to see the Beacon," said Miss Lasky coming up behind them. "Miss Paulet, you must come to the Beacon too."

But Sylvia would not leave her aunt.

"Hard luck. But you must come another run. I've chucked my plans and am staying on. I think this is so delectable."

Sylvia was not sure that she wanted to be third with Miss Lasky.

Rain set in later in the day. The motorists were back soon after tea. She heard their voices, but she did not go down.

"Don't stay up here with me, dear," said her aunt. "I am perfectly well now, and I shall be quite comfortable." She too had heard Rex's voice.

But Sylvia felt almost morbid, determined not in any way to seek Rex.

In the evening, after a few commonplaces about the run being cut short, she went away to another part of the room and talked to Micheline Lacey.

Micheline began a little flow at once.

"I'm looking at *Film World*, Mummy sends it me at school every week. That's Madie Davis. She features in lovely things, generally with Gus Barney, but sometimes with Percy Mayne, he's her husband, no he isn't though, it's Little Tubby-Tite, he's her husband just now. A girl and me at school wrote and asked her what were her favourite parts, and she wrote back such a sweet letter, and said Ola in 'Temptation.' She said she sobbed for half an hour one day in the studio because it was such a sad piece, and her eyes are blue not brown, because someone asked last week, and you see here's the answer to 'Jeanie mine.' 'You have been misinformed. Miss Davis's eyes are not brown, but blue of a very deep violet-shade, and she has been divorced twice.' "

"Miss Paulet, do come," called Miss Lasky from across the room. "Rex and I are having a heated argument about roads. Yes, it's scandalous to take the liberty of calling him Rex, but one can't bike with someone for two days and not call him Rex at the end."

She had thought of him as Rex, she had said the name to herself, but not to him. Once he had called her Sylvia. She had not known before she was jealous, and now she knew it with a vengeance. She looked towards the fire where they were sitting, and made some sort of answer. He did not speak; he had not spoken to her for three days. His head was buried in a map.

Mrs. Lacey came up. "Has my small daughter been boring you? She's quite mad on films, but I think they're such a common lot, not at all the people I like to associate with." She jumped on to something else. "Miss Paulet, excuse me for mentioning it, but I should be careful of that Miss Lasky. I know that sort; being a married woman, I suppose I've come across them. She's not like a straight English girl. I should say she's a German Jew; you know that sort, that never let a man alone; and Mr. Glen's such a nice boy."

Sylvia's heart turned cold; her unacknowledged thought was confirmed. But what could she do, or what would she wish to do? Nothing.

Mrs. Lacey spoke from a wider knowledge of men and women than Mrs. Oxenford with all her marriages and engagements. She had spent her life for some years in fighting for men with other women, and knew the hotness of battle.

But by the next day the success of Miss Lasky's attack was becoming manifest even to the doubting. Mrs. Oxenford, with men at her province, did not like to be found making a mistake, but she had to own there was danger.

"I *never* have seen such barefaced hunting down of a man," said she. "It will be quite against his will, poor boy, but nice men are so weak, when it comes to unscrupulous women."

"I don't think it will be against his will," said Miss Carlyon, speaking more freely now Mrs. Gibson and Mrs. Lacey were not there. "Men usually like the most unsatisfactory sort of women."

"I think it's the motor bikes," said Miss Watford in her prim little voice. "His has fallen in love with hers, and motors decided everything now."

That day Sylvia had a headache, a long, heavy headache, which meant she had time to dread the future, interrupted by loud visits of her aunt on tip-toe, till dinner. At nearly eleven she heard the motor bikes under the window.

Next morning she was well, and her aunt was well. She was down early. Lilith was standing in the passage with hat and coat on. "Rex has just gone to see about the bikes," said she. "We shall have a jolly ride, shan't we?"

There was no suggestion of Sylvia's coming to-day. It was bright and windy, too chill for old age sitting out of doors, just right for youth. She and Miss Watford were together most of the afternoon. She heard with envy of the hard drudgery of Form IV B. There would be no time to think.

On the fifth morning after Lilith's arrival Sylvia was late for breakfast. When he aunt was deposited with a host of occupations round her in the lounge, she went out for a walk by herself. She took a sequestered turning, and plunged into a green coppice. She came to a clearing, a fallen tree trunk, and Lilith and Rex in one another's arms.

"Sylvia," cried Lilith, springing up, "don't tell anybody; it's a secret. The most perfect thing in the world has happened; we're engaged."

She glanced at Rex; he looked drunk with happiness, not as she had ever seen him before. She thought he hardly knew she was there.

"Engaged," she said. "Are you? I congratulate you. I congratulate you both." These words must do, she could not quite think what they meant. She turned and left them.

Oh, to be certain of solitude. But this was charabanc day. A procession of them, looking like bulls, had been streaming down the black road. The contents wandered from tea shop—cup of coffee and cakes—to the tobacconist, the picture postcard shop, the sweets and chocolate shop, and the fancy shop, back to the tea shop for tea; or else sat under the shade of the large unsightly corrugated iron garage, and ate sandwiches. But there were always some rash spirits who wandered out into the heather, and suppose one of them saw her, and caught her crying. Perhaps her room was safer, but the walls were thin. She went back; she sat down on the chair in front of her dressing-table, saying now and then to herself: "I knew it would happen. I knew it." By chance she saw herself in the glass. She knew she was pretty. The girls had often told her so at school. Grief, indignation, agitation had lent movement to her sweet, calm looks. Her silky flaxen hair, her palely tinted cheek, her grey eyes shedding soft beams, she could see all her charms before her. The lounge had been quite wrong; it judged of what had been admired in its youth. Times change. Gentle, sweet, dignified, good, she had not the smallest chance against the newcomer.

She did not notice how time sped. There was a knock at the door and Lilith came in.

"Sylvia," said she, "I've come to say good-bye. We're going to town as soon as the gong rings. He's breaking it to his mother this minute. I told him to provide out-size handkerchiefs. She doesn't love me, and there'll be some gnashing of teeth. I just wanted to say, forgive me for taking him."

"I don't think there is anything to forgive," said Sylvia, not looking at her.

"Yes, there is, because you know I've taken him from you."

"In that case we needn't talk about it."

"Yes, we must. Do you mind? I want you to know I'm not quite the beast I seem. The very first minute I saw him—that was in the morning of the day I spoke to you, he walked past me, when I was sitting under a tree—I knew in an instant he was the man I ought to have. I always have known there was a special someone, and I've been disappointed so often. I'm not awfully young; I'm twenty-seven, two years older than he is, and of course men have sometimes been in love with me—I think I rather easily can get people in love with me—and each time I've hoped, and it's been a most horrible let down, and this time it's absolutely, absolutely right. And if it's right for me, it be must be right for him, do you see,

Sylvia, so I ought to take him. You're so awfully sweet, but you're not really his sort. Marry some jolly High Church curate, and you'll be frightfully happy. That's why I spoke to you the first evening, and said the bike was out of order. I was waiting for him. I got the bike out of order on purpose, and I never wanted to get to Basingstoke."

Sylvia was quite powerless against Lilith, even her reason succumbed. She believed that she was not the right sort.

"Come and say good-bye to him," said Lilith. "We're starting from the garage. Packing and paying the bill—they overcharged me—and getting engaged is too much for one morning."

Still under the influence of Lilith, she was able to give his hands a friendly grasp, to wish him happiness with a feeling of sincere exaltation. He said: "Thank you very much," but he did not look at her.

Mrs. Glen did not come down to lunch. It transpired that she was busy crying in her own room, and was having some Bovril later. Sylvia got the business of telling her aunt over as soon as possible. Her aunt was not demonstrative nor very talkative. She was of the old school, whose emotions kept themselves to themselves, but she became red with indignation, and said two or three times: "I can't think what your mother will say."

At last Sylvia said: "But mother does not know anything about it."

Her aunt's red turned into a blush of guilt as she answered: "Yes she does, dear, because I told her."

"Did you, Aunt Agnes? but you won't tell her about this will you?"

"Oh no, dear, certainly I wouldn't. I shouldn't mention it at all."

She thought of the many morning chats she had had on the subject in the lounge.

"Shall we go on with the reading, Aunt Agnes?"

"Thank you, dear, if you are not tired."

"Oh no, I'm not in the least tired."

But as she read, she felt tired to death of life. The exaltation had died down rapidly, now they were gone, and left her sick at heart.

Her aunt watched her with a curious feeling of shyness. She had been just a sweet, nice, unselfish girl, like thousands of girls in the past generation, like hundreds now when the type is less common. Suddenly in a moment from the dear little great niece, the daughter of dear warm-hearted Helen to whom Aunt Agnes could say anything, she had turned into someone unapproachable like her cold father. Grief had cut her off. Her aunt longed to comfort her. She and old age had become used to one another; she no longer regretted youth. Now she yearned for it again, that she might understand Sylvia as only a contemporary could.

"Would you care to go for a few days to Crowborough?" she said tentatively. "I know of a nice hotel there."

"That's just as you like, Aunt Agnes, but it hardly seems worth while just to change for three days."

She would not understand what Aunt Agnes meant.

They had tea upstairs, and then she slipped out unperceived to walk alone. But after dinner she could no longer avoid the full discharge of sympathy.

Mr. Gibson (the two husbands had been told all) put an extra log on the fire. "Come here, dear," said someone, and she found herself placed in the largest chair. There was a kind of dressing of the wound in the tone of Mr. Oxenford's reading aloud of *Punch*, as though it was specially for her. And her bad cards were pitied and her good cards applauded at bridge, as if she were a dear little child with a toothache. Rex's and Lilith's names were scrupulously banished. There was the less sacrifice, as the engagement had been the uninterrupted topic of the lounge from tea to dinner. All Mrs. Glen knew she had at once related to Mrs. Gibson, and Mrs. Gibson to everybody she came across. Mrs. Glen had now been put to bed with a boiling hot water bottle and a cup of peptonized cocoa.[67] When she said good night, Sylvia hoped fervently no one would be so sympathetic as to kiss her. She would not recognize any squeeze of her hand. She also had an offer of peptonized cocoa, but declined it.

She went to a solitary nook in the heather next morning. To-day its peace was not likely to be molested. She had a book in her hands. She had tried to read, but her mind could turn to but one subject: if Lilith hadn't come.

While she was there, Miss Laura Carlyon came and sat down beside her.

"I hope I'm not disturbing you," she said, "but my sister and I are going this afternoon, and I wanted to say good-bye."

"Are you?" said Sylvia. "I'm sorry. But we're going too on Saturday. I suppose everyone will be going soon."

This topic lasted for two or three more sentences. Then Miss Carlyon said: "I'm going to be very impertinent, but you must forgive me, for I feel you are like a little sister. I had a sister, my favourite. She died when she must have been about your age, and you are so like her, or her daughter." What would Mrs. Lacey have felt, if she had heard she was like Miss Carlyon's sister? "I have felt all this for you so very much, because the same thing happened to me, so I know all about it." Her voice shook, and she spoke

[67] Pre-digested, intended for use by invalids.

with difficulty. This opened the floodgates, which Sylvia had kept too long closed, and she sobbed.

"But I expect you were engaged," she wept. "I shouldn't mind it so much if we'd been engaged, I would much much rather. Then I could have had a kiss, and now I have nothing at all."

"No," said Miss Carlyon. "I think it was worse. It made one feel more bitter. But you're stronger than I am, better altogether, so you won't let yourself get hard as I did, making that sister of mine so anxious that she really lost her health worrying about me. I allowed myself to think that life was over and everything was sour, much too long. Don't waste time doing that, because it does grieve the kind people round one so much, and it isn't true. In your case there's still less need; besides, I don't think that nice boy will be taken in for long."

"Yes, I think he will. I think he cares for her more than he did for me, if he did care for me. I could see the look in his eyes."

"Well, I'm not Mrs. Oxenford. Men are not my speciality. It's later than I thought. Good-bye. Don't let's lose sight of one another. Will you come and stay with us? We're in a dreadfully dull part of town, and two elderly old maids are very unexciting, but it would give us a great deal of pleasure."

Sylvia returned with warmth the kiss she had dreaded the night before.

Those long three days before they left, long and very empty they looked in prospect, rather long and empty they were when she reached them. She helped Micheline paste film stars into her film album, and she tried sketching. She at once became prey of all the idle.

"Oh, you're sketching," cried Mrs. Oxenford, "That's right. I'm so glad, it's such a nice interest. I used to be fond of it until I married, and then, as my husband said, I had something better to do. But when one gets into country like this, I feel I must get out my paint-box. Isn't that tree too tall? It never could be as tall as that."

Mrs. Lacey came and leaned over and dilated on Miss Lasky's goings-on with "that poor boy, *ever* so late I heard them one night. I didn't think it a bit nice, not in a really select house like this." Then another topic. "Oh, those Carlyons, I'm glad they're gone. Weren't they old maids, really old maids? I've known awfully jolly women, not married, really almost jollier than what were married, but they seemed to put on side, because they were old maids, particularly Laura, and I don't see anything to set yourself up about in that, do you? Rather the reverse."

In Hilda Watford, her own generation, Sylvia found, as her aunt had thought she might, some solace.

They had been talking quietly and confidentially of one another's lives. Looking back, Sylvia could not remember how it came in that Hilda said, "I think you're to be envied. *I* envy you frightfully. I mean—" She broke off and began again. "You see you had something, even if it's gone, and anyhow you've got your own love and that will last. You'll be amused, but if I had had the smallest, what the Victorian novels call encouragement—I like that word encouragement, don't you?—I should have been quite absurd about him. Only one can't for absolutely nothing. He said one word to me once: 'I'm sorry, I didn't know that was your paper.' "

"You mean…?" said Sylvia.

"Yes, it's my one and only lapse. In six weeks three girls were in love with him. Men *are* spoilt."

Sylvia said good-bye to Mrs. Glen, who went home shattered the day after Rex's and Lilith's departure. Her slightly fretful tearfulness and fondling, meant so kindly, made Sylvia draw back into herself. Her response sounded stiff, and Mrs. Glen said to Mrs. Gibson: "I don't believe she really cares."

This grew to be the general feeling. Sylvia lost some of her popularity in her last three days. If only she had told someone something and they could all have grieved about it! And Mrs. Gibson found out from Aunt Agnes that she had not said a word even to her. The authority, Mrs. Oxenford, spoke out: "The fact is she's a very nice girl, but she is cold and he found it out. There is just the little wounded vanity." Mrs. Oxenford herself had jilted, not been jilted. "But it has not gone far, her heart has never been really touched. But that's just the modern girl. They are so cool."

The last day came. The season was over. Mrs. Long and Kate were smiling good-byes and receipting bills all the morning. Cards and "We *must* meet in town" were being exchanged in every corner of the lounge; the cards to be lost presently in the train. The guests departed with mixed feelings. Some were glad the difficult business of holiday making was over, and they could get back to routine. Some were so torpid they took each half-hour as it came, and couldn't say whether they enjoyed any. Mrs. Lacey's heart bounded that she need no longer be on her best behaviour. Mrs. Gibson's mind was on half a crown wrong in her bill; she had hardly leisure to say any of her civil things. The men were wandering up and down the passage. They were often rather restless before and during a journey. Two of the married couples were going on to other hotels; hotels, eternal holiday hotels and their routine. Hilda Watford said to her friend who came to fetch her: "The relief of getting back to a human being *at last*."

There was only one person who was heartbroken at leaving, that was the calm Sylvia in her neat tweed travelling coat, her brow as smooth as her hair. She was picking up the little bags that dropped from her Aunt's fingers as she counted the change, and asking Kate pleasantly if she would not be glad to have them all gone, as though nothing had happened to her at all. Kate went over to the popular side and said, "she never cared a straw for that boy."

Sylvia had taken a last look before breakfast at the spot where she had hoped he would say the something he had to say. The sun shone on it, it looked its sweetest, most smiling self. She couldn't bear leaving it, but she did not think she could bear to come again.

THE DEAD LADY

It was one night a hundred and thirty years ago. The lady lay upon her bed, her breath came in heavy gasps, and she spoke with difficulty. When at times her faltering tongue failed her, her large eyes, fixed upon her husband, spoke the words she could not utter.

She knew that she was dying, and she told him once again her last desire. She feebly raised her left hand to her lips. On it were two rings, the gifts of her husband, an enamel posy ring on the little finger, a ruby on the third. She kissed them both. She murmured to herself: "True love dost last for ever." It was the motto engraved at the back of the ruby ring, which he had given her on her wedding day.

"Let them be buried with me," she said to her husband.

He promised her.

"Where is Nurse?"

"Mrs. Cummins is very ill, my lady," said Mrs. Barbery, her woman, who stood at the foot of the bed.

"Nurse ill," she said, hardly comprehending. "And I can't say good-bye to her."

She again looked at her husband.

"It is *very* hard to part," she said.

He hid his face, and shook convulsively from head to foot.

"But the time has come," she continued, breathing with more difficulty. "Before I die, I thank you, dear, dear husband, for all your goodness. I have been a happy wife."

"I have not been good enough, not worthy of you." He pressed her to his heart.

"Do not grieve for me too much. I could not bear it. I should have to come back to you." A smile, a faint, faint reflection of the transporting smile of her youth rested on her face an instant and faded away. What more last whispering words she essayed were hardly audible. She lay speechless with her hand in his; he watched her silently. The heart grew feebler, at length it stopped entirely.

"Mrs. Barbery," he said, "give her something to drink." She put the cup to her lips in vain.

"Let me give it to her," said he, "she will drink it then."

"It is no use, Sir Harry,"

"What are we to do?" he cried.

At this moment the door opened, and Doctor Mimm was ushered in.

"Grieved to have been so long delayed, Sir Harry. My horse cast a shoe coming across the moor. I had to walk to Padewy Forge before I could get another."

"Come here, Doctor, come here quickly," said Sir Harry. "Look at her."

The doctor came, walking heavily and uncertainly. He gazed upon the lady. He took her hand and felt the pulse. His eye rested on the ruby, and his thoughts may have been more intent on that than on his patient.

"Umm," said he. "I was afraid, Sir Harry, I was very much afraid. Alas, her ladyship has paid the debt to nature. What I anticipated has occurred."

"Why didn't you come before?" said the husband turning angrily upon him.

"Nothing could have saved her," replied Doctor Mimm, solemnly shaking his head. "It was decreed. And now, my dear sir, let me persuade you to come with me. I have Mrs. Tibbits below. Let her come up and perform her sad office."

The husband went with him as in a dream.

"In such melancholy circumstances," said the doctor, when they had reached the dining-room, "I invariably recommend a little nourishment to the bereaved survivor. It is particularly necessary that they should be sustained. A glass of port wine, or two or three or more, as the physician advises. You will allow me, Sir Harry." He rang the bell and ordered the butler to bring up wine. "The best you have in the house. On this distressing occasion Sir Harry must have nothing but the best."

While he regaled himself in the dining-room, Mrs. Tibbits fortified herself upstairs in a like manner with gin. Two hours later the doctor left for home. He spoke to the butler at the door.

"Where is Mrs. Tibbits? I wish to speak to her."

"Mrs. Tibbits is gone, sir."

"The devil she has, and I ordered her not to stir from here till I'd seen her. Out of my way, you blockhead. Let me pass, sir. Can't you see I want to get out at the door?"

"You're to step round at once to my master's, Mrs. Tibbits," said the doctor's man late in the afternoon, "and I wouldn't be in your shoes, my lady, for you're out of favour."

"Now then, you," said the doctor when Mrs. Tibbits appeared, "what did you promise me?"

"Oh, sir, I tried so faithful, I did indeed, but how could I get the ring when Mrs. Barbery was there watching of me? She's a very proud prying woman, sir. Mrs. Cummins herself couldn't have been more so. She has locked the door, took the key, and give it to Sir Harry."

"Very well, Mrs. Tibbits, if you can't perform your promise, nor can I. No cash."

"Oh, sir," falling on her knees, "and when I put the powder you gave me for Mrs. Cummins so comfortable in her tea, just as you bid me, and she was very upset, so that every one of them thought she was dying, and I have not a penny to pay the rent."

He dismissed her with imprecations.

"I must have the cursed ring," said he. "It's my one hope. If Dallas doesn't get his money, he'll expose me. Let no man hope for a grain of mercy from Dallas." He sat lost in cogitation.

Sir Harry sent for his man of business that night, and asked that arrangements should be made for the funeral at the earliest date.

"But, Sir Harry, you will hardly allow time to make your more distant neighbours acquainted with the sad intelligence. His Grace for instance would wish to be represented at the obsequies."

"Then we must dispense with their kind attention. I would rather have it over and done with. What care I for my neighbours?"

Mrs. Barbery inquired whether he wished to take a last farewell before the coffin was closed down.

"No, no," he replied hastily. "Do not ask me."

Lady Wild was laid in the mausoleum of the family, which was situated in the park adjoining the church. After the ceremony, when all had dispersed, the sexton locked the gates and made his way home.

But at ten o'clock at night, when the village was asleep, he rose up softly, put on his clothes, took a key from its place, with a crowbar, a lantern and a small sharp knife, and hastened back to the park. It was midsummer, and there was still a faint aftermath of light in the horizon, by which he was able to see his way without the aid of his lantern. As he reached the gate of the mausoleum, the moon rose in the heavens. He stood and waited, his knees shook, and he would fain have turned back home. At length he unlocked the gate and the inner door, and went in. He put down his lantern and began with determined haste to unfasten the lid of the coffin.

The moon to his guilty eyes shone with a baleful light. It illuminated the interior of the mausoleum, and cast long, curious, and very black shadows upon the statuary and memorial tablets of the family, so that it seemed to the impious intruder that the effigies of the deceased gazed upon his wicked design.

When he had exposed the body, he took the left hand, which lay upon the breast, and began fearfully to cut at the finger on which was the ruby ring. As he proceeded, it seemed to him that a tremor passed through the body. He threw down the hand in terror, drank at his brandy, murmured it was strange what a man could fancy there alone at night, and braced himself anew to his task. Blood came oozing forth; then there rose a faint cry from the coffin. He tugged violently at the ring and wrenched it off; he sprang affrighted to the door; he fled into the park, and in his extremity he dropped the ring and the key.

The lady, roused from a long deathlike trance into which she had fallen, stirred and opened her eyes. At first her confused senses refused to aid her; she knew nothing. She spoke faintly. "Where am I? Tell me, where am I?" Again her senses travelled far away, her eyes closed. The pain she was suffering recalled her to life. She saw that blood was flowing; she endeavoured to staunch the wound. She shuddered, she was cold as marble. She struggled, she extricated herself and stepped forth. She drank some of the brandy left by the sexton. This gave her strength to look round, and at length to recognize with horror where she was. She knew not how she had penetrated to that sad abode. By degrees memory returned. Now she recollected what had happened. She uttered a piercing cry:

"Alas, I am dead." As she glanced fearfully round the place of terror, she caught sight of the ring which glittered in the moonlight. She picked it up and put it on her right hand. She found she could walk with tottering steps. She struggled to the door. There the balmy air of night fanned her cheeks and gave her strength. She stepped out into the park. The full and radiant moon shed its beams abroad. Their light seemed friendly to her. The path to the house was clear as day and bright like silver. Long and painful was her journey. Her feeble limbs sank beneath her, often she must stop to recover her breath, but love urged her on, the picture of her husband forlorn and solitary.

The small door which led to his private apartment was open to the garden. He was in the habit of walking late. How often had she on the fair mild nights of June paced the lawns with him, leaning on his arm. She went in, she hastened along the little passage, she opened his door.

"My dearest one," she cried, but the words died on her lips, for she saw her husband was not alone. Kate Wicks the daughter of the innkeeper was on his knee.

He caught sight of her though the girl did not. He cried loudly: "*You!*" His face turned ashy pale. The lady saw his expression of horror. She stepped back instantly into the darkness and shut the door. As she did so, she heard the rude, untutored accents of the woman. "Why, Sir Harry, what ails you?"

"Nothing ails me," he said, "but it's chill, though it's June. Fill up my glass."

The lady sped on. The moonlight streamed through the great window on the staircase, and lighted her way along the corridor upstairs. She did not know how she reached her own room. There she could sit for a brief space, and bewail her misery.

But she saw that she was not alone; her old nurse was kneeling by her bed weeping and crying out:

"Oh, my lady, my own sweet lady, what can I do without you?"

She came near and said: "Nurse."

The old woman shrank from her with a cry.

"Do not turn from me, Nurse, do not be afraid. I am not dead, alas, I am not dead. Kiss me nurse, and warm me, for I am perished with the cold."

Then the nurse kissed her. "Oh, my own sweet dear lovely lady, oh, my lamb. Oh, thank God you have come back to me. But there's blood on your dear hand and blood stains on your gown. Come and I'll put you in your bed. Barbery shall get it ready for you."

"No, stop, Nurse. No one must know I am here. Let me go to your room, there we shall be undisturbed."

The nurse lit the fire, undressed the lady, wrapped her in blankets, gave her hot wine to drink, and dressed her wound, weeping and wailing over it.

"But what have they done to you? Who has done it? Some wicked wretch has torn your poor finger."

"I know nothing. I came to myself, and I was alone."

"Alas, that I should have been ill that night of all nights. I thought I should have been the one to go first. I warrant I shouldn't have allowed them to nail you down in a coffin."

Lady Wild accepted the ministrations and caresses of the nurse in silence. She said no word of her husband, nor did the nurse dare say a word of him to her.

"Now I must sleep," said the lady, "but promise me to wake me at dawn, for there is much I have to do."

The nurse sat by her bed, and when the first light began peering through the windows, she woke the lady according to her promise.

"You were sleeping so deeply, my poor lamb, I could not bear to rouse you."

"I shall soon have a long rest," said Lady Wild.

She looked earnestly at the nurse, and said:

"How is my husband, Nurse?"

"Poor man, he's sleeping. I heard him go to his room very late. These past two nights he has been walking up and down his room for many hours together. Shall I call him?"

"No, why should you trouble him? I know he has consoled himself. I saw him with her. It is my fit punishment. I would not resign myself to leave my husband. I rebuked the summons of my Maker. Therefore He has let me return to life, to see that in no more than twenty-four hours my place has been filled. Perhaps I was mistaken, perhaps in life I had no place. My son and my daughter with families of their own do not need me. My work was over."

"Oh, there are many, many, that need you. All the village are speaking of you," cried the nurse.

Lady Wild shook her head.

"Tell me the truth as you love me: was this the first time he—?"

"Oh, my lady, don't ask me."

"It was not the first time."

"You know the Wilds have always been followers of women."

"Yes, I should not have deemed myself exempted."

"But this night of all nights in the year, and to bring her into the house. They are saying that he means to marry her. Some say that——"

"It is not for them or for you to discuss your master and my husband. Now attend to me carefully. I am going away. I shall never trouble my husband again, and he must not know I came back. He thinks he saw my spirit. Give me a dress and cloak of yours, Nurse. No one must recognize me on my journey. But first you must go to the mausoleum and take a hammer with you and set all in order, so that nothing may be suspected. There is no time to lose. Get me the dress at once."

"Dearest Madam, stay and rest a little longer. Where are you going?"

"A long journey, I don't know where, but I believe I shall find home at last. Kiss me, dear, faithful, kind friend of all my life, and, Nurse, stay with him always, and love him for my sake, as you know how dearly I loved him. Go now, I shall not rest till you return."

She lay back upon the bed.

But when the nurse was gone, she rose up quickly, took the ruby ring from her finger and found some ink and paper. She wrote this one sentence: "Doth true love last for ever?" She wrapped the ring in the paper. Then she went into the corridor and down the great stairs to Sir Harry's room. She listened at the door. He was breathing loudly; he was a heavy sleeper, difficult to rouse. She stole in and came to his bedside; he was in a profound sleep. She took his hand which lay on the counterpane; she softly opened it, put the paper containing the ring within it, and closed the fingers. She looked upon him for the last time, kissed him, and left him. She hastened away, she went out at the little garden door and walked as rapidly as she could towards the lake.

It shone like bright gold, and the birds all around her sang with joy. The merry morning smiled upon her. She bade it and earth farewell, and with one prayer for her husband she commended her soul to God, and threw herself into the lake.

Very early that morning Dr. Mimms was at the sexton's cottage.

"I was expecting you last night," said he.

"Oh, sir, I can't justly bear to tell you, but I haven't nothing for you."

"Nothing, curse you. How's that?"

"I carried out your instructions, Doctor. I took with me that little knife you give me, Sir, but as true as there's stars in the sky, when I begin, that moved, yes, that moved, Doctor. I wa'nt daunted, I'm a man no one can daunt, on I went again. The blood came out, and oh, she gave a screech, such as you never heard. I had the ring, Sir, don't you think that I didn't take it, but something in white came and spirited it out of my hand, and I was driven forth out at the door."

"You liar, you're keeping the ring."

"No, Sir, as far as my knowledge is concerned, the ring's left in the mausoleum, and you can fetch it yourself, Dr. Mimms, for I wouldn't go back to the place for a sight more money than you can give me."

"Give me the key of the mausoleum."

"So I would, Sir, willing, but I haven't got it. It dropped from my hands, as I went out of the tomb, Sir, and I haven't had the heart to seek for it."

"You and Tibbits are the choicest couple of rogues it's been my fortune to meet."

Dr. Mimms went immediately to the park. He looked about him carefully to see that he was not observed. Then he hurried to the mausoleum, but the door was locked. In despair he searched for the key, crawling on his hands and knees in the long grass. He searched in vain. Mrs. Cummins had brought it back with her to the house.

When Sir Harry woke, he found the packed in his grasp. He read the words written by the hand of her who was lately dead.

Sweat poured from his face and he shook like a leaf. He rang his bell violently.

"Someone entered this door last night, Greaves," said he to his man. "Who was it?"

"No one has been here to my knowledge, Sir Harry."

"Send Mrs. Barbery to me."

"Was not the ruby ring on her ladyship's finger when she was laid in the coffin, Mrs. Barbery?"

"Indeed it was, Sir Harry, to my certain knowledge, for I watched beside her to the last."

Then he sent for Mrs. Cummins, but to his questions she only answered, "I can tell you nothing, I know nothing."

He shuddered, he put the ring carefully away, and he told himself that it must be returned to the hand which had worn it faithfully for five and thirty years.

He sent to the vicarage that afternoon, and requested the attendance of the incumbent.

"I had the intention of waiting upon you to-day, Sir Harry," said Mr. Grisby, "to offer my sincere condolences on the decease of her ladyship. I would endeavour to direct your thoughts to those heavenly consolations which are provided by religion, and also to urge that the blow with which the Almighty has smitten you may be turned to your soul's profit by an amendment to your life, of which, Sir Harry, if report speaks truly, there is, even at this solemn and melancholy hour, a serious necessity."

"I am grateful to you, Mr. Grisby, You see before you one who is sincerely affected. And I ask your counsel, sir, in a special and private matter in which I could consult no other than a minister of religion."

"What of ghostly aid I can give you is at your disposal."

"Do the spirits of the dead revisit this earth?"

"You ask me a question to which no certain answer has been vouchsafed. Such visitants, it is true, are mentioned in the Scriptures and were known among the ancients. In the time of their ignorance God winked at them, but in these less enthusiastic and more rational days such appearances rest on the evidence of the rude and vulgar. The uneasy conscience can, however, of itself create an airy vision, which is alike a punishment and an admission."

The words of the austere clergyman alarmed Sir Harry, but in spite of them he was cherishing a secret guilty purpose in his heart. There was another who hankered after the ring besides the doctor. The designing Kate Wicks had desired it from the moment she saw it on Lady Wild's finger in church. When it was known in the village that the lady was dying, she set her heart on extracting it from Sir Harry, over whom by her imprudent boldness and coarse flattery and handsome person she exerted an unbounded influence.

By noon a strange tale went about the village. Mrs. Barbery whispered to the housemaid that she had spied the ring that very morning on Sir Harry's bed. In the evening Kate Wicks again came privately to Sir Harry through the little garden door. She used all her wiles and begged and prayed.

"I haven't got it," said he, "you know already that I haven't got it."

"But I know that you have," said she.

"The devil you do. How do you know it?"

She laughed and begged him the more.

"Not to-night," he answered. She entreated him still further.

"To-morrow, possibly to-morrow," he said in a low voice. "Leave me to myself."

He went to his room, he opened the drawer and took out the paper. He read again the sentence his wife had written' "Doth true love last for ever?" He tore it into a hundred pieces and threw them out of the window. But the words rang in his ears all the more. He went to bed and slept. He opened his eyes, and it seemed to him that he was in the park and in front of him he saw the mausoleum. The door opened, the gate opened, his wife came forth in her shroud. It was night, but he could see her clearly. She walked past him, moving slowly; she made her way in the moonlight to the house. He saw her face, she was smiling, and immediately he was in his room with Kate Wicks. His wife opened the door and looked upon him. Again he was with her, as she mounted the great staircase and went weeping to her room. Then he saw the nurse with her, but though he listened intently he could not hear what they said to one another. She came out and down the stairs, and now he was in his bed, and she was bending over him, touching his hand, and giving him the ring. He felt her kiss on his brow, he tried to take her hand, but she was gone, and he caught sight of her in a bonnet and cloak. Her countenance was mournful as he had never known it, her eyes were wild. She was walking swiftly along the woodland path which led to the lake. He tried in vain to overtake her. He called, she neither turned nor answered. She seemed to him to walk still faster. She came to the lake, she stood at the brink. He heard a loud noise; it was morning, and his man was knocking at the door.

Throughout the day the remembrance of his dream oppressed him. A hundred times he asked himself, "What was she doing at the side of the lake? Had my dream lasted but an instant longer, what should I have seen?"

His bailiff desired to see him, his steward, there were urgent matters he must decide, he dismissed them, he was very much occupied with business. He sat in his chair doing nothing. Late in the afternoon the butler came to him: "Goodrich is below, Sir Harry, he begs leave to speak to you." Goodrich was the gamekeeper.

"Send him away, I am too busy."

"He asks very particular to see you, Sir Harry; there is something it is his duty to tell you."

"I can see no one."

The butler went out, and returned.

"He begs leave very earnest indeed. He asks me to give you this."

He put in Sir Harry's hand the posy ring which Lady Wild had worn on her little finger.

"Great God," cried Sir Harry, "am I to have no peace, no peace to the end of my days? Send Goodrich here."

"This morning," said the gamekeeper, "so please your honour, me and Bill Haynes rowed over to the island to see his traps. The boat was clogged in some weeds and when we tried to get off—not to take up your valuable time, Sir Harry—there was a dead body in the way. We lifted it out, there was no recognising the face, but the dress was a woman's black coat and bonnet, and on the little finger there was her ladyship's ring."

He gave them money for their services and sent them away.

"That is what she had in her hand," said he to himself. "I knew it, I knew it was so."

He sent for Mrs. Cummins.

"Her ladyship came back here," said he, "the very night of her burial, and you saw her. You swore to me you knew nothing."

"How did you hear she came back, Sir Harry? Not a soul saw her save myself. I alone knew. She made me promise so solemn I would never tell."

"It is no concern of yours how I heard. Tell me all you know."

Then the nurse related her story. "She kissed me, she bid me come back to her as soon as possible, but though I made all speed, when I returned she was gone."

When he was alone Sir Harry suffered the agony of profound remorse.

This was the hour Kate Wicks would come stealing to the little garden door; now Greaves discreetly whispered she was waiting.

"Curse the woman," said Sir Harry. "Let her not venture to set foot within this house again."

That very night the body of a lady was again carried to the mausoleum. The door was ajar, and a light could be seen shining within. The doctor was already there. He had at length with Tibbits' aid secured the key. He was bending down intently searching for the ring, with his back towards them, but at the sound of their entrance he turned round sharply. At the sight of Sir Harry he became white as ashes.

"What business have you here, Sir?" cried Sir Harry.

For answer Doctor Mimms whipped out a pistol, fired, and hit Sir Harry in the leg. Sir Harry fell, and in the confusion which followed the doctor was able to make his escape into the park. He fled from the village that night. His whereabouts were eagerly enquired after by the many to whom he was in debt, but he was never more heard of.

From that time Sir Harry fell into a melancholy, never going outside the gates of the park, refusing to see anyone, turning from the door the friends that visited him. The once jovial house, the merriest in the neighbourhood, became silent and forlorn. Sir Harry was to be met walking continually from the mausoleum to the lake and back again, retracing the steps his wife had taken on her last journey. He talked to himself ceaselessly on his way, even murmuring the sentence she had written on the paper: "Doth true love last for ever?" And "Do not grieve for me too much, I should have to come back to you," her last conscious words to him. Then he would answer: "Alas, my wife, you should not have come back," and began again his melancholy discourse.

Thus he passed long fair summer days and no one could rouse him. Now came the great gales of autumn, the dark rushing rain, and the grey impenetrable mist, never lifting from the dark wood. His servants entreated him to stop indoors. Mr. Grisby exhorted him to face with more manly fortitude the portion meted out to him by Providence. He heeded not. "My wife is gone," he said frequently, "and I am hurrying fast to follow her. Do not delay me."

He shrank into a bent, infirm old man; it was clear that his time would not be long. Then winter came, and thick snow covered the bleak flat expanses of that desolate portion of the Midlands. A harsh iron frost bound the land.

His body was found one morning close to the spot where his wife had drowned herself. The son in India, hearing of the sad fate of both his parents, made no haste to come home and take possession of his inheritance, so that the house, the park and the gardens fell into decay, and the village people shunned the place, and said Sir Harry might be seen at nights walking by the lake. And mother after mother, as generations followed each other, related the strange story of the lady who returned to life, and concluded with: "They say, those that know, that it's wonderful unlucky for any to come back when their time has come. It's better to lie quiet and at peace."

MISS DE MANNERING OF ASHAM

"Oct. 9.

"My dear Evelyn,

"As you say you really are interested in this experience of mine, I am doing what you asked, and writing you an account of it. You can accept it as a token of friendship for, to tell you the truth, I had been trying to forget it, whatever it was. I hope in the end to bring myself to the belief that I never had it, but at present my remembrance is more vivid that I care for.

"Yours affectionately,

"MARGARET LATIMER."

. . . . . .

You remember my friend, Kate Ware? She had been ill, and she asked me to stay in lodgings with her at an East Coast resort. "It is simply Brixton-by-the-Sea, with a dash of Kensington," Kate wrote, "but I ought to go, because my aunt lives there, and likes to see me. So come, if you can bear it."

"I think we might take a day off," said Kate one morning, after we had been there a week. "Too much front makes me think there really is no England but this. Let's have some sandwiches, and bicycle out as far away as we can."

We came to a wayside inn, so quiet, so undisturbed, so cheerful in its quietness, that we felt at last we had found the soothing and rest we were in need of. Yes. I suppose our nerves were a little unstrung; at any rate, being high school mistresses, we knew what nerves were. But hitherto I have felt capable of controlling mine, only, as Hamlet says, I have had dreams. And

Kate is rather strange by nature; I do not think her nerves make her any stranger.

"Now," said Kate, when we had finished our meal—she always settles everything—"I propose we borrow the pony here and have a drive. I don't like desecrating these solitary lanes, which have existed for generations and generations before bicycles, with anything more modern than Tommy."

Kate generally wants to have a map, and know exactly where she is going, but to-day we agreed to take the first turn on the left, and see where it led to. It was a sleepy afternoon, and Tommy trotted so gently that we were all three dozing, before we had gone a mile or two. Then we came to what had been magnificent wrought iron gates with stone pillars on either side. The pillars were now ruined, and the wall beyond was falling down. Kate said, "Let's go in." I said it was private, but we did go in.

We came to an avenue of laurels, resembling the sepulchral shrubberies with which our fathers and our fathers' fathers loved to surround their residences, only those were generally more serpentine. It must have been there many years, and had had time to grow so high as to block out almost all the sky. It was very narrow, and the dankness, the closeness, the black ground that never gets dry, which have always oppressed me in such places, seemed almost intolerable here. I thought we should never get out to the small piece of white light we saw at the end of it. At the same time I dreaded what I expected to find there; one of those great, lugubrious, black mausoleums of a mansion, which so often are the complement of the shrubbery. But this avenue seemed to have been planted haphazard, for it led only to another gate, and that opened on a neglected park. We saw before us an expanse of unfertile-looking grass, and then the horizon was completely hidden by ridges of very heavy greenish-black trees. There were other trees scattered about; they looked very old, and some had been struck by lightning. I felt sorry for their wounds; it seemed as if no one cared whether they lived or died.

There was a small church standing at the left-hand corner of the park, so small that it must have been a chapel for the private worship of the owners of the park; but we thought they could not have valued their church, for there was actually no path to it, nothing but grass, long, rank and damp.

I do not know when it was that I became so certain that I abhorred parks, but I remember it came over me very strongly all of a sudden. I was extremely anxious that Kate should not know what I felt. However, I said to her that grandeur was oppressive, and that after all I preferred small gardens.

"Yes," said Kate, "one might feel too much enclosed, if one lived in a park, as if one could never get out, and as if other things…"

Here Kate stopped. I asked her to go on, and she said that was all she had to say. I don't know if you want to hear these minute details, but nearly everything I have to tell you is merely a succession of minute details. I remember looking up at the sky, because I wanted to keep my eyes away from the distant trees. I did not like to see them—it seems a very poor reason for a woman of thirty-eight—because they were so black. When I was six years old, I was afraid of black, and also though I lived in the country, I used to feel a sense of fear and isolation, if the sun was not shining, and I was alone in a large field; but then a child's mind is open to every terror, or rather it creates a terror out of everything. I thought I had as much forgotten that condition as if I had never known it. I should have supposed the weight of my many grown-up years would have defended me, but I assure you that I felt all at once that I was—what after all we are—as much at the mercy of the universe as an insect.

I remember when I looked up at the sky I observed that it had changed. As we were coming it had had the ordinary pale no-colour aspect, which it bears for quite half the days in the year. Some people grumble at it, but it is very English, and if you do not like it, or more than like it, relish it, you cannot really relish England. The sky had now that strange appearance to which days in the north are liable; I do not think they know anything about it in Italy or the south of France. It is a fancy of mine that the sudden strangeness and wildness one finds in our literature is due to these days; it is something to compensate us for them.

If I said the day was dying, you would think of beautiful sunsets, and certainly the day could not be dying, for it was only three o'clock in the afternoon, but it looked ill; and the grey of the atmosphere was not that silvery grey, which I think the sweetest of all the skies in the year, but an unwholesome grey, which made the trees look blacker still. I should have felt it a relief if only it had begun to rain, then there would have been a noise; it was so utterly silent.

Just as I was wondering where I should turn my eyes next, Tommy came to a sudden stop, and nearly jerked us out of the cart. "Clever," said Kate, "you're letting Tommy stumble."

But it was simply that Tommy would not go on. He was such a mild little pony too, anxious, as Kate said, to do everything one asked, before one asked him.

"Tommy's frightened," said Kate. "He's all trembling and sweating."

Kate got out, and tried to soothe him, but for some time it was very little good.

"It's another snub for the men of science," said Kate. "Tommy sees an angel in the way. Animals are very odd you know. Haven't you noticed dogs scurrying past ghosts in the twilight? I am so glad we haven't got their faculties."

Then Tommy all at once surprised us by going on as quietly as before.

We drove a little further, and we came to the hall. It was built 150 years before the mausoleum period, but it could not well have been drearier, though it must formerly have been a noble Jacobean mansion. It was not that it looked out of repair; a house can be very cheerful, in fact rather more cheerful, if it is shabby. And here there was a terrace with greenhouse plants in stucco vases placed at intervals, and also a clean-shaven lawn, so that man must have been there recently; nevertheless it seemed as if it had been abandoned for years.

I cannot tell you how relieved I was when a respectable young man in shirt sleeves made his appearance. It is Kate generally who talks to strangers, but the moment he was in sight I felt I must cling to him, as a protection. I felt Tommy and Kate no protection.

I apologized for trespassing in private grounds.

"No trespassing at all, miss, I'm sure." He went on to say he wished it happened oftener, Colonel Winterton, the owner, being hardly ever there, only liking to keep the place up with servants, and "if there wasn't a number of us to make it lively, one room being shut up and all," he really did not know——

It did not seem right to encourage him on the subject of a shut-up room; we changed the conversation, and asked him about the church.

He said it was a very ancient church, and there was tombs and that, people came a wonderful way to see. Not that he cared much about them himself.

Kate, who is fond of sight-seeing, declared she would visit the church.

I would not go, though I should like to have seen the tombs. I said I must hold the pony. The young man said he was a groom, and would hold the pony for us. Then I said I was tired: Kate said she would go alone. She started.

"Don't go down there, miss," said the groom, "the grass is so wet. Round by the right it's better."

His way looked the same as her's to me, but Kate followed his advice.

I talked to the groom while Kate was away, and I was glad to hear that he liked the pictures in reason, and that his father was a saddler, living in the High Street of some small town. This was cheerful and distracting to my thoughts, and I had managed to become so much interested that it was the young man who said, "There's the lady coming back."

"Well," I said, "what was the church like?"

"It was locked," Kate answered, "however, it was nice outside."

"But Kate," I said, "how pale you are!"

"Of course I am," said Kate. "I always am."

The young man hastened to ask if he should get Kate a glass of water.

"Oh dear no, thank you," said Kate. "But I think we might be going now. Is there any other road out? I don't want to drive exactly the same way back."

There was, and we set off. As soon as we had said good-bye to the young man, Kate began: "About Grace Martin; what do you think of her chances for the certificate?" and we talked about the Certificate until we got back to the inn. As to that oppressed feeling, I could hardly imagine now what it was. It had passed, and the world seemed its usual clear, safe self, irritating and comfortable. It was clearing up, and the trees and hedges looked as they generally look at the end of August. They were dusty and a little shabby, showing here and there a red leaf, occasional bits of toadflax, and all those little yellow flowers whose names one forgets, but to which one turns tenderly in recollection, when seeing the beauty of foreign lands. My thoughts broke away from our conversation now and then to wonder what I could possibly have been afraid of.

They gave us tea at Tommy's home, and the innkeeper's wife was glad to have some conversation.

"Yes, the poor old Hall, it seems a pity the Colonel coming down so seldom. He only bought it seven years ago, and he seems tired of it already, and then only bringing gentlemen. Gentlemen spend more, but I always think there's more life with ladies. It's changed hands so often. Yes, there's a shut-up room. They say it was something about a housemaid many years ago and a baby, if you'll excuse my mentioning it, but I'm sure I couldn't say. If you listen to all the tales in a village like this, in a little place you know, one says one thing and one another. I come from Norwich myself."

"The church looks rather dismal," said Kate. "The churchyard is so overgrown."

"Yes, poor Mr. Fuller, he's a nice gentleman, though he is so high. First when he come here there was great goings on, services and antics. He says to me, 'Tell me, Mrs. Gage, is that why the people don't come?' 'Oh,' I says, 'well, of course, I've been about, and seen life, so whether it's high or low, I just take no notice.' I said that to put him off, poor gentleman, because it wasn't that. They won't come at all hardly after dark, particularly November; December it's better again; and for his communion service, what he sets his heart on so, we have such a small party, sometimes hardly more than two or three, and then he gets so downhearted. He seems to have lost all his spirit now."

"But why is it better in December?"

"I'm sure I couldn't tell you, miss, but they always say those things is worse in November. I always heard my grandfather say that."

I had rather expected that what I had forgotten in the day would come back at night, and about two, when I was reading Framley Parsonage with all possible resolution, I heard a knock at the door, and Kate came in.

"I saw your light," said she. 'I can't sleep either. I think you felt uncomfortable in the park too, didn't you? Your face betrays you rather easily, you know. Going to the church, at least not going first of all, but as I got near the church, and the churchyard—ugh! However, I am not going to be conquered by a thought, and I mean to go there to-morrow. Still, I think, if you don't very much mind, I should like to sleep in here."

I asked her to get into my bed.

"Thank you, I will," said she. "It's very good of you, Margaret, for I'm sure you loathe sharing somebody's bed as much as I do, but things being as they are——"

The next morning Kate was studying the guidebook at breakfast.

"Here we are," said she. " 'Asham Hall is a fine Jacobean mansion. The church, which is situated in the park, was originally the private chapel of the de Mannerings. Many members of the family are buried there, and their tombs are well worth a visit. The inscriptions in Norman French are of particular interest. The keys can be obtained from the sexton.' Nothing about the shut-up room; I suppose we could hardly hope for it. We must see the tombs, don't you think so?"

Kate was one who very rarely showed her feelings, and I knew better than to refer to last night.

We bicycled to the Hall. It was a very sweet, bright, windy morning, such a morning as would have pleased Wordsworth, I think, and may have brought forth many a poem from him.

"Now," said Kate, "when we get into the park, we'll walk our bicycles over the grass to the church."

I began: then exactly the same feeling came over me as before, only this time there could be nothing in calm, beautiful nature to have produced it. The trees, though dark, did not look at all sinister, but stately and benignant, as they often do in late August, and early September. Whatever it was, it was within me. I felt I could not go to the church.

"You go on alone," I said.

"You'd better come," said Kate. "I know just what you feel, but it will be worse here by yourself."

"I think perhaps I won't," I said.

"Very well," said Kate. "Bicycle on and meet me at the other gate."

I said I was a coward, and Kate said she did not think it mattered being a coward. I meant to start at once, but I found something wrong with the bicycle. It took quite half an hour to repair, but as I was repairing it all my oppression passed, and I felt light and at ease. By the time I was ready, Kate had visited the tombs, and was coming out of the church door. I looked at her going down the path, and saw there was another woman in the churchyard. She was walking rather slowly. She came up behind Kate, then passed quite close to Kate on her left side. I was too far off to see her face. I felt thankful Kate had someone with her. I mounted; when I looked again the woman was gone.

I met Kate outside the church. She always had odd eyes; now they had a glittering look, half scared and half excited, which made me very uncomfortable. I asked her if she had spoken to the woman about the church.

"What woman? Where?" said Kate.

"The one in the churchyard just now."

"I didn't see anyone."

"You must have. She passed quite close to you."

"Did she," said Kate. "She passed on my left side then?"

"Yes, she did. How did you know?"

"Oh, I don't know. We give the keys in here, and let's bicycle home fast, it's turned so cold."

I always think Kate rather manlike, and she was manlike in her extreme moodiness. If anything of any sort went wrong, she clothed herself in a mood, and became impenetrable. Such a mood came on her now.

"I don't know why I never will tell things at the time," said Kate next day. It was raining, and we were sitting over a nice little fire after tea. "It's a sign of great feebleness of mind, I think. However, if you like to hear about Asham Church, you shall. I saw the tombs, and they are all that they should be. I hope the de Mannerings were worthy of them. But the church; perhaps being a clergyman's daughter made me take it so much to heart, but there was a filthy old carpet rolled up on the altar, all the draperies are full of holes, the paint is coming off, part of the chancel rail is broken, and it seems an abode of insects. I did not know there were such forsaken churches in England. That rather spoilt the tombs for me, also an uncomfortable idea that I did not want to look behind me; I don't know what I thought I was going to see. However, I gave every tomb its due. Then, when I was in the churchyard, I had the same feeling as last time; I could not get it out of my mind that something I did not like was going to happen the next minute. Then I had that sensation, which books call the blood running chill; that really means, I think, a catch in one's heart as if one cannot breathe; and at the same time I had such an acute consciousness of someone standing at my left side that I almost felt I was being pushed, no one being there at all, you understand. That lasted a second, I should think, but after that I felt as if I were an intruder in the churchyard, and had better go."

One afternoon a week later, the great-aunt of the smart townlike landlady at our lodgings came to clear away tea. First of all she was deferential and overwhelmed, but I have never known anyone have such a way with old ladies and gentlemen of the agricultural classes as Kate. In a few moments Mrs. Croucher was sitting on the sofa with Kate beside her.

"Asham Hall," said she. "Why, my dear mother was sewing maid there, when she was a girl. Oh dear me, yes, the times she's told me about it all. Oh, it's a beautiful place, and them lovely laurels in the avenue, where Miss de Mannering was so fond of walking. It was the old gentleman, Mr. de Mannering, he planted them; they was to have gone right up to the Hall, so they say. There was to be wonderful improvements, he was to have pulled down the old Hall and built something better, and then he hadn't the money. Yes, even then it was going down, for Mr. William, that was the only son, that lived abroad, he was so wild. Yes, my mother was there in the family's time, not with them things which hev a-took it since."

"You don't think much of Colonel Winterton, then?"

"Oh, I daresay he's a kind sort of gentleman, they say he's very free at Christmas with coals and that, but them new people they comes and goes, it stands to reason they can't be like the family. In the village we calls them jumped-up bit-of-a-things, but I'm sure I've nothing to say against Colonel Winterton."

"Are there any of the family still here?"

"Oh no, mum. They've all gone. Some says there's a Mr. de Mannering still in America, but he's never been near the place."

"It's very sad when the old families go," said Kate sympathetically.

"Oh, it is, mum. Poor old Mr. de Mannering; but the place wasn't sold till after his death. My mother, she did feel it."

"Was there a room shut up in your mother's time, Mrs. Croucher?"

"Not when she first went there, mum."

"It was a housemaid, wasn't it?"

"Not a housemaid," with a look of important mystery. "That's what they say, and it's better it should be said; I shouldn't tell it to everybody, but I don't mind telling a lady like you; it wasn't a housemaid at all."

"Not a housemaid?"

"No; my mother's often told me. Miss de Mannering, she was a very high lady, well, she was a lady that was a lady, if you catch my meaning, and she must have been six or seven and forty, when she was took with her last illness. And the night before she died, my mother she was sitting sewing in Mrs. Packe's room (she was the lady's maid, my mother was sewing maid, you know) and she heard Doctor Mason say, 'Don't take any notice of what Miss de Mannering says, Mrs. Packe. People get very odd fancies, when they're ill,' he says. And she says, 'No, sir, I won't,' and she comes straight to my mother, and she says, 'If you could hear the way she's a-going on. "Oh, my baby," she says, "if I could have seen him smile. Oh, if he had lived just one day, one hour, even one moment." I says to her,' says Mrs. Packe to my mother, ' "Your baby, ma'am, whatever are you talking about?" It was such a peculiar thing for her to say,' says Mrs. Packe. 'Don't you think so, Bessie?' Bessie was my mother. 'I'm sure I don't know,' says my mother; she never liked Mrs. Packe. 'Miss de Mannering didn't take no notice,' Mrs. Packe went on, 'then she says, "If only I'd buried him in the churchyard." So I says to her, "But where did you bury him then, ma'am?" and fancy! she turns round, and looks at me, and she says, "I burnt him." ' Well, that's the truth, that's what my mother told me, and she always said, my mother did, Mrs. Packe had no call to repeat such a thing."

"I think your mother was quite right," said Kate. "Burnt! Poor Miss de Mannering must have been delirious. It is such a frightful…"

"No, my mother didn't like carrying tales about the family," said Mrs. Croucher, engaged on quite a different line of thought. And whether it was that she had heard the story so often, or whether it was that they are still more inured to horrors in the country—I have observed far stranger things happen in the country than in the town—Mrs. Croucher did not seem to have any idea that she was relating what was terrible. On the contrary, I think she found it homely, recalling a happy part of her childhood.

"Then," went on Mrs. Croucher, "Mrs. Packe, she says to mother, 'You come and hear her,' she says, and my mother, 'I don't like to, whatever would she say?' 'Oh,' says Mrs. Packe, 'she don't take any notice of anything, you come and peep in at the door.' 'So I went,' my mother says, 'and I just peeped in, but I couldn't see anything, only Miss de Mannering lying in bed, for there was no candle, only the firelight. Only I heard Miss de

Mannering give a terrible sigh, and say very feint, but you could hear her quite plain, "Oh, if only I'd buried him in the churchyard." I wouldn't stay any longer,' says my mother, 'and Miss de Mannering died at seven in the evening next day.' Whenever my mother spoke of it, she always said, 'I only regretted going into her room once, and that was all my life. It was taking a liberty, which never should have been took.' "

"But," said Kate, framing the question with difficulty, "did anybody——? Had anybody had a suspicion that Miss de Mannering——?"

"No, mum. Miss de Mannering was always very reserved, she was not a lady that was at all free in her ways like some ladies; not like you are, if you'll excuse me, mum. Not that I mean she would have said anything to anyone of course, and she had no relations, no sisters, and they never had no company at the Hall, and the old gentleman, he'd married very late in life, so he was what you might call aged, and the servants was terrible afraid of him, his temper was so bad; even Miss de Mannering had a wonderful dread of him, they said.

"There was a deal of talk among the servants after what Mrs. Packe said, and there was a housemaid, she'd been in the family a long time, and she remembered one winter years before, I daresay eighteen or twenty years before, Miss de Mannering was ailing, and she sent away her maid, and then she didn't sleep in her own room, but in a room in another part of the house not near anyone, that's the room they shut up, mum. And they remembered once she was ill for months and months, and her nurse that lived at Selby, when she was very old, she got a-talking as sometimes old people will, she died years after Miss de Mannering, and she let out what she would have done better to keep to herself.

"It wasn't long after Miss de Mannering's death they began to say you could see her come out of that there room, walk down the stairs, out at the front door, down through the park, along the avenue, and back again to the house, and then across the park to the churchyard. And of course they say she's trying to find a place for her baby. Then there's some as says Mr. Northfield, what lived at Asham before Colonel Winterton came, he saw her. They say that's why he sold it. Mr. Fuller they say he's spoke to her; they say that's why he's turned so quiet.

"Then there's some say, Miss Jarvis—she kept The Blue Boar in the village, when I was a girl—she used to say, that Miss Emily Robinson, the daughter of Sir Thomas Robinson, who bought the place from Mr. Seaton, who bought it after Mr. de Mannering's death—he wasn't much of a 'Sir' to my mind, just kept a draper's shop in London, the saying was—she was took very sudden with the heart disease, and was found dead, flat on her face in the avenue. Of course the tale was, she met Miss de Mannering and she laid a hand on her. The footman that was attending Miss Robinson—she was regular pomped up with pride *she* was, and always would have a footman after her—he says he see a woman quite plain come up behind her, and then she fell. He told Mr. Jarvis. Poor Mrs. Dicey—they was at the Hall before the Northfields—she went off sudden too at the end, but she was always sickly, and I don't hold with all those tales myself.

"But people will believe anything. Why, not long ago, well, perhaps twenty years ago, in Northfield's time, there was a footman got one of the housemaids into trouble, and of course there's new people about in the village since the family went, and they say the room was shut up along of *her*. It's really ridickerlous."

"Did you ever see her, Mrs. Croucher?"

"Not to say see her, mum, but more than once as I've been walking in the park, I've *heard* her quite plain behind me. That was in November. November is the month, as you very well know, mum,"—I could see Kate was gratified that it was supposed she should know—"and you could hear the leaves a-rustling as she walked. There's no need to be frightened, if you don't take no notice, and just walk straight on. They won't never harm you; they only gives you a chill."

"Did your mother ever see her?"

"If she did, she never would say so. My mother wouldn't have any tales against Miss de Mannering. She said she never had any complaints to make. There was a young man treated my mother badly, and one day she was crying, and Miss de Mannering heard her, and she comes into the sewing-room, and she says, 'What is it?' and my mother told her, and Miss de Mannering spoke very feeling, and said, 'It's very sad, Bessie, but life is very sad.' In general Miss de Mannering never spoke to anybody.

"My mother bought a picture of Miss de Mannering, if you young ladies would like to see it. Everything was in great confusion when Mr. de Mannering died. Nothing had been touched for years, and there were all Miss de Mannering's dresses and her private things. No one had looked through them since her death. So what my mother could afford to buy she did, and she left them to me, and charged me to see they should never fall into hands that would not take care of them. There's a lot of writing I know, but I'm not much of a scholar myself, though my dear mother was, and I can't tell you what it's all about, not that my mother had read Miss de Mannering's papers, for she said that would never have been her place."

Mrs. Croucher went to her bedroom and brought us the papers and the portrait. It was a water-colour drawing dated Bath, 1805.

The artist had done his best for Miss de Mannering with the blue sash to match the bit of blue sky, and the coral necklace to match her coral lips. The likeness presented to us was that of a young woman, dark, pale, thin, elegant, lady-like, long-nosed and plain. One gathers from pictures that such a type was not uncommon at that period. I should have been afraid of Miss de Mannering from her mouth and the turn of her head, they were so proud and aristocratic, but I loved her sad, timid eyes, which seemed appealing for kindness and protection.

Mrs. Croucher was anxious to give Kate the portrait, "for none of 'em don't care for my old things." Kate refused. "But after you are gone," she said, for she knows that all such as Mrs. Croucher are ready to discuss their deaths openly, "if your niece will send her to me, I should like to have Miss de Mannering; I shall prize her very much."

Then Mrs. Croucher withdrew, "for I shall be tiring you two young ladies with my talk." It is rather touching how poor people, however old and feeble, think that everything will tire "a lady," however young and robust.

We turned to Miss de Mannering's papers. It was strange to look at something, written over a century ago, so long put by and never read. I had a terrible sensation of intruding, but Kate said she thought, if we were going to be as fastidious as all that, life would never get on at all, So I have copied out the narrative for you. I am sure, if Mrs. Croucher knew you, she would feel you worthy to share the signal honour she conferred on us.

MISS DE MANNERING'S NARRATIVE

It is now twenty-two years since, yet the events of the year 1805 are engraved upon my memory with greater accuracy than those of any other in my life. It is to escape their pressing so heavily upon my brain that I commit them to paper, confiding to the pages of a book what may never be related to a human friend.

Had my lot been one more in accordance with that of other young women of my position, I might have been preserved from the calamity which befell me. But we are in the hands of a merciful Creator, who appoints to each his course. I sinned of my own free will, nor do I seek to mitigate my sin. My mother, Lady Jane de Mannering, daughter of the Earl of Poveril, died when I was five years old. She entrusted me to the care of a faithful governess and nurse, and owing to their affectionate solicitude in childhood and girlhood I hardly missed a mother's care. Of my father I saw but little. He was violent and moody. My brother, fourteen years older than I, was already causing him the greatest anxiety by his dissipation. Some words of my father's and a chance remark, lightly spoken in my hearing, made an ineffaceable impression on me. In the unusual solitude of my existence I had ample, too ample, leisure to brood over recollections which had best be forgotten. Cheerful thoughts, natural to my age, should have left them no room in my heart. When I was thirteen years old, my father said to me one day, "I don't want you skulking here, you're too much of a Poveril. Everyone knows that a Poveril once, for all their pride, stooped to marry a French waiting-maid. That's why every man Jack of them is black and sallow, as you are." I fled from the room in terror.

Another day Miss Fanshawe was talking with the governess of a young lady who had come to spend the afternoon with me. They were talking behind us, and I heard their conversation.

"Is not Miss Maynard beautiful?" said Miss Adams. "I believe that golden hair and brilliant eye will make a sensation even in

London. What a pity Miss de Mannering is so black! Fair beauties are all the rage they say, and her eyes are too small."

"Beauty is a very desirable possession for a young woman," said Miss Fanshawe, "but one which is perhaps too highly valued. Anyone may have beauty; a milkmaid may have beauty; but there is an air of rank and breeding which outlasts beauty, and is, I believe, more prized by a man of fastidious taste. Such an air is possessed by Miss de Mannering in a remarkable degree."

My kind, beloved Fan! but at fifteen how much rather would I have shared the gift possessed by milkmaids! From henceforth I was certain I should not please.

Miss Fanshawe, who never failed to give me the encouragement and confidence I lacked, died when I was seventeen and had reached the age which, above all others in a woman's life, requires the comfort and protection of a female friend. My father, more and more engrossed with money difficulties, made no arrangement for my introduction to the world. He had no relations, but my mother's sisters had several times invited me to visit them. My father, however, who was on bad terms with the family, would not permit me to go. The most rigid economy was necessary. He would allow no guests to be invited, and therefore no invitations to be accepted. The Hall was situated in a very solitary part of the country, and it was rare indeed for any visitor to find his way thither. My brother was forbidden the house. Months, nay years passed, and I saw no one.

Suddenly my father said to me one day, "You are twenty-five, so that cursed lawyer of Poverils tells me; twenty-five, and not yet married. I have no money to leave you after my death. Write and tell your aunt at Bath that you will visit her, and she must find you a husband"

Secluded from society as I had been, the prospect of leaving the Hall and being plunged into the world of fashion filled me with the utmost apprehension. "I entreat you, sir, to excuse me," I cried. "Let me stay here. I ask nothing from you, but I cannot go to Bath."

I fell on my knees before him, but he would take no denial, and a few weeks after I found myself at Bath.

My aunt, Lady Theresa Lindsay, a widow, was one of the gayest in that gay city, and especially this season, for she was introducing her daughter Miss Leonora.

My father had given me ten pounds to buy myself clothes for my visit, but, entirely inexperienced as I was, I acquitted myself ill.

"My dear creature," said my cousin in a coaxing manner that could not wound. "Poor Nancy in the scullery would blush to see herself like you. You must hide yourself completely from the world for the next few days like the monks of La Trappe, and put yourself in Mamma's hands and mine. After that time I doubt not Miss Sophia de Mannering will rival the fashionable toast Lady Charlotte Harper."

My dear Leonora did all in her power to set me off to the best advantage, to praise and encourage me, and my formidable aunt was kind for my mother's sake. But my terror at the crowd of gentlemen, that filled my aunt's drawing-room, was not easily allayed.

"I tremble at their approach," I said to Leonora.

"Tremble at their approach?" said Leonora. "But it is their part to tremble at ours, my little cousin, to tremble with hopes that we shall be kind, or with fears that we shall not. I say my little cousin, because I am a giantess," she was very tall and exquisitely beautiful, "and also I am very old and experienced, and you are to look up to me in everything."

I wished to have remained retired at the assemblies, but Leonora always sought me out, and presented her partners to me. But my awkwardness and embarrassment soon wearied them, and after such attentions as courtesy required they left me for more congenial company. Certainly I could not blame them; it was what I had anticipated. Yet the mortification wounded me and I said to my cousin, "It is of no use, Leonora. I can never, never hope to please."

"Those who fish diligently," she replied, "shall not go unrewarded. A gentleman said to me this evening, 'Your cousin attracts me; she has so much countenance.' Captain Phillimore is accounted a connoisseur in our sex. That is a large fish, and I congratulate you with all my heart."

Captain Phillimore came constantly to my aunt's house. Once he entered into conversation with me. Afterwards he sought me out; at first I could not believe it possible, but again he sought me out, and yet again.

"Captain Phillimore is a connexion not to be despised by the ancient house of de Mannering," said my aunt. "There are tales of his extravagance it is true, and other matters; but the family is wealthy, and of what man of fashion are not such tales related? Marriage will steady him."

Weeks passed by. It was now April. My aunt was to leave Bath in a few days, and I was to return home; the season was drawing to its close. My aunt was giving a farewell reception to her friends. Captain Phillimore drew me into an anteroom adjoining one of the drawing-rooms. He told me that he loved me, that he had loved me from the moment he first saw me. He kissed me. Never, never can I forget the bliss of that moment. "There are," he said, "important reasons why our engagement must at present be known only to ourselves. As soon as it is possible I will apprise my father, and hasten to Asham to obtain Mr. de Mannering's consent. Till then not a word to your aunt. It will be safest not even to correspond." He told me that he had been summoned suddenly to join his regiment in Ireland and must leave Bath the following day. "I must therefore see you once more before I go. The night is as warm as summer. Have you the resolution to meet me in an hour's time in the garden? We must enjoy a few minutes' solitude away from the teasing crowd."

I, who was usually timid, had now no fears. I easily escaped unnoticed. The whole household was occupied with the reception. At the end of a long terrace there was an arbour. Here we met. He urged me to give myself entirely to him, using the wicked sophistries which had been circulated by the infidel philosophers of France; that marriage is a superstitious form with no value for the more enlightened of mankind. But alas, there was no need of sophistries. Whatever he had proposed, had he bidden me throw myself over a precipice, I should have obeyed. I loved him as no weak mortal should be loved. When his bright blue eyes gazed into mine, and his hand caressed me, I sank before him as a worshipper before a shrine. With my eyes fully open I yielded to him.

I returned to the house. My absence had not been observed. My cousin came to my room and said with her arch smile, "I ask no question, I am too proud to beg for confidences. But I know what I know. Kiss me, and receive my blessing."

I retired to rest, and could not sleep all night for feverish exaltation. It was not till the next day that I recognized my guilt. I hardly dared look my aunt and cousin in the face, but my demeanour passed unnoticed; for during the morning a Russian nobleman attached to the Imperial court, who had been paying Leonora great attentions, solicited her hand and was accepted. In the ensuing agitation I was forgotten, and my proposal that I should return to Asham a day or two earlier was welcomed. My aunt was anxious to go to London without delay to begin preparations for the wedding.

She made me a cordial farewell, engaging me to accompany her to Bath next year. "But, Mamma," said Leonora, "I think Captain Phillimore will have something to say to that. All I stipulate is that Captan and Mrs. Phillimore shall be my first visitors at St. Petersburgh."

Their kindness went through me like a knife, and I returned to Asham with a heavy heart.

"Where is your husband?" was my father's greeting.

"I have none, sir," said I.

"The more fool you," he answered, and asked no further particulars of my visit.

Time passed on. Every day I hoped for the appearance of Captain Phillimore. In vain; he came not. Certainty was succeeded by hope, hope by doubt, doubt by despair. Ere long it was evident that I was to become a mother. The horror of this discovery, with my total ignorance of Captain Phillimore"s whereabouts, caused me the most miserable perturbations. I walked continually with the fever of madness along the laurel avenue and in the Park. I went to the Church, hoping that there I might find consolation, but the memorials of former de Mannerings reminded me too painfully that I alone of all the women of the family had brought dishonour on our name.

I longed to pour out my misery to some human ear, even though I exposed my disgrace. There was but one in my solitude whom I could trust; my old nurse, who lived at Selby three miles off. I walked thither one summer evening, and with many tears I told her all. She mingled her tears with mine. I was her nursling, she did not shrink from me. All in her power she would do for me. She knew a discreet woman in Ipswich, whither she might arrange for me to go as my time approached, who would later take charge of the infant. She suggested all that could be done to allay suspicion in the household and village.

At first my aunt and cousin wrote constantly, and even after Leonora's marriage I continued to hear from Russia. My letters were short and cold. When I knew that I was to be a mother, I could not bear to have further communication with them. My aunt wrote to me kindly and reproachfully. I did not answer, and gradually all correspondence ceased. Yet their affectionate letters were all I had to cheer the misery of those ensuing months. I shall never forget them. Although it was now summer, the weather was almost continuously gloomy and tempestuous. There were many thunder storms, which wrought havoc among our elm trees in the Park. The rushing of the wind at night through the heavy branches and the falling of the rain against my window gave me an indescribable feeling of apprehension, so that I hid my head under the bedclothes that I might hear nothing. Yet more terrible to me were the long days of August, when the leaden sky oppressed my spirit, and it seemed as if I and the world alike were dead. I struggled against the domination of such fancies, fancies perhaps not uncommon in my condition, and in general soothed by the tenderness of an indulgent husband. I could imagine such tenderness. Night and day Captain Phillimore was in my thoughts. No female pride came to my aid; I loved him more passionately than ever.

On the 20th of November some ladies visited us at the Hall. We had a common bond in two cousins of theirs I had met frequently in Bath. They talked of our mutual acquaintance. At length Captain Phillimore's name was mentioned. Shall I ever forget those words? "Have you heard the tale of Captain Phillimore, the all-conquering Captain Phillimore? Major Richardson, who was an intimate of his at Bath, told my brother that he said to him at the beginning of the season, 'What do you bet me that in one season I shall successfully assault the virtue of the three most innocent and immaculate maids, old or young, in Bath? Easy virtue has no charms for me, I prefer the difficult, but my passion is for the impregnable,' and Major Richardson assures my brother that Captain Phillimore won his bet. Mr. de Mannering, we are telling very shocking scandals; three ladies of strict virtue fallen in one season at Bath. What is the world coming to?"

My father had appeared to pay little heed to their chatter, but he now burst forth, "If any women lets her virtue be assaulted by a rake, she's a rake herself. Should such a fate befall a daughter of mine, I should first horsewhip her, and then turn her from my doors."

During this conversation I felt a stab at the heart, so that I could neither speak nor breathe. How it was my companions noticed nothing I cannot say. I dared not move, I dared not leave my seat to get a glass of water to relieve me. Yet I believe I remained outwardly at ease, and as soon as speech returned, I forced myself to say with tolerable composure, "Major Richardson was paying great attention to Miss Burdett. Does your brother say anything of that affair?"

Shortly afterwards the ladies took their leave.

I retired to my room. I had moved to one in the most solitary part of the house, far from either my father or the servants. I tried in vain to calm myself, but each moment my fever became more uncontrollable. I dispatched a messenger to my nurse, begging her to come to me without delay. I longed to sob my sorrows out to her with her kind arms round me. The destruction of all my hopes was as nothing to the shattering of my idol. My love was dead, but though I might despise him, I could not, could not hate him.

Later in the day I was taken ill, and in the night my baby was born. My room was so isolated that I need have little fear of discovery. An unnatural strength seemed to be given me, so that I was able to do what was necessary for the little one. He opened his eyes; the look on his innocent face exactly recalled my mother. My joy who shall describe? I was comforted with the fancy that in my hour of trial my mother was with me. I lay with my sweet babe in my arms, and kissed him a hundred times. The little tender cries were the most melodious music to my ears. But short-lived was my joy; my precious treasure was granted me but three brief hours. It was long ere I could bring myself to believe he had ceased to breathe. What could I do with the lovely waxen body? The horror that my privacy would be invaded, that some intruder should find my baby, and desecrate the sweet lifeless frame by questions and reproaches, was unendurable. I would have carried him to the churchyard, and dug the little grave with my own hands. But the first snow of the winter had been falling for some hours; it would be useless to venture forth.

The fire was still burning; I piled wood and coal upon it. I wrapped him in a cashmere handkerchief of my mother's; I repeated what I could remember of the funeral service, comforting and tranquilizing myself with its promises. I could not watch the flames destroy him. I fled to the other end of the room, and hid my face on the floor. Afterwards I remember a confused feeling that I myself was burning and must escape the flames. I knew no more, till I opened my eyes and found myself lying on my bed, with my nurse near me, and our attached old Brooks, the village apothecary, sitting by my side.

"How do you feel yourself, Miss de Mannering?" said he.

"Have I been ill?"

"Very ill for many weeks," said he, "but I think we shall do very well now."

My nurse told me that, as soon as my message had reached her, she had set out to walk to Asham, but the snow had impeded her progress, and she was forced to stop the night at an inn not far from Selby. She was up before dawn, and reached the Hall, as the servants were unbarring the shutters. She hastened to my room, and found me lying on the floor, overcome by a dangerous attack of fever. She tended me all the many weeks of my illness, and would allow none to come near me but the doctor, for throughout my delirium I spoke constantly of my child.

The doctor visited me daily. At first I was so weak that I hardly noticed him, but my strength increased, and with strength came remembrance. He said to me one morning, "You have been brought from the brink of the grave, Miss de Mannering. I did not think it possible that we should have saved you."

In the anguish of my spirit I could not refrain from crying out, "Would God that I had died."

"Nay," said he, "since your life has been spared, should you reject the gift from the hands of the Almighty?"

"Ah," I said in bitterness. "You do not know——"

"Yes, madam," said he, looking earnestly upon me, "I know all."

I turned from him trembling.

"Do not fear," he said. "That knowledge will never be revealed."

I remained with my face against the wall.

"My dear Madam," he said with the utmost kindness. "Do not turn from an old man, who has attended you since babyhood and your mother also. My father and my father before me doctored the de Mannerings, and I wish to do all in my power to serve you. A physician may sometimes give his humble aid to the soul as well as to the body. Let me recall to your suffering soul that all of us sinners are promised mercy through our Redeemer. I entreat you not to lose heart. Now for my proper domain, the body. You must not spend your period of convalescence in this inclement native country of ours. You must seek sun and warmth, and change of scene to cheer your mind."

His benevolence touched me, and my tears fell fast. Amid tears I answered him, "Alas, I am without friends; I have nowhere to go."

"Do not let that discourage us," he said with a smile, "we shall devise a plan. Let me sit by my own fireside with my own glass of whisky, and I shall certainly devise a plan."

By his generous exertions I went to visit his sister at Worthing. She watched over me with a mother's care, and I returned to Asham with my health restored. Peace came to my soul; I learnt to forgive him. The years passed in outward tranquility, but in each succeeding November, or whenever the winds were high or the sky leaden, I would suffer, as I had suffered in the months preceding the birth of my child. My mind was filled with baseless fears, above all that I should not meet my baby in Heaven, because his body did not lie in consecrated ground. Nor were the assurances of my Reason and my Faith able to conjure the delusion: yet I had——

Here the writing stopped.

"Wait, though," said Kate, "there's a letter."

She read the following:

"3 Hen and Chicken Court,
"Clerkenwell.
"March 7, 1810.

"Madam,

"I have been told that my days are numbered. Standing as I do on the confines of eternity, I venture to address you. Long have I desired to implore your forgiveness, but have not presumed so far. I entreat you not to spurn my letter. God knows you have cause to hate the name of him who betrayed you. Yes, Madam, my vows were false, but even at the time I faltered, as I encountered your trusting and affectionate gaze, and often during my subsequent career of debauchery has that vision appeared before me. Had I embraced the opportunity offered me by Destiny to link my happiness with one as innocent and confiding as yourself, I might have been spared the wretchedness which has been my portion.

"I am Madam, your obedient servant,
"FREDERIC PHILLIMORE."

I could not speak for a minute; I was so engrossed with thinking what Miss de Mannering must have felt when she got that letter.

Kate said, "I wonder what she wrote back to him. How often it has been folded and refolded, read and re-read, and do you see where words have got all smudged? I believe those are her tears, tears for that skunk!"

But I felt I could imagine better than Kate all that letter, with its stilted old-fashioned style, which makes it hard for us to believe the writer was in earnest, would have meant to Miss de Mannering.

"To-morrow is our last afternoon," said Kate. "What do you think," coaxingly, "of making a farewell visit to Asham?"

But though Miss de Mannering is a gentle ghost, I do not like ghosts; besides, now I know her secret, I could not intrude upon her. So we did not go to Asham again. Now we are back at school, and that is the end of my story.

"THERE SHALL BE LIGHT AT THY DEATH"

It was more than a hundred years ago, when an old lady, Mrs. Bailey, and her great nephew were conversing together in a neat parlour.

"My dear James," said she joyfully, "I can hardly believe it is you. You know it is three long years since I have seen you. Not that I can see you now, or hear you talk, for my senses are wearing out, nor can I taste much for the mater of that, but I am just as happy as if I could. I take it very kind of you coming to visit me like this, for I shall not be here much longer, and I yearned to speak with you once more before I die."

The young man, James Clarkson, murmured that he was glad to come, and the old lady went on: "I have set everything in order. The house and furniture are to be sold, and the lawyer tells me that will fetch a good sum. There's a little in the Funds too; that will make eight hundred pounds for you, and two hundred for your dear sister, who does not want much, as she has a kind husband to look after her."

Clarkson's face fell, "I am sure you are very good to me, Aunt," said he, "but could you not manage that I might have some of what is coming to me now? It would be very handy, more than handy. I am in want of money."

He spoke loudly and urgently, for it was to ask for money, and not for love of her, that he had come that day. In site of her deafness he made her understand. She was a trifle alarmed, but drew herself up, and said it was impossible; the lawyer had settled everything for her, and nothing could be altered without his assistance.

"Cannot you give me anything, Aunt?" he said. "Give me a hundred pounds; give me fifty pounds."

"I can give you five pounds, my dear," she aid, fumbling in her bag. "There is no more in the house, but you shall have that and welcome."

He took it, and hardly thanked her.

"Come, I must go," said he. "I must catch the coach at Dereham."

"Oh, James," said she, taking his hand, "you must not leave me without some refreshment after that long journey. A good neighbour has sent me a pound of delicious tea from London, just off the ship. You were always fond of tea."

"I must go," he reiterated.

She begged him again, and he said roughly he would stay.

"Call Betsy, my love," said she, "and tell her to bring it in. I gave orders that it was to be ready on the hob."

He called, and called again; no one came.

"The poor thing is in her tantrums to-day. She is a good girl, but when she gets into her tantrums, she is like a mad creature. She said she would poison me with rat poison one day; we are plagued with the rats, the house is so near the wood. People say she is crazy and that it is not safe for me to live with her, but poor Betsy does not mean anything. And with your sister living in the village, I have no fear."

He had not appeared to listen to this rambling; now an idea seized him. "I will bring in the tea myself."

"You, my visitor; no, indeed," said she, smiling; "I'll go." But he was already gone.

He went into the kitchen, it was empty. He heard the servant moving in her bedroom overhead. The tray, with two cups ready, stood on the table. He looked about, and found a bottle marked poison; he took the teapot off the hob; he read the instructions on the bottle and poured some of its contents in the teapot. Many and many a day afterwards he thought of this action, and he always recollected how, as Mrs. Bailey spoke of Betsy, an impulse, clear as a command, had come to him: "Money you must have. There is rat poison in the kitchen; give it to her. No one will suspect you; all will be well." What struggle to resist there had been, who shall say? If fierce, it was brief. He took the tray in. She poured out tea for him and for herself. He contrived to throw the contents of his cup into the grate. He heard the hiss, when the water touched the fire. It sounded to him like the whistle of a great wind. He felt the sweat streaming down his face. The old lady knew nothing, and gazing at him, said sweetly, "Now, James, is not this delicious?" for she could taste nothing. The answer stuck in his throat, but he muttered a sullen assent. She drank her own cup, and was satisfied; she offered him a second. He took it, and again threw the tea away; she drank a second cup.

"I must go, I must go," he said.

She put her arms around him, and pressed him to her.

"Good-bye, dearest nephew. Thank you again and again. I hope we shall meet in another world."

It was dark when he came out into the road. There was no other house near. He walked to Dereham without meeting a soul; he caught the coach, and reached Norwich late in the evening. He tossed in his bed all night, and by next morning he had taken the coach back to Dereham. He would have given the world to have kept away, but that mysterious fatality, which transports the murderer to the scene of his guilt, drove him to his aunt's house. The pale face of his sister greeted him. He murmured some excuse for his presence.

"James, thank Heaven you are come. I was longing for you, but knew not where to write. Betsy tells me you were with my aunt yesterday afternoon. Was she well then?"

"Perfectly well."

To himself his voice sounded hesitating, but she observed nothing.

"She is very, very ill now, and the doctor says she cannot live through the day."

The horror and alarm on his face were not assumed, and in her agitation the sister did not mark that he expressed no surprise.

"You must see her. She is very weak, but she may recognize you."

"I cannot see her," he said, shuddering.

"Dear James, it is the one comfort we can give. She loved you so fondly. Remember you were her godchild."

An irresistible impulse carried him up to the bedroom. His aged aunt lay on the bed as if in a lethargy, and her eyes were closed.

His sister gently drew the curtains aside, and begged the brother to call her by name.

He could not speak. She pressed his hand, and whispered, "Poor James." Then she bent down, and said, "Aunt, here is dear James come to see you."

The aunt opened her eyes, turned her head towards him, and fixed them earnestly upon him, as if she would pierce his heart's core. Never had her mild eyes cast on him a glance so searching. Then she said with remarkable solemnity: "There shall be light at thy death."

She lay her head back on the pillow, closed her eyes, and spoke no more.

These strange words affected him indescribably. The chill almost of death seemed to freeze his frame; all sensation ceased save horror. He stood rooted to the spot.

His sister spoke to him.

"I was sure she would recognize you, her favourite."

He stammered something, and turned his face away.

Now a heavy gasp came from the bed, a second, and all was over. His aunt was no more.

When his mind recovered itself, he left the room, and hurried down the stairs, calling to his sister, "I cannot stay longer."

"Dear James may be rough outside," thought the sister, "but he has a feeling heart within."

And now he could do at once what he desired to do. Making use of his great-aunt's last gift, he posted to London with all speed, repaired to Jew moneylenders in the city, and at exorbitant interest, on the strength of his promised legacy, borrowed six hundred pounds. He then hastened to the office in which he was employed. Three days before in an act of madness he had, when putting by the week's profits in the safe, embezzled a large sum to discharge his gambling debts. Payment for them had been vociferously demanded. He was a friendless man, and none of his boon companions would put themselves out to relieve his distress. He had been tortured with the thought that in his absence the theft would have been discovered, but the heads of the firm had been indolent and indifferent. Nothing was suspected, and with the money restored he could again breathe freely.

The cause of Mrs. Bailey's death was so mysterious that there was a post mortem examination. It was then discovered that she had been poisoned, but disease of the heart was also so far advanced that her existence could not have been prolonged more than a few weeks at most. The only two persons who had been with her on the day preceding her death were her nephew and her servant, Betsy Allgood.

Clarkson's attendance was required at the inquest. With his guilty knowledge, all clearly pointed to him as the murderer, but suspicion seemed to glide off him and fix itself on the servant, who, though devoted to her mistress, had been frequently heard to utter threats against her. Her own remembrance of the afternoon was faint. Her memory seldom retained a recollection of what occurred during her outbursts of temper. The unsatisfactory explanation, which was all she was able to offer, warranted her commitment for trial at the March Assizes.

Clarkson felt he could bear no more. He feigned illness, and was not present at the funeral. "Dearest James," his sister wrote, "I had no notion how fondly you returned the love of one whose affectionate thoughts turned so often to you. Comfort yourself with the recollection that her last dying look and words were for you. And such words: 'There shall be light at thy death.' More than once she spoke to me with sorrow that of late years you had cared so little for the welfare of your soul, but they say at the moment of death a special insight is sometimes permitted. She saw with the eye of faith that it shall be well with you at the end."

He thrust the letter immediately into the fire, for it was his frantic desire to banish all recollection of his aunt for ever. In his secret soul he believed her last words boded no good to him, though, as he assured himself a dozen times a day, they were but the wandering, meaningless utterances of a being in the very act of dissolution.

"She was old," he would reflect, "her time was at hand. I did but advance it by a few weeks, a few days, perhaps a few hours. It could not be regarded as equivalent to the death of one with years of life to run; Heaven could not so regard it."

The day of the Assizes came. The trial was soon over. Clarkson again found that, in spite of the most searching examination, he emerged scatheless and unsuspected. The wretched woman was declared to have done the deed. Her reiterated denials, her grief and horror at Mrs. Bailey's decease, were of no avail; she was condemned to death. It seemed as though Providence was intervening on Clarkson's behalf. He heard the prisoner's doom pronounced with satisfaction. With her death all danger of discovery would be at an end.

His sister, who visited Betsy Allgood in her cell, begged him to exert himself to secure her reprieve. The rector of the parish was infirm, the squire an absentee, the doctor a drunkard, the farmers ignorant, her husband incapable at the moment from illness. Clarkson alone could act.

"My dear Emily," said he, "I would gladly do all in my power. But a poor clerk, of what use could I be?"

"Ask Mr. Luckly or his brother." They were the heads of the firm in which Clarkson was employed.

"That would be a liberty on my part."

"But think. The life of a poor innocent woman may depend on it. The dreadful act was not done by intention. Never was a creature more devoted than she. I implore you to help her."

"I will do my best," said James, but he did nothing. When his sister inquired, he said Mr. Luckly's application has been fruitless.

"I have a favour to ask you," said she some days later. "The execution is to be at Norwich on Wednesday morning. Poor Betsy has a strong desire to see you: she has something to say to you, which she can say to no one else."

"I cannot see her," said her brother quickly. "Any alleviation in her unhappy condition allowed by the prison authorities I shall be happy to pay for, but I cannot see her."

"You shrink from the thought, but indeed, since the chaplain has been praying with her, she is resigned to her lot. You will find her perfectly composed."

"Say no more," he said. "I cannot see her."

"James," said his sister earnestly, "if you refuse me in this, you will show yourself devoid of the humanity that becomes a Christian."

"That may be," said he, "I shall not go."

Nor would he be persuaded. Yet he was at Norwich on the Wednesday morning. He had sworn to himself again and again he would not see her, but he was compelled to see her. He was one of the crowd which watched the cart carrying the prisoner to the gallows. Her gaze was mournful and abstracted. She looked on the concourse of faces without seeing them. Suddenly however her eyes met Clarkson's. They were large and glowing. How large they seemed now, and how intense was their fire. Her lips moved; she spoke to him. He was too far off to hear the words, but what need was there to hear? He knew them. On the mind's ear they fell with a mysterious distinctness, unknown to waking life. "There shall be light at thy death." He struggled violently, but he could not repress a cry. He fought his way out of the crowd.

He returned to London as soon as possible, and by an orgy of gambling, into which he plunged to drown reflection, he soon brought himself to as desperate straits as those he had fallen into before his aunt's death. He was forced to fly the country. Yet even his wretched situation could not at first divert his thoughts from that twice-repeated sentence. He told himself often that the meaning, if meaning there was, must be propitious. But in the dark night his reasonable surmise had little weight with him. Remorse too visited him, and he would cry out in his misery: "Only twenty-seven years old, and hung on the gallows," so that more than once his fellow lodgers knocked at his door to ask what was the matter. But time, which levels and alleviates all, at length calmed his fears.

He lost sight of his sister. He ceased correspondence with her when he went abroad, and he never saw her again. His way of life went from bad to worse. He became a drunkard, and he was shunned by decent society and associated with companions lower than himself. He had come from a stock of respectable provincial attorneys. At first he felt shame at his fall, but gradually his gross nature became indifferent to his entire loss of social regularity and comfort. And had his guilty soul no private thoughts of horror or repentance? None. In the harsh struggle for bare existence, which became his lot after he left England, he had room for no sentiment, not even superstition. Once and only once, in a life prolonged beyond the allotted span of seventy years, was he reminded of his sin.

He was at sea, working as a common sailor. One night he was troubled by a bad dream. He thought that he was drinking at an inn in a room full of people, and that someone, he knew not who, gave him a folded paper. He was certain that it contained writing, which he desired above all things not to read, yet he could not forbear opening the paper. He saw that there was one short sentence. Before he had time to gather its purport, he awoke. And with the teasing persistency of a dream his mind throughout that day and the next was busy surmising what the sentence had been.

A week later, driven by contrary winds (he was on board a small sailing vessel) he landed at a seaport town on the coast of Lincolnshire. It was night, and he was drinking with some of his shipmates at the inn. Suddenly there appeared among them a gentleman of commanding appearance; his clothes were handsome, his gold watch fine enough to attract the attention of a thief, who sat in the corner. It seemed even to that dull and unimaginative society that he had come to them in some mysterious manner. Yet the landlord had ushered him into the room, and his words were still sounding in their ears: "You'll forgive it's being a poor place, sir, but it's better than nothing, such a night as this." The fire, which had been red and glowing, burst up at his entrance into brilliant flames. The eye of fancy might have conceived them darting out at the bars to greet him. Either the fire, or some other light, illuminated the faces of the company, and it seemed that they were pale. The tales and laughter ceased; silence fell, but for an uneasy shuffling of the feet.

"My friends," said the stranger, looking upon them. "I did not come here to spoil sport. Ring the bell, and let us have whisky, plenty of it, and the best they have in the house. You were cheery enough when I entered, you were telling stories, I believe. Let us continue them."

But even the superfine spirits could not enliven them; the silence continued, and each man looked at his neighbour.

"Come, it seems I must provide the entertainment myself. I will look into the fire, and there I shall see the picture of what each man here is thinking of. You, my friend, for instance," he said, turning sharply to his neighbour, who edged away from him; "I see a dish of fat pork chops, dropping with richness, and plenty of sage and onions."

This made everyone laugh, but it was the laugh of the slave who desires to propitiate.

"And you," he said to the thief. "I see a shop, and a till, and some sovereigns. Then I see a diamond ring, a lady's hand, and a pawnshop. Is the picture correct?"

The thief's face grew white. The gentleman jested thus for a few minutes. Then he looked at Clarkson, and speaking with more deference, as to one in a higher position than the others, said, "And you, sir, if I may venture to guess your thoughts, were they not turned to a small, white house near a wood? I see an old woman, and is there not a tea-tray and two cups of tea, one drunk and the other thrown into the fire? Then an old woman lying on a bed, and oddly enough there is a gallows."

"I don't know what you see, or what you don't see," said Clarkson vehemently. "It's no matter to me, but you have seen no concerns of mine."

"No, then I am mistaken, and must ask your pardon. I am also mistaken in this probably."

He took out a scrap of paper and a pencil, wrote some words on the paper, folded it, and handed it to his neighbour.

"Have the goodness to pass this to the gentleman; I have not the pleasure of knowing his name."

Clarkson for a moment was overmastered by that sensation, so dreadful and disquieting, when the waking world seems visionary and the dream real. He knew that he had already seen the room and the company a week ago. He had too already seen the folded paper. He refused to take it, striking fiercely at the man who passed it to him.

"Let me read it then," said the stranger. "It will divert our friends."

"No, no, no," he cried out. "Give me the paper."

The problem which had baffled him was now clear as day; he was certain what the sentence would be. He opened the paper, and it stared him in the face: "There shall be light at thy death." He shook all over, though he endeavoured to control himself with all his powers, that the stranger should not be aware of his agitation.

"I fear," said the strange gentleman, "that what was meant as a jest to while away a winter evening is a cause of unmerited suffering to our friend."

Clarkson cowered, and could answer nothing.

"And now good night, my men," said the other rising abruptly. "I have a long way to journey to-night; I must delay no longer. I thank you for my entertainment. Farewell."

He bowed and smiled, and made his way out of the room. At his departure the fire died down. They drew a long breath of relief, and at last the bravest soul said timidly: "Did anyone hear tell what the gentleman's name was?"

"You take care what you're asking, young chap," said an old sailor. "It's better by far not to know his name."

Clarkson roamed about the town the whole night, heedless of the rain and wind, dreading discovery, dreading still more he knew not what. The day broke; his shipmates received him as usual. Nothing was suspected, and the stranger had left town. He had posted to London, the ostler reported, and Clarkson saw him no more.

Years passed, and the time drew near when the guilty man must die. He had retired to an old, battered cottage in the Midlands, far from the scene of his former crime. His surly disposition made him no favourite with the villagers. He became infirm, and seldom passed the threshold of his cottage.

"What relations have you?" asked the doctor who was attending him. "They should be sent for without loss of time."

"There is no one. I had a sister, but she may be dead; I have not heard of her in thirty years. It was my fault, she was a good sister."

"Is there no one you would like to see?"

"I should like to see the vicar."

The vicar came, and sat beside the bed. Hitherto Clarkson had spurned his ministrations.

"Have you anything on your mind, of which you would wish to unburden yourself before the time comes when you must go hence?"

"There is one thing," said Clarkson, endeavouring in his demeanour to Mr. Lawford to return to the respectable class from which he was now an outcast. He paused. "Do you think it is a man's first duty to discharge his debts?"

"Undoubtedly it is."

"At whatever cost?"

"At whatever cost. A man is a thief who does not discharge his debts."

"It might perhaps be at great, at enormous cost."

"Even at great cost," said Mr. Lawford, not comprehending. "It is better to enter into life maimed than to be cast into hell fire."

"Ah, but I have paid my debts. Six hundred pounds it was, and I have paid it all."

"Then let us give thanks to the Almighty for His mercies, and for giving you peace at the last," said Mr. Lawford. Knowing that the mind frequently becomes clouded at the approach of death, he opined that the sick man was wandering.

Clarkson shut his eyes, and the clergyman prayed.

"I must be going now," said Mr. Lawford, rising. "There was nothing more you wished to say to me?"

"Nothing," returned Clarkson; but as the clergyman opened the door, he called him back. "If you could come again, sir, there might be something I could say, but not now."

"Mr. Clarkson," said the clergyman solemnly, "to all appearance the time of your dissolution draws nigh. Do not, like

Felix,[68] postpone repentance to a convenient season. That convenient season may never come."

"Yes, but I cannot say more now," replied Clarkson with agitation.

"I am summoned to a dying woman at Carlton-le-Moor; I will come this evening, when I return from thence."

The doctor, seeing the solitary condition of the sick man, sent a woman, Nurse Trimby, to attend on him. And in her words shall the closing scene be described, for she told the tale over and over, and no detail was forgotten.

"He was quiet when I came first, that might have been six o'clock. I tidied things up, and I lights the fire. 'Oh, dear,' he says, 'whatever you do, don't light that fire. I don't want no fire.'

" 'Stuff-a-nonsense,' I says, 'not light a fire, and how am I to warm your broth, and where am I to sit this winter's night, if not by a nice warm fire?'

" 'Don't let me see it then,' 'e says, and I put my shawl in front of his eyes.

"Suddenly 'e says to me, 'Nuss, are you there?'

" 'Lor, 'ow you did startle me,' I says. 'I thought you was asleep.'

" 'There's some words I 'eard once,' he says, 'or it might perhaps be twice. I was just a-wondering what they meant.' He didn't say nothing more just then, and I didn't take no notice of him. It's no good your takin' too much notice, when they're ill. They're just like children.

"He started a-stammering, but at last 'e gets it out.

"'There shall be light at thy death,' 'e says. 'What do you think that means?'

68 Felix, the Roman governor who procrastinated and missed his opportunity to repent. Acts 24:24-27

" 'I'm sure I don't know,' I says. 'Light at thy death. Dark I should say, for they can't see, when they're a-dyin'.'

" 'No,' he says, 'of course it must be nonsense, utter nonsense.'

" 'Come to that,' I says, 'it may be more sense nor what we think for, after all. There was my sister married a Yorkshireman, and she tells me they was very partic'lar there to 'ave a light at the corpse's 'ead, kept off the spirits, it did. They was wonderful terrified with a candle.'

" 'Thank you,' 'e says. 'That makes it all plain.' Then 'e says: 'Nuss, will you light a candle and put it by me.'

" 'Well,' I says, 'you're beginning' early. You're not a corpse not yet.'

"'E settles down quite quiet after that for half an hour or so, then 'e says, 'Nuss, what's that smell I smell?'

" 'Oh,' I says, 'it's only just a little brandy, as I have here on the mantelpiece. Doctor told me to be sure to 'ave it 'andy in case you felt fainty like.'

" 'It ain't brandy I smells,' 'e says.

" 'You shall 'ave a drop,' I says. And I give 'im enough to send him to sleep, but there 'e was a minute after, 'Nuss, is there anybody a-walkin' along the road?'

"I looks out of the window, but it was a dark night, and I couldn't see nothin'.

" 'I daresay it's James Parkins comin' home from work,' I says, just to humour him. 'Yes, I can 'ear 'im quite plain, and now he's gone past the 'ouse.'

" 'There's the steps again,' 'e says.

" 'That'll be Mr. Ryder,' I says, 'and 'e's gone past too.'

" 'No,' 'e says. 'Them steps never go past the 'ouse, they're always comin' nearer.'

" 'Oh dear,' I says, 'if you talk so silly, I shall 'ave to speak very sharp to you. Do lie still and go to sleep.'

"Restless. How 'e did toss, to be sure. And mutter, always a-mutterin' somethink. 'Twenty-seven years old and to die on the gallows.' I heard him say it as plain as I 'ear you now. I give 'im some more brandy, but I couldn't get 'im quiet.

"Lor, how 'e kep' asking me what the time was.

" 'If I've said it's 'alf-past eight once, I've said it a dozen times.'

" 'If Mr. Lawford would but come in time and I could tell 'im.'

" 'The doctor'll be coming soon,' I said.

" 'I couldn't tell him, 'e says.

" 'Well,' I says, 'I've seen many a dyin' bed, but never such a to do as you make.

"Then 'e begins again worse than ever.

" 'Is the curtain drawn?' 'e says. 'There's a light in the sky what I don't like.'

"I looked out of the window, and I see just a little faint speck of light.

" 'Why,' I says, 'it's only a star. What harm can that do you? Turn your face to the wall, and you won't see it.'

"In a minute 'e says, 'That light's getting brighter.'

"I looked again. The cottage stood all by itself by the road, and you could see the road stretchin' for miles, there was no trees in the way. 'Ah,' I says, 'it's the moon risin'.' though how he saw it I don't know. 'It's going to be a lovely moon this frosty night.'

" 'No,' 'e says, 'that ain't no moon. Shut the shutters as far as you can to keep the light out.'

"Well, I was shuttin' the shutters, when that light I saw in the distance seemed to grow bigger; and when all was made fast, mark my words, if that there light didn't come in at the window, and shine in the room.

" 'Oh,' he cried, 'put the clothes round me tight, Nuss. That light will be my death. And these steps a-comin' up the stairs, and that wicked smell. Oh, my sins, my sins,' 'e says, 'what shall I do?'

" 'You come with me into the other room.' says I.

"I took him by the arm to try and help him. I got him out of bed, but pore thing, 'e was too weak to move further.

" 'It's no use,' 'e says; ' 'elp me back to bed, Nuss.'

"I could hear the steps myself quite plain. 'That's the doctor,' I says, but mind you, I didn't think it was.

" 'Oh, if I had but told Mr. Lawford.'

" 'I'll go and see the doctor,' I says.

" 'Don't leave me, Nuss,' and he ketches hold of my arm; 'e got it so tight, I 'ad a job to make him drop it. 'In God's name, don't leave me.'

"But you don't think I was going to stay in the room with all them goings on, that light as bright as day, when it was nine o'clock at night.

" 'I'll come back,' I says. 'Don't you be afraid.'

"I went out, and as I was a-goin' out, somethink pushed past me. Ah, you may prick up your ears, but it did, give me a push it did, I felt the place all that night, and I see no one at all, but the smell—brimstone and sulphur—I won't say more than that, but it was a smell no Christian souls has any cause to smell.

"Up comes the doctor that very moment.

" 'How is he, Nuss?'

" 'He seems rather queer, Sir. I was a-thinkin' it would be only right to call and ask you to step in.'

"He opened the door, went in, and shut it after him. In a moment out he came.

" 'Why, Sir,' I says, 'you do look upset.'

" 'I am,' says he. 'I am terribly upset. You'd better go home, Nuss,' says 'e. 'This ain't no place for a woman.'

"But there, I thinks I'll stay outside the door.

"Then there came a cry from the room: 'Oh, help me. Help me.'

"The doctor says, 'We can't desert him, poor, miserable wretch,' and he turned the 'andle of the door, but that there door it wouldn't open. He pushed with all his might, but it wouldn't open. While he was a-pushin'. I looked through the key-'ole. The light was as bright as ever, and I see someone a-movin' inside. Widder Green, she says I says I see a tail, but that's a thing she's no call to say, for I never said it. I said I seed *somethink* a-movin'. Then the pore man on the bed gives a holler, it gives me a shiver to think of it now; and the doctor, 'e puts his 'ands to his ears, and he calls out: 'God help me, I can't bear it.'

"Then he turns and sees Mr. Lawford comin' up the stairs.

" 'Mr. Lawford,' 'e says, 'we're in a terrible strait. The wretched man is in the anguish of death, and the door cannot be opened. I left him in my miserable cowardice, and now the door cannot be opened.'

"Mr. Lawford's a gentleman, we know, but 'e's not at all free. 'E went up to the door, without saying so much as a good evening to me; if there was some brandy missin' when Mr. Robbins died, I can't see it's right to remember it against a pore, 'ard-workin' woman. He says, 'Peace be to this house, and to all that dwell in it,' turned the 'andle, opened the door as easy as easy and went in. I heard the sick man say, 'Thank God.' Mr. Lawford said he give a sigh and died quite easy. We went in too, and there was the room quite dark but for the candle on the mantelpiece; the fire was almost out. Mr. Lawford was a-holding of him in his arms. There was a smell of brandy, for I had forgotten to put the cork in, but nothink else, no smells as there shouldn't be. Mr. Lawford, 'e said a prayer, which was very right and proper 'e should, and there are some thinks his comin' in handy like when he did made the 'ouse quite sweet and clean for Christian souls to live in. But it's not a house I likes myself, nor yet that part of the road neither, not after dark. And that's the whole story, as true as the gospels, and if anyone knows, I do, for I see it all."

LE SPECTRE DE LA ROSE

Two ladies were drinking coffee after lunch on Sunday afternoon. They sat in a Kensington drawing-room, and from the portraits of nineteenth, eighteenth, and seventeenth century gentlefolks surrounding them, and the engravings and water colour sketches of different aspects of an old house in a park, one might surmise that the owner of the drawing-room, or the owner's family, had not always lived in Kensington, but came from the country, and from that special section of the country which is called "county."

One, Miss Davenant, was aristocratic, stout and seventy. The younger, her cousin, was twenty-eight, and though now thin, she would grow into just such another as Miss Davenant bye and bye. Both had this characteristic in common: one felt sure they would be, as they deserved, honoured and regarded with true affection, but not adored.

"Now," said the younger, Miss Janet Holmes, "I must go and pay my respects to Aunt Lucy."

"Do," said Miss Davenant. "There she is near the window. I feel so at sea in this cramped-up Kensington and she reminds me of the Hall more than anything. I put her a little out of the way as she might not be harassed by eyes profane. Poor Aunt Lucy!"

"Aunt Lucy" was the portrait of a young lady, who might have been sixteen or seventeen at the time she was painted. One guessed this from the youthful delicacy of her tints, but she had nothing of either the leanness or clumsiness of sixteen. The period must have been the years between 1820 and 1830, when the world really cared for female beauty and, really caring for it, was given it. Probably the painter would not have had the heart to make any young lady plain, and he had employed all the resources of the most limpid blues and pinks, airy curves, silken wisps of ribbon, and flowing tresses to assist the sitter. But she had no need of his assistance, being in herself perfectly lovely. She was, besides, the embodiment of grace, innocence, and tenderness, the three feminine qualities particularly in favour with her generation. To have combined all this in one person seemed sufficient, but in addition she possessed, not what was so much valued at the end of the last century, a sense of humour—humour requires a power of criticism which was alien to her—but 'a spirit of artless glee,' as her contemporaries would have called it, which played round her mouth; the extreme kindness and friendliness were shining in her dark blue eyes.

"Well, do you love her as much as ever?" said Miss Davenant, coming up and standing by her cousin. "You could not bear to say good-bye to her at the Hall, when you were a little girl of six. Do you remember how you wept? Why, Janet," as she caught sight of Janet's face, "I believe, if you are not actually weeping, that is a tear I see wanting to roll down your cheek."

"It is very ridiculous," said Janet, "I can't think why she should have that effect on me. I assure you I don't usually cry at pictures, but she is so perfectly, *perfectly* beautiful, and when one is plain oneself——"

"Are you plain, my dear? I'm sure I never noticed it."

"Was she really as exquisite as that?"

"It was just like her, her sister Charlotte told me."

"I love that look she has, as if she were above all the scramble of the world. People so often seem to use beauty as a sort of money to buy pleasure and success, you can see it in their faces, and she hasn't a trace of it."

"I don't believe she did have a trace of it. I think she thought too lowly of her beauty for that, and too highly of herself, if I make my meaning clear. I heard so much about her from Aunt Charlotte, I almost came to feel I knew her myself. Did I ever show you my other picture of Aunt Lucy?"

"No, I didn't know you had another. I should like to see it."

Miss Davenant brought a small chalk drawing and some letters from the cupboard.

"That was done three years later, when Aunt Lucy was nineteen, a week or two before she died. Aunt Charlotte did it."

The sister was not expert like the artist, but she had, what the amateur often possesses in such a high degree, the power of getting a likeness. Here the likeness was almost painful. There were not only the physical symptoms of decay, but the expression was changed. Both the radiance and the trustfulness were gone, and instead there was a look of dejection, almost of wildness. In spite of all, the sovereignty of beauty was still upon Lucy; she might be dethroned, but she was as much a queen as ever.

"I don't think you ever heard the story about her, Janet. I heard it often from Aunt Charlotte. She was Lucy's special sister. She outlived the rest of the family, and she became lonely at the end of her life, as all we old maids do, and not only the old maids, everybody old, I suppose, becomes rather lonely. She was very fond of me, she had a loving nature that must be fond of someone, and I used to be fond of her, and she told me her sister's story again and again. But although I know it so well, I never could fathom it. It remains one of the mysteries. As one goes on, the mysteries of life increase. The miracles have never been a stumbling-block to me, when one thinks with what strangeness one is everywhere encompassed."

"I have always loved your stories, Cousin Eleanor."

"This is rather a long one, so I daresay you will get tired of it. You must wait a little, while I arrange my papers, and then I shall be ready to begin." After a pause Miss Davenant continued: "Your mother, of course, has told you about the family: my grand-parents, your great-grand-parents, were flourishing at Davenant Hall early in the last century. When I say 'flourishing' I mean they had a large family of those great-aunts and uncles of yours, whom you don't remember, and not much money to bring them up on. Charlotte and my father headed the family, and somewhere in the middle came your grandmother and two extravagant brothers, and then Lucy. Some of the older ones had married, not as richly as they might have done; in fact if my father had not found a good manager as well as every other perfection in my dear mother, the Hall would have been sold long ago; and Frank and Richard were swallowing up their father's patrimony, when we come to the year 1821, Lucy being then sixteen, and Charlotte twenty-eight. A great ball was given in June by the Duchess (do you remember driving to the Castle, when you were a little thing? No, you hardly would) to celebrate a daughter's coming of age. Lucy was very young (you must put in 'Aunt', Janet, I really cannot trouble about 'Aunt' every time) but my grand-parents felt this was a chance not to be missed. They hoped her unusual beauty might retrieve the fortunes of the family. 'I was away at the time,' Aunt Charlotte often said to me afterwards, 'my eldest sister was expecting her confinement. If only I had gone to the ball, I might, perhaps I might, have prevented what happened.'

"Lucy sent Charlotte long letters to acquaint her with her doings. As the life of a not very prosperous squire's daughter was monotonous in those days, she had leisure both of hand and head to write with considerable detail. I like her letters; they are full of the extreme simplicity and innocence which, Aunt Charlotte told me, were to be her undoing. Here is one about the ball:

> 'Oh, that my beloved sister could have seen me this afternoon! My mother, Barton, Nanny (the maids) and I were all sewing at my dress as hard as it was possible to sew. You recollect that the Duchess commanded us all to go in fancy costume, and after long thought my mother has determined that I shall be winter; then we can employ my Uncle Frederick's India muslin with good effect, and not waste money. Miss Marset has made the gown, but we are sewing the pearls on at home. The pearls are flakes of snow or sleet, whichever you please, or perhaps rain. I think I am thawing winter. I know my Charlotte will not accuse me of Vanity if I tell her that when I was dressed in my gauze with the pearls in my hair (more thaw) old nurse kissed me, and said I was too beautiful to live. This you know, was a great deal from old nurse, as I have never been the favourite at all with her; it was always Richard or little Emma. My father, too, when I presented myself before him said, "This beats even your mother on her wedding day." '

"I think that was delightful of your great-grandpapa, Janet, for great-grandmamma from her youthful portraits must always have been exceedingly plain. Well, to go on with Lucy's letter:

> 'I looked at myself in the glass, and I did think in that dress I was beautiful. Later. The compliments encouraged me

very much for a while, but I have been ready quite an hour and a half before the carriage, and I have had time for all my courage to ooze away. You will think me a fool, I know, but I shook with fright at the prospect of the ball. In fact I am shaking with fright as I write. I am employing the waiting time in writing to you. Shall I have *one single partner*? The mortification of sitting down the whole evening would be so great. Oh, my dear sister, if you were by my side to laugh me out of my terrors!'

"Here also is her mother's letter after the ball:

'My dear Charlotte,

'You cannot conceive what a sensation our little Lucy created as she passed through the hall to pay her respects to the Duchess. Never have I seen the hall so resplendent as that night, the myriads of wax candles being reflected on the polished surface of the dark panels. It was thronged with dancers; there must have been close upon five hundred, but in all this splendour our little Lucy shone as Queen. The Duchess was attended by her daughter, the statesque Lady Harriet Conyers (you recollect her famous ivory complexion) and her niece, Miss Adelaide Fortescue, whose sparkling eyes, they say, are the toast of two counties.'

"I think grandmamma rather fancied her letter writing, don't you, Janet?

'Her Grace, when she had saluted us all very graciously, called Lucy back, and embracing her affectionately, said: "I must kiss this lovely child." Then she turned to the young ladies, and said: "You two girls must look to your laurels. Here is one who, I think, will carry all before her." "My dearest Mamma," said Lady Harriet, "we may be vain, but we are not so vain as all that. We capitulate at once. Miss Davenant, please reckon us among the first and warmest of your admirers." Lucy was immediately surrounded by a band of gentlemen, and I was told afterwards that a duel was nearly fought for the possession of two or three pearls, which came unfastened from her dress. Lord Maudesley danced with her several times, and expressed his admiration of her to the Duchess in the highest terms. Mr. Lowther and others showed themselves to be very devoted, but the most assiduous was a young man, attached, I think, to Lady Charles Wilbraham's party. As you know, all were in fancy costumes, and he wore a rose-coloured doublet and tights and a black velvet cap with a rose-coloured plume. He was strikingly handsome, and never have I seen anyone dance as he did. It is not only a mother's partiality, but when he and Lucy were partners, the rest of the dancers seemed to make a space for them, and stopped to admire. The sight was so charming that your father and I forgot our cares and the aches of our elderly bones, so much so that it was actually Lucy who was ready to go first. Dearest child, hear head was not turned, as mine would have been if I had such a triumph at my first ball, but I do not remember that anyone took particular notice of me except your father. She is as simple as she always was, a shade pensive perhaps this morning, but no wonder, she has plenty to be pensive about! Captain Ffolliot actually made her an offer yesterday, but she had the good sense to refuse it. He is not a desirable man. I shall welcome you back on Friday, for of course one cannot expect your father to have observed all the little shades of attention with a mother's eye, and I would not disturb dear Lucy's simplicity for the world.'

"Lucy herself wrote less triumphantly of the evening:

'It is after the ball, and I am very, very, *very* weary. Of course it was wonderful. Everyone made much of me and was kind to me. I don't know how you can say you dislike young men. I have never met such delightful creatures. It was the "red letter day" of my life, nothing will ever happen like it again. I cannot express to you what it was, but I am not sure—I wish you were here, I do wish you were here. I will say no more. *Adieu*, till Friday.'

"When Charlotte came back, she had Lucy's triumphs poured into her ear by both father and mother, and again and again her mother described the young man in the rose-coloured doublet. 'He was not of Lady Charles' party. That I have ascertained. Mrs. Hartley thinks he came with the Whartons from the other side of the county. Lord Maudesley called yesterday: it is clear he is very much attracted.'

"It struck Charlotte that Lucy, who had hitherto confided her smallest thought, was reserved about the ball. She talked with animation about the dresses and the beauties, but she said little of her partners, and not one word of the rose-coloured gallant. At last Charlotte started the subject, and to her surprise the gentle Lucy answered almost with asperity: 'There is nothing to say, nothing at all.' At night, however, she spoke. The sisters shared a bedroom. 'Now that there is nobody but you, and me, and the moon, I will tell you. I don't know why I hesitated, or rather I do know, but even with you, my sister of sisters, I feel afraid. I don't know if you will understand. I liked all my partners very much, particularly Mr. Lowther, though I think thirty is very old. I had just finished dancing with him a second time, when the man you enquired about came up and engaged me. He was not introduced; it was the Duchess's desire that we should all be unknown to one another, only some partners told us their names. You have said I am a light dancer, and others said so at the ball; but, oh, Charlotte, what it was to dance with him! I felt I was flying, and so strong that I could have danced to the end of the world. No one else made me feel this. He did not talk to me much. He said once, "If only this could go on for ever," and I said, "If only it could." Was that too much?'

" 'I don't know,' Charlotte replied. 'I can't tell you. I am a clumsy dancer, no one would ever wish to dance for ever with me. I think I wish you had not said it.'

" 'Then what will you say to the rest? But I must go on now.'

" 'But did he tell you nothing about himself?'

" 'Nothing. Nothing whatever. I don't know how often we danced. I only know after I had seen him I cared for no one else. I counted the minutes for his dances; they were like a blissful dream too good for the world. We had finished a dance, and we went to an ante-room, leading out of the hall. There was a glass door, which opened on to the garden, and we could see the dawn coming over the trees; the dawn pale, pale green, and the trees very dark. He unfastened the door, and the scent of the roses was wafted in by the night air. I have never smelt such roses; they were not like earthly roses. He leaned out, and picked me two.

Then he said: "Give one back to me, and I will keep it, till I see you again." He looked at me, and he said, "You love me?" and I said, "You know I do." Don't reproach me, oh, don't reproach me, Charlotte, I could say nothing but the truth, when he looked at me so penetratingly.'

" 'My poor Lucy,' said the anxious Charlotte, 'what can I say? You have been so imprudent, so forgetful of your own dignity. How could you?'

" 'Say no more,' said Lucy, 'I am punished enough.'

"She got into bed, turned her face away, and pretended to sleep.

" 'You cannot conceive,' Charlotte used to say to me, 'what a pang I felt that that little sister-daughter of mine, whose every thought I believed known to me, should be turning from me.'

"Lucy woke Charlotte later in the night. 'I am sorry to disturb you, Char, but I have a weight like lead on my mind. I have not told you all. What will you think of this? After he said: "You love me?" he drew me to him and kissed me. That kiss, I cannot describe it. For the first instant it was rapture, and then a chill ran through me, and I felt as if all my strength was drawn out of my body. He said: "There is the dawn. I must go. I will come back when it is time. You will wait for me?" I tried to say "yes," but I had no breath, I could only whisper. His face, I fancied, changed. I noticed his pallor, and his eyes—I had thought them so beautiful, Charlotte—they seemed almost to devour me. Then he stepped out at the door, and sprang down the steps of the terrace. He sprang so lightly that it was as if he were carried by the wind. I watched him, but the shrubbery must have been nearer the house than I thought, for in an instant he was gone, vanished in the blackness of the trees. I felt overcome with such weakness that I believe I nearly fainted. I could think of nothing and feel nothing. I do not know how long I waited in the ante-room. Then I came to myself, and had such a longing for him that I could hardly contain myself. The thought of any other partner was unendurable. I determined to find my mother, and beg her to let me go home. I went back into the hall, and was claimed by Mr. Lowther. I explained that I was tired and looking for my mother. He was very kind and found her almost at once. The crowd was thinning, guests were already departing. I think my mother was vexed that I did not wish to stay longer. My father however said: "She looks dead beat. Remember what a little young thing she is, bed is the place for her." I felt that I was deceiving them, but I could not tell them any more. Now, Charlotte, you know absolutely all. Forgive me if you can, but if you can't, there is no help for it, for I must go on loving him.'

" 'Whatever you did, you know I should forgive you,' said Charlotte. 'But think an instant. Would any honourable man conduct himself as this man has done? He forced you to avow your love, but he said not a word of his love for you.'

" 'Ah, but he does love me, Charlotte.'

" 'You don't know that he does.'

" 'Then why should he say I was to wait for him? No, he does love me, he does love me. You shall smell his rose.'

"Lucy took the rose from her work-box, and gave it to Charlotte. Charlotte told me the rose had a very strange perfume. There was something mysterious and aromatic about it, besides the usual scent of roses. It was by no means unpleasant, but she said it filled her with an extraordinary repulsion. The rose had been bright red, but the petals were of course now brown and falling.

" 'I smell it constantly,' said Lucy, 'and it brings him back,' closing her eyes in the softest ecstasy, and then smiling on Charlotte. 'It makes me feel as if I were dancing still.'

" 'You know how beautiful she was,' my aunt used to say. 'But her beauty at that moment I have no words to describe. She never looked so beautiful again, except the morning after she was dead. But I thought her eyes too bright, her cheek too flushed, for serenity of mind or health of body. I felt forebodings even then that she would rue this day, and miserably true my forebodings proved.'

" 'I will tell my mother,' said Lucy, 'but let me wait a little, Charlotte. I want to be alone with my secret. I did not like telling even you, you know, but then I was wretched at not sharing everything together.'

"After her confession, Lucy lay down again, and was soon sleeping, but Charlotte was awake for hours. Ought her mother to be told? Mrs. Davenant, I gathered from Charlotte, was an active woman, busy with her husband, house, and younger children, too busy for sympathy with the older ones. Though an affectionate, she was also a formidable mother. She would have had no pity on Lucy's story. As for the father, he indulged himself in the ungovernable temper which then was rather admired. Charlotte could only hope that the affair was an exaggerated fancy of Lucy's youthfulness, which would be soon forgotten.

"Mrs. Davenant took Lucy with her to pay a state call on the Duchess. Lucy went into the garden with Lady Harriet. They walked, as Lucy told her sister, past the door where she had stood with her partner, and Lady Harriet gave her one of the red roses. It smelt as other roses smell. The trees were further than they seemed at night, but the light of dawn plays mysterious tricks with Nature. Now in noonday all looked gay, placid and unromantic. Lady Harriet recounted tales of the limitless admiration Lucy had aroused at the ball, and she was astonished and almost irritated that Lucy did not show more excitement. 'It was unnatural,' she said afterward to Charlotte; 'here was I, a recognized beauty of three seasons, entitled to have a certain fuss made about me, and I assure you I was much more flattered by my few compliments than she was by the thousands lavished on her.'

"Mr. and Mrs. Davenant however were excited enough. The talk turned naturally on the rose-coloured young man.

" 'We have been wondering about him,' said the Duchess, 'and we are all agreed that he was the handsomest man present, and he and your little Lucy by far the best dancers, but no one can say who he was, or where exactly he came from. The Langhornes say their cousins know him, and he has two good places, one in Northamptonshire. I heard he is attached to some embassy, Madrid I think, and they say he is starting for Spain immediately. Neither of my girls danced with him, and in all the crowd and excitement I somehow missed his farewells. But unless I am very much mistaken you will see or hear from him again. I do not think he will be content not to meet his fair partner very soon.'

"Charlotte also made many enquiries. She had never been so energetic before in riding over the county to visit neighbours in remote villages, but the result was always the same. The Wilbrahams were certain he came from the Whartons, and the Whartons were certain her came with the Wilbrahams. There were countless surmises, but not one word of definite information. And amongst the many young ladies who had enthusiastic memories of the ball, Charlotte found none who had danced with him.

"In course of time Lord Maudesley proposed and Mr. Lowther also, but Lucy refused both. The splendour of the one offer, with its prospect of the share of an earldom, the comfort of the other, with the suitability of a park not ten miles off, seemed to have no attractions for her. She had never been vain. It was one of her virtues to be indifferent to her own attractions, and warm in her enjoyment of other people's. Charlotte would have been disappointed in her if she had changed, yet like Lady Harriet she felt that for Lucy to show a little interest in her first conquests would have been more natural, more understandable.

"These rejections were vexatious and ridiculous to the parents, and her mother begged Charlotte to remonstrate. Charlotte had known that Lucy was tenderly affectionate, especially towards herself; but she had supposed that, like many other girls, though fastidious up to a certain point, she would have had little difficulty in attaching herself to any agreeable young man who had the merit of being devoted to her, and that at her early age, if one proved faithless, she would be able, without undue suffering, to transfer her love to another. But she found that she had not known Lucy, for when she began pleading with her, Lucy said: 'How can you think, when I have told a man I love him, that I could receive the addresses of another? How *could* you think that of me?'

"Charlotte then felt it necessary to explain to her parents how Lucy had been attracted and had had every reason to suppose her affection returned. She entered into no details. Remembering that the young man's praises were in everyone's mouth, and not unmindful of his two good estates, Mr. and Mrs. Davenant were pacified, and supposed he would come and make his offer in due course. But days passed, then weeks, then months, and he did not come.

"Gradually, how who can say, public opinion became unfavourable towards him. The Langhornes repudiated all knowledge of him; the man their cousins knew was a Mr. Hartley. At last one day at a party Charlotte heard Mrs. Wharton's loud voice. 'Oh, but you know that man Lucy Davenant danced so much with at the ball was a dancing master dressed up. Friends of the Fenwicks told them it was a fact. Their butler's cousin keeps a public house at Worthing, and the man has often been seen there.' This story on investigation—its beginnings were lost in obscurity—proved as baseless as 'the two good places.' Unfortunately it reached the Davenants' ears and, even when discredited, the sting remained. Mrs. Davenant indignantly charged Lucy to give up all thought of her partner. Lucy remained silent, and Mrs. Davenant gladly took silence for consent. With time interest subsided. The county forgot the affair, and even forgot to pity the young lady.

"But a more sinister shadow fell on Lucy's love affair.

"Charlotte once described to me the exact moment, when it came upon her that the unknown stranger was not of this world.

" 'One early morning in June, I had been nursing little Emma for some childish complaint. I had watched her through the night. Our anxiety was over, and she was sleeping peacefully. I could refresh myself for an instant by standing at the window in the corridor and looking at the dawn, which was now appearing above the trees in the coppice close by. The unearthly beauty of the scene entranced my gaze, when swift as lightning my thoughts turned to the Duchess's ball, to Lucy and her favourite partner. I saw in a flash the scene of their farewell, his strange and secret departure, and the conviction darted into my mind with the most astonishing vividness that he was not a creature of flesh and blood. I remembered that he would not stay, when the dawn was coming. I saw too why it was we had never been able to trace him, and why the rose had been abhorrent to me. I was so certain that I had no room for the possibility of doubt. I shuddered, and at the same time I suffered a most powerful revulsion against Lucy. That she could lavish her pure passion on what? A spectre? I felt as if I could not go to our bedroom and meet her, as if I could not bear to touch her. I dreaded her. In a moment or two the certainty was gone, and I felt aghast that I had been harbouring a fancy, which was as wicked as it was contrary to reason, but from time to time it recurred. It recurred, Eleanor, and alas, with it came that same dread and turning against Lucy. I think, I trust she never knew it, but even now I cannot, cannot bear to think of it!'

"I remember now, Janet, how my dear, good, self-controlled Aunt Charlotte shook all over as she spoke."

"Aunt Charlotte *really* thought that? How utterly amazing! Was she that sort of person, Cousin Eleanor? I had imagined her the prop and stay of the family."

"I cannot say I know what 'that sort of person' is; I have no experience. Aunt Charlotte had seen the 'Weeping Lady' at the Hall, but so have I, and so have most properly constituted Davenants, and I don't think myself deficient in common sense. I am vain enough to think I am the other way about."

"I'm sure you are," said Janet, conscious that she had seen no "Weeping Lady." "Do go on. I won't interrupt again."

"Things continued as I have described for about a year. Lord Maudesley soon consoled himself with someone else, but Mr. Lowther's love was of a different sort. After six months he asked Lucy again, and again she refused. He told her, faltering so that he could hardly speak, that he would wait; he could not give up hope unless she married. 'Unhappily for me,' he said, 'or rather happily, for I would sooner love you and fail than love another and succeed, we Lowthers do not change.'

" 'I wish it was not so,' Lucy answered. 'I am not in the least worthy of your love. But I had better tell you, for you will understand. I am like you; there is someone to whom I have given my heart, and I shall not change either.'

"Following upon special extravagance on the part of Frank, Lucy refused a third rich offer. Her father burst out into abuse of her. Charlotte told me that she herself, tall, strong, and determined, was always terrified at her father's rages, but Lucy, although she trembled and her voice was very low, answered without much hesitation: 'I cannot marry, because I love that man I met at the ball.'

" 'What? That monkey of a dancing master? But you were ordered to give him up long ago.'

" 'Father,' said Charlotte, 'you know that story was not true.'

" 'I know no daughter of mine shall ever marry a man who has that sort of story told about him. Why, you don't even know his name. What is his name?'

" 'I don't know,' said Lucy. 'But I cannot marry anyone else.'

" 'Do you mean you are engaged to him?'

"She did not speak for a minute, then she said: 'No, I am not engaged to him, he never asked me to marry him.'

"Her father continued to rain at her, but she was entirely unchangeable. You may have observed, Janet, that it is the timid-looking of this world who have the iron wills. Charlotte thought her resistance unnatural and alarming. She told me that, ever since her return after the ball, there had been a curious change in Lucy. At first it was hardly perceptible, but, as months passed on, it could not but be seen. She had never had great powers of mind; her charms were of the heart; but Charlotte thought she observed a diminution in what powers she had, a want of concentration. The beauty which had dazzled her on the night Lucy spoke of her love blazed out from time to time, but in the intervals Charlotte was struck by her languor. 'Then I could perceive, I who knew her face by heart, that her expression—I have never told anyone, and I can hardly tell you even now, Eleanor, forty-five years after—it became more vacant, and at the same time hungering and unsatisfied.' Her zest in life seemed gone. She was less affectionate even with Charlotte. Charlotte believed that her mind was never really concerned with anything but the stranger. She came to connect her peculiar flashes of beauty with smelling the rose. Its perfume seemed to give her a hectic, fervid charm, which presently died down, and left her as it were extinguished.

"Life at home became more and more unhappy. At last Mr. Davenant decreed that, if Lucy would not marry as her parents wished, she should be turned out of the house. This meant that Charlotte was turned out too, for she would not leave Lucy."

"How outrageous fathers were in those days!" said Janet.

"Still don't you think even now Lucy's conduct would be thought very exasperating? A child of seventeen to 'afficher' herself as attached to a—whatever the creature was—who made no sign at all of being attached to her.[69] I feel a certain sympathy with Mr. Davenant.

"The sisters went to stay with your grandmother. How long their visit lasted I don't know. I fancy your grandmother was not sympathetic to Lucy. While she was there, she caught cold; the seeds of consumption were sown, and they sprang up very rapidly. Whether her infatuation was a cause or symptom of consumption one cannot say, but I think it must have undermined her powers of resistance to the disease. Of course then mildness and warmth were thought the only remedies. The father regretted his violence now, and funds from his very scanty savings were forthcoming.

"The sisters went to Rome. One of the wild brothers escorted them; he troubled himself very little with them once they arrived.

---

[69] Afficher: to display or parade oneself.

They had a cousin, a wife of someone connected with the Embassy. Through her they were asked to the balls, and were introduced to several people. An old governess of the family, Miss Monks, tried to support herself by taking boarders, and they lodged with her. There was a large colony of English in Rome then, larger than now very likely, with many students of art and music.

"The two girls led a strange, forlorn existence. Charlotte eked out the money by various devices. She even helped Miss Monks at times. That was a come-down for her. We Davenants have always held our heads high. Even now in these democratic days I should not want to be maid of all work to Bohemian young men. And Aunt Charlotte was an aristocrat of the aristocrats. She got some money by portraits too, she told me, and copying pictures. They had to have money to buy dancing dresses. Lucy would go to the balls. She had a sort of hallucination that she would meet that miserable partner at one of them. It was all she went for. Hostesses were delighted to have her. She was continually at the Embassy, but beyond invitations our cousin troubled herself with very little about them. Consumption every month was slowly working its ravages upon her, but they hardly diminished her beauty, only altered it. There was a perfect furore about her. The Italians adored her for her fairness, but Charlotte used to say; 'I don't think the English were behind. It was all nothing to her, less than nothing, and her indifference made her still more irresistible. I remember people used to say the opera was twice as brilliant if she was there to grace it. All the fatigue and late hours were very bad for her, but the doctor said it was better not to thwart her. She used to come back utterly spent, and sick with disappointment, but she would go again and again. Her adorers overwhelmed her with flowers. Those she could not wear I sold to a florist, a faithful creature, so kind in his humble way to Lucy. I do not know that I was naturally clever with flowers, but necessity gave me some special knack, which took people's fancy. When she was lying resting after those terrible balls, I used to sit far on into the dawn making up bouquets. Often it was I who had arranged the tributes presented to her beauty. I did not tell her all my expedients to get her money. She was proud for me; it would have added to her sufferings. I was too anxious to have any pride left; nothing mattered to me. Not that she cared about costly dresses, and her beauty was far beyond the extraneous attraction of fashionable clothes. She wore plain white muslin again and again, relieved simply by sashes and flowers. We had no jewels. Those I brought out had to be sold.'

" 'Affairs went from bad to worse at home. My kind parents would have done all they could for Lucy, but your Uncle Frederick's extravagance was impossible to restrain. What those dreadful months were to endure! All the beauty of Rome was thrown away on us. I hated its beauty; its strangeness, its unfriendliness, and its endless sunshine; those horrible great marble statues and palaces, and those wicked monks everywhere, droning through their noses.' Charlotte was an excellent Protestant. 'And Lucy, who had loved Davenant so much, now pined for the sweet winds and cloudy sky! Nothing would have made her get well, I know, but I think she would have suffered less in her own England. Miss Monks was not very kind; she might have been kinder, but an invalid is a burden in a house like hers, though Lucy was never exacting.'

" 'One day I had been bathing her foot to cure some little bruise, and her fearful thinness struck me so that I cried out: "Oh, my own, sweet, dearest sister, on my knees I entreat you to give up this infatuation. It can come to no possible good. It is now nearly three years since the ball. If he had truly cared for you, he would have come, he would have written. Let me clasp you in my arms, and I will tell you what I think. I believe he is—what shall I say?—not of this earth. *What* exactly, I cannot tell; I only know that it is the greatest misfortune in the whole world that you ever saw him." '

" 'I thought she would have been shocked and alarmed at my words, but instead she answered: "Do you think so, Charlotte?" Turning on me a glance of utter mournfulness: "Sometimes I think so too. But you see I *have* met him, and I cannot change." '

" 'But you can, Lucy. By God's grace you could. Pray for help to struggle against it.'

" '*You* could, Charlotte, because you are strong. But I could not; I am utterly weak.'

" 'At any rate, let me have the rose; you smell your little strength away into it.'

" '*Must* you have it?'

" 'If you love me, give it me.'

" 'You have given up everything for me, for you *did* love Mr. Raymond. Of course you shall have it.'

"Mr. Raymond was a gentleman whom they met in Rome and, while all the world was adoring Lucy, he set his heart on Charlotte. She loved him also, but she would not leave Lucy, and she would promise nothing for the future.

"So Lucy gave up the rose, but, if it had the fatal influence Charlotte imagined, the influence was removed too late. There came no fresh spring of health and hope.

" 'One thing I can say with thankfulness,' Charlotte would tell me, 'after that there was never a shadow between us; the dreadful feeling was all gone.'

"The doctor's hopes, if he had them, were not fulfilled. Lucy grew worse. One afternoon the sisters were in their squalid apartment, a kind of dingy elongated greenhouse, Charlotte described it to me. Grandeur and space are necessary to Italy. I think squalor there is more squalid than in England. It was the end of July, and the fever-laden heat was particularly oppressive to Lucy. They could not afford to leave Rome, as the more prosperous English had done. Their brother Richard had been sent to convey them home to England for the summer, but, though less wild than Frederick, he was incapable of resisting any whim; and fancy, Janet, he stayed on week after week at some German gambling establishment, putting off his journey from day to day, spending the money supplied for them, and they were compelled to wait, helpless, until he came to his senses. The inconvenience of the situation was only equalled by the degradation. All Lucy's admirers were away at baths and watering-places. What would they have thought to see their wondrous goddess, who awed them, yet enchanted them, panting on a hard, musty sofa, alone with the Italian servant; even Miss Monks had fled from the heat. It was in that week that Charlotte made the drawing of Lucy.

"They never now discussed her infatuation. Charlotte had lost hope of her marriage, and in her heart all hope of her recovery. She was reading to Lucy, though it was evident Lucy was not listening. Her mind was wandering back to the meadows and woods near their home. Just then the Italian servant announced 'a gentleman from England to see you.' Lucy flushed scarlet all over her face, but, when Mr. Lowther entered the room, she had turned so pale that her sister felt a pang of fear. 'Oh, Mr. Lowther,' said Lucy, and then burst into tears. 'I was thinking of Davenant, longing for it. It's like a piece of Davenant seeing you.'

"His joy, and at the same time his anguish, at the sight of her made him hardly able to speak. He soon rose to go, and Charlotte made an excuse to accompany him. They went into an old garden near and, seizing her hand, he said: 'Miss Davenant, you must have some pity on me. To see her thus, to be powerless! Tell me is there any remote, any smallest hope for me? If she were my own, if I could watch over her and give her everything, I think I could——'

"Emotion stopped him.

" 'You can imagine the pang,' Charlotte used to say to me, 'to feel that he could give her what, with all my love, I could not. But I would not be jealous. I told him that I would try persuading, "but I have almost stopped trying, I think it torments her to no purpose." '

"She spoke to Lucy that evening. To her astonishment Lucy said: 'If he wants me, I will marry him. I see now too late that what I hoped was—I do not know what it was, but it was more elusive than a dream. I have spent three years going after a shadow, and I have vexed everyone, and above all you, my own one, and now it is too late I can see it all.'

" 'But it is not too late.'

" 'Yes, I think it is. I don't believe I shall live long, and you don't either.'

" 'But you can't leave me, Lucy.'

" 'I think I shall be glad to rest; I am so tired. But in what time I have left I will try to do better, and to please him whose faithful heart I have grieved so much.'

" 'I never saw anyone in such ecstasy as Mr. Lowther,' Charlotte would say to me. In the morning he brought her the choicest fruits and wines, and set about making arrangements for them to travel to fresher air. He wanted to start that very day, but Charlotte said the fatigue would be too great. They took Lucy into a garden near, and then she asked to be left alone.

" 'I would really rather be alone,' she said, taking Charlotte's and Mr. Lowther's hands. 'There is much I must think about.'

"Mr. Lowther rode into the country to complete arrangements; he was to return the following day; and Charlotte left her in the charge of Benedetta, Miss Monks' servant, 'a good creature,' Charlotte used to say, 'but a papist, and, I am sorry to say, very bigoted,' while she went to do some necessary shopping for the journey. She was detained and, when she reached home, she was distressed to find Lucy not returned, for it was sunset.

"She hastened to the garden. On her way she met a man advancing towards her. 'Never, never, shall I forget him, Eleanor,' she used to say. She wrote down her recollections of him; it was not necessary, for she knew them by heart, but I will read them to you. 'He was tall and strikingly handsome, and so young that he still retained the slimness and the delicate tints of boyhood. He was dressed in the favourite black cloak and wide hat of the Italians, the cloak flung across his shoulder displaying the remarkable grace of his form. The colours of the declining sun in Italy, so incomparably richer than those in our northern clime as to be sometimes almost overpowering, were on this evening of an exceptional splendour. They illumined the face of the youth so that it seemed to shine with an almost unearthly glow. As we met, a breeze arose laden with scents of spices and roses, which I thought rendered the languid air still more oppressive. He seemed to feel no oppression however. His lustrous eyes turned on mine; they smiled, they danced, they almost spoke to me, as if asking me to share some private source of satisfaction. He was walking rapidly, yet with no appearance of hurry. He turned, after he passed me, and waved his hand. I did not realize till afterwards at whom; then his light, bounding step carried him out of my sight for ever. As soon as he was gone, I was possessed by the most powerful sensation that what I had seen was an illusion, a figment of my own disturbed imagination. Whether it was, who can say? If it were an illusion, the remembrance of it still remains to me now, Eleanor, when I am old and have forgotten so much, clearer than reality.'

"Charlotte walked on as quickly as possible and met Benedetta running towards her. She could hardy listen to the tale the old woman panted out to her: that, as they had been turning homewards, a very handsome, tall gentleman had come up to the dear young lady and spoken to her. Lucy had started, and Benedetta at first thought she was frightened, but then she smiled and laughed, and seemed asking him to stay, but in a minute he was gone.

" 'He came down this path, you must have met him.'

"Charlotte asked if he was wearing a cloak and broad hat.

" 'Yes, that was the gentleman,' said Benedetta, 'and his smile was as innocent as a baby's.'

"Benedetta had tried to make Lucy go home, but she had begged hard that she might remain a few minutes longer, and then Benedetta, seeing Charlotte in the distance, had hastened to ask her leave.

" 'No, no,' said Charlotte. 'It is madness for her to delay after sunset.'

"And now Lucy herself was seen coming towards them. Poor, frightened Charlotte ran, and clasped her in her arms.

" 'My darling,' she said. 'How could you have stayed out so long?'

" 'Oh, Charlotte, Charlotte,' cried Lucy, not seeming to hear her. 'I have seen him. He has kept his promise.'

"Her face was radiant; she looked as she had not looked for years.

" 'He, that man, who smiled on me, as I passed?' said Charlotte. 'Impossible.'

" 'Yes, Charlotte, it was, it was.'

"The next moment Lucy gave a cry, and fell back. 'At that very instant, I believe,' Charlotte used to say, 'she ceased to breathe.'

" 'I did not realize it then. Benedetta and I carried her home. We put her to bed, and applied restoratives. I sent Benedetta for the doctor. He was delayed in coming, and during those long hours I did not cease from my efforts. I suppose I was almost beside myself, for, all exertions were in vain. I would not allow myself to believe her dead. All that day I had foolishly abandoned myself to hope that my little sister might yet enjoy some months of happiness before her end. It was Mr. Lowther on his return next morning, who, with a tenderness I can never forget, at last compelled me to own the truth.' " Here is an extract from Charlotte's diary.

" 'I torment myself continually thinking of her last piercing cry. Did that same malignant fate, which had wasted her short life, molest her even in death, or was it but the painful struggle of the soul, tearing itself free from the frail mortal covering? When I remember that I saw *him* smiling and happy but the instant before, and she! Oh, to think of all her anguish of suffering. That bitter, bitter hope deferred, and then, when it seemed life might dawn anew for her! But it is fruitless agony to dwell longer on the subject.'

"Charlotte said the expression on Lucy's face after death was troubled at first, 'but as her features became more composed, she looked more beautiful than anything I ever saw in life, or could ever conceive. I had admired the most celebrated works of antiquity and the Christian era, but never was there anything to compare with her, never, *never*.'

"Mr. Lowther stayed and helped Charlotte, until her return to England. Lucy lies in Rome. Money could not be afforded to bring her to England. He gave Charlotte a brother's kiss when they parted.

" 'I shall see you again, Charlotte,' said he, 'for you are part of Lucy, but I cannot face England just yet without her.'

" 'But I never did see him again,' Charlotte told me, 'for he caught a fever and died abroad.'

"Charlotte went back, and after a long illness became the stay of her family, as you called her. But the joy of her life was over, and Mr. Raymond never came back to her. He was not a Mr. Lowther; he had taken her at her word, and married someone else. That is the whole story. I think, and at the end Aunt Charlotte would say every time: 'I believe some people had the cruelty to say that Lucy was—was out of her mind. But she never was that, only on the one point a very little clouded.' "

"I suppose Aunt Charlotte never saw the young man again?"

"No, never. He, 'the spectre,' as she called him, simply passed out of her existence. 'Spectre,' it's an old-fashioned word one doesn't hear now. I remember reading that poem of Gautier's, 'Le Spectre de la Rose'; I at once thought of Aunt Lucy and her 'spectre.' It gave me a turn against the poem, so that I couldn't even bear the pretty ballet those Russian people did a few years ago."[70]

"It is an unutterably sad story," said Janet. "Poor, *poor* Aunt Lucy."

"Poor indeed in those miserable last years, but surely not so poor to have died young, although I am very glad not to have

[70] The short ballet *Le Spectre de la Rose*, written by Jean-Louis Vaudoyer, was based on a verse by Théophile Gautier. It premiered with the Ballets Russes de Monte Carlo in 1911.

died young myself, and like life extremely even now. Sometimes I think the gods take the geniuses in kindness. A stale, elderly genius is not very charming. In the same way it must be very difficult for beauties to grow old. They have to do it, I know, but it must require great strength of mind. Perhaps Lucy might not have had it. Her loveliness made her fill a wonderful place in her short life. When I was a girl, and very full of Aunt Lucy, all beautiful things made me think of her. I'm not sure that they don't now. Early morning in spring, and music, and especially the sunsets we used to see, as we came back home from hunting. Only I used to think she had something in her better than them, far beyond them—you know what romantic fancies girls get—and her influence seems to last on still, so many years after, for it's making me try to be poetical, and as for you, you are head over ears in love with her. Perhaps it is not only the 'actions of the just,' but also the beauty of the innocent, which smells sweet and blossoms in the dust."[71]

Janet did not speak for a minute or two, but when she went to bid the portrait good-bye, Lucy's own enchanting smile, smiling it seemed especially for her, dispersed her unhappiness like sweet autumn sunshine.

---

[71] From the poem 'Death the Leveller' by James Shirley (1596–1666).

LIFE IN A TOURING COMPANY

By One Who Has Tried It

The Queen, The Lady's Newspaper, 8 April 1905

The middle-class girl, whose life has passed in the usual round of parties, travel, games, or philanthropy, will find touring in a second-rate theatrical company a quaint experience. The whole thing is such a queer scramble that at first it is difficult to realise that one is occupied with a great and serious art. People say the stage is being swamped by outsiders; but surely in that case the wealthy amateur would be able to make the mode of life conform a little to the ordinary standard of comfort. The theatrical world is a world apart. It has its own slang, hours, and code of manners. The profession is largely hereditary, and the outsider who embraces it embraces its idiosyncrasies as well. I have never seen an actor or actress (long on the stage) who was quite like an ordinary person; and usually members of the profession are very unlike indeed. A girl went to a highly reputed agent in London and asked for work. "No, dearie," said he, laying his hand tenderly on her shoulder, "nothing to-day except panto, and you would not like that, I know." "Dearie" was only another word for madam. But is there any other profession where "Dearie" is the official form?

On tour an actress depends entirely on the company for intercourse, and there is a great deal too much time for talk. Fourteenth-hand gossip about celebrated actresses, and minute details of the current rows are the staple topics. There is a theatrical type which haunts most companies—the confidential type. It records the story of its life to the nearest ear it can find. These intimate secrets at first sight make the listener bashful, particularly if they are shouted out in the presence of a large mixed assembly. It is astonishing how many actors and actresses have something in common with this type.

I suppose in every profession there is a danger of becoming narrow and one-sided, but theatrical people for the most part have no interests beyond the stage. In conversation with an outsider they literally have nothing to say, unless they are allowed to babble of their own affairs. I once heard an actor mention politics; he wondered how a war might affect the run of his play! The majority read very little beyond theatrical papers and the works of one or two sentimental novelists.

One feature of the stage world is the absence of class distinction. The members of the company are always talked of as "ladies and gentlemen." It is quite likely that the carpenters and dressers have relations in the profession, or they may have been in it themselves. The stage is truly democratic. A world-wide actor may rise from the meanest beginnings, and education and refinement are no help to success, though they need not necessarily be a hindrance.

But if there is no class distinction there is part distinction—a far more serious affair. The manager, the great man who "runs the show," wields an absolute sway. In their contracts the members of the company promise to undertake cheerfully whatever they may be called on to do. The leading lady and gentleman are great, too. They have the best dressing-rooms, and it is advisable to listen with avidity to their legends about the parts they have played. Exactly according to their position on the programme will be the standing of every member of the company. Woe to a small part that hangs her clothes on the peg before a greater than she has established herself. They will be violently torn off and flung on the floor, and so she will be taught her place. The etiquette in these matters is rigid, and half the inevitable battles on tour range round pegs.

The discomforts of touring are many. The companies generally stay a week at each town, travelling on Sundays. Engagements not being booked to suit the actors' convenience, they may have to appear one night at Woolwich, the next at Edinburgh, spending the whole of Sunday shunting in and out of stations, and arriving at length with lodgings to find at eleven o'clock at night. Fit-up companies, which carry their own stage, are worse still; for they visit the little out-of-the-way places capable of only a one-night audience. Life is then one rush of packing, unpacking, room-hunting, and travelling—killing work to most girls. But the little towns have their compensations. They are not blase from over-amusement. They receive with reverent appreciation whatever is provided for them, though sometimes they are serious minded, when a scientific lecture or a missionary meeting will entice most of the audience away.

Getting rooms is often a wearisome business. There are only a limited number of theatrical lodgings in each town, and all the decent ones may be already secured. The prudent traveller collects the names of reliable lodgings at the beginning of each tour, and writes beforehand for rooms; but most actors, not being prudent, simply trust to luck. As a rule, theatrical lodgings are inferior. Nice landladies dislike pantomime girls, who will dance on the table. One has to put up with mustiness, clammy cooking, and impertinence. Provincial theatres in small towns, being neither shops nor factories, are not inspected, so dirt and bad smells abound. Some theatres are really insanitary, but companies bear meekly the ill-health thus engendered, knowing it is useless to complain. The profession is so overstocked that actors are absolutely at the mercy of their employers. One might fancy it was to the interest of the manager that the actors and actresses should look as presentable as possible. However, everything is done in the dressing-rooms to prevent this. There may be one dim, cracked looking-glass—very likely none—no chairs, the gas out of order, no water for washing, no hooks to hang dresses on, a room suitable for one forced to hold ten ladies. I never saw any dressing-room in which everything wanted was there, and was there unbroken. One gets used to the discomfort after a time, and ceases to notice it; but it is amusing to see the gorgeous gold and crimson of the front of the house, and think of the squalor behind.

At first it is a little difficult to get through a theatrical day, but loafing soon comes easy. Breakfast, 9.30 till eleven, or later; loaf, go to theatre for letters, meet the rest of the company, and loaf there; buy dinner, and look in at shop windows—dinner, eternal chop or steak. After dinner loaf, go and buy tea and to-morrow's breakfast, go out to tea or entertain members of the company, loaf with them till it is time to go to the theatre. After the play supper (not the orgie usually conceived of, but bread and milk or cocoa), then dawdle about for an hour or so chatting to friends who have dropped in, and at last loaf off to bed. So ends the dissipated day. Actresses mend their clothes besides; actors who cannot do this have no compensating occupation. Neither sex cares for athletics. Some managers try to start games, but they are not taken up warmly. There are country walks and excursions sometimes, and going to the photographer's, which is a great treat, and furnishes conversation for weeks; but on the whole the life is very monotonous.

There is not much sending of notes and bouquets, nor is there a frantic crowd of admirers at the stage door, or stage-struck youths in the wings. That sort of this is left to musical comedy. In most places strangers are not allowed inside the theatre. A few loafers collect sometimes up and down the platform, looking in at the windows of the theatrical "special," where a large notice is posted up—" 'Her Greatest Sin' Company, reserved carriages." Actors and actresses in private life are in their own opinion an unfailing source of interest to the public. When they are taken notice of they bridle, arrange their hair, and, assuming an elegant attitude, remark sadly that "the public never will learn that actors and actresses are mere flesh and blood like themselves, after all." "It is so awkward; people will be recognising one in the streets," I have heard actresses say. But it never is awkward, for people never do. In university towns there is a mild pursuit of the prettier members of the company. Undergraduates even go to theatrical tea parties, when the actors and actresses, having no idea what to say to them, talk stage gossip very loud, and the embarrassed visitors are left out in the cold. Tea parties are very funny. You play "Consequences," coupling the names of the present company, and reading the results aloud, with the blinds drawn up, "so that you can see their blushes." Afterwards each one speaks his piece, and on the way home we say in confidence that "we cannot think how So-and-So has the face to recite if he can't do it better than that."

Nowhere is jealousy so frank and undisguised as on the stage, but then, often the struggle is desperate, and the victim who falls behind may literally have to face starvation. An actress I knew was playing some pathetic scene with the manager. He had a great speech, to which she listened in tears. Her tears were so attractive that the manager discovered that the audience were looking at her and not at him. This did not do. He sent for the actress, and explained to her that for the future she must sit with her back to the house, that nothing might disturb its contemplation of him. "But my friends are coming to-night," said she. "Mayn't I show just this once?" "No," said he. "I've waited twenty-five years for my chance, and I've got it now. Do you think I'm going to have you soil it? You can wait twenty-five years, too."

A manager can successfully dispose of competition; a plain actor has to resort to slander. Strange stories will be circulated against the unfortunate who has "taken his laugh," reliable details will be forthcoming as to when and where he was drunk; this holds good of actresses, too. But the next day something happens to put the aggrieved one in a good temper; he forgets his revenge, so does everyone else, and all is loving-kindness—till next time.

Theatrical people have very little reserve. Actresses cry in the middle of the stage perfectly unabashed. Most high school girls feel they have lost their self-respect if they cry in class. But I have heard of rehearsals where all the ladies of the company will be in tears regularly at the severity of the manager.

Some managers make a point of bullying. They feel it upholds their dread authority. "What do we want your ugly flat face here for?" was the remark one poor girl had to endure. Managers also foster their dignity by taking the only seat and leaving the girls standing; but on stage this is not only a managerial trait. You must expect actors to smoke in your face and keep their hats on in your presence. Familiarity does doubtless breed a little contempt between the sexes. Still, there is a very pleasant comradeship and men are kind in helping girls—much kinder than girls are in helping one another. Actors and actresses are jealous of their own sex as possible rivals, but they can afford to be pleasant to one another. So also a tragedian will count up a comedian's "laughs" with as much enthusiasm as if he had scored them himself; but two tragedians will regard one another's "calls" with the bitterest hate.

The happy-go-lucky living in the present of actors is surprising. As a rule they depend on their earnings for their bread, and have no savings. Prospects of engagements are always uncertain, and some performers seem perilously near the workhouse. But they never get depressed; there is an atmosphere of perpetual youth and merriment, even amongst the quite elderly, who do really seem to remain at the fictitious age they employ for advertisements. You would think they had not a responsibility in the world, certainly no children to support and start in life.

Perhaps it is that wonderful atmosphere which makes theatrical life, with all its discomforts and squalor, with all the spite and vanity which it engenders, so peculiarly attractive. It has a fascination which does not by any means disappear when one gets behind the footlights, and, however much actors may grumble at its drawbacks, if they have to leave the stage they hanker after it still.

www.ingramcontent.com/pod-product-compliance
Lightning Source LLC
Chambersburg PA
CBHW020932310726
48980CB00007B/736/J

* 9 7 8 1 7 3 9 3 9 2 1 0 9 *